THE BOOK OF FAITH

THE BOOK OF FAITH

a novel

Elaine Kalman Naves

Cover design: Debbie Geltner
Author photo: Monique Dykstra
Book design: WildElement.ca
Printed and bound in Canada.

Permissions:

The following publishers have generously given permission to use quotations from the work of Yehuda Amichai: from *Open Closed Open*, copyright © 2000 by Yehuda Amichai, translations by Chana Bloch and Chana Kronfeld, published by Harcourt, Inc. Reprinted by permission of Houghton Mifflin Harcourt. From *The Selected Poetry of Yehuda Amichai*, copyright © 1986 by Yehuda Amichai, translations by Chana Bloch and Stephen Mitchell. published by Harper & Row. Newly revised and expanded edition by University of California Press, 1996. Reprinted by permission of University of California Press. From *Great Tranquility: Questions and Answers*, copyright © 1983 by Yehuda Amichai, translation by Glenda Abramson and Tudor Parfitt. Reprinted by permission of HarperCollins Publishers. Permission to quote from "Picture in a Frame" (Waits/Brennan), copyright © 1999 by Jalma Music, c/o peermusic Canada. All rights reserved.

Library and Archives Canada Cataloguing in Publication

Naves, Elaine Kalman, author   The book of faith / Elaine Kalman Naves.

Issued in print and electronic formats.
ISBN 978-1-927535-74-5 (pbk.).--ISBN 978-1-927535-75-2 (epub).--
ISBN 978-1-927535-76-9 (mobi).--ISBN 978-1-927535-77-6 (pdf)

I. Title.

PS8627.A93B66 2015   C813'.6   C2015-901851-X
                                 C2015-901852-8

The publisher gratefully acknowledges the support of the Canada Council for the Arts and of SODEC.

Linda Leith Publishing Inc.
P.O. Box 322, Victoria Station, Westmount QC H3Z 2V8 Canada
www.lindaleith.com

For Jessica and Rebecca
For Linda and Norm
and for Archie

Prologue

...a life
that was meant to be a long one came to its end.

—Yehuda Amichai

On a sweltering afternoon in the late summer of 5760, corresponding to the year 2000 of the Common Era, most uncharacteristically for Jews, who are a tardy people, it was standing room only at Paperman's a full half-hour before the scheduled funeral service.

The long, stark room held four banks of pews into which six hundred people were crammed. An enormous mahogany carving in the shape of a shield dominated the chapel. It may have represented the Wailing Wall or, more prosaically, a gigantic gravestone.

No one likes doing business with Paperman's, but it's the only game of its kind in town. Ever since Lazar Paperman converted a volunteer burial society into a business a century ago, Paperman's has held the monopoly on the final passage of Montreal's Jews. Heeding the founder's motto, his descendants continue to deliver the traditional rites gracefully, tastefully, and affordably.

In the fourth row, a couple of seats in from the aisle, Helen Stern turned her shellacked head and scoured the hall. Her eyes glowed with satisfaction.

"Isn't this something?" she announced. "Of course, I did call everybody," she added.

Her voice carried over the subdued murmuring in the room, and a woman with a blaze of auburn curls topped by a black lace doily gave her a withering look from the row directly in front.

Helen erased the smirk from her tawny face. "If it were up to me I'd be at the very back of the room, but Jeff—" here she indicated her husband at her side with a nod, "is a pallbearer."

The redhead whipped her head back to face the front. She did not utter a word, but her rigid spine expressed outrage.

It's not where you're sitting that's my problem, Helen. It's that you actually think it's because of you that we're all here.

Like a gust of cold air, silence fell over the room. A black-suited funeral director had entered by a side door.

"Please rise."

A collective gasp swept the hall at the sight of the gleaming oak casket rolling into the chapel. It was as if everyone had inhaled in unison and then been instantly strangled.

"You may be seated."

Rabbi Kaufman took the podium, accompanied by a cantor.

The young cantor, a beautiful tenor, chanted the Twenty-third Psalm. Next to him at the lectern, Nate Kaufman surveyed the crowd. A lanky man with a neat chin beard, he wore a tiny crocheted black kipah. A close observer would have noted red and swollen eyes behind his owlish glasses.

The rabbi began in a barely audible voice.

My eyes flow copiously,
My heart is confounded with grief,
My whole being laid waste
Over the ruin of the daughter of my people.

His voice gathered strength: "This verse from the Book of Lamentations is an outpouring of grief bemoaning the destruction of Jerusalem and the Temple in the sixth century BCE. Traditionally we read it on *Tisha b'Av*, one of the saddest days on our calendar.

"In Hebrew the Book of Lamentations is called *Eikhah*.

"*Eikhah* means *how*? Surpassing even the agony of loss we are experiencing, we are overwhelmed by our shock, horror, and disbelief. *Eikhah*—how could it be that we are here to cry out at the tragic passing of such a keenly alive, such a *spirited* human being? *How could this have happened?*"

Part One

The Jewish people read Torah aloud to God
all year long, a portion a week,
like Scheherezade who told stories to save her life.
By the time Simchat Torah rolls around,
God forgets and they can begin again.

—Yehuda Amichai

1

"It had to be a man who dreamed up *Simchat Torah*," Rhoda said.

"Well, obviously," Faith said. "The entire religion thing is rooted in patriarchy."

Rhoda continued as if she hadn't heard. "No woman is stupid enough to invent another holiday on top of four weeks of breast-beating and gorging on brisket and honey cake."

"But *Simchat Torah* isn't at all about breast-beating," Erica said.

The three friends were walking along Netherwood towards the Baily Road shul on a crisp October evening as fast as the considerable foot traffic allowed. Statuesque, silver-haired Rhoda was in the middle, with Faith and Erica hustling to keep up with her long stride.

"It's a holiday designed to make everybody look like a fool." Rhoda was on a roll. "*Hakafot!*" She practically spat out the Hebrew word. "Please! All those self-important *machers* parading around with the Torah, and the kids running wild with their flags, and those half-hearted horas. As for the rabbi, don't even get me started!"

"We won't." Faith smothered a full, cherry-lipped

smile, catching Erica's eye. "He *was* in good form," she added.

"He was *drunk,*" Rhoda said, but she did drop her voice. It was one thing to criticize Nate to Faith and Erica, another to be overheard by the general public.

"You're *supposed* to be a little high on *Simchat Torah,*" Erica said. She had her reasons for being partial to Nate, who had been exceptionally understanding at the time of her mother's death.

In a rare blaze of intra-denominational goodwill, this year the Rabbinical Board of Montreal had decreed a community-wide *Simchat Torah* celebration, centred on the Baily Road shul, the biggest synagogue in the twin boroughs of Hampstead and Côte St. Luc. Each congregation in the area had been invited to bring over Torah scrolls for a street festival.

The three women crossed Harrow Crescent and nearly tripped over Jeff and Helen Stern. "Ah, our three lovely Graces. Thick as thieves as always," Jeff muttered under his moustache, as the trio stepped off the sidewalk to pass. It was Jeff, the former president of Congregation Emunath, who had once dubbed them the Three Graces at a party, and the moniker had stuck.

"*Putz,*" Rhoda cracked, when they were out of earshot. Beneath her prickly shell beat a loyal heart, and she still nurtured a grudge against Jeff Stern, for ignoring Faith's very presence at the annual general meeting. The one investing her as the new president. Caught off-guard by Rhoda's expletive, Faith gave a rich belly laugh, while

Erica shook her head in mock disapproval, her auburn curls shaking.

"We have to behave," Faith said, wiping her eyes.

"Only you have to behave, Madame la Pres," Erica said. "The rest of us can be as bad as we want."

"Hello, Faith. Hello, Rhoda. Hello, Erica."

"Hi, Marty," the Graces responded in unison as Marty Riess, one of the stalwarts of the shul board, came up behind them and then pulled ahead.

Faith waited for Marty to be swallowed by the dark. "Odd to see him without Leona," she observed.

"What's odd about it?" Rhoda arched an eyebrow. "Hershy didn't see fit to come. And, for that matter, neither did your Al."

Faith stopped midstride for a moment, placing her hands on her hips. "They weren't sitting together during the service, either," she said.

"Maybe Leona was with friends," Erica said.

"Leona doesn't have friends," Faith retorted. She and Leona Riess had had a spectacular run-in a year ago when Leona was the editor of *The Shul Monthly*. "I still think it's very odd. It's not like them at all."

"You're *such* a yenta," Rhoda scolded, just as they reached the shul. Outside her flesh and blood, Faith was arguably Rhoda's favourite person in the whole world.

A crowd was milling about in the street, people's breaths forming small clouds in the brisk night air. A cluster of women spun madly in the middle of the road, surrounding a girl clutching a Torah to her breast, as if afraid someone would pluck it from her arms.

"Look at all those guys in their black hats and white leggings up there on the stairs. I think they want to tear her limb from limb," Faith said.

"Oh, but there's Nate with Rabbi Shulman!" Erica exclaimed, giving a little wave.

"Don't tell me they're going to let Nate speak here," said Rhoda.

"They're not," Faith said. "He's standing up there with the dignitaries, but they're never going to let him open his mouth. They think Reconstructionists are heathens!"

Rhoda sniffed. "I smell weed. I wonder who's responsible for that?" She paused and then asked, "Faith, how much longer do we have to stay? Surely we've shown our faces long enough."

Erica's toes were tapping. "I want to dance," she announced. "You're supposed to dance." Having come to Judaism by a roundabout route, Erica was big on tradition.

"Go right ahead."

Erica hesitated, shy of breaking into the circle without her friends. A writer isn't a natural joiner by habit or temperament, but she was a good dancer and she had taken a stand. Pulling back her narrow shoulders in resolve, she approached the dancers, a slightly built, almost dainty figure melding into the ring.

"You're being way more of a curmudgeon than usual tonight," Faith said, crossing her arms beneath her generous bosom. Short and stout, she was a good head shorter than Rhoda. The two of them continued to appraise the scene, slightly to the side of the crowd. Reisa Kaufman, Nate's wife, her head wrapped turban-style in a scarlet kerchief, was beckoning them to join a new band of twirling women.

"My tolerance for glorifying a piece of parchment dressed in old velvet has just about run its course," Rhoda said.

"C'mon, we're supposed to dance!" Erica had broken free and now grabbed Faith by the arm, tugging her towards Reisa's group. "*Am Isroel, am Isroel, am Isroel chai!*" *The people Israel lives*, Erica sang, linking hands with Leona Riess. Torn between Rhoda's truculence and Erica's enthusiasm, Faith wavered before allowing herself to be pulled into the circle, her face lit by a huge smile.

Rhoda moved out of the way of the dancers, casting a sceptical eye on a knot of kids from the shul youth group. They were clustered around a banner held up by a girl on one side and a boy on the other. By the gleam of the street lamp, she recognized the girl as Ilana Stern in a tarty miniskirt and bomber jacket. The boy had an earring and a two-day stubble, and was in shirtsleeves despite the chill, his head covered by a baseball cap worn backwards.

Is Faith right that I'm being a killjoy?

It was an article of faith with Rhoda to be strictly, maybe even brutally, honest. Direct and outspoken, she didn't hold with the current wisdom that being judgmental was a bad thing. She rather prided herself on judging and pronouncing. But it wasn't her intent to be a party poop-

10

er; certainly not to rain on Faith's parade. Her sense of fun was at least as well developed as Faith's and Erica's. So why was she being such a wet blanket? The thought popped into her head that she'd once been a rabble-rouser marching against a war—not towards a synagogue. And in the same era she had taken part in a sit-in for *McGill français*. She didn't want to do the arithmetic on how long ago that had been. The war she had protested was Vietnam, and she'd never actually voted for the Parti Québécois. But now here she was, toeing the line of convention and tradition, a three-day-a-year Jew rubbing elbows with a crowd of religious fanatics. Not that Faith and Erica were religious fanatics (though Erica with her peculiar, crypto-Jewish background did try too hard sometimes). Nor for that matter were Rabbi Nate or Reisa. But these guys with the *tzitses* and the *payes* and the white stockings and the air of superiority—what was she doing among them?

Rhoda reminded herself that she wasn't here for them. She was here for Faith.

And Faith was here because she was the new president, and the presidency had its price. Sure, it had its public highs, which clearly she enjoyed, her smile enormous as she hauled the Torah around the sanctuary at Shabbat services. Or when she addressed the entire congregation in full motivational flight on Rosh Hashanah. She had been so engaging and effective that, besides harvesting many compliments on how well she had spoken, people were now calling the shul office to volunteer to serve on the new committees she had urged them to join.

But there were other duties Faith found onerous, to-night's street festival being a case in point. She had de-clared she couldn't face it without Rhoda and Erica.

Friendship too has its price, Rhoda said to herself. So why then be so grudging about this nocturnal expression of loyalty? Perhaps she ought even to look on the bright side and acknowledge that the weather added a sheen of grace to the proceedings.

Rhoda loved this time of year, loved the distinctive sweet fragrance of decomposing maple leaves. She in-haled deeply and threw her head back to gaze up at the stars that were beginning to glitter.

The singing stopped abruptly, and a flock of black hats began mounting the podium. Rhoda's moment of bliss dissipated. Faith had promised they would leave be-fore any speeches, but clearly it was too bloody late for that.

2

Faith stood in front of the full-length mirror in her bed-room, looking wistfully at her image in bra and black tummy-control Spanx panties.

"I'm putting on weight again."

"No, you're not." Accustomed by long experience to Faith's losing battle with embonpoint, Al didn't take his eyes off *The National*. He himself was on the bulky side, a rumpled giant with a weakness for junk food. As a profes-sor of political science, he considered his preoccupation with the politics of the presidential penis a professional interest.

Faith sucked in her stomach and shifted position so she could view her form in profile. "I look four months pregnant."

Al tore his eyes away from the image of Monica Lewinsky. "You look adorable."

"Oy, Al!"

"I mean it. Come here and tell me all about your evening. How was the street festival? How was shul?" He rummaged about Faith's side of the bed, clearing away an empty bag of potato chips along with the *Gazette*, the *Globe*, and Sunday's *New York Times* to make room for her. He muted the volume with the remote, silencing Independent Counsel Kenneth Starr mid-sentence.

"It was okay, considering the venue. Rabbi Shulman actually invited the other *reboinim* to say a few words."

"That must have been very interesting."

Faith laughed her rich belly laugh. "It wasn't *very* interesting, but it *was* good PR. Rabbi Shulman's pretty liberal for the Baily shul. Speaking on the same podium as a Reconstructionist must have been a big step for him."

"One small step for orthodoxy, one giant step for mankind?"

"Well, but what do you think he makes of our stated lack of faith in a supernatural God?"

"I don't know what to make of it myself. It *is* a concept that's a little hard to wrap your mind around."

Al pulled Faith close to him, and she snuggled in,

molding her body against his. He gave her waist an affectionate squeeze. "So it went well? There was a good turnout?"

"Very good! The street was packed with people from all over. Al, you'll never guess. Marty and Leona Riess weren't sitting together during services, and then they both went to the Baily separately."

"So?" Al pivoted around, presenting his broad back. "Would you mind scratching my back?"

"I think they've split up."

"Marty and Leona? They're together a hundred years!"

"I've always heard it was a *horrible* marriage."

"Really? Well if that's what you've heard, it must be so. Uhmmm, that is so good …. And so, how do you feel now that the holidays are finally over? Has a great weight been lifted off your presidential shoulders?"

"What a question! I suppose I do feel a bit relieved that we're back to normal, whatever that is. But I'm sure Nate's going to throw me a new kink soon."

"In other words, you're loving every minute of it. Faithie, have I ever told you that no one in the world can scratch a back like you?"

"And who else has been scratching your back lately?"

3

Erica sat up in bed, heart pounding. There were tears in her eyes, and she couldn't tell if she was hot or cold. Her toes felt frigid, but her armpits were clammy with sweat.

The digits on her alarm clock blinked 2:42. She had gone to bed a couple of hours earlier, having put in some time at her computer after coming home from the Baily. Now she tried to collect her thoughts so that the hammering in her chest might slow. The dream that had woken her began to play back in bright swatches of colour. A restaurant decorated with swag drapes in burgundy velvet, the table set with white cloth and silver, a man in a tux holding a glass of red wine, as if for a toast.

Erica reached for the switch on the bed lamp. She groped for the *Tanakh* on the night table, almost knocking over a glass of water. She willed herself to resist following the dream to its source, her extravaganza of a fiftieth birthday celebration. If she went there now, she'd never get back to sleep.

The Bible fell open at Psalm 116.

Once, in an unguarded moment, her father had let slip that her grandfather used to recite the Psalms in times of trouble. When his creditors were pressing him hard. When her grandmother was fighting for breath during a bout of pneumonia. Erica had tucked away this rare piece of lore about the ways of the orthodox. After she and Ricky split up a year ago, it had taken weeks before she could sleep through the night. She got into the habit of reading Psalms to calm herself when she woke from a nightmare.

No orthodox Jew would have called Erica observant, and she would have felt silly applying the label to herself, but it felt natural, even soothing, to fall back on tradition in a crisis. When she began to feel more settled, she had put the Bible back on the bookshelf in her office. But then, last spring, she'd been diagnosed with a malignancy.

Return, O my soul, unto thy rest;
For the Lord hath dealt bountifully with thee.
For Thou hast delivered my soul from death,
Mine eyes from tears,
And my feet from stumbling.

The language was beautiful and apt. She particularly liked the part that came next, about walking in the lands of the living. Of course it was overdramatizing to imagine she'd been delivered from death, when it was just of a small nodule on her thyroid. The next verse also fit. Sort of. "I said in my haste: 'All men are liars.'" She didn't think that all men were liars, just because Ricky was one. (But he was a barefaced liar, a jerk. He had toasted her in front of everyone at the party; he had made a glowing speech. All a sham, and she like a fool had lapped it all up.)

Stop it! Erica said out loud, "Stop it right now."

She snapped off the light and began deep breathing. In. Out. Inhale s-l-o-w-l-y. Exhale. Release tension in shoulders against pillow. Allow legs to feel heavy. Breathe in. Breathe o-u-t. *Concentrate on feeling better than ever before.* Concentrate on the breath. *Inhale* through the nostrils. *Exhale.*

4

Rabbi Nate Kaufman dialled Faith's work number and got her on the first ring.

"Developmental Psych."

"Faith, is this a bad time?"

Faith rolled her eyes. Nate called her several times a day, both at home and at work. It was seldom a good time.

"How did you think it went last night?" he asked. "The turnout from the shul was poor," he added, without giving her a chance to reply.

Faith could just picture him furrowing his brow and wringing his hands. Literally, not metaphorically, wringing. "I thought we had a very good turnout," she said briskly. "And I liked your speech."

"Which parts?"

"Uh, well, you know … the bits about building bridges and finding common ground. And Rabbi Shulman made the right sorts of noises, too. I mean for someone orthodox."

"But not everyone who was at Hakafot showed up."

"Well you can't expect everybody to be as enthusiastic as you are about this sort of thing. Nate, I'm seeing a client in five minutes."

"I actually called to ask you a favour."

Faith smothered a sigh.

"Would you come with me to see Melly Darwin about the capital campaign?"

Faith prided herself on having an intimate and encyclopedic knowledge of her community, but was momentarily at a loss for words. Accustomed to anticipating Nate's agenda well in advance, she was caught completely off guard. Melly Darwin was one of the shul's wealthiest members. Enlisting his help for financing a possible new building before canvassing the rank and file was a foxy move. She was quite chagrined at being taken by surprise.

If you had asked Faith why she had accepted the mantle of the presidency—and pressed her to be serious about her answer—she might have said something about liking the idea of being a small cog in the large wheel of Jewish continuity, of helping in a modest way to perpetuate the positive values of Judaism. Not the stupid, nitpicking, obsessive-compulsive minutiae of kashruth or Sabbath observance, but the institutions of synagogue life and, yes, the tribal closeness of a people that had foundered for millennia and yet had stubbornly persisted in—being. Just being Jewish. It was her way of doing her bit for her people. That's what she would have said as to why she hadn't turned down what she knew was bound to be a demanding job.

She probably would not have mentioned that there were intangible perks to the office of the president. It was a truism, practically a truth universally acknowledged, that no one knew as much about a person as did their lawyer or their accountant. Maybe not even their shrink. But a shul president was also advantageously positioned to obtain some fine insights. Performing the mitzvah of visiting a shiva house, she might bear witness to the most astonishing family meltdowns. Reviewing a report from the membership chair, she had privileged dope on the deadbeats: the members, not necessarily of the ranks of the impoverished, who shamelessly drifted from year to year mooching off the public weal, without paying their fees.

Gaining unexpected entry into the Darwin household as an incidental perk?

"I guess I could come," she said slowly to Nate, with an unusual note of indecision in her voice. She didn't know Darwin to speak to, although he came from the same town in Poland as her parents did. Outside of the High Holidays, she had never seen him in shul.

She had always been curious about Melly. Slightly resentful of him, too. It would be intriguing to pay a call on him on shul business. Especially if they were to visit him at home. Melly Darwin's colossus of a house was a landmark in New Hampstead, an area not renowned for restraint in architecture.

"So I'll set up an appointment with him for the two of us?" Nate pressed.

"Just make sure it's in the evening. By the way, Nate," Faith couldn't resist asking, even though she heard voices in the waiting room. "Leona and Marty weren't together at Hakafot. Or at the street celebration. Do you know what's going on? Or is this something confidential?"

Nate gave a small, discreet cough. "Well, I don't believe it's a secret any more, They're separating."

"I knew it," Faith said with satisfaction, not because

she rejoiced at marital break-ups but because her hunch had been dead on. "I just knew it."

5

Email from faithrabinovitch@mch.org to rhoda.kaplansky@lbpsb.ca

October 13, 1998, 12:55 p.m.
   The Reb has confirmed that Leona and Marty are *fini*. What do you think of him as a candidate for Erica?

Email from rhoda.kaplansky@lbpsb.ca to faithrabinovitch@mch.org

October 13, 1998, 12:57 p.m.
   Why don't you get a life? What exactly do you know about Marty? Even if Erica wasn't still stuck on ridiculous Rick, what makes him suitable? A Y chromosome?
   P.S. Don't you ever work?

6

Melly Darwin lived a ten-minute walk from Congregation Emunath, in a mansion that stood at the corner of Hillpark and Briarcliff on what must have been at least a triple lot. Faith pulled up and parked on the opposite side of Hillpark. Waiting for Nate, she dimmed her lights but kept the engine running because of the evening chill. As always when she saw this house, she felt a mixture of envy, admiration, and scorn. What gave Melly and Bubbles Darwin the right to live in such opulence, while her parents, who were of the same generation and background, had always struggled to get by?

In its oversized boxiness, the three-storey brown brick building looked more like an embassy or even a small synagogue than a private residence. Arched windows edged a huge skylight above the burnished wood squares of the front door. Every detail shrieked money.

She and Nate had decided in advance that he would do the talking, which meant she could sit back and take stock of the meeting. This was something she was used to doing at work and knew she was good at. In fact, she tended to do it automatically, managing to observe a great deal more than a particular situation required and squirreling away surplus information to mull over later. She did this without premeditation or ulterior motive. She had a vast curiosity about the world and the people around her, and she genuinely enjoyed sharing the knowledge she acquired through a kind of recreational sleuthing. So when she saw Nate pull up behind her, she was as astonished as she was annoyed to find her pulse quickening.

She scrambled out of her car and waved to him. "I can't believe it," she said softly as they walked up the flagstone path, "I've actually got butterflies."

Darwin answered at the first chime of the bell, as if he had been waiting by the door. He was burly and bull-necked, a seventyish man of medium stature and florid complexion, exuding both authority and urgency in his jerky movements. He had a head of wiry iron-grey hair, a humped nose, and fleshy lips over prominent, very white teeth. In his short-sleeved polo shirt and dark cotton pants, he looked as if he were about to play golf rather than conduct a meeting. Faith wondered, not for the first time, what had attracted him to Congregation Emunath. Perhaps it was merely his home's proximity to the shul. He didn't strike her as an ideological Reconstructionist, inspired, like the founding members, by notions of social justice and the overarching importance of Jewish culture.

"Come in, come in." He greeted them with a geniality at odds with the searching beam of restless brown eyes that darted away quickly after taking their measure.

"You want we should go to the conference room, or maybe first a tour?" His accent reminded Faith of her parents' idiomatic English inflected by equal measures of Polish and Yiddish.

"The conference room," Faith blurted, "unless of course you'd rather—"

"Yes, yes, it would take too long to show the whole house," he gestured grandly with both arms. For an instant she caught a glimpse of a smear of blue on his left forearm.

"Perhaps you could just show us this floor," Nate said. Faith, still unsettled by the sight of Melly's number, felt her jaw drop as she stared at the rabbi. *Isn't that just like him? He's as much dying to see the place as I am, but I'm too embarrassed to say so. And he isn't.*

"On this level we have three thousand"—he pronounced it t'ousand— "square feet. I'm not boasting— a businessman always thinks numbers. Numbers like dollars, naturally, but also numbers like square feet. Altogether this house is ten thousand square feet. It's a nice property," he added with a sudden, almost ingenuous smile. "Mine wife says I shouldn't blow mine horn. I'm not, I swear. I'm just giving facts. How d'you like so far? Here's the living room—it's big enough for a party for one hundred."

"Who plays?" Faith asked, eyeing the grand piano in the corner wistfully.

"Mine wife used to. A bit. But now she'd rather play cards with the book club ladies …. And this here's the dining room. I like everything should be solid, real substantial. Like it's been here forever. I don't want people should think I'm—how you say?—nouveau riche. This here table's solid oak. Custom built for me. I'm gonna tell you something, Rabbi, around this table sometimes we get *t'irty* people for the Seder, no extension needed!"

For a moment his voice wobbled. "Though I don't want you should think anything can replace all mine family that died. Never."

He fought to regain his composure, the bull neck stiffening, his colour high.

"But I made a new family here in Montreal and now

23

we are—like it says in the Bible, nearly as numerous as the stars in the sky."

His face cleared, and he managed a brief smile, his teeth flashing.

"This here's one of the guest powder rooms. We got six bathroom in the house and four powder room. And this here's the den. How do you like the plasma screen? The *ainecklach* when they visit, I got a whole entertainment centre for them. DVDs, a sound system, a videocam. Mine kids call it the House of Fun." This last was said with less bombast and a sudden disarming modesty, as if the good opinion of his children were a validation of a special order.

"And the kitchen—with the big island and all the conveniences for mine wife. Not that she spends too much time in here. We have the help for that. So come, come, we go to the conference room so we can talk."

They retraced their steps in the direction of the entrance. Darwin paused for a moment at the foot of the curved staircase and leaned on the balustrade to yell upwards. "Bubbles!"

There was no response. He drummed his fingers against the shiny block of wood and called out again, "Sweetheart! The Rabbi is here!"

There was the sound of a door opening upstairs and then the click of high heels above. "I'll be down soon," a contralto voice sang out.

The conference room was across the hall from the living room and looked out on the street through one of the arched windows Faith had observed from outside. It was simply furnished with a long table in rosewood, surrounded by a dozen chairs. The artwork in the room was at odds with the utilitarian furniture. Oil paintings of classical female figures draped in flowing, gossamer garments vaguely evoked Aphrodite. Alongside the sylphs and goddesses hung photographs of stripmalls and shopping centres. Faith recognized a new mall on the South Shore that had been profiled recently in the Business Section of *The Gazette*. The mall was notable for containing both a Chez Darwin, a new addition to the line of women's wear shops that had initially made his fortune, and a La Lace boutique, his subsequent wildly successful lingerie franchise.

In a corner by the window, just behind the chair to which Melly now headed, stood a striking bronze bust of a man gazing into the distance. An excellent likeness—the hawk nose and fleshy lips were dead giveaways—it projected an image of decisiveness and strength.

Darwin took the chair at what was clearly the head of the table. He gestured to them to sit on either side of him.

"Would you like something to drink? Ginger ale? Tea?"

"No, no," Nate replied. "We just ate."

"I will ask the obvious question: why you want to put up a new building?"

Nate leaned forward to rest his elbows on the table and laced his fingers together. He cleared his throat and shot a tentative smile at their host.

"I'll give you the obvious answer, Melly. We've out-grown our building. It was put up nearly thirty years ago when our community numbered sixty families. As you know, we added the library and the balcony ten years later—by then we were two hundred families. Now we've got four hundred families, and we're bursting at the seams. We anticipate much growth in the years ahead. It's only natural, since we're expecting Reconstructionism to gain strength among Jews with time. Even as it is, we can't accommodate our membership adequately, let alone new members."

As Nate warmed to his topic, he began to talk faster, and his timidity evaporated. "On the High Holidays we're obliged to hold extra services at the Y, because we can only fit about six hundred people into the building. We need better facilities for programming; we need a proper social hall, we need air conditioning—"

"Pardon me for butting in, Rabbi. I'm gonna tell you something, Rabbi—I'm not sold on this idea of growth. You know I'm a plain man with no education. But mine eyes are sharp. Here where I live, I watch mine neighbours. They're all *frum*, and they seem to be getting *frummer* all the time. They don't come to our shul, even though they live around the corner. On *Shabbos* they walk to the Baily or the Adath. What I think is this, it's the Orthodox that are growing by—how you say?—leaps and bounds, not us."

Nate furrowed his brows and swallowed. He wished he'd asked for something to drink after all. He had to tread carefully. It was only a foolish or inexperienced rabbi who came hat in hand to his richest congregant and then made mincemeat of his arguments.

"When it comes to demographics," Nate said, taking a deep breath and smoothing his trim goatee with one hand, "of course the numbers can be interpreted in a variety of ways. With all due respect, though, Melly—and you may have little education, but you're one very smart man—with all due respect, I would argue that the trend is towards the expansion of liberal Judaism. You are quite right that the ultra-Orthodox *are* gaining ground and that there's also a resurgence in the modern Orthodox movement. But the mainstream movements—Conservative and Reform and traditional Orthodox—all of them look tired today. For thoughtful, contemporary Jews, our movement has so much to offer. Things like full egalitarianism for women and girls and dynamic, participatory services. And of course our emphasis on Jewish culture instead of blind faith—these are just some of the values that make us so special. And," added Nate, pleased with his eloquence, "if we had a new, beautiful building, with appropriate function rooms, I believe we would attract many more young families with children who will need bar and bat mitzvahs. In fact, I have many, many ideas on how Congregation Emunath could become the leading synagogue in the city. But of course first we must have better facilities."

"It all sounds very fancy," Darwin drummed his fingers on the shiny surface of the table. "How much d'you think it'll cost?"

Nate tugged at his beard nervously. "Five million, maybe five and a half, according to our preliminary feasibility study." He expected an outburst from Darwin, but when none came, he pushed on. "We are certain we can raise half that from the membership at large. We also believe it's very important that the members feel a sense of ownership, of proprietorship. So we're only going to propose that you help us with the other half."

Darwin screwed up his face and slapped himself on the forehead dramatically. "I've got to hand it to you, Rabbi. You've got more chutzpah than me—and that's saying something. One moment please." He strode to the door and almost collided with it, as it was thrown open from the other side. A tall, handsome woman in a flowing black lounging costume swept in. Every black hair of her upswept coiffure was glued into place. Her air of assumed majesty implied that, at the very least, a fanfare of trumpets was in order.

"*There* you are, Bubbles. I was just going to get you."

"I *told* you I was coming. You're always so bloody impatient, Melly!" There was no immigrant accent in her diction; she wore the smug confidence of the born-and-bred Montrealer who, half a century earlier, had traded on her sex appeal to land a *greener* who worshipped her and who had fortuitously fulfilled his part of an unwritten contract: he had made good. "Excuse my language, Rabbi—how *are* you? And how are *you*, Faith? No, no, don't get up. I'll just sit here next to you, Rabbi. So, what have you decided amongst yourselves?"

"You know, sweetheart—," Melly shot her one of his mercurial glances before training his eyes back on Nate, "our Rabbi's a bit of a joker. He's asked us for nearly three million dollars. But perhaps, Rabbi, you are not really a comedian, just a very able negotiator. Perhaps you're asking a lot more than you expect to get?"

There was a pregnant silence. Somewhere in the house a clock chimed the quarter hour. Nate wondered if he should say something. Faith sneezed.

"*Gezuntheit, gezuntheit,*" Darwin said heartily, then turned to his wife once more.

"What should we say to them, Bubbles?"

Bubbles studied her flawlessly manicured coral fingernails, then propped her chin on her hands.

"Rabbi, as you know, we have a beautiful family. Our girls, God bless them, we couldn't ask for better. Besides both of them being in the business—and so good at it—they've made fine marriages: two doctors, Rabbi, imagine! One's a pulmo ... pulmonologist, the other's an intensivist, that's intensive care, you know. Charlene has two children and Anita, so far only one, but we hope for more. Now our son, Glen, he's also quite wonderful, but maybe a little bit unsettled, a little rebellious. He and his wife are expecting their first baby in the spring. You know, Rabbi, I think if you could persuade our *shiksa* daughter-in-law to convert by then, Melly would be more inclined to help you out."

"Now, *Bubbles!* Hold on, hold on, under no circumstances I pay for half the building! Conversion, no conversion, I'm not the only member with some change. So what do you say Rabbi?"

Nate's eyebrows had shot up and his freckled cheeks had turned pale. Faith had only seen him ashen like this after the *Avoda* service on Yom Kippur.

"What do I say to what?" he asked faintly. "You're not seriously suggesting that I should convert someone who's reluctant? You surely don't mean that I should take this on as some kind of challenge? In Judaism, we *discourage* Gentiles, we turn them down three times. A rabbi doesn't make deals." He tugged at his beard. "Perhaps I misheard you, Melly. Maybe you're asking me to comment on other large donors?"

Again there was a long pause, during which the rabbi blinked furiously. Faith had never seen him so off balance.

"We're saying," Darwin finally spoke, "that there are many considerations here, many services for exchange." He cocked his head in Faith's direction. "I heard you had a friend—what's her name, Bubbles? She writes in the paper."

"Molnar," Bubbles drawled.

"That's it. Erica Molnar. Is she a friend of yours?"

"Yes," Faith said, nonplussed. "Erica's a very good friend of mine."

"She writes some kind of stories or something?"

"She writes a column, Melly," Bubbles dripped sarcasm. "A literary column."

"But she writes books too, no? Am I not right she

writes books? Tell your friend, I want her to write a book about me."

"Erica's a professional writer." Faith fairly bristled with indignation. She automatically drew her hands to her hips, a pose she usually adopted when on her feet and in a combative frame of mind. "Erica doesn't come running just because someone asks."

"I'm not *someone*. I'm Melly Darwin. Meyer Melech Darwin. That's what I want, a professional. Bring her to me. I have a story like she's never heard before. She makes up stories, right? Mine story she couldn't make up! No one could make up a story like mine. Right, Bubbles?"

7

Nate unbuttoned his shirt slowly, then slung it in the wicker hamper in the corner of the bedroom. He sank onto the bed, reaching for his folded pyjama top beneath the pillow. Without bothering to button himself up, he slid under the covers next to Reisa, unclipped his kipah, and took her into his arms. "Unbelievable," he sighed into her neck. "Quite unbelievable."

"But I'm still not clear what happened," Reisa said, extricating herself from the embrace, and sitting bolt upright against her pillow. "Did he turn you down or did he say yes?"

Nate rolled onto his back and stared up at the ceiling, painted navy with little silver stars. *Maybe that was a touch too eighties? Maybe they needed to repaint, redecorate?*

31

"Bubbles muddied the waters, first by bringing up the issue of the conversion of Glen's wife. And then *he* implied that if Erica wrote a book about him, he'd be more amenable."

"Are they playing good cop, bad cop?"

"They're both bad cops. Erica isn't going to write a book about Melly. And I can't convert Glen's wife."

"I don't see why not. If she came to you and asked, you could and you would."

"A, she hasn't come. And B, I don't do conversions on demand. You know people study for years with me!"

"Some people study for years with you, and others do it more quickly. There's a lot at stake, Nate."

"You don't have to tell me that!"

"And as far as Erica is concerned, everyone has their price. I'll bet you she has hers."

8

Thursday evening after supper Faith held a debriefing for the Graces at Rockaberry's on Queen Mary Road.

"Nate's got to have it," Faith said, sipping her latte and shaking her head. "He's had a bee in his bonnet ever since he got back from California. Nice job, Rhoda."

Rhoda grinned, revealing the crowded uppers that gave her smile a charming irregularity. She inclined her silver head modestly. She had just finished carving one slice of very berry pie and another of apple crumble into three surgically equal slivers. "This isn't San Diego," she said, passing the plates around. "And anyway we've got an entirely acceptable building."

"That meditation retreat in California had a huge impact on him," Faith mused. "Maybe it's some kind of mid-life thing, y'know what I mean? He's meeting up with his classmates from rabbinical college after something like twenty-five years, and they're probably all showing off with their big fancy American shuls. What a come-down our little hovel must seem after all that!"

"I don't think it's about his trip to California at all," Erica said, pouring tisane into her cup from a green ceramic teapot. "I think it really is about the building. My kids call it a barn. And, Rhoda, it's not true that it's perfectly acceptable. The roof leaked badly last winter."

"So fix it! Patch it or do whatever you're supposed to do with a roof! And what if it *is* like a barn? It's supposed to be. The original design was modelled on a French-Canadian farmhouse."

"It costs way too much to renovate," Faith said. "And it's not worth it. The feasibility study said so."

Rhoda put down her fork, wiped her lips, and arched a finely-shaped eyebrow. "Take us out of that building and we're going to be like every other synagogue in Montreal. Full of ourselves. Stuffy. Self-serving."

Faith scanned the diners at the neighbouring tables, nearly all of them boisterous teenagers. A grey haze enveloped the room, even the No Smoking section where they were seated. She lowered her voice and leaned forward conspiratorially. "This is in the strictest confidence."

33

The other two nodded gravely, deliberately avoiding each other's eyes. If they didn't snicker or otherwise throw Faith off course, a juicy tidbit was likely to follow. Faith turned towards Erica. "You're in for quite a surprise. The rabbi's going to put the touch on you to write a book about Melly."

"Are you crazy? I've never laid eyes on the man."

"Well, he's heard about you. He has you in mind for his biographer."

"C'mon Faith, what you been smoking?"

9

A couple of bearded blackhats were leaving the butcher shop by the back door when Erica entered by the front. At the counter, Noam, the butcher, a burly fortyish man with a slight stoop, dressed in blue jeans, a lumberjack's shirt, and a diminutive kipah, was fingering the blade of a cleaver and grousing under his breath. "The *Va'ad*'s going to be the death of me."

It wasn't clear whether his dark musings about the Jewish Community Council's kosher supervisory arm were being addressed to a young woman at the counter or at Erica behind her.

"That's the third time they've come to check me out this month. Twenny years in the business, they think I dunno how to salt a chicken! What can I do for you today, Bella?"

"I don't know what to feed them already," the woman called Bella whined, as she balanced a baby on her hip, while a little girl at her knee tugged on her stylishly cut mid-calf skirt. Erica couldn't decide whether the blonde hair beneath the dark snood was real or a very good wig.

"Avrumeleh wants only chicken fingers," Bella sighed dramatically, wagging a finger at a boy of about five who had his nose stuck against the glass door of one of the freezers by the wall. "Avrumeleh," she pleaded, "If I buy some minute steak, will you eat?"

"I *hate* steak!"

Bella gave another long-suffering sigh. "See what I mean? And my daughter won't touch chicken fingers."

Noam stared impassively in front of him. Erica cocked her head to catch his eye.

"Shall I come back later? I just need a couple of things."

"I'm almost done," Bella said. "So throw in three pounds of chicken fingers, I've got to feed them something! You've no idea what a struggle it is. I don't wish it on anybody. And my husband won't eat either," she added, a helpless look on her blandly pretty face. "And after *yontiff* they're more picky than ever."

Erica watched Noam's reddened fingers dance over an assembly line of boneless chicken breasts on the stainless steel counter, turning glistening slabs of meat into a mound of neat slices in seconds. With economy of movement, he divided the pile in three, heaping each onto a styrofoam tray, then sealing it in plastic wrap.

Erica was fond of Noam and his shtick. He spoke a

smattering of oddly-inflected Hungarian which he liked to practise on her. Born in Israel, to parents who, like hers, were Hungarian, he was Lubavitch without being stridently so. She got a kick out of his earnestness and the homespun bits of philosophy he dished out along with the best kosher meat in town. Or at least Faith and Rhoda said it was the best, and she ceded to their expertise. Having come to kashruth by the back door relatively late in life, she herself had no basis for comparison.

As Bella and her brood trooped out, Erica gave Noam a sympathetic smile.

"*Szervusz*, Erica."

"You're a patient guy, Noam."

"What am I gonna do? They're my bread and butter. And the Rebbe, *olav ha shalom*, when I used to visit him in Brooklyn, he used to say what's the point in *davening*, if we can't get along with each other? God must get awfully bored listening to us every day the same thing, if we don't do the right thing. Maybe the *Moshiach* won't come until Bella finds something to serve her husband and kids that they'll eat."

"I guess you're doing your bit then to make him come."

"I'm trying. Don't joke about it, Erica. This is serious. The Rebbe said that what God wants most from us is in the work of our hands, that's the way we'll fix the world. And the *Moshiach* will come only if we're all doing the *mitzvot*."

Erica thought she'd better order before Noam got himself truly worked up about the *Moshiach*.

"Two chickens cut up, no skin, please. And could you please give me some soup bones and chicken bones as well?"

"And a little liver for Cinnamon? I figured you're due to come in, so I've been putting some aside. How's he doing, by the way?" Noam hated cats, and his solicitous enquiries about Erica's geriatric pet were always couched in tones of tender scorn.

"Holding his own pretty well for an old gentleman."

10

Erica backed out of her driveway on Saturday morning in some haste. It was five past ten—she would have to hustle to make it. Since Faith's investiture as president, this had become their routine. Instead of lingering over the fat Saturday paper, catching up on phone calls, or doing the groceries, they were off to shul together.

Erica had learned to be on time for these outings; Faith was starchy if kept waiting. "On time," though, meant a calibrated degree of lateness. Services started at ten, but being there for *Mah tovu*, the first of the morning prayers, showed greater eagerness for religion than Faith deemed necessary. On the other hand, she considered arriving after 10:20 bad form for her new presidential status. A decorous entrance before the *Amidah*, the standing prayer, was just right.

Erica pulled up in front of Faith's brick and stone split-level on Rosedale, just as Faith, who'd been watching for her from inside, came sailing down the stairs.

"A new outfit?" Erica asked her as she buckled up.

"Rhoda and I found it on sale at BCBG. It was a steal."

"That leopard print is very you, but however do you manage on those spiky heels?"

"They're not that high, Erica, really. Not when you're as short and round as me. How was your Friday night?"

"Just Tamara and my father. The usual."

The usual now. Erica allowed her mind to wander. It used to be both her parents and Raichie and Ricky as well. But her mother had passed away, Raichie was working in Toronto, and Ricky—Ricky was gone. What was his used-car heiress serving him on Friday nights? Lobster bisque? Steak tartare? The heiress, the kids had let drop, was a very good cook.

Erica transported herself back from a vision of Ricky feasting on a heaping platter of verboten shellfish, an oversized serviette tucked into his starched white shirt. Faith was asking her something that she hadn't heard the first time.

"Melly Darwin? Are you still riding that hobbyhorse?"

Faith chuckled from the depths of her belly. Erica's arcane turns of phrase gleaned from who-knew-where were a source of merriment to her and Rhoda.

11

Erica and Faith entered the sanctuary just as Rabbi Nate was intoning the *yotzer*. The square room was hinged towards the east, its focal point a row of slender stained glass windows above the *Aron Kodesh*. Through the narrow panes the sun cast prisms of colour onto the *bimah*, both illuminating Nate's face and tingeing it with a hint of mystery. His expression flickered in an almost imperceptible greeting—from past experience, Erica knew that after the service he would be able to give an exact accounting of who had been present, even on Shabbatot when there were a couple of hundred congregants in attendance.

She was faintly surprised when Faith took her arm to steer her towards the central section of the sanctuary rather than their habitual spot on the left side. "O God, you have created us in your image and have made us to share in your work of Creation. You have given to each generation the task to shape the future of humankind," the rabbi was reciting as Faith made a beeline for seats directly in front of Marty Riess and Abigail Rosen, checking to make sure that Erica was in tow. Erica's puzzlement grew. Why had Faith brought them into such proximity with Abigail, who as Faith was well aware, was no fan of Erica's.

A poet of uncertain renown, Abigail, in fact, disapproved mightily of Erica, for having merely congratulated her on the publication of her latest collection, instead of rushing to interview her for *The Gazette*—as she clearly believed was her due. That had left Abigail with no alternative but to call Paul Ladouceur, Erica's editor, who in turn wounded her by being unfamiliar with her name and oeuvre.

Even worse, Ladouceur then assigned the collection to young Guido Vincelli, who mustn't have had a dram of poetry in his punk soul. In an omnibus review, the wretched Vincelli had dismissed Abigail's years of effort in one line ("*Reaching the Pinnacle* strains for the heights but scales no peaks").

Abigail had had to content herself with a rave review in the *Canadian Jewish News* ("Abigail Rosen wears her Jewish heart on her sleeve and brings to life the joys and sorrows of a Montreal-Jewish childhood") and the triumphant satisfaction that a Spanish publisher had not only bought the translation rights but had invited her to attend the launch in Madrid the following spring.

Having located the exact seats for her purpose, Faith nodded briskly at Erica, and the two of them sat down, Erica still wearing an expression of bemusement.

12

Bent on a little clandestine matchmaking research, Faith wondered what Marty was doing next to Abigail, who was at the very least eighty-five and neither charming nor beautiful. Was it his well-known and unabashed admiration for the arts? Did he have a mother complex? During the *Shema*, she noted that he had a pleasant singing voice and good Hebrew pronunciation. At the same time, she was taking mental stock of those in attendance.

It was a surprisingly large group, for the Shabbat following the holidays. In the front row on the right hand side, ancient and bent, Moish Stipelman, founding rabbi of Congregation Emunath, with Sylvia, his battle-ax of a second wife. A few rows behind them, the sleek blonde page boy of Leona Riess—*that* was it! Leona had staked claim to the family pew, forcing Marty to relocate beside Abigail. Then there were a few youngish couples, all accompanied by prepubescent children, the next crop of bar and bat mitzvah candidates. Faith made a mental note to greet and welcome each of them at the *kiddush* after services.

"The Shatzes are here," she whispered to Erica.

"Uhuh," said Erica, her nose in her *siddur*.

"Haven't you heard?"

"What?" Erica, apparently lost in prayer, sounded vaguely exasperated.

"The son's having an affair with the Golda character in *Fiddler*."

"What?" Erica nearly dropped her *siddur* as she turned to stare at Faith in a most satisfying display of attentiveness

"You do know the Yiddish Theatre is doing *Fiddler*?"

"Yeah. So?"

"So Jason Shatz, and the father—Mike Shatz—*and* his father, old Solly Shatz, are all in the play. And Jason's sleeping with Barbara Walfish, the woman playing Golda."

"So what?" Erica's voice kept rising as Faith expertly reeled her in.

"What d'you mean, so what? He's twenty-four and she's forty-seven! And married! Or was, till recently. Apparently she's having to give back the Mercedes."

"I should think so!"

"The Shatzes all think it's great, Jason having the sexual prowess to satisfy a sex bomb like Barbara."

Erica's shoulders began to heave with the effort of suppressing the storm of laughter that threatened to erupt at the idea of puny Jason Shatz in the guise of Don Juan. Faith was quite content at the effect she had produced. But before she could supply another lubricious detail, Erica's features contorted in a grimace of pain. Startled, Faith snapped her head around. Abigail's arresting liquid brown eyes—her one fine feature—were burning at her with wrath. She wagged a bony finger—the one that had just poked Erica between the shoulder blades—in her face.

"Grow up, you two," Abigail hissed amidst a scraping of feet as the congregation rose for the *Amidah*.

13

Nate was about half way through the *d'var torah* when a couple of the stranger members of his flock began filing in.

Each year it was a challenge to come up with a fresh reading of the Creation story, particularly after the exertions of the High-Holiday sermons had, as usual, leached him of his best ideas. And yet each year he loved this moment of wrestling with the ancient and majestic text—it was too inflated to compare himself to Ya'akov and the angel, but still .... Engaging with the thinking of the great rabbis through the ages, hoping to come up with some small fragmented truth of his own that might speak to a questing mind or two, these were the reasons he had entered the rabbinate.

He was warming to his theme that the *parsha* presented two Creation stories, one centred on God and beginning appropriately with the birth of heaven, then of earth, and the second focused on humans, reversing the order. "That magnificent sentence introducing *Bereishit*," he was saying, "that sentence we can all quote: 'In the beginning God created the heaven and the earth,' speaks first of the creation of the sky, *hashamayim*. But when the story is reprised in Genesis 2 and God forms man from the 'dust of the ground,' the order of the words is inverted and we learn that this was the day on which God 'made earth—*haaretz*—and heaven.'

"The late great modern-Orthodox rabbi and philosopher, Joseph Soloveitchik, gives a brilliant and profound interpretation of these two Creation stories in his classic essay *The Lonely Man of Faith*. In it he says that the answer to why there are two different accounts isn't because of, what he terms, an 'alleged and imaginary dual tradition.' Rabbi Soloveitchik, as an Orthodox rabbi, doesn't examine the Torah as a literary text that can and often does incorporate different sources from different eras. He sees it as the actual revealed word of God. Thus for him the two accounts arise directly out of what he views as a real contradiction in the nature of man.

"We as Reconstructionists are of course open to the study of the Torah as a rich compilation of various texts from different eras. But we are also at liberty to study the

43

gleanings of Soloveitchik and to learn from them."

Nate was an unassuming speaker, not given to oratorical flourishes, but his voice inadvertently grew louder as, looking up from his notes, he observed Rozalee Zelniger and Simon Herscovitch making their entrance into the sanctuary, more or less together. Rozalee, her fronds of dyed carrot hair more than usually dishevelled, was pushing a steel frame walker in front of her. Why the walker?—Nate puzzled to himself, momentarily distracted from his sermon. Rozalee wasn't especially old, maybe in her mid-fifties. To date, she had merely declared herself blind, not halt, a claim bolstered by the coke-bottle lenses of her horn-rimmed glasses, but open to challenge, since she also professed to be a visual artist and had occasionally been sighted behind the wheel of a car. Thin to the point of gauntness, chin thrust forward, Rozalee was proceeding down the aisle with a normal gait, but as she neared the centre of the front row where she insisted she needed to sit on account of her impaired vision, she gathered up the walker in her arms and fairly sprinted to her seat. Simon, her octogenarian husband, dressed in a faded but freshly pressed Mao jacket from the 60s, was making his stately progress several paces behind her, dragging one leg and using a cane.

Nate took a deep, steadying breath and resumed speaking. "So that in Genesis 1, we read, 'And God created man in His own image...; male and female created He them. And God blessed them; and ... said to them, Be fruitful and multiply, and fill the earth and subdue it, and have dominion over the fish of the sea, over the fowl of the heaven and over the beasts and over all the earth.'

"The Rav calls the Adam of Genesis 1 Adam the first. This Adam is—we are told—created in the image of God. Rabbi Soloveitchik suggests that humanity's likeness to the divine expresses itself in our striving and ability to be creative beings. The first Adam is boundlessly curious in his mission to subdue his environment and to gain control of nature.

"The creation of the second Adam is quite different. The text in Genesis 2 speaks of God breathing the breath of life into Adam's nostrils and giving him a soul. This Adam doesn't create a world of his own or dominate nature so much as he looks with wonder upon God's garden and nurtures it.

"So we can view the first Adam as a social, creative being, who emphasizes the artistic aspect of life. Rabbi Soloveitchik also points out that this Adam is never alone, not even on the day of creation. He emerges into the world together with Eve, while the second Adam stands alone and is spiritually oriented.

"I am simplifying the Rav's thesis, but let me now conclude with my view that the Torah, including the Creation story, is not an either-or proposition. Rather it gives a rounded picture of the world and of our own human nature within it. We are neither the first Adam nor the second. We are both practical and spiritual, creative and nurturing."

Nate looked up from his notes to scrutinize his congregants. There were fifty or sixty people in the room, a respectable number for this particular Shabbat, though as always he wished that the fervour of the High Holidays would carry over into better attendance in the new Jewish year.

"Are there any comments or questions?" he asked diffidently, though he was quite pleased with how he had developed his tentative thoughts.

Rozalee bounded to her feet before the words were out of Nate's mouth. Thin chest quivering, she throbbed with indignation. "As a vegetarian and a Reconstructionist, I wish to disassociate myself from the idea that we as humans are superior to the members of the animal kingdom. When God tells Adam and Eve to rule over the fish and the birds and the other creatures, that's the beginning of all evil in society! I myself am a vegan and I think the fact that Shabbat *kiddush* includes eggs and fish, and even *cheese* from time to time, is an implicit act of aggression towards the creatures who we share the earth with. And cruelty towards animals begins right here in the Torah, in *Bereishit*."

"Thank you, Rozalee," Nate said, looking around the room for help from any quarter.

"Rabbi," Abigail sang out, without standing up. Her sonorous voice could carry from any part of the room.

"Yes, Abigail," Nate said, bracing himself. Participation by the congregation was a fundamental tenet of Reconstructionist Judaism. He believed in it wholeheartedly. Why was it, though, that the most trying individuals tended to hog the discourse?

"I find the title of Rabbi Soloveitchik's book really evocative, Rabbi: *The Lonely Man of Faith*, that's wonderful. As a writer myself, I know how difficult it is to choose a really good title.

"I remember reading the book some time back. The part that especially spoke to me was the personal element. He wrote about his own loneliness. I was surprised that a man of such piety could sound so tormented, could feel so alone in the world, abandoned by all, even by God. Why do you think that is, Rabbi?"

In the row in front of Abigail, Faith and Erica exchanged a long appreciative look.

"You got to hand it to her," Faith whispered.

Erica, forgetting Abigail's recent attack for an instant, nodded. "I bet she's the only one here besides Nate who's read Soloveitchik."

Nate leaned forward on the lectern, cupping his chin with one hand and stroking his beard slowly. "I think, Abigail, that in today's secular society, having faith is to feel at odds with the rest of the world. But paradoxically, a feeling of loneliness can also send the man or woman of faith towards God, through the avenue of prayer. And feelings of loneliness can propel you towards others, as a way of creating connectedness as well as community." Nate glanced sidelong to his right, where his cherished Reisa was sitting in the front row. "There's an essential loneliness to living, but it's mitigated by the profound loving connections we are capable of forging. The first Adam is not alone for even a single day. He and Eve emerge into the cosmos together. And let's not forget either that the Rav dedicated his book to Tonya, his wife of many, many years. Despite his feelings of marginalization, he was far from being alone."

"But that's not really the point, is it?" Abigail persisted. "That's about subjectivity, but I was talking objectively, or existentially, if you prefer."

Nate scanned the room to see if there were any other hands in the air. But Abigail wasn't done.

"Rabbi," she called out. "I want to add one more point, Rabbi. If we're going to be subjective." She paused for effect. "Again, that haunting title. I really think it fits you to a T, Nate. I've always thought so. The Montreal Jewish community is one big Orthodox sea. That leaves you a very lonely figure. I mean, the way you don't fit in with the other rabbis in town. And I just want to say how much you mean to me: you are in your own way a heroic figure."

A subdued titter rippled through the room.

"God, she's impossible!" Erica mouthed to Faith, rubbing the shoulder that was still tender from Abigail's thrust. Faith rolled her eyes in response. "She makes a great point and then she blows it."

"Well, thank you, Abigail," Nate said. He tugged at his beard, looking unsure as to whether he wanted to burst out laughing or weep. Surveying the room once more, he glanced up at the balcony, and then said perfunctorily, "If there are no more comments or questions, then let's return the *sefer* Torah to the Ark."

14

The folding screen separating a spartan social hall from the sanctuary was pushed aside for *kiddush*. Conversation hummed briskly around tables set with the usual array of Shabbat fare: gefilte fish and herring, party sandwiches, pita, hummus. Marty Riess juggled a plate of gefilte fish and purple horseradish in one hand and a glass of red wine in the other. He cocked his head from his great height towards Erica.

"I was quite embarrassed by Abigail's behaviour," he said apologetically.

She looked up at him with a wry smile, revealing a small dimple on her left cheek. "I wasn't behaving particularly well myself."

"I was thinking about you during the *d'var torah*," he said, his expression earnest and his deep-set eyes serious.

"You were? Why?"

"A creative person like you must feel like God, no?"

"Like *God*?"

"You know, writing, making up stories, bringing things into the world that weren't there before."

"It's really just what I do, my work."

"I'd like to ask you more about it some time."

"Well, okay," Erica said, offhand. She had once served on the shul program committee with Marty and found his ideas deadly dull. She turned away, and, for want of something to do with herself, reached for a celery stick.

"I understand we're in the same boat," Marty persisted.

"What boat is that?"

"Leona and I are separating. I heard you and your husband also."

"I see. That boat."

"And—I was sorry to learn that you've had an operation."

"Thank you." *Really, did he have to rub salt into all her wounds?* "Would you excuse me, Marty? I wanted to say something to Nate."

Erica spun around and scanned the room for the Rabbi, who was trapped in conversation with Rozalee. Rozalee had exchanged the walker for Simon's cane, and was making a point by bashing it into the floor. Nate appeared grateful when Erica materialized at his elbow.

"That was a very interesting *d'var torah*, Nate."

"You think? Have you read the Rav?" He looked sorrowful when she shook her head.

"At least now I've heard of him. I found your summary of his ideas fascinating."

"Well, thank you. I've been meaning to call you, Erica. Do you know Melly Darwin?"

Oh, God! I escaped Marty only to land on this particular mine.

"No. But I've heard about him too."

Nate frowned. "From Faith, I suppose."

"Wasn't she supposed to say anything?

"Did she tell you he wants to speak to you?"

Erica was silent.

"Okay, I guess if I'd called you earlier, you wouldn't

50

have heard it from Faith first. Melly Darwin has a writing proposition for you. A business proposition that he was, uhm, *shy* to bring you himself. Can he call you about it?"

"What kind of writing?"

"A biography or something like that. He's an unusual man who has had an extraordinary life. You might both benefit from collaborating with each other."

"It's not my sort of thing at all," Erica said with a hint of irritation. "I'm a novelist. Or at least I was one once."

"Maybe it's time for you to branch out?"

15

Marty nodded at the liveried doorman wishing him "*Bonsoir.*" In theory, he didn't mind the idea of a doorman—if one were obliged to give up one's home, it might as well be for a place with a touch of class, like the Rockhill. The gold-braided uniform, though, was not his style at all. Marty shrugged. He wasn't going to stay here forever, solo in a studio apartment.

At the elevator he ran into Kim Tran, his next-door neighbour. They smiled at each other. Dressed head to toe in black, Kim was carrying a couple of plastic grocery bags from Épicerie Atlantique. He guessed her to be in her early thirties, perhaps a bit more; he found it hard to tell with Asians. Very attractive.

Marty had met her when he moved in a couple of weeks ago and she'd brought him a pot of green tea as he was unpacking. Now as they rode upstairs together, she asked if he was all settled in.

"More or less. But I don't feel comfortable until everything is where it's supposed to be, and I'm not quite there yet."

"I know what you mean."

They got out on the fourth floor and walked to their apartments in silence. Placing her groceries on the carpet, Kim rummaged in her purse for her key and, just as Marty was about to step inside his place, asked in a burst, "D'you have plans for dinner?"

Marty sucked in his breath in surprise. In his new life, he had resolved not to lie about anything, not even the tiniest white lie. But he suddenly was overcome by the feeling that if he told the truth, he would slide off a precipice straight into some kind of trap.

"Actually, no. I was going to maybe order in."

"I just picked up a few things for supper," Kim said, craning her neck back to meet his eyes, her own wide and limpid. "Why don't you come over, and I'll make us something simple."

"Well, okay," Marty said. He realized he must sound churlish. "When should I come?"

"In half an hour? Maybe we could have a glass of wine and you could give me a hand?"

"Well, okay," Marty repeated, and dove through his front door.

She's feeling neighbourly, he told himself, hanging up his coat and throwing his gym bag into the cupboard. He was so distracted, he forgot to take out his shorts and wet towel. Neighbourly, that's all. She couldn't be much older than his boys. His heart was thumping.

What was he going to take her? You couldn't go to someone's house empty-handed. His mother had drummed that into him along with social pieties like "Always wear clean underwear." Marty blushed, chuckled, told himself he was crazy, as he lunged into the bedroom and yanked a fresh pair of briefs from a drawer. Changing underwear was of course only a precaution, but while he was at it, it wouldn't do any harm to shave as well. He was prone to five o'clock shadow. Claiming he was too scratchy, Leona had occasionally kicked him out of bed to shave in the middle of love-making.

Working up a good lather with his shaving brush, Marty stared at himself in the mirror. He grimaced at the sight of the dark pouches beneath his eyes, took stock of his beak of a nose and thinning crown. *A ruin, positively cadaverous.* He screwed his face up against the mirror, searching for evidence of nose hairs. Cheered that he couldn't find any, he sucked in his gut and tried a sidelong boyish smile. Really, his remaining hair was mostly dark. And he had his own teeth after all. He didn't need to wear glasses if he wasn't fussy about reading street signs (he didn't need to, since he knew them by rote anyway). He dabbed his face free of cream, patted on some aftershave. In your early fifties, there was still time to compensate for the failures of the past, *self-actualize*, like Dr. Winters kept on harping about.

Marty tapped on Kim's door and, when she answered,

handed over the bottle of Beaujolais that he'd settled on from his small supply. (Leona liked Chardonnay.) Again that cheery smile. She had reapplied her lipstick and was wearing Asian pyjamas, black with burgundy trim. She was pretty in a petite and unobtrusive way, her makeup flawlessly applied, her body slim. She had beautiful heavy black hair, cut blunt to shoulder length, and straight bangs that gave her the air of a serious child. But beneath the bright chandelier of her hallway, he could detect two jagged frown lines in her wide brow. Perhaps she was a bit older than he had initially thought.

"Do you like shrimp?" she asked. She had a clear little voice, slightly tinged with an accent. "I bought fresh shrimp."

"Love it."

"Come and give me a hand then."

Her place was bigger than his studio, with two closed doors that he assumed were bedrooms off a long corridor, and a spacious living room and minute dinette, both sparsely furnished. She shepherded him into the small square kitchen.

As if she were reading his mind, she said, "My boyfriend and I split up last month. He took most of his stuff with him to Toronto."

"I'm sorry," Marty said, feeling awkward. "Were you together a long time?"

She handed him a corkscrew and gave him back the bottle of wine.

"A couple of years. Long enough. But it's okay. If

something isn't meant to be, it's not meant to be."

"But how do you know it isn't meant to be, if you don't work at it for longer than that?"

"I go with my gut feeling. That's what Oprah says."

Marty poured wine into the two glasses sitting on the counter. It was a philosophy that might have saved him a lot of grief in his marriage. Only he couldn't remember ever having clear gut feelings. More like major pain in the belly.

He wondered if he should clink glasses with her, thought better of it, lest it seem too eager or romantic. What was he doing here with this unknown woman anyway? He took a gulp of wine, then watched her purposeful preparations, rinsing the shrimp under running water, chopping ginger and garlic, fluffing rice with a fork. Apparently her comment about his helping had been rhetorical. Just as well, since he was a total klutz in the kitchen. He offered to set the table, a small civility he no longer bothered with for himself, but that had been one of his favourite domestic tasks in his former life. She waved him in the direction of a cupboard.

Over dinner—which was very good, a stir-fry of shrimp, bok choy, and snowpeas—he asked what she did for a living and learned she was a hairdresser. She had recently bought the Westmount salon where she had been working only a few months. Before that, she had spent several years in a bigger place in the Town of Mount Royal, where she learned the ropes and built up a sizable clientele that followed her to the new place. She became quite animated when describing her work, said she had lots of plans for the business. Her face clouded over when he inquired about the boyfriend.

"I don't talk about him. We were partners in the store, and then he left for Toronto. He said he wasn't going to play second fiddle to any woman." Marty realized that he had been extremely tactless.

"Where are you from?" he took another tack.

"Why do people always ask that? Just because I'm Oriental!" She had trouble pronouncing the word, skipping the "r." "I came in 1979."

"You mean from Vietnam?"

She nodded.

Marty said, "I used to work for a needle-trade company that sponsored a family of boat people around that time. A very nice family, the Phams. They'd gone through some tough times, but they adjusted really well to life here."

Her face grew stony. She glared at him.

"I'm sorry. Did I say something wrong?"

"I never talk about those things."

"Why not?"

"Too sad, too hard to think about. No point."

Marty began to wonder how he could gracefully make his exit. He supposed he ought to offer to help with the dishes, but he suddenly felt bone tired, probably from the wine. Or maybe because he was altogether too familiar with the process of trying to pull teeth from an uncommunicative woman. *No thanks. Been there. Done that.*

He stood up. So did Kim. She closed the gap between them, rose to her toes and drew his head down, her hands cupping his ears. Their lips met. She tasted sweet and sexy. He struggled with himself for a second. It was so deliciously voluptuous to have those small breasts pressing against him. He pulled back, letting her go.

"What's the matter? Don't you like me?"

"How can I not like you?" he said, gallant. "It's not that I don't like you. I don't know you. And I have a feeling you may be younger than my children."

"How old are they?" she asked, tapping his cheek with a finger, her eyes mischievous. She was clearly enjoying herself.

"My older son is almost thirty-two," Marty said. "My younger boy's thirty."

"You've just made my day! I'm thirty-nine."

"Oh well, in that case…," he said, and they both laughed. His last thought before entering the bedroom was that he was a lucky man. Being single was a whole lot easier than he had anticipated.

16

"That's him," Faith hissed, "That's Melly Darwin!"

Three Graces accompanied by two husbands were queued up at the Egyptian for *Life Is Beautiful*. Because Rhoda was a stickler for punctuality, they were near the head of the line, which snaked some distance behind them.

"Who the hell's Melly Darwin?" Hershy asked. Balding and barrel-chested, he was half a head shorter than Rhoda, a Mel Brooks to her Anne Bancroft, with a zany sense of humour to match.

"A member of our congregational family," Al said under his breath, "and one with a lot of chutzpah at that."

Darwin, in blue jeans and an expensive-looking trench coat, was dragging a reluctant Bubbles by the sleeve. In a seamless manoeuvre, he shoved her forward to the head of the row. There was a slight commotion, but then the line opened up to accommodate them.

"Did you see what he just did?" Faith placed her hands on her hips and nudged Erica with her elbow.

"Uhuh. And *this* is the guy you and the Rabbi have in mind for me?"

"Will someone please tell me what's happening?" Hershy bugged out his eyes and hunched his shoulders in imitation of a puzzled half-wit. Erica, who had a chronic weakness for his routines, burst out laughing.

"Our Erica's going to ghostwrite his war memoirs," Al said, chucking her under the chin. "It should be quite the story."

"He should be so lucky," Rhoda said, trying to keep a straight face with some difficulty. "Erica's a woman of principle."

The line began to move. "You're not going to do it, are you?" Rhoda asked after they'd bought their tickets.

"I don't even know what it's about! I suppose I'll have to speak to him."

"Good luck," Rhoda flashed her crooked smile. "That should be fun. Do you guys want popcorn? My treat."

After the movie, they trooped out, pensive. Few subjects dampened their group energy, few topics left them speechless. A movie about the Holocaust could do it, but only if it was good. Faith and Erica were the children of survivors; the other three looked upon the wartime suffering of their families with a reticent respect.

"Coffee?" Rhoda broke the silence.

"There's Ben's around the corner," Al said. "I could go for a smoked meat."

"Oy, Al, we already ate," Faith patted her tummy and shook her head.

"Okay, okay, so coffee."

They emerged at the corner of Peel and de Maisonneuve. The air was nippy, the streetlights glimmered. A car hooted nearby. As they crossed the street, heading towards Stanley, Erica glanced upwards. "That's the Hermes Building. You know, where Ricky has his office."

"Ricky Who?" Hershy said, deadpan. The somber mood was instantly shattered. Al punched Hershy's shoulder. "Good *gezucht*." The three women stood beneath the windows of Richard Aronovitch et Associés and laughed and laughed. Tears rolled down Erica's cheeks.

By the time they arrived at the Van Houtte on Stanley they were engaged in animated conversation.

"My parents loved this movie," Faith said, sitting down and shrugging off her jacket. "To my surprise. It's like no other Holocaust film I've seen." She turned towards Erica. "How about your father?"

"Oh, he hasn't seen it," Erica said. "Before my mother died he might have gone, but it's impossible to get him to take in anything to do with the Holocaust now. Speaking of my father, isn't this the old Tokay restaurant?"

"Yeah," Al said. "I used to come here all the time when I was at school. You couldn't get an espresso anywhere in this town except in the Hungarian joints. Here or the Pam Pam, or the Coffee Mill. By the by, I hear you and Marty Riess are in the same boat."

"God, Faith," Erica said. "Really, you're a regular Deep Throat."

"You've only just discovered this?" Rhoda grinned lopsidedly.

"He's got his eye on you," Al teased.

"I shouldn't think so. He's probably already got somebody."

"Why d'you say that?"

"Because in my experience that's what the male of the species does. Dumps his wife of thirty years for someone new."

"Ouch!" Al exclaimed.

"Present company excepted, of course."

"You could do worse than Marty," Al persisted. "I told Faith. Just ask her."

"Excuse me," Erica said. "What else do you do besides talk about me?"

"Marty's a good egg. And he's a lot more cultured than you think. Faith and I ran into him and Leona at

Stratford last summer. You shouldn't be so snooty because a guy sells real estate for a living. I bet he knows way more than you do about the bard."

"You're all ganging up on me!"

"*Ricky Who* isn't the only man in the world," Al said. "Not even the only man in town. When Marty calls, my advice is don't brush him off too fast."

"What makes you think he's going to call?"

"A hunch. Just a hunch."

17

It was after eleven when Erica got home. Cinnamon Cat yowled a disgruntled greeting and slithered around her ankles as she walked through the door. She bent down to stroke his head and he began purring loudly, pressing his furry neck against her fingers, and then meowing again, this time more urgently.

"You silly animal," she scolded, but headed for the fridge and threw a few cubes of liver into his dish. "You can thank Noam for this." There was a note from Tamara on the microwave shelf, saying she was sleeping over at her boyfriend Bob's place.

Erica smiled wistfully, hearing her father's voice in her head, "First love, true love." She pictured Tammy and Bob on the living room couch as she'd come upon them once, cradled in each other's arms fully clothed, tuckered out, content. She gave a rueful shake of her head. *Lucky them*.

It was too early for bed. The aura of the film clung to her, the yearning strains of the Barcarolle from *Tales of Hoffman* still in her ears, the final image of the mother and child united at the end of the war particularly haunting. She thought it an improbable ending; the little boy would never have survived a concentration camp. Yet the film's point about the power of the father's love to inspire and keep the faith in his wife and child was incredibly moving. Maybe if she and Rick had lived through those times, their love would have burned stronger, instead of fizzling out. She shook her head—what an insane idea!—and hung up her poncho in the hall closet, then stepped into her office, which opened from the kitchen.

The phone on her desk was blinking. One message was from a deep-voiced male with a Polish accent. "Mine wife tells me that you were at the movies tonight. I would be interested in your opinion about *Life Is Beautiful*. I would like also to discuss with you a business proposition. Call me tomorrow at home, or on Monday at the office." He left three numbers, home, office, cell. There was also a call from her father in his usual telegraphic delivery and strong Hungarian inflection. "Thank you for supper. It was vonderrful. As usual. Tamara is a darling. I love you, sveetheart."

On her desk lay a galley copy of a book for review that she had begun in the afternoon. She really wasn't sleepy. She could read a few more pages; she was behind schedule, her piece was due Monday afternoon. She carried it to the living room, turned on the light, uprooted

Cinnamon Cat from the leather armchair, and sat down. He eyed her, aloof, and began licking his haunch disdainfully. She patted her lap to placate him, and after giving her a long considering look, he jumped up and began purring loudly. She recalled once yelling at Ricky that she got more fulfillment from the cat than from him. *Why grieve the loss of such a man?*

The novel wasn't bad. Paul, her editor, had been right when he thought it would appeal to her. The author, a young man, had won a short-story prize a couple of years earlier and had turned the story into a novel. The original version was set in Montreal at the time of the last referendum. She recognized a scene at the Atwater Market that had made the leap directly from the old piece into the new text.

It resonated with her when she'd read it the first time. She shopped regularly at the market and thought she recognized the belligerent farmer with whom the book's protagonist got into a political slugfest. The author evoked the ambience of that period well, the tension, the anxiety about the outcome of the vote. Also the market itself with its bounty of produce, profusions of bedding plants and cut flowers.

Ricky shared her enthusiasm for markets. Wherever they travelled they sought them out. Arles had been the best, the Boulevard des Lices on a Saturday morning. Years and years ago, Tamara hadn't even been born, they had left Raichie with her parents to take a fall trip to France. Rick had shot two rolls of film that morning; the slides must still be upstairs somewhere, but she didn't need them to conjure up the sprawling street bazaar with its flowers and crates of vegetables and olives and cheeses. Meat roasting on spits, stands of baguettes, croissants, melons, apricots, plums. There had been wire cages of squawking chickens and turkeys. People took the birds home live in cardboard boxes, to wring their necks, she supposed, shuddering. What a hypocrite she was, as if meat sprang painlessly on to her plate via Noam's shop.

On another trip there was the covered market in Oxford with its high rafters and suckling pigs and rabbits hanging from hooks in one butcher shop after another. And the enticing smells of coffee and fresh sage warring with the distinctly off-putting odours of fish and souring produce.

She shut the book with a bang, startling the cat, who bounded from her lap. Why was she mooning like this? The good memories were more painful than the bad ones. And since there were plenty of those, she ought to reflect on them and be glad to be rid of him. Just like Rhoda and Faith said.

Later that night she dreamt she was on a bus riding up Côte-des-Neiges. All around her, the landscape was blanketed by a thick crust of green-grey ice. Vista upon vista, it spread before her eyes, like an enormous glacier, like the Columbia Icefields that she and Ricky had toured when they'd gone out West. The bus ground its way upwards, making laborious progress, its wheels spinning and crunching. At the crest of the hill, pushing through the yellowish boulders, flowers of every kind swayed in the biting wind. She could make out purple hyacinths and red tulips and snowdrops and crocuses as well as exotic blooms she had no names for. She felt a sense of wonder at how they could be sprouting in such forbidding terrain. When she woke up to pee, the images stayed with her, vivid and startling. "But that's where the cemetery is," she thought. "Isn't that weird?"

18

For the past five years, Marty Riess's week had begun with an eight o'clock session on Monday morning with his analyst, Dr. Willard Winters. Over that period Marty periodically reminded himself of all the reasons he was grateful to Dr. Winters. Guiding him in shaking certain unfortunate habits. Helping to extricate him from an awful marriage. Even encouraging him to join the synagogue that had come to mean so much to him.

Marty had to remind himself of these positive aspects of his association with Dr. Winters, because Winters was no gentle, empathic therapist. Once upon a time he must have studied Freud, Jung, and Adler, but he'd clearly decided to forge his own philosophy of what could best be termed tough love. And Dr. Winters was definitely at his most bloody-minded and intransigent this particular Monday. No sooner had Marty stretched out on the couch—in the past five years he couldn't remember it being cleaned even once; the tweed headrest stank of decades of patients' hair oil—and no sooner had he begun his recitation of the events of his Saturday night, than the old killjoy was at his throat.

"What the hell do you think you're up to?"

"What d'you mean?"

"Is this your idea of how to embark on a meaningful relationship? Is this what you left your marriage for?" The old coot was practically spitting.

"I don't know what you're getting at. Kim is lovely."

"She's young enough to be your daughter."

"She isn't. I told you, she's thirty-nine."

"Can you see introducing her to Jason and Ian?"

Marty was silent.

"She's not Jewish." Dr. Winters sounded like a prosecutor addressing a courtroom.

"Neither are you. Neither is 99.9 per cent of the human race."

"Can you see taking her to one of your community's potluck dinners? Did you happen to mention to her that you're a grandfather?"

"It didn't come up," Marty said weakly. He stayed quiet some more. Then he said in a very small voice, "That's not the only thing that didn't come up." In the cinema of his mind, he unspooled the ignominious moving frames in Kim's bedroom, the entangled limbs, the mussed bed clothes, his repeated aborted attempts at entry.

He had a near palpable sense of Dr. Winters gloating behind him. He wondered if he was rubbing his arthritic joints in glee.

"No kidding. Sounds like your cock's smarter than your head."

"God, what have I done to deserve you?" Marty allowed the words to tumble out. "I can't believe I'm paying for this."

Dr. Winters let it go. "Look, correct me if I'm wrong, but the idea was that, besides being one nasty number, Leona was no match for you in intelligence or interests or substance. The idea was that at your age you don't have a hell of a lot of time to waste. The idea was that you'd look for a worthwhile partner to spend the rest of your days with."

"Just because someone's a little bit young and of a somewhat different background doesn't mean they're not worthwhile."

"That's very true. Do you happen to know anything at all about this… this *Kim*? If she hadn't flung herself at you because she was at loose ends on Saturday night, would you have given her a second look? I know you pride yourself on having come a long way, Marty, but boy, do you still have a long way to go!"

19

When the phone rang at 8:45 Monday morning, Erica had already been at her desk for an hour. At that delicate stage of writing a review, when derailment could still happen, she resisted the urge to pick up the receiver. But then of course she succumbed to playing back the call a couple of minutes later. Listening to the voice of Melly Darwin's office manager, she congratulated herself on not having responded. But then shortly after, Jennifer Blaine, her agent, also left a message, mentioning Melly's name and asking Erica to call back.

This is one pushy Jew! Erica horrified herself by the thought that had just popped—from where?—into her head. One of her classmates at Sacred Heart, where no one had had the slightest clue about her origins, once said it within her earshot about their bossy Moroccan-Jewish French specialist. And she, like a coward, never breathed a word of protest. And now for such a thought to surface in her own mind? Hers, Erica Molnar's, author of *The Shadowed Generations?*

The man was pushy because he was pushy, not because he was a Jew!

But was he ever pushy, to worm his way through a crowd to the head of the queue at the movie. What good could come of associating with such an individual? *No good.*

She broke into a hot-flash sweat, removed her sweater, and made herself return to her keyboard. At eleven thirty, she saved the completed review to a diskette, popped the diskette into her purse, and got in her car. She had a lunch meeting with Paul to discuss a batch of new columns.

They met at their usual sushi counter on rue Notre-Dame in Old Montreal, a chrome-and-mirrors place that was reasonable enough for the Books Editor to treat a columnist on his expense account the odd time. Paul was perched awkwardly on a high stool at one of the tiny side tables. He was a big man, with broad shoulders, a shock of greying hair, and bushy dark eyebrows. He stood to give Erica a brief hug.

Erica sniffed suspiciously as she emerged from the embrace. Technically Paul was her boss, but they'd worked together several years and become buddies. Her eyes fastened on his shirt pocket, where a box of Marlboros stuck out.

"I thought you'd stopped."

"I had," he glared at her, as if daring her to continue.

This of course was the stereotypical Paul Ladouceur, the one who cultivated the air of a crusty misanthrope and whom his colleagues twitted about his oxymoronic surname. Sweet he was not.

"Sorry," Erica said, looking away. "I thought you'd been feeling better."

"Let's drop it for today, okay?"

"Okay." She felt herself flush. Paul wasn't usually gruff with her. She bent to the floor, as much to hide the tears that had leapt unbidden to her eyes as to rummage in her purse on the floor. *Idiot! Rick was right, you gush like a fountain at the least provocation.*

Face recomposed, she surfaced with her diskette. "Before I forget, here's my review."

Paul slipped the diskette behind the Marlboros in his shirt pocket.

"Thanks," he said. He seemed not to have noticed a thing.

They consulted the menu with exaggerated interest, and then noted their orders on the little pad on the table.

Erica was wondering how much longer she could avoid looking up, when Paul coughed. His lips formed a wry smile. His dark eyes remained bleak.

"Sorry I bit your head off. The past week's been lousy. For the sake of my svelte form, I opted for smokes instead of booze. It was going to be one or the other. Just for a while."

They discussed the line-up of future columns. One of the books on the Giller shortlist had not yet been reviewed. The author of the Atwood biography was coming to town and should be interviewed; so too the gay Jamaican writer whose second novel was three weeks off. Paul had brought her the advance copy. She stowed it under the table.

"I need to pick your brains," she said to him, as the waiter brought their order. "This brash old guy at my synagogue has some idea that I should be writing a book about him."

"Which parts of my brain are we picking?"

"I'm not sure. I don't really know what it's all about. He's sent messages through my Rabbi and Faith. You know, my friend Faith. And on the weekend he called while I was out."

"So who is he?"

"Someone rich and maybe influential. A Holocaust survivor from Poland. Maybe I should pass him off to you. You at least know something about Poland."

Paul's mother was Polish and had played an active role in the Resistance. He had a serious interest in the history of World War II, and from time to time brought the wrath of *Gazette* management upon his head for his generous coverage of books dealing with the war. The powers that be viewed him as an egghead lacking the common touch, more likely to give coverage to Norman Davies than to John Grisham.

"Erica, you started working for me because you were blocked. Maybe writing a book like this would get your juices flowing again."

Erica bit her lip. Paul hadn't nagged her in a while about what he saw as her true calling. Ten years earlier, she'd written a novel. *The Shadowed Generations* had been widely and generously reviewed and, implausibly, sold several thousand copies at home. This was regrettably a little before the German literary public fell headlong into its romance with the Holocaust, but just as America was waking up to its appetite for the subject. There had been a U.S. edition and a British one, as well as a cross-Canada tour. But there had also been major personal fallout.

"You mean," she said, "that you don't think it would be like prostituting myself?"

"*Prostituting?* As opposed to what? The clean-cut, sanitized world of the media?"

"But that's to make a living!"

"*Precisely*. If he's got a good story and he pays appropriately, what's the harm?"

"It doesn't feel right somehow."

"What's with you, Erica? Are you making such a bundle in alimony?"

Erica laughed mirthlessly. "From Ricky? Please."

71

"So treat it like any other gig. It's not like you not to go after a story."

"That's just it. I like going after a story. Here the story seems to be chasing me."

"And here I thought women were into being pursued."

She smiled, a dimple appearing on her left cheek. "*Touchée*. Okay, okay, I'll think some more about it."

"What's this sugar daddy's name?"

"Melly Darwin."

"What's Melly short for?"

"Who knows? Melvin maybe."

The phone was ringing as Erica unlocked her front door. She caught it on the last ring.

"*Erica!*" Jennifer's voice was an accusation. *Good heavens*, Erica thought. Only the most pressing business would induce her agent to call twice in one day. She visualized Jennifer dressed in some kind of dramatic outfit, a mass of cornrow braids sculpted to her head, grey-green eyes narrowed. Her fingers would be drumming on the desktop.

"I've been bombarded by calls about you all day. Why are you incommunicado? How am I supposed to do my job?"

Jennifer was good at her job. She was attentive to her clients, super-efficient, and followed through on the small print. She and Erica hadn't spoken in a while—they had had no reason to. Erica had forgotten how ruffled Jennifer could get if kept waiting.

"I've been out since crack of dawn," she lied. "I just got in."

"Don't you call in for your messages?"

"I'm not usually in such demand. What's up? How're you?"

"Okay." She didn't ask how Erica was, so she was still miffed. "I've had no fewer than three calls about you." A current of excitement crept into her voice. "Wait till you hear. Both Kaitlin Gardiner *and* Tamas Esterhase are interested in the story of some Holocaust survivor in Montreal. And then this guy's secretary calls saying you're not returning his calls! You can't live off a broken heart forever, Erica. This could be a big opportunity for you."

"Slow down! I've no idea what you're talking about."

"You must know who this guy Darwin is."

"He's a member of my synagogue."

"Supposedly, he's got a story. And he's got to be *very* well connected, because Kaitlin says that if you agree to get on board, she'll publish it. And Kaitlin apparently is all buddy-buddy with Tamas. Who says he's interested in film rights."

"Hold on. If Tamas Esterhase wants to make a movie about Melly Darwin, he doesn't need me."

"That's where you're wrong. Without a book, no screenplay, no film."

"But why me?"

"Why not you? You're a decent writer. Don't blow this off, Erica. Kaitlin says he's going to offer a low six-figure advance. I might be able to hoist that upward a bit

… Are you still there?"

"I am, but my head's spinning. That's a lot of money for the likes of me. Did they say what makes this story so extraordinary?"

"Don't you think you should call Mr. Darwin and find out for yourself?"

"Where did *you* leave it with them?"

"That you'd call his office and have the courtesy to sit down with him and discuss it. Did I do wrong?" This last was said with a distinct edge.

"No," Erica said, properly meek. "No, you did not. Thank you."

20

Rhoda tapped on the door of Lasalle Elementary School's kindergarten A, and without waiting for a response poked her head in. "Is Sean ready for me?"

"I'm ready for you," Sherry-Lynn said. "Just look at him." Rhoda adored Sherry-Lynn, a born teacher, brimming with youth and energy. Her eyes followed the pointed finger. The children were seated on the floor in a circle. All but Sean Callaghan. Wiry, small for his age, and coiled for action, Sean was running his fingers through the hair of a pony-tailed little girl in a pink jumpsuit. As his victim twisted to shrug him off, he got a purchase on her elastic and yanked it from her head.

Pandemonium broke out. Pink Jumpsuit leapt to her feet, stepping on the hands of the boy next to her, who began to holler. Sean in the meantime twirled the elastic—it was one with a shiny red bauble in the centre—in the air and began dashing triumphantly on the outside of the circle, Jumpsuit in hot pursuit.

Rhoda took three quick steps in Sean's direction and grabbed him, just as he was about to collide with the piano. Over her shoulder, she saw Sherry-Lynn bound towards the screaming little boy on the floor, scooping up Jumpsuit in her arms on her way.

Keeping a firm grip on Sean's wrist and choking back a surge of hilarity—she always found it next to impossible to keep a straight face in situations like this—Rhoda marched him to her so-called office, a cubby she shared with the school nurse. She braced her back against the examination bed, squatted to his level, and arranged her features into what she hoped was a stern expression. Prising his clammy fingers apart, she extracted the elastic. Sean's eyes filled with tears.

"Tell me the name of the little girl whose elastic this is, Sean."

"Sawah."

"How do you think Sarah feels right now? C'mon, Sean! Is she happy or sad that you took her elastic?"

"Wan' i'."

"What do you want?"

"Eyasti'."

"I can't give you the elastic because it's not yours. But maybe when we go back to class, you'll give it back to Sarah yourself? That might make her feel better?"

He pouted, gazed down at his sneakers, ground the toes of his left foot into the tile floor.

"Know what?" Rhoda said, "Let's sit down and look at some of our words."

She sincerely hoped no one would find out what she was about to do, because it certainly didn't qualify as appropriate pedagogic or speech therapy methodology. She took a pink barrette still sheathed in its plastic wrapper out of the pocket of her denim skirt.

"I've got something special for you. If you try extra hard today."

In the past she had rewarded him at the end of a session with stickers, as she did with all her kids, but stickers did zilch for Sean.

Rhoda cupped her chin with one hand and studied him.

The child furrowed his brow as he concentrated. Slowly, a radiant smile began to light up his face.

Rhoda slipped the barrette back into her pocket and stashed Sarah's elastic away in the outside compartment of her purse. She zipped it up and stowed the bag in her grey metal locker. With luck, out of sight would be out of mind. For a while anyway.

Sean was repeating kindergarten, and this was her second year working with him. A thick sheaf of documentation attested to the fact that he was an unusual kid with an exotic history. His mother was a large, raw-boned bleached blonde in her late forties. Bridget Callaghan had flown to Bucharest seven years ago to collect Maureen, the daughter she was officially there to adopt. Apparently, at a year Maureen was the size of a six-month-old but somehow the orphanage had managed to convince Bridget that the tiny scrap of humanity sharing Maureen's crib was her brother. Wrinkled and covered with fur-like hair all over, Sean had small simian eyes and looked more like some small woodland creature than a two-month-old baby. Overcome with pity, Bridget Callaghan had brought both children home.

The first year was a nightmare of colic, ear infections, and night terrors, yet she had, it seemed, not only coped but thrived, her longing for children finally slaked. The problems, however, continued to mount, and when Sean was nearly three and Maureen four, the community clinic where she took them for check-ups referred them to Charles Levitan. A pediatrician at the Children's, Levitan had begun to build a reputation as a specialist with Romanian adoptees. Bridget took an instant loathing to him because he was the first person to apply the word "delayed" to Sean.

"Ya mean retarded?" She had the shoulders of a quarterback and towered over the doctor.

"That is not a word we use anymore."

Over time Bridget became a militant advocate for Sean. She got him on to all the waiting lists. She had his hearing and vision tested. She dragged him to rehabilitation centres because she was determined that if he had "delays," he must catch up before he truly fell behind. After meeting with her, Rhoda felt equal measures of compassion and exasperation. The woman simply would not accept her son's deficits.

Sitting across from Sean at a child-sized table painted psychedelic orange, her long legs wound around the chair legs, Rhoda wondered if she could have mustered the patience to work with him if he'd been less cute. He really was adorable in his red plaid shirt and brown cords. Very Romanian looking, in what she thought was a classical Romany Gypsy way. Dark olive skin, eyes of an unusual yellowish cast. His hair was still a thick and coarse thatch. You could easily imagine him to have been an exceptionally hairy baby.

To get a handle on Sean, she had repeatedly pored over his chart, gone out of her way to read up on Romanian orphans, and acquired a great deal of anecdotal detail from Faith, who worked alongside Charles Levitan at the Children's as a child psychologist. It wasn't unusual for Rhoda and Faith to have overlapping caseloads, since Rhoda's schools fell into the Children's catchment area. Having her best friend so strategically deployed gave Rhoda a more rounded view of a child and the opportunity to talk over cases with Faith, whose judgment was keen.

Over the course of the previous year, she had scratched her head as the experts vacillated between flavour-of-the month diagnoses. Developmental delay, pervasive developmental delay, intellectual handicap. The doses of Ritalin varied accordingly. She persisted on working on his articulation, vocabulary, and story-sequencing, and was gratified by his improved concentration, though his classroom behaviour remained disruptive. The obsession with little girls' hair ornaments was a fresh kink. She had no idea where it came from or what it meant.

Of course he hadn't forgotten about the elastic she'd confiscated. Three turns at the flash cards (one dog, two dogs, etc.), and he was fidgeting on one leg, then wandering off towards the locker.

"Is i' time?"

"Not yet."

They sat down and took three more turns with the flash cards, this time trying to build a story around the puppy. He grinned at her and said, "Doggie wan' bawwe'. Ge' my bawwe' now?"

"Barrette, Sean."

His sassiness was irresistible. Though there remained ten more minutes to the session, she stood up to give him his reward.

21

Faith was taking the history of a child from a type of family that invariably made her cringe. Orthodox Jews from Outremont, the Fishbeins were decked out in full Hasidic apparel. All Berel Fishbein—the father—needed to make him look at home at the court of the Baal Shem Tov were mid-calf britches and white stockings. Otherwise he was perfectly attired for the part of an eighteenth-century disciple of the founder of Hasidism. He had a shaggy, greying beard straggling down to his sternum, abundant dark *payes* coiled around his ears, a black top hat squished low over his brow, and *tzitzis* peeking through his unbuttoned frock coat.

By contrast, Faigie Fishbein, the mother, appeared completely contemporary—even elegant—but for her droopy posture and pained expression. She wore a very good honey-coloured wig in a layered cut and an orange shawl over a camel jumper that was just starting to show signs of what she reported was her seventh pregnancy. They had brought their two youngest offspring—a toddler girl in her father's arms, and the presenting child, a boy of three, sitting in his mother's lap and dangling his feet rhythmically against her shin. Yossie was on referral from his pediatrician as being possibly autistic. He had enormous, thickly fringed green eyes that focused just slightly over Faith's shoulder, no matter which way she swivelled in her chair.

Faith was able to pay close attention to clients while simultaneously conducting a private mental slide show. The Fishbeins lived on Stuart near Lajoie; she had spent her first years of life a few blocks away, on de l'Épée, corner Bernard. She had probably passed by their two-storey 1920s brown brick cottage a half dozen times a day on her way to and from the Girls' entrance of Guy Drummond School, or to *cheder* at Beis Sarah afternoon Hebrew School on Bloomfield.

Faith at forty-eight knew she looked a lot like the way she looked at ten. She was still short and zaftig, still had a baby face, hazel eyes, and a smile that spread from ear to ear over large teeth. Only her hair had changed. In her late twenties she had made the decision to fight the premature grey she had inherited from her mother, and now gold streaks frosted the pixie cut of her youth.

For Faith, the Fishbeins, like other Hasidic families that filed through the Children's, evoked the history of her mother's family in Poland—the little that she knew of it. Her maternal grandparents had been Hasidic. Faith viewed Radobice, the ancestral shtetl, through unsympathetic eyes, her opinions shaped as much by her imagination as by her parents' terse accounts. As Berel Fishbein yanked on his earlocks and Faigie responded in sullen monosyllables to her questions about Yossie, Faith wondered if her grandparents might have been a carbon copy of this couple.

There were grounds for this sort of speculation, since not so much as a tiny snapshot remained of them. When Erica's novel caused such a stir a few years ago, she had shown Faith an album of sepia family portraits extending back generations. They depicted prosperous squires with sideburns and Franz-Joseph moustaches, matrons with elaborate braids, boas, and bustles, girls in buttoned ankle boots and white hair ribbons at garden parties and tennis matches in the Buda hills. Faith was enchanted and much impressed. Afterwards she described the photographs to her parents. Her mother's reaction took her completely aback. Lips narrowing, Freda Guttman, as a rule so sunny tempered and upbeat, spat out, "Ah, yes, the Hungarian Jews, they at least have pictures." Faith had stared at her uncomprehendingly. "Their war was a picnic compared to ours."

But no, Faith mused, of course her grandparents wouldn't have looked like the Fishbeins, what an insane idea. Faith's grandfather had died when Freda was five, poisoned, so Freda said, by the stench of the tannery where he had eked out a living. Her grandmother would never have been able to afford an expensive wig like Faigie Fishbein's. She would have had her head shaved and have covered her stubbled scalp with a kerchief or a coarse headpiece of horsehair. Freda had never badmouthed her mother to Faith. But she had also never let her lift a finger around the house as she was growing up, not even to vacuum her room or dry the dinner dishes. "It's not for children," she would say to Ziggie, if he protested that she was working too hard, putting in long hours in the family bakery, then tackling the housework. Freda had been the only daughter in a family of five boys. While her brothers memorized endless Torah commentaries, it was she—a delicately built girl, all eyes and a cloud of hair— who had carted the coal for the stove and shouldered the slopping buckets of water from the well. *Like a servant*.

Faith slipped her notes on the interview in a file folder, and began writing out referral slips for a barrage of tests for Yossie. In a neat, slanted hand she filled out an appointment card to a follow-up clinic in six weeks' time.

"But it's nothing serious, right? He *will* outgrow it?" Faigie asked. For the first time there was some emotion in her voice as she searched Faith's face for reassurance.

Faith found this sort of professional moment excruciating. It never failed to remind her of how blessed she was with her two wonderful children, her doting husband, her near perfect life. It wasn't up to her to say that Yossie Fishbein was autistic. At least not at this time. Depending on what the tests showed, depending on what the team concluded, she might yet have to break bad news to this family. Even if they irked her by token of who they were, she felt considerable empathy for them right now.

"We will do everything we can for Yossie, but we must first obtain a proper diagnosis—"

Faigie didn't wait for her to complete the sentence. She twisted her mouth into a moue of distaste and shook Yossie from her lap.

"—in order to help him …." Faith's voice trailed off as Faigie grabbed the baby from her husband and stuffed her into the stroller. They stormed out of the office without a backward glance and without saying goodbye.

Faith dialled her parents' number with one hand while unwrapping her tuna sandwich with the other. Freda answered on the first ring. Faith pictured her sitting by the wooden kitchen table, staring into space.

"Hi, Mummy.

"How come you never call anymore?"

The reason that Faith's life was merely near-perfect and not completely perfect had to do with this apathetic voice and its edge of groundless reproach.

"Mummy, we talked yesterday. And the day before."

"No. We didn't."

"*Yes*. Remember you told me that Rivka and Anna had dropped by for a visit yesterday?"

Faith felt Freda straining to recollect.

"Oh, yeah." Was she actually remembering or making an adroit recovery?

"Have you been out?"

"Soon we're going. Daddy's cleaning up from lunch."

"May I speak to him?"

"Okay. Ziggie! It's … it's our daughter."

Oy! This is new. She can't remember my name.

"Faithie? How nice," her father boomed in her ear. He sounded delighted to hear from her, as if it were a pleasant surprise, and not a daily event at this time.

"How's everything?"

"Fine, fine. Mummy ate a good lunch. I made noodles and cottage cheese, and now we're going for a walk. It's a nice bright day."

Maybe if he complained, maybe if he admitted that caring for Freda was not just wearing him down but turning him inside out, she wouldn't feel such guilt on his account. But if she suggested a day program for her mother or perhaps Meals on Wheels, he acted as if she were criticizing him for the way he was managing.

"Good. Maybe I'll drop by on my way home. D'you need anything?"

"No, no. Denk you very much. I was already by the bakery. But you come, come, we will love to see you."

A wave of gloom washed over Faith as she replaced

the phone in its cradle. She tossed her unfinished sandwich in the waste bin, disregarding her mother's voice in her head chiding her about wasting food.

Had she not always had such an enviable relationship with Freda, perhaps she would be able to accept her illness better. But once Faith emerged from adolescence, they'd become as much friends as mother and daughter. They loved chewing over the latest gossip in their overlapping circles, while doing the sales at Ogilvy's or window shopping at Holt Renfrew. Afterwards, they'd extend the outing with a bite at the Pavillon Atlantique or Chez Pauzé.

When Andrea was a toddler, Faith went back to university to get her Master's. At around the same time, Freda started night school. It was yet another point of connection between them, breeding a strong mutual respect. Freda had been sixteen when the war broke out. All her life she put personal ambition aside, first channelling it into struggling to stay alive, and then into making a living and raising children. Acquiring knowledge for its own sake was like quenching a deep thirst, and she began to indulge in it in earnest after she and Ziggie sold the bakery. She breezed from high school to college, deliberately trying to compensate for her starved youth by a diet rich in the classics and philosophy. Then, ten years ago, she enrolled in a degree program at Concordia and unaccountably began getting lost on the way to classes. That was the first sign.

And the worst part of it, Faith thought, her lower lip trembling as it always did when she was upset, the *worst* part was the rage now always bubbling beneath all her interactions with her mother. She was furious at Freda for allowing this to happen to her. She was equally furious with herself—a supposed specialist in the dysfunctions of the mind—for her fury. But she couldn't help herself. She couldn't bear to see Freda day after day in the same soiled paisley silk blouse, *Freda* who had always been so fastidious. Dainty Freda, a stickler about table manners, now wiping greasy fingers on her skirt.

Round face clouded, Faith stared unseeing past the neat pile of patients' charts on her desk, beyond the narrow window at the smoke billowing from a ventilation stack below. She told herself it was counterproductive to harbour such anger. Even more counterproductive to put the kind of energy she was putting into agonizing over how many years she had left before she began to get lost herself. (Seventeen.) Of course that was not her sole source of worry. She fretted about Al's asthma and about Rhoda's blood pressure. She fussed over Max's psoriasis and Andrea's cramps. And, although she made the most encouraging pronouncements to Erica about the innocence of thyroid cancer, her heart constricted every time Erica was due for a checkup.

She looked at her watch. She had just enough time to have a quick word with Erica.

But when she dialled, Erica brushed her off. "Can't talk. I'm about to call your pal Darwin."

Faith perked up. "Okay! I'll call you later."

22

Email from faithrabinovitch@mch.org to rhoda.kaplan-sky@lbpsb.ca

October 20, 1998, 12:45 p.m.
Erica's calling Melly Darwin as I write. What do you think?

Email from rhoda.kaplansky@lbpsb.ca to faithrabino-vitch@mch.org

October 20, 1998, 3:10 p.m.
I think I hope she knows what she's doing.
An indelicate question: do you ever work?

23

Melly Darwin clearly didn't believe in niceties or preambles. That is, judging by his conversation with Erica, which went like this:

Melly: You probably want to know about mine name. Mine name was Wiener before it was Darwin. That means from Vienna, right?

Erica: I guess—I ... never thought about it.

Melly: Well I'm gonna tell you I been to Vienna, I lived in Austria after the war. When I come to Canada, I don't want to be called by those places. I want to call myself Winner but Bubbles wouldn't hear of it. That was before we were married. I listened to her more then. So around that time I heard about this guy Darwin, you know him?

Erica: (weakly) Charles Darwin?

Melly: That's the one. He had some theories (he pronounced it *teeries*) that made sense to me. Survival of the fittest, you know? That's what I want you to write about, mine story of survival. And the Melly comes from Melech. You know what *that* means, right? In Hebrew.

Erica: (even more weakly) Yes. It means king. Did you change your first name too?

Melly: Nah. Melech is my real name, my middle name. I was born Meyer Melech. In the camp when I was on by mineself alone I start calling myself Melech. It's a much better name .... Are you still there?

Erica: I am.

Melly: So do we make a deal? What d'you say?

Erica: But what exactly are you proposing?

Melly: You write the book. I pay. Isn't that how it works in your trade?

Erica: (laughing) Well, yes. But also, no. The money part you discuss with my agent, and she'll talk it over with me, and then if we can agree on that, we could go ahead. But before we get to the money question, I need to know more about who you are and what your story is. And why I should be writing it.

Melly: So come over to mine house. Come Sunday afternoon. The whole family is here Sunday. You meet everybody, I tell you a little bit about mine story. And I tell you why you should write it.

24

Every second Thursday, Rabbi Nate met Moish Stipelman for lunch. They took turns choosing the venue. It being Moish's turn this Thursday, they were at Snowdon Delly, *aka* Snowdon Dell, or as the official sign put it distinctly in French, DeliSnowdon.

Moish had three reasons for always picking the Snowdon Dell. First, for its haimish ambience of fifties diner: oxblood vinyl booths, paper place mats, shiny metal napkin dispensers, and comfortably corpulent aging waitresses.

Next, he loved the smell. The ripe aroma of cured meat, garlic, and brine, the sweet tang of coleslaw, and above all the clinging, reassuring odour of sizzling fat gave him a buzz. Naturally he never touched the succulent smoked meat, pastrami, rolled veal, or the sublime chopped liver. Not only because it wasn't kosher—if he'd given in to his cravings, he could have indulged in cold cuts at Ernie and Elly's, a restaurant that specialized in a hideous combo of kosher deli and Cantonese dishes. But when he'd turned eighty his cardiologist had sworn him off cholesterol. Moish was about to have his ninety-third birthday in three weeks and he wasn't arguing with success. He was somewhat deaf, a bit lame, and, in the past year, his erections had turned a tad unreliable. Otherwise he was in fine form, thanks—in his mind at least—to the fact that smoked meat hadn't crossed his lips in thirteen years.

The same could not be said about French fries. The third reason Moish frequented the Snowdon Dell had to do with the fries. They were the best in town, cut in thick wedges, deep fried to golden brown crispness, and—really and truly—they weren't greasy.

"Joel Jacobson ought to taste these," Moish said to Nate, referring to his cardiologist. He said it every time they ate there.

Nate smiled wanly. He wasn't a great fan of the Snowdon Delly for the very reasons it appealed to Moish. The place was about as unhip as you could find, a step up from a fast-food joint. He poked his fork suspiciously into the gargantuan mound of whitefish salad on his plate and swallowed. The truth was—and he always forgot this between visits—the food wasn't *bad*.

"I've been thinking," Moish said, dabbing at his little pencil moustache with a napkin. He had a round face dominated by a bulbous nose and jowls reddened by a network of broken blood vessels. The few wisps of silvery hair sprouting from beneath his blue silk kipah gave him a cherubic expression. But the grey eyes behind the oversize bifocals were keen. Nate had chosen Thursdays for their regular rendezvous because he devoted Thursday to working on his sermon. More than once Moish had pointed him to just the right *midrash* or reference in the Talmud. Not to mention the occasions when he had steered him with shrewd intuition in the right direction in more worldly matters.

"A cocktail party," Moish was saying, "someone should organize a cocktail party for you." He tapped the table with his forefinger for emphasis. "Twenty, thirty people. Melly Darwin to be on the guest list, of course. And five or six other really influential guys. And girls, too, of course," he added with a sly smile. "You're going to need all the big guns behind you before you float this notion of a new building to the membership."

Nate nodded. "I know. That's a good idea, actually. But it's a little bit awkward. I can't just ask someone to make a cocktail party for me."

"No, you can't. But I can," Moish said. He patted his moustache again, then added, "I'll speak to a few people." By which he meant—and Nate knew he meant—that he'd speak to his daughter. Frances Stipelman was married to Mark Tannenbaum, son of Sam of grocery empire fame. Mark was a most successful corporate lawyer. They entertained lavishly and lived very nicely in an old crenellated high rise perched on the crest of Côte-des-Neiges. The trouble was Frances. Moody and skittish, if she weren't his daughter, Moish might have called her a witch or worse. He would have to catch her in a rare expansive moment.

The old man gave a belch, smirked, then smoothed his kipah. "It would be a fine thing for you Nate, to have a new building."

Nate's sandy eyebrows shot up and his brow wrinkled. He managed to look delighted and anxious at the same time. "It would, wouldn't it?"

91

Driving home (badly) in his battered '87 Ford Taurus—his great-grandkids called it The Heap—Moish reflected that, for a smart man, Nate could be very thick. Imagine enlisting him in the back-room lobby for the building campaign! Didn't he realize what the building—at thirty-odd years, it wasn't even remotely old—meant to him? No, of course he didn't. Because despite his brains, Nate could be so obtuse. And insensitive.

When he had arrived from Toronto in 1980, a callow boy with shoulder-length locks and a guitar slung over his shoulder, Nate was practically handed Congregation Emunath on a silver platter. Dewy-eyed from Rabbinical college, he was embraced as a plucky mascot by the demoralized congregation, then reeling from the defection of a third of its members after the election of the Parti Québécois four years earlier. At a time when Anglos and head offices escorted by Brinks trucks were streaming in panic down the 401, any young English-speaking professional arriving from the opposite direction was acclaimed a hero. The hiring committee lapped Nate up. They offered him the position of assistant rabbi with the understanding that if everything worked out, he would replace Moish within the year.

Which he did, while Moish stayed on as Rabbi Emeritus. Over time, Moish grew quite fond of Nate, seizing every opportunity to declare that he loved him like a son. Which didn't negate his resentment that Nate had inherited—even after the losses—a decent-sized congregation, a modest but perfectly adequate building, and a whole synagogue infrastructure: a secretary, a caretaker, and a host of helpful volunteers. He had in fact fallen heir to the house that Moish built.

And now he wanted to tear it down.

A mad klaxoning from some crazy driver in a red Mazda heading south on Lavoie alerted Moish to the fact that he'd run a stop sign. He was almost home, but the jolt of adrenaline coursing through him like a shot of schnapps as a result of this little excitement persuaded him that he wasn't yet ready for home. Sylvia would be at her customary mahjong game with the girls; he was a free man. He passed St. Mary's Hospital and considered paying a quick visit to Lorne Silver, an old friend laid up with some mysterious ailment, but decided to phone instead. He felt quite energized and ready for adventure.

Moish had been a traveller in his heyday. At one time he'd plied the Caribbean, visiting Jewish communities in Havana and Santiago and Curaçao; he'd gone behind the Iron Curtain with his suitcases filled with *mezuzot* and boxes of *matza* well before the followers of the Lubavitcher rebbe had thought of reigniting the faith of Soviet Jewry. It grieved him that no insurance company would give him coverage nowadays if he stepped out of the country. He would have loved to have made contact with the Jews of Bombay and Cochin and poked around China where, according to a recent piece in the *Canadian Jewish News*, there were still members of the tribe who looked entirely Chinese, yet eschewed pork and shellfish and lit candles on Friday night, without any idea why.

At Côte-des-Neiges, he veered south. The dazzling sunshine blinded him, so he couldn't make out the colour of the traffic lights, but he decided to sail through the intersection, concentrating on keeping up with the Mercedes in front of him. He crossed Queen Mary with aplomb, and congratulated himself. A destination was taking shape in his mind. It had been ages since he'd visited the old neighbourhood near the river, where he had spent his childhood.

Moish was a toddler when his family fled Kiev in the wake of the pogroms of 1906. He had only the shadow of a memory of a man in uniform on the train from Quebec City, who miraculously addressed them in Yiddish. *Sholem aleichem*, the newsie said to his father, and gave him, free, a stale copy of the *Keneder Adler*. That was their first taste of the new country, the gift of a stranger.

They rented a cramped little frame cottage with cardboard walls at the corner of Cadieux and Craig. Dirt cheap because of the unremitting clanging of streetcars from the nearby terminus, it had no setback and seemed to grow straight out of the band of wooden sidewalk.

His dad was a *mohel* and a *shoichet* by trade, a scholar by avocation. To feed the family, his mother converted the front room into a grocery store, peddling brown paper packets of sugar and flour and penny candy.

Moish was the golden boy, the only one of four brothers with a taste for both Torah and secular learning. The big turning point of his life was winning a scholarship to the Jewish Theological Seminary in New York, right out of a BA from McGill. He wasn't committed to being a rabbi, just flirting with the idea. At the Seminary he fell under the spell of Mordecai Kaplan, his professor for both *midrash* and philosophy of religion. Kappy was a lovable megalomaniac, vain, egotistical, brilliant, charismatic. In later life, he looked like Colonel Sanders, with his silver goatee and moustache, high forehead, wire-rim glasses, and cap of white hair. But in the mid twenties, when Moish was a regular at Kappy's Friday-night table, he was still youthful, full-lipped, handsome, his blazing blue eyes mesmerizing. He had yet to write *Judaism as a Civilization*, but he was already well on his way to standing Judaism on its head. In his sermons at the Society for the Advancement of Judaism, he was already expounding his theory of God as divine process. It was an astounding concept: God, not a supernatural being, but a dynamic force facilitating creativity, beauty, justice, and love.

Moish's favourite memory of Kappy from that period was the Purim when he'd danced the Charleston in the uniform of a Ku Klux Klan wizard, a blue Star of David emblazoned on his white hood, and the words *Grand Kugel* embroidered in red on his chest. That was Kappy for you, always a ball of fire, always irrepressible, stubbornly convinced that the synagogue wasn't just a place for worship but for every aspect of Jewish life—song, dance, sport, what have you—at least as much as prayer.

In the midst of this mellow reverie, Moish gave a sudden yelp of pain. A cramp torqued his right calf in a vise-like twist, and his foot sprang off the brake. The harsh blare of a horn behind him transformed itself into the blast of the shofar on Judgment Day. The Judgment Day that for him was mere metaphor. His head jerked forward and smacked against the windshield. Afterwards, he'd remember nothing of the accident but a resounding voice proclaiming, as if from a great distance, *"We bring our years to an end as a tale that is told."*

25

Erica rang the doorbell of the Darwin residence at 54 Hillpark. She had dressed for the occasion with excessive care: a new loden jacket over cuffed wool pants, a cream sweater set and—way over the top for a poolside invitation on Sunday afternoon—a string of pearls (from Ricky for their twenty-fifth anniversary). She was well aware of the irony of trying to hold her own vis-à-vis Bubbles Darwin, whose husband's fortune was originally built on fashion, and who, according to Faith, was a fashionista *par excellence*. But Erica wasn't above vanity or competition, even if the competition was a millionaire old enough to be her mother.

She pulled her shoulders back and told herself she was dressed for success. This was not a social visit.

No one came to the door. She rang again, then rapped smartly with the lion-faced knocker. It reflected back a distorted image of herself with fat cheeks and a potato nose. She stared at it in indecision, her heart leaping at the idea that she wouldn't have to face this interview. Her thoughts skittered this way and that. She had no illusions about a commissioned biography of a crass and wealthy businessman. It was a recipe for professional disaster, no matter what Paul and Jennifer said. It would be way more work than anybody anticipated and would end up reflecting badly on her. The critics would eat her alive. Darwin was bound to take advantage of her lack of experience in the business world. And really and truly, did she need another troubling guided tour of the Holocaust? That no one was answering the door was an omen. She should turn on her heel and leave.

But then what would she say to Jennifer? And just think of how disappointed Faith would be if she returned without so much as getting through the door.

She assessed the scene. A tall cedar hedge cut through the front garden on a diagonal. In front of it bloomed a few lingering rose bushes and the neatly mowed lawn sloped gently towards the street. But a gap in the hedge at the side of the house might gain her entry through the rear. *Here goes*, she thought and squeezed through the opening, shaking her hair free of twigs.

In the back, the lot was enclosed by the same cedar hedge which, though six feet high, couldn't obscure the enormous brick houses built to the edge of their property lines to maximize every inch of living space inside. One good thing she could say about the Darwins, they had green space. A lot of it. Enough for a central pergola and a nice sized patio. She headed along the flagstone path in its direction.

Mystery solved.

Peering through sliding glass doors that opened to the patio from inside, through a haze of steam, she made out an aquamarine swimming pool and a clump of people around it. A trio of small children wearing floaties were chasing one another round the tiled room.

Erica banged on the glass with the flat of her hand. The children, two boys and a girl, stopped in their tracks to gape at her, as if she were an object of rare curiosity. A tall, willowy woman with an upswept hairdo sauntered over, a long white terry robe loosely belted over her black swimsuit. Appearing mystified, she pulled the sliding door open. Erica recognized her from the movie theatre.

"I'm so sorry," Bubbles said, as Erica stammered, "I tried the front door."

"It's my housekeeper's day off. We should've put a note on the door for you"

She turned her back on Erica and shouted in the direction of the pool, "Melly! *Melly!*"

A man with a powerful crawl continued his progress until he'd completed the lap. Hoisting himself up onto the side, water streaming from his trunks, he grinned and waved.

"Wanna swim?" he yelled. "We have all sizes bathing suits."

"No thanks." Erica unbuttoned her coat. She was ridiculously overdressed. Literally and figuratively. So much for success.

"I come out then."

He waded to the stairs at the corner of the pool and emerged, shedding droplets of water. Grabbing a towel off a hook on the wall, he wiped his hands, then wrapped it around his middle. Padding over to Erica, he extended a hand and crunched her fingers. She was acutely aware of the matted dark hair on his chest as she felt him inspecting her. For a man of his age, he radiated a startling masculine charge.

"So you came to see me," he said. The smile was self-congratulatory.

"Are you surprised? You did ask me."

"A little bit. A famous writer like you." He looked her up and down. "And such a beauty! No one told me that about you."

Erica blushed, taken aback by the unexpected gallantry. "I think you know who's famous here," she said, trying to regain her poise.

"You mean me? I'm just a little Jewish guy from Poland who made a pile of money."

"Is that why you invited me here?"

"I ask you here, I want you should meet mine family. Glenny! Charlie! Annie! The writer lady's here. Where are the *ainecklach*? Matthew, Chelsea, Ryan, are you hiding? And the rest of you big boys and girls, where are you?" He clapped his hands and screwed his head around. *"Where the hell is everybody?"*

"Right here, Zaidie," the small girl in floaties tugged at Melly's towel.

He bent towards her, beaming as he gathered her in his

arms. "This here's Chelsea, mine Charlene's daughter." He patted the fair head of the little boy who had sidled up beside him, hooking his arm around Melly's knee. "Shake hands with the lady, Mattie. Say hello."

Mattie hung his head, mute.

Erica crouched to eye level. "Hi Matthew. I'm Erica. How old are you?"

The child held up four fingers, while his head remained bowed, studying his bare toes.

A tall, slender young woman in perfectly tailored jeans materialized behind the child and placed her arm around his shoulders, while extending a hand towards Erica. Erica was struck by her shining black eyes. "I'm Charlene Darwin, Matt's Mom. And Chelsea's."

Erica straightened up; they shook hands. By now others had arrived and introductions were made.

"I got fifteen more laps," Melly said. "Make yourself at home." He dived into the pool, spattering her pant legs.

Sweating, she removed her cardigan and piled it with her coat on a canvas deck chair. She sat down, crossing her ankles neatly, as she'd been taught long ago by the nuns at school—a pose she reverted to whenever ill at ease. A pretty young woman with lovely creamy skin and eyes of a deep, almost violet blue, took a seat next to her.

"I'm Margo."

"Are you a daughter, too?"

"Daughter-in-law. Glen's wife. I'm their big problem."

"You don't look like a problem. Why are you a

problem?"

"I'm pregnant."

"That's not a problem. Mazel tov!"

Erica's eyes slid down the girl's body.

"You're not *very* pregnant," she smiled. Margo looked to be perhaps her daughter Raichie's age, mid-to-late twenties. Her bright red bikini revealed a great deal of cleavage but only a small mound of belly. "Why would being pregnant be a problem?"

"I'm not Jewish. Glen and I didn't have a Jewish wedding. His parents want my baby to be born Jewish."

"For Reform or Reconstructionist Jews, it's enough if either parent is Jewish."

"It's not enough around here."

"Ah," Erica said. "You're the one they'd like to convert."

They were silent, watching the activity in the pool. Chelsea and Mattie were doing the dog paddle in the shallow end. The little one, Ryan, was on Bubbles' lap, watching the other two intently, his thumb in his mouth. Melly was on his back now, sweeping his arms and legs in strong Vee formation.

"I'm a convert," Erica said softly.

"*You*? I heard you were some kind of Jewish writer."

"I am. But I'm also a convert. Not many people know."

"When did you convert?"

"Oh, a long long time ago. Before my children were born."

"Because your husband made you?"

"No, nothing like that. It's a somewhat complicated story."

"What did your family make of it?"

"My mother had a hard time with it. She never really got over it."

"And have you ever been sorry?"

"No ... I don't think so—"

They were so absorbed in their tête-a-tête that they hadn't noticed Melly climb out of the pool. Now he stood bending over them, in flip-flops and white robe. "I just need to shower." He held up his hand for emphasis. "Five more minutes. Margo, take her to the conference room."

Contemplating the glass of ginger ale in front of her, Erica drummed her fingers on the big rosewood table. Her eyes took in the goddess paintings on the wall and the bust of the master of the house on its pedestal. (*What conceit! What ego.*) She could just make out the real live Melly on the phone in the next room, his voice muffled by the din of a hockey game on television. From time to time, someone poked a head through the door, ducking out again at the sight of her, alone. *What a bunch of boors.* She would count to ten and then leave.

At this point Melly and his three children trooped in. They arranged themselves around the table by some predetermined order, with Melly at the head and Glen at his father's right, opposite Erica. Thickset and fair like his father, Glen had close-cropped dirty blonde hair, a snub nose, and his mother's dark eyes. He wore a permanent frown, as if it took all his powers of concentration to sustain attention to the matter at hand. Charlene, the oldest child, slipped into the seat next to him. Tall, slender, and immaculately groomed, she had Bubbles's olive skin and wore her black hair drawn into a ponytail. Anita, the baby of the family, who looked to be in her mid-thirties, hesitated before sitting down next to Erica. She was short and bosomy, with a head of light brown curls, and wire-rimmed glasses. Erica cast her a sidelong glance when she observed her pulling a small pad out of her pants pocket. She began doodling, and in a few seconds the outlines of a flimsy garment began to take shape beneath her pencil.

Glen cleared his throat. "We're not a literary family," he said.

"Speak for yourself," Anita said. She had inherited Melly's broad and fleshy mouth and his air of coiled energy. "Mom's a great reader and a regular at her book club. Not to mention that she's cousins with Leonard Cohen."

"*Third* cousins, Annie," Charlene observed with a small smile. Of the three siblings, she seemed the most comfortable in her own skin. "He has never exactly cultivated the connection."

"Guys, cut it out. Let me tell the lady what I want." Melly put his palms together and leaned forward. "I want you should write a book about mine life."

"I know this already, but why, Mr. Darwin?"

"Call me Melly. Please. I want you should write a book about mine life to teach people. Also for mine family. For mine girls and their husbands, and for Margo, who should know more about the Jewish people. For the *ainecklach* I already have and the ones I'm gonna have ..." He broke off for a minute and looked out of the corner of his eye at his son. "To tell them about where I come from. Radobice. Have you heard of Radobice?"

"A little."

"Good. *Very good*. I told you all she's smart. Most people in Montreal never heard of Radobice, it's not a big place. How come you know?"

"I don't know very much. My friend Faith's parents are from there. I've heard them speak of it from time to time. Not with a lot of affection."

"I want you should write where I come from and about mine beautiful family that they killed off everyone, everyone except me." He took a checkered handkerchief out of his trouser pocket and blew his nose.

"Daddy," Charlene uncrossed her legs and in one lissome movement pushed away from the table and darted behind her father, encircling his head with her arms. "Please, Daddy, don't upset yourself."

"Charlie, sit. I have to say what I have to say." He blinked rapidly, then regained his composure.

"I was just a kid when the war broke. And then terrible, terrible things happened—some things mine children know and other things I've not told no one, except mine wife. How I was ripped away from the side of mine parents." He gulped and wiped his eyes. "The best mother, the best father .... How I was by mineself, with tough guys, no one to trust. How a miracle happened to me, a real miracle! And how I escaped with a friend I made, except we nearly died." He paused again, bored his eyes into Erica's, and squared his shoulders, "I come out of all that afterwards. I do a little black market after the war is ending. There are adventures, lots of adventures. And then I come first to New York and then here to Montreal because of mine wife, who I meet in New York, but she's from here, and I work like an animal to prove to everybody that I am somebody. And then I have an idea from which to make a little money and then I start mine first store, and then I have another idea and we get La Lace. And then in the last few years when the children are big and they start to be mine partners, I begin with the properties. And I make a big management company— big property management with stores and commercial and residential. And that way I make a real fortune. That roughly is mine story. But the interesting things is in the details. Which I will tell you later."

In the oppressive silence, Anita fidgeted in her chair and Charlene extracted a tissue from her elegant jeans. She wiped her eyes surreptitiously.

Glen cleared his throat. "I'm not sure, Daddy, that this is a good idea for you. Stirring up all this old stuff, going back over these terrible things." He looked hard at Erica on the other side of the rosewood table.

"Tell me something. Do you think this writing project will be good for my father's health?"

"I have no idea," Erica said, startled. "I don't know

your father."

"Well, you should know that he has a heart condition."

"Glenny, Glenny, you're such a good boy, but this is foolishness."

Glen scowled. "All this digging up of the past, what's the point? It will open up all those wounds again for you. Isn't it enough that we know that you suffered and that there was nobody left from your family? Why go into more detail? The whole point is, you made a new life here. A really good new life. That's who you are, the life you made is who you are, Daddy. To write a book about it, you're going to have to relive every agony, every single loss. I'm seriously worried about what that's going to do to your heart."

"That's enough!" Melly slammed his fist on the table. "I have made a decision about this book. And here now I have a writer. You're gonna scare her off before she's even started. She shouldn't be worrying about mine health. And neither should you. I am with the very best cardiologist, mine two son-in-laws say so. And this discussion has no place here, Glenny. Of course I made myself a new wonderful life. But mine family that was, I want them remembered. And also all that I went through, I want there should be a book. This is worth it to remember forever."

Erica leaned forward, searching out Melly's eyes and holding them with her own. "I have a great deal of sympathy for the suffering that you endured Mr.—Melly. More than I can possibly communicate now. My own family—"

"I know from your family. I know. Bubbles tells me you write a book—"

"Yes, but it wasn't a story like you want. It wasn't true in all the details. I'm a novelist, I've never written along those lines."

"What's the use to make up stories to fool the people?"

"Sometimes you can tell a greater truth by saying the story is made up."

"Are you telling me no?"

"Let me ask you something very crass. There are a great many books written about suffering and survival in the Holocaust. What's going to distinguish your story from all the others?"

"This is a very good question. I figure you ask, so I already thought about it. One, it's going to be about *mine* life. *Mine!* And two, you're going to write it. That's what will to—how you say?—distinguish. That is *genick*, enough, for me."

26

That evening Erica met Faith and Rhoda for coffee at Franni's on Monkland.

"And so then he said that all he cared was that it should be about his life and that I should write it."

"And then?" Faith leaned forward, her ample chest nudging the sugar bowl.

"There wasn't too much after that."

"You mean you folded just like that?" Rhoda said.

"*Folded?* He made his case. I heard him out and then I left."

"But you're going to do it?" Faith asked.

"We're a long way from that. His lawyer's going to get in touch with Jennifer. And I don't understand how come a high-powered screenwriter and publisher are interested in this story. There doesn't seem to be anything so out of the ordinary about it. We'll have to see."

"Did you at least like him?" Rhoda pressed.

"He's really arrogant. I was pissed off at the way he kept me waiting, and by the way everything revolves around him at home, and probably everywhere else, too. But there was something very touching about how his children rallied around him, kind of protective. And even about the way he presented the outlines of his story to me."

Faith set her bowl of *café au lait* down carefully. "You know I've been campaigning for you to do this. It's high time you wrote another book." Her lower lip began to quiver. "But I think it's going to really bug me if you write about this guy. I mean, why him? Why's his story more remarkable than my parents'? The only reason Melly's going to get a book about him is because he's disgustingly rich and can afford the services of someone like you. It's *horrible*!"

There was a moment's lull. Then Rhoda cracked her enigmatic sidelong smile. "I love the way that word rolls off your tongue, Faith. No one does indignation better than you."

"But she's right," Erica said. She turned towards Faith. "So you don't think I should pursue it?"

"Oh, you should. Definitely. Don't mind me. I must be pre-menstrual or something. In fact, I am. I've got this deep craving for cheesecake. Who'll join me?"

Grinning like conspirators, they pushed their chairs back and filed over to the glass counter at the front of the coffee shop. After a short but passionate discussion over the merits of the four kinds of cheesecake on display, Faith and Rhoda agreed to split a slice of double chocolate, while Erica opted for a carrot muffin. A young waiter carried their order over and set it out ceremoniously on the table.

As always, Rhoda performed the precise cutting ritual, then savoured a mouthful. "Orgasmic," she sighed.

Erica laughed, a dimple creasing her left cheek. "To change the subject radically, how's Moish, Faith?"

"Amazing. He's over the concussion, and the ribs are supposed to heal in a couple of weeks. Nate says he's in fine form. Doesn't want to hear of giving up his licence."

"That won't be up to him," Rhoda said, huffy. "The very idea that he should continue driving! Talk of chutzpah. If the old bastard wants to kill himself, that's one thing. Mercifully, he crashed into the guard rail and not a human being."

"This might interest you," Faith said. "Guess who Al and I saw last night at Chao Phraya?"

"Who?" Erica asked, without enthusiasm. Faith had a

huge circle of acquaintances, most of whom Erica didn't know.

"Marty Riess and Carol Cape."

"I told you he had someone."

"Erica, sometimes you're really dense. Carol Cape's a *date*, not a someone."

"I'm sure there's some deep truth in that, but it escapes me."

"Carol Cape's been divorced twenty years. She's a Westmount real estate agent—and a member of the shul. You'd recognize her. She comes to services from time to time. Tall, quite attractive, brown hair pulled back ..."

"How do you know she and Marty haven't been conducting a torrid affair for years?"

"The body language. There's a certain comfort level between a man and a woman who've slept together. These two were way too stiff. I'd bet my head they haven't done it."

"It's always an education chatting with you. So much for Al's theory that he's going to ask me out."

"Al says he's working up to it."

"Well, I'm not interested. He's just not my type at all. Physically, I mean."

"I suppose Ricky with his flat gut is," Rhoda broke in. "It's that convent background of yours, Erica. The nuns turned you off the body type of the mature Jewish male."

"*What?*"

"Marty," Rhoda enunciated carefully, as if she were

building a child's vocabulary. "Marty has a Jewish body. He's got a bit of a pot but he's still a nice looking man. I mean, for his age. Ricky, on the other hand, has a goyish body.

"For God's sake. What new theory is this? Rick's Jewish, not goyish."

"Yeah, but he's built like a white-bread boy. All neat and fit and skinny."

Part Two

Inside the synagogue
is me.
Inside me
my heart.
Inside my heart
a museum.

—Yehuda Amichai

1

"Al! For Heaven's sake!"

Al surfaced slowly from the morning paper. Faith's irate squeal was impossible to ignore.

"What's the matter?" he yelled, stumbling to his feet in the breakfast nook and ambling out of the kitchen. Faith stood at the top of the stairs in a yellow turtleneck and rust skirt. She was hopping on one foot, a pair of panty hose in her hands.

"What's the *matter*?! Did you walk Seymour this morning?"

"Yes," Al said, glad to be off the hook. "Yes, I did. But he wouldn't shit."

"How long did you stay out with him? Two seconds?"

"It's freezing outside, Faith. I'm sorry, I'm sorry. Didn't you look where you were going?"

"Obviously not. *Bad* dog!" This was aimed at the black standard poodle cowering guiltily in the hallway.

Al began dabbing at the carpet ineffectually with a sponge. The stench was awful.

"The French regard stepping into dog shit as lucky."

"In that case, I hope they wallow in it. By the way, did you notice that one of the back stairs to the garage is

114

wobbly?"

"No, but I'll look at it. Sorry about Seymour."

"Okay, okay."

Faith swore under her breath as she stepped outside. The sky was the colour of pewter, and little pellets of freezing rain gnawed at her cheeks as she began scraping off her windshield. A sheen of ice had already begun to coat the bare branches of the trees and shrubs, transforming them into filigreed sculptures of crystal and silver.

The roads were snarled all the way to the hospital. Since last winter's paralyzing ice storm, weather like this turned her to jelly. But when the sun broke through the glowering clouds and outlined the trees along The Boulevard, she sucked in her breath involuntarily at the beauty of the display.

She was twenty minutes late and sweating as she rode up the escalators at the hospital. Clinic was already in progress, and Charles Levitan ignored her as she slipped into the room.

Over the course of the morning he and she had a series of brittle exchanges that made her want to throttle him. To cheer herself up, she kept on thinking of her upcoming lunch date with Rhoda.

At eleven Rhoda called, begging off on account of the weather. Later, when Faith checked in with her parents, Freda unaccountably hung up on her. Faith pressed the redial button, and Ziggie picked up, sounding frazzled. Her heart sank as he suddenly conceded that perhaps, after all, a day program was something they should look into for her mother. "I'll ask around," Faith said, her lower lip quivering.

In the late afternoon, just as she was thinking of knocking off for the day, she got a call from a hysterical sounding Bridget Callaghan demanding another consultation for Sean.

"But we just saw him last month."

"I want him seen again. The pills don't work."

"It takes a while for them to kick in."

"Youse always say that. I wanna see results. I want him re-evaluated."

"Mrs. Callaghan, our department has limited resources. We're quite unable to see Sean again so soon after his last appointment. There's a very long waiting list for kids we haven't evaluated even once."

"I won't have him repeating kindergarten again."

"I'm almost certain he won't have to do that."

"You're just trying to get rid of me. You don't give a good goddam. None of youse does." She began to cry into the phone.

"We certainly do care. *I* care."

"You don't know *nothing* about what it's like." For a second time that day the phone slammed down on Faith.

"*Fuck*. How badly did I handle that?" she said out loud to the empty office. How insincere she must have sounded. "*We certainly do care. I care,*" she mimicked herself, her voice hollow even to her own ears. How much, after all, did she *really* care? Not a tenth of what she felt

116

for Freda, for instance. And the woman was right. She didn't have a clue about what it was like to live with a kid like Sean. Not what it was *really* like. Day in and day out, a kind of pre-Alzheimerish nightmare, with the prospect of more of the same forever.

But seeing him again so soon after the last appointment wouldn't do a thing. He'd have to wait. She slammed her agenda shut with unnecessary force, put on her coat and hat, and locked up.

Outside, a ferocious wind had dried up the morning's ice and rain. She had to fight the gusts that threatened to lift her bodily, and was breathless by the time she reached her car. The city was at its ugliest this time of year, filthy patches of snow crusted to the sidewalks and lanes. Still, the days were getting longer, and it was bright once more at five. In fact a burst of sunshine greeted her as she turned up Côte-des-Neiges, perhaps an omen of spring. She flicked on the radio and debated whether to keep heading north and pop in to see her parents, or take The Boulevard west and put her feet up for a few minutes at Rhoda's. She glanced at her watch. Rhoda mightn't be home yet, and Ziggie had sounded really bad at lunchtime.

Her parents owned a duplex on de la Peltrie, a side street near the Jewish General. She and her brother Daniel had grown up in this little brick square with its front door always painted apple green. She still carried a key to the house, though she seldom used it. She rang the outside doorbell, waiting to be buzzed in. When there was no answer, she rang again, straining to hear the sound of the chimes inside. Her parents' ancient Chrysler was parked on the street—they had to be home. Her heart began to hammer as she rummaged in her purse for the key, dropping her gloves on the stone threshold.

She bounded up the four steps in the hallway and knocked. The sound of Ziggie's muffled voice was reassuring. She was about to unlock the interior door, when she heard Freda shuffling on the other side.

"Who is it?"

"It's me. Faith."

The door opened a crack. Freda in slippers and knee-highs bunched around her ankles, wearing the reviled pink and blue paisley blouse, hung onto the door for support and surveyed her with an expression that might have been puzzlement or alarm. She was still a pretty woman in spite of her years and her illness. Thin bleached bangs framed her mild brown eyes. She had an upturned nose and the same generous mouth and good teeth as Faith.

"Daddy ...," Freda began, then trailed off, looking over her shoulder at Ziggie stretched out on the rose-patterned living room couch.

Faith strode in, without removing her boots. Ziggie rose on an elbow as if to try to stand. He was very pale, but otherwise appeared normal.

"Don't get up," Faith said, trying to conceal her fear. "What's wrong?"

"I was maybe a little bit dizzy."

"I think he had a heart attack," Freda said, more cogent than Faith remembered her in months. She extracted an old tissue from the pocket of her skirt and began rubbing it between her fingers.

"No," Ziggie said in agitation. "No heart attack. I was a little bit dizzy. Mummy wanted too many things. All at once. That's all."

"Did you have chest pains?" Faith asked.

"No! No chest pains!"

"Don't get excited, please, Daddy. I'm just trying to find out what happened."

"I told you already. I lay down because I wasn't feeling well."

"And how do you feel now?"

"A little better."

"I think he had a heart attack," Freda repeated, shredding the kleenex into strips. Faith and Ziggie exchanged a long look. He threw his arm over his eyes in a gesture of defeat.

Faith checked her watch. Ten past six. She was due at the synagogue at seven thirty.

She realized she was still wearing her coat. She flung it into the hall closet and headed to the kitchen to call Al. She hoped he hadn't turned off his cell. He had a departmental meeting at the end of his day and had been planning to eat at the university. When he picked up, she apologized for interrupting, and filled him in rapidly.

"Do you want me to come over when I'm done here?" Al asked, clearly concerned.

"Would you?"

"I could be there by seven thirty, quarter to eight lat-

est. You're going to leave there around when, seven fifteen?"

"That's if I'm going to be on time. I'm supposed to be
chairing this thing."

"I know. You feel okay leaving them to their own de-
vices for a few minutes?"

"I'll have to see."

An hour later—having helped Ziggie to his feet,
opened a can of soup, and made grilled cheese sandwiches—Faith watched the colour return to his face as he
munched slowly. She decided to risk leaving them until
Al arrived.

Outside, the wind had abated. Big puffy snowflakes
flew hypnotically towards the windshield. She wanted
to concentrate on the agenda for the meeting but all she
could think of was the apprehension in her father's eyes,
his uncertain steps. He had had these dizzy spells before
without lasting ill effects. But he was older now and frailer than he let on. If he were to get sick, what would she
do with Freda?

She turned the radio on. A bracing shot of Bachman-
Turner Overdrive on the Golden Oldies station jolted her
system nicely, and she began humming along to *Takin'
Care of Business*.

The snow was getting woollier, muffling the din of
traffic rising from the gully of the Decarie Expressway, as
she crossed over it at Van Horne. Imperceptibly her body
began to unclench, and her thoughts drifted to the meeting ahead.

All in all, she had to admit that she was surprised at how much progress the building campaign had made in recent weeks. Frances Stipelman's soirée a month ago had been a turning point.

Who had convinced Frances to convene a cocktail party remained a mystery—although Faith suspected that Nate must have pulled old Moish's strings. Anyway, it had been rather fun, not least because she had treated herself to a flouncy and flamboyant scarlet number (at regular— which was to say outrageous—price at Scandale on the Main). A necessary extravagance, given the high flyers in the room. To further bolster her confidence, Rhoda had loaned her the heavy gold choker her father had designed for her fortieth birthday.

The venue had been swish, to say the least. A private elevator whisked guests to the tenth floor of the Water-loo, a grand old building perched on the western haunch of the mountain with a stunning view of the city below, all aglow in twinkling lights. A waitress in black and white uniform took their coats and boots, and ushered them down a corridor to the living room painted a deep red. The vibrant colour of the walls made a surprisingly effective backdrop for the art on display, an eclectic mix of old and new. There was an idealized portrait of Frances in her youth surveying the world with hauteur as she leaned on a mantel that held a blue and white bowl of oranges. There was a Saul Steinberg line drawing of a Japanese vase whimsically nodding at a rocking chair. A. Y. Jackson's signature adorned a Laurentian winter landscape, and on a marble pedestal a monstrous Inuit carving of a snowy owl flapped its wings ominously.

Noting Faith's interest in the artwork, Mark Tannenbaum, their host, took her by the elbow and steered her down a corridor to show her a couple of rather gaudy Old Masters—their names meant nothing to her—who, he explained with evident pride, were of the Florentine school. She wished she could appear nonchalant in the face of such wealth and ostentation, but she was impressed and said so. A look of naked self-love flitted across Tannenbaum's sallow, tight-featured face. "One of our sons-in-law works for Sotheby's in New York. He tipped me off about these two in advance of the auction."

A waitress—a different girl than the one who had greeted them at the door—swooped in with a tray of canapés. Faith took an endive stuffed with tapenade and sauntered back into the living room, leaving Tannenbaum to greet new arrivals. She was curious about the guest list. Nate had kept her in the dark about it. Perhaps he wasn't sure himself. Of the executive, only she (escorted by Al, always ill at ease among the *machers*), the Sterns, and Marty Riess had been invited. Marty had recently been parachuted into the treasurer's thankless position upon the sudden resignation of the former incumbent, Lorne Silver, for reasons of health. The presence of the Sterns was entirely predictable.

There were those who thought smooth, sleek, and supercilious Jeff Stern should have opted for the rabbinate instead of pharmacology because of his deep love of

Torah, passion for ritual, and obsession with synagogue politics. Others held that it was just as well—a good rabbi needed compassion and humility more than the ability to strategize. As it was, Jeff spent so much time on shul business that rumour had it his pharmacy was on the skids.

Hershy Kaplansky, Rhoda's husband, was the one who had originally dubbed Helen Stern "the Lovely Helen of Troy." The moniker was cruelly shortened by the Graces to The Lovely. For The Lovely was anything but. Suspicious and eagle-eyed behind Nana Mouskouri tortoiseshell frames, that night she wore an elasticated top in a hot pink diamond-shape pattern over a tight black skirt that emphasized her squarish, rather butch build. She had stiff, varnished chestnut hair, a prominent overbite, and a wide mouth painted purple. Her most distinctive feature was her skin, an unusual shade of copper. Rhoda liked to conjecture about The Lovely's skin colour. Was it makeup? Was it bronzage? Why didn't it—whatever it was—extend to her neck? "Someone," Rhoda liked to point out, "should tell her that, whatever it is, it should follow through to her neck."

The Lovely's parents had been founding members of the shul, with a long history of involvement at the board and executive levels. Faith's presidency could be viewed as but a blip in the stranglehold of the Stern dynasty's leadership. This was vividly illustrated when—chairing the last annual general meeting of his presidency—Jeff neglected to introduce her as the next incumbent until he was prompted to do so from the floor. Earmarked to replace Faith when she would eventually step down, The Lovely was named first vice-president at the same meeting. The two Stern progeny held key positions in the youth group and participated regularly at Shabbat services. It would only be a matter of time until they took their places on the board. All this would have been viewed as commendable had the Sterns at least tried to mask their complacency with a veil of modesty, had they been just a little less obvious about their assumption that Congregation Emunath was their private fiefdom.

Sushi and chicken teriyaki on a skewer were being passed around when the Darwins arrived. A few minutes later David Himmelfarb ambled in.

"Shylock," Al whispered wickedly to Faith, and she pinched his arm in warning. Himmelfarb, a paunchy, balding geezer with a white spade of a beard, was in the mortgage business, an occupation Al insisted was a euphemism for usury. Sally Lightstone, a retiring little woman who made a career of good works based on her share of her father's fortune in school supplies, was the second to last person to arrive. The last was Aaron Leibovitch, a tall skinny beanpole of about fifty, the scion of a family that was still holding its own in the fur industry. He was a good friend of Nate and Reisa, his wife, like Reisa, a professor of Jewish studies at McGill.

The nitty gritty part of the evening consisted of an inspirational address by Nate, which he launched into as soon as Aaron walked in. It seemed to Faith that of late, whether at board meetings, Friday night potluck dinners, or shul services, Nate was honing the art of the stirring pitch to perfection. At the cocktail party he knocked off a little homily with the ease of a circus barker.

"My dear friends, you know why we're all here, so I shall be brief. You may have heard this little story from me before, because it's one of my favourites. It's about an apocryphal Hasidic rebbe and two mischievous *cheder* boys. These boys were notorious for always being up to some kind of scamp, and the rebbe had a reputation for being able to best them. But on this occasion, they appeared to have cornered him.

"'Rebbe,' the one called Yankev said, 'Itzik has a bird under his arm. Tell us, Rebbe, is the bird dead or alive?'

"The rebbe was stumped. He knew if he said the bird was alive, the boys would smother it to prove him wrong. But if he said the bird was dead, they'd let it fly out and also prove him wrong.

"So the rebbe thought for a moment and then said quietly, 'Boys, the bird is in your hands.'"

Nate paused and cocked his head. There was silence.

Sally Lightstone tittered nervoursly. Then Melly Darwin chuckled.

Nate repeated in a stronger voice, "Ladies and gentlemen, the bird is in your hands."

He sat down to smiles and polite applause. Marty got up and spoke briefly from prepared notes. He said he had taken over the treasury at a particularly delicate time. According to preliminary designs, the building would cost in the vicinity of five million dollars. In addition, he thought it prudent to budget an additional million as an endowment fund for long term maintenance. "Our congregation is not by and large wealthy. However, I think it's no secret that in this room are gathered those members of our community who have the ability to make or break this project. It behooves us to listen carefully to our rabbi. Like he says, the bird is in our hands. We can either kill it or we can give it wings."

Marty had done quite well. Faith liked him for taking his new duties seriously and for shaping up as an ally.

Turning south on Dufferin Road, Faith reflected that tonight's meeting of the executive committee was crucial as a reality check. Some decent pledges had already come in from the wealthy contingent. In fact, half of the projected costs, just under three million, had been promised either by those at the party or by a subsequent solicitation of the most likely prospects. A professional fundraiser, a brash young man by the name of Elliott Namer, had been hired, and a team comprised of him, Helen Stern, and the rabbi had already canvassed fifty members.

In Faith's opinion—and she knew from a quick exchange with him at services last Saturday, in Marty's as well—the preliminary design was overly ambitious. It was beautiful and elegant—and expensive. The design embodied all the rabbi's dreams. Nate had practically drooled at the sketches of the building's outside cladding of Jerusalem stone. The architect's renderings depicted a gorgeous four-storey interior: the sanctuary with an antique marble arch and oak pews, a dedicated social hall, several conference rooms, a bridal chamber for formal functions, spacious administrative offices, a panelled rabbi's study, a roomy, fully equipped kitchen, not to mention tiled bathrooms.

Faith nabbed a parking space right in front of the shul; lo and behold she was actually five minutes early. The meeting was being held in the library, a dingy room upstairs, off the rabbi's (unpanelled) study, and used on Saturday mornings for a children's program. She hung up her coat, then cleared a pile of newsprint and coloured pencils off her spot at the head of the long table. Nodding greetings to the early birds, she pulled a sheaf of agendas out of her briefcase. She began passing them around as the Sterns slid into their seats, and as Maureen Segal—the committee's secretary—entered, out of breath, muttering imprecations about the weather.

Faith smiled her all-encompassing smile, managing to make eye contact briefly with everyone around the table. "I'd like to put a time limit on tonight's meeting. I'm sure you'd all appreciate being out of here by nine." There were murmurs of assent.

"Marty, I'd like to move up your report to first item on the agenda."

Marty was sitting at Faith's left, across the table from the rabbi. He glanced at his notes, cleared his throat, then said, "It's my sense everyone here's enthusiastic about the building project and the preliminary concept. I share that enthusiasm myself. But as the treasurer, my first priority is the bottom line, not the design. To date, half the

estimated cost has been pledged, with all the major giv-
ers already canvassed. That's good as far as it goes"—here
he wrinkled his brow and paused for a moment before
continuing—"but where's the other half to come from?
If half has been pledged with all the major donors having
spoken, it's clear the rest has to come from the congregation at large."

"If I may speak?" said Elliott, sitting at the rabbi's
side. Faith nodded.

A short, plump young man sporting a blue satin kipah
slightly off centre on his close-cropped head, Elliott had
a puffed-up manner and spoke with undue vehemence.
"In the world of fundraising we always refer to the twen-
ty/eighty formula. That's to say twenty per cent of any
group—the most affluent portion of a cohort—pays
eighty percent of the bill, whereas eighty percent—those
of more restricted means—pay twenty percent."

Faith said, "Marty, you still have the floor."

Marty said evenly, "I am well acquainted with that
particular equation, Elliott, but it doesn't apply to us. In
our case, it's the eighty percent of people of more restricted means who will be obliged to foot not twenty percent
but half the bill." He reached for the file folder in front
of him and withdrew a stack of papers. "This here's our
membership list. I've done a little preliminary survey. We
have close to 300 full-paying members. We expect this
group to cover three million dollars. The numbers speak
very plainly: that's in excess of $12,000 per family."

Faith broke the moment of stunned silence.

"We're in an awkward and sensitive position vis-à-vis the membership," she said. "At last week's board meeting, the members of the board had a chance to look at the conceptual design. I expected all sorts of reservations, but everybody loved it. They were all oohing and aahing over the drawings.

"The trouble is, we happen to have a very docile board this year. No one asks tough questions. In fact no one really asks any questions. Which means that board meetings go smoothly. But that's going to make it very sticky when the whole congregation gets a hold of this plan."

Drumming her fingers on the table, The Lovely Helen said, "So how can we get them on side? We absolutely need them to be as keen as we are."

Marty said, "We have to give them the numbers."

Jeff Stern snickered. "You're going to see the room clear very fast if you do that."

Marty said, a slight edge in his voice, "We need to know where we stand. If we can't afford the project because the membership won't pay, it's a lot better to know it now. I'm not in favour of going behind people's backs or pussyfooting with the numbers. If we can't raise the rest of the money, maybe we've got to go back to the drawing board. Otherwise we're going to spend a bundle on additional architects' fees and feasibility studies, only to kill the whole thing. This design, for instance, could be modified, made more modest—"

"Well, speaking of modesty," Faith broke in, forgetting her role as chair, "I'm sure it'll be lovely to have a façade of Jerusalem stone, but what's it going to cost to ship that stone here from Jerusalem?"

"But it's so gorgeous!" Nate exclaimed. "Think of what it says to us about who we are, and what it says to the whole community."

"I agree, Nate," Marty said, "but who's going to pay for it? You've canvassed a sampling of the members—what's your sense of the people you've talked to so far?"

Nate furrowed his brow, looking ill at ease. "I expect it would be unrealistic if it was all smooth sailing. Not everyone has given as generously as they might." He slumped back in his chair. "Some people—I won't mention any names—showed us the door, people who I *know*"—here he yanked his beard ferociously, "I *know* are in a position to help. But," he brightened, "we've canvassed fifty people and raised three million. Fifty people donated three million. That's very good."

Marty said, "You can't use those figures the way you're using them, because one third of the three million came from Sally Lightstone. There isn't another person in the congregation to match that million-dollar gift."

Nate said, "I was very disappointed in some of the reactions. I expected a great deal more from Melly Darwin."

"Melly Darwin's no fool," Marty said. "When he tells us he's lending us $300,000, he's letting us know that we can't sit pretty and expect him to foot the bill by himself. That's what he's really saying. But I bet he'll make that into a gift in the end, if the rest of the money's raised."

Marty gestured towards the rabbi. "What's your sense, Nate? Do you really believe people are going to be ready to fork over $12,000 per family?"

Nate looked perplexed. Before he could open his mouth, Jeff said impatiently, "Melly Darwin can afford to do way better than $300,000 and should be encouraged to do so."

Faith managed to keep her voice devoid of emotion. "It's not that easy to coerce a person into generosity. Time will tell whether Marty's right or not about Melly. What I'd like to get a sense of tonight is whether we're in favour of toning down some of the more extravagant aspects of this design."

There was a brief silence. Outside the wind howled and Maureen, the secretary, looked up from her notes to peer anxiously at the window.

Nate asked in an aggrieved tone, "By extravagant, you mean the Jerusalem stone?"

"Among other things."

"Like what?" He began cracking his knuckles.

"Perhaps," Faith said gently, "three storeys instead of four."

The Lovely narrowed her lips. "But that will alter this design radically."

"It might not have to," Marty said. "If we consulted with the architect and asked what would have to be sacrificed to shave off a million dollars from the estimated costs, it might be instructive to hear his answer."

Nate sighed. Jeff said grudgingly, "Well, there's no

harm *asking*."

"So do I have consensus around the table," Faith asked, "that we recommend to the board that it request a consultation with the architect about the possibility of an alternative execution of the design concept?"

There were nods all around.

As the room cleared at nine precisely, Nate hung back for a moment, trying to catch Faith's eye. Marty kept fiddling with his papers and made no move to leave. Irritated, the rabbi shrugged and then stomped off to his office across the hall.

Faith put on her coat. "Thanks, Marty, for playing the heavy. It made things easier for me."

"You don't have to thank me. I was just doing my job." He continued fidgeting with the membership list on the table. "I was wondering ..., Erica wasn't at services the past two Saturdays."

"She hasn't been well," Faith said guardedly.

"It's nothing serious, is it?"

"She had to have a treatment, and it's been unpleasant."

"She had a recurrence?" He looked so distressed, his eyes so puppy-dog earnest that Faith said impulsively

"No, no, nothing like that. You knew she had an operation? Well, her doctor didn't want to put her through a follow-up treatment at the time, until she'd fully regained her strength. It's nothing really drastic, just a one-shot thing. Sort of an innocuous potion, you just drink it down. But preparing for it's been *horrible*. She had to go off her meds and that's made her weak as a baby. But she swallowed the cocktail a couple of days ago and she ought to be fine in a few days."

"You'll give her my best?"

As soon as Marty was gone, Nate stuck his nose through the door. "Faith, why didn't you tell me I was going to get the shaft tonight?"

"Really, Nate! What a thing to say! You didn't get the shaft."

"Well, what would you call it?"

"I would call it checking out reality! As in buying what you can afford as opposed to mortgaging not your own future but that of everybody else around you. And just so as you know, I personally have had a *horrible* day. Among other things, my father was quite ill this afternoon. If you don't mind, I've got to go over to my parents' and see how he's doing."

"I'm very sorry, Faith. I didn't know. Is there something I can do?"

Yes, get out of my way before I knock your head off.

2

Ricky held Erica in a tight embrace, slathering her face with kisses. His hands massaged her nipples in that particularly expert way he had. "What are you doing here?" she asked him drowsily. He continued caressing her, as he murmured into her neck, "I love you more than ever, even with all this nonsense about divorce."

"How did you get in the house?" Erica sputtered,

pushing him away. "You gave me back the key."

"I have my ways."

Erica felt a wave of rage bubbling up as Rick smiled his charmer smile. "And I've come for the Inuit sculptures, the Mozart CDs, and all the photo albums." The phone blared in her ear. Erica started awake and reached for it, knocking over the glass of water on the bedside table.

"Oh God," she groaned, her voice thick, propping herself on an elbow.

"This is Marty Riess, Erica. Am I calling too late?"

"What time is it?" Erica said, completely woozy. She shook her head in disbelief over where her unconscious was capable of spiriting her.

"Nine thirty … p.m. I'm terribly sorry. You must have been asleep."

"I was reading in bed. I've been a bit under the weather—"

"I, I know. I hope you don't mind. Faith told me about it at the meeting tonight. That's why I'm calling. To say I hope you'll be better soon."

"That's kind of you. Thank you."

"This might not be the right time," Marty said in a rush, "but I've been meaning to call you … I've been re-reading your book, Erica. I think it's wonderful. And of course it gives a certain insight into you. Which of course you don't have of me. But we have one thing in common, at least on a superficial level. We're both on our own, after many years of marriage. That's to say," he paused and swallowed audibly, "if you're not with someone."

Erica smiled weakly. "I'm not with anyone." *Not when I'm awake, anyway.*

"Well, then, how would you feel about dinner on Saturday? That's if you don't have other plans."

"I don't have other plans. But I'm not sure if I'm up for dinner. I don't know what Faith told you, but the whole process leading up to this treatment has played havoc with my system. I have zero appetite, for one thing." She gave a small laugh. "That's not so bad for my figure, but the thought of a restaurant meal is daunting."

"Coffee?"

"Coffee sounds fine."

"How about I pick you up at eight?"

Erica hung up the phone and lay back against the pillow. She felt a foolish smile plastered on her face. She dialled Faith's number.

3

Al picked up the phone. "Faith's just coming through the door," he said, bringing Erica up to speed about Ziggie. "She tucked them both into bed after the meeting and promised to call his cardiologist tomorrow. Here she is."

"Is he okay?" Erica asked Faith.

"I hope so. I'm bushed. How come you're calling so late—are you okay?"

"Don't be such a worrywart. Are you sitting down? Guess who called?"

"Who?"

"Marty."

Faith began screeching. "Oh my God, Al! Oh *my* God."

The dog leapt off the bed.

"What's wrong?" Al exclaimed.

There was an ear-to-ear grin in Erica's voice. "We're going for coffee on Saturday."

Faith held a hand to her heart and jumped up and down. "Erica has a date with Marty."

"Will you please stop wailing like a banshee," Al patted her on the fanny. "You're gonna scare the shit out of Seymour again."

He grabbed the phone. "I hope you remember who predicted this way back when."

"I can't believe we're carrying on like this," Erica said, trying to sound stern. "It's strictly high school."

"High school?" Al said. "Lucky you."

He hung up, pensive. "There's something very nice about the idea of starting all over again, like a kid."

Faith was in the bathroom, blotting her eyes with a cotton pad. "You think? And here I thought you were happy with me."

"Faithie," he materialized behind her and kissed her bare shoulder. "Of course I am. It's just the idea of being young again."

"We're younger than Erica and Marty."

"You're right," he said and began waltzing her around the room. They collapsed on the bed in a heap on top of the dog and piles of newspapers. Seymour crawled out from under them, yapping with great excitement, and fell to licking Faith's face until she made Al put him away in his basket on the floor at the foot of the bed.

4

Melly Darwin's office was located on Graham Boulevard just south of the Metropolitan in a new medium rise, enclosed by banks of green-tinted windows that from a distance mirrored the billowing morning clouds. When Erica had first begun interviewing him in January, Melly lost no time informing her that he didn't just manage the building but owned it.

She pulled into the parking lot at nine o'clock, berating herself for being overly ambitious in scheduling this meeting for today. She was still feeling the effects of withdrawal from thyroxin, even though she was back on it now. The experience of the treatment had given her a renewed respect for the thyroid, that bland piece of tissue whose existence she had barely suspected until it required excision. As she got out of the car, her heart thumped as if she had just run a marathon. She had to will her rubbery legs into motion lest they collapse beneath her.

As she pressed the elevator button for the fourth floor, which was occupied in its entirety by Les Entreprises Régales, she wondered if her addled brain—fed a steady diet of *I Love Lucy* videos for the past week—would rise to the occasion. Upstairs, a pleasant reception area with large plants and leather armchairs led to a rabbit warren of offices accommodating Melly's children, an office manager, an in-house lawyer, and other support staff. Melly's secretary led her to his corner suite, which though large, showed none of the ostentation of the house on Hillpark. One set of floor-to-ceiling windows looked towards the concrete columns of the Metropolitan, another over the snow-covered gardens of the sedate residential properties below. The walls held photos of Chez Darwin and La Lace ribbon-cutting ceremonies, tony condo buildings, and grandchildren in various angelic poses. There was also a framed and laminated copy of a *Gazette* article about the South-Shore mega mall containing the Chez Darwin and La Lace flagship boutiques.

Erica began setting up her tape recorder on Melly's huge and messy desk, as the secretary, who introduced herself as Marie-Paule, brought her coffee in a styrofoam cup and told her that Melly would be with her shortly. Erica sipped the coffee—it was weak but at least hot— while glancing over her notes and list of questions for Melly. This would be their fourth interview, and she was less than satisfied with their progress. Ever boastful, Melly had yet to reveal the "story like no other" he had promised. Which didn't mean that she wasn't powerfully drawn to the snippets and anecdotes that he launched haphazardly at her, frequently doubling back over material he'd already recounted. He was quite incapable of adhering to a chronological spine on which to hang his tales. She had no idea how she would piece together a sustained narrative based on what he was telling her.

Glen stuck his close-cropped head in the doorway. "Are you busy?"

Erica shrugged. It was obvious she wasn't.

He edged into the room and, sliding behind his father's desk, observed casually, "So how's it going? How soon before we see the book?"

"Not so soon."

"You know I'm not crazy about this idea of my dad's, right?"

She raised her eyebrows, casting her mind back to her meeting with the family. "When I met you the first time, you seemed worried about his health."

"The story of how my father became a wealthy man, I think that would be way more interesting. Has he talked about that at all?"

Erica shook her head. She wished Melly would hurry up.

"My dad's a genius at business. He started out here from scratch in a shoe factory among a bunch of Pepsis—"

"Pardon? Do you mean French-Canadians? Francophones?"

"Yeah, don't mind me. It's just a joke. Margo, my wife is French, you knew that, no? She speaks perfect English but she's a Pepsi. So anyways, my dad's working among all these women in a factory in the East End and he overhears them gabbing about looking for bargains. Like nice clothes they can afford. And it gets him thinking. He's got some buddies in the *shmatte* business, maybe he can use his connections with them. And so he goes and fetches samples, skirts and blouses and later dresses, all good quality, no junk. And at lunchtime at the factory he peddles the stuff to the girls he's working with. He's got good taste, and he also gets my mom involved because she's got great taste, and after a while he builds up this little business, while he's still working away at the sides of leather and the clickers and the sewing machines, and all the shoe crap …. Hey, Erica, don't you want to turn on your tape recorder?"

Erica bent forward and obediently pressed the red record button.

"When he opened up his business, the very first Chez Darwin on Masson Street in Rosemont, it was with money that he borrowed from those women. *This* is the sort of thing you should be writing about, Erica. This is the sort of thing that's interesting to people."

Glen's face had reddened during this speech, and his voice had become husky with emotion.

Erica bit her lip and thought hard. "You seem upset that he wants to go public about his Holocaust experiences," she said, picking her words carefully. "But it's clearly very important to your father to put his story out there. I'm sure he'll get around to telling me about his life in Montreal, too, eventually."

Glen jumped up, towering over her, barely able to control himself. His hands—which were directly at her eye level—were shaking. She recoiled in her chair, alarmed by his level of agitation.

"Religion just divides people! And all this stuff should be, if not actually forgotten, not dwelt upon." His voice was strangled. "I don't want my children to carry this sort of baggage, to live in the shadow of countless horrors. Judaism, Catholicism, it's all built on ignorance. When I have time, I read about science, I watch nature documentaries about deep time. *That's what life's about.*"

She stared up at him in astonishment. "I have no idea what you're talking about. What's this deep time?"

He glowered down at her. "The world wasn't created five thousand years ago like it says in Genesis but billions of years ago. That guy Darwin whose name my dad chose for us, that's what I'm talking about! Our family history starts from then, from when he changed his name to Darwin. All these years, he made a great life without looking back." He lowered his voice, visibly trying to regain his composure. "Of course, I'm terribly sorry that he suffered so much and of course I'm deeply grateful that he survived. I wouldn't be here if he hadn't. Case closed."

There was a click as the door swung open. Erica had never been so happy to see Melly. Mock angry, he clapped his son on the shoulder. "Glennie, you been talking her head off?"

Glen gave Erica a warning frown that implied their conversation had been private, before rearranging his features to bland normality for his father's benefit. "Nah, I was just keeping her company till you got here. I'm on my way to the condo in St. Lambert. So long, you guys."

Melly slipped behind his desk, and leaned back in his

chair, arms hooked behind his head in a relaxed and re-flective pose that suggested he had not overheard Glen's outburst. He was dressed in a well-cut grey suit, his white shirt open at the neck. Without any small talk and look-ing at the wall behind Erica's head, he began to speak with a deliberate air.

"Today I want to tell you about mine father and mother. They were sent away from mine town during the liquidation, to Treblinka.

"Mine mother, she was a very beautiful human be-ing. Beautiful in her looks, for sure, although a young boy don't think about his mother's face or figure, is she a beau-tiful woman? She was then just mine mother. But I real-ize now she was. She was tall and slim, and had dark hair she wore pinned up in a bun, mine father didn't want she should cut it. And she had dark eyes like burning coals, they were so black and so shiny. Mine Charlie looks a lot like her. Especially now, after she's had a couple of kids." He paused, as if departing from a prepared script, a shad-ow falling over his face. "Charlie turned forty this year. Mine mother, she must've been around that age when they took her away." For a moment his restless brown gaze fell upon Erica, and just as suddenly he focused again on the wall. She wasn't certain, but she thought his eyes had filmed over.

"Mine father was a special good man. A business-man. Very honourable and respected. We had a very el-egant ladies' wear store on the main street in Radobice. Mademoiselle de Paris. It wasn't like a Chez Darwin, it was much more exclusive. More like a Holt Renfrew—only for classy people, mostly not Jews." He gave a small, sad smile. "He got some flak from the Jews, because he kept it open on Saturdays. Not that he went in himself on Shabbos. We had a Polish manager, he opened and supervised on Saturdays." Again his face clouded over. "When the Germans occupied us, that man took over the store, mine father was no longer the boss. And soon after, a German replaced the Polak. And mine father I think began to shrink into himself, that was the beginning, when we lost the store. And then of course they took him for the forced labour …. Have I already told you about this?"

"In the time of the ghetto? After you were pushed out of your apartment?" She leaned forward to check that the cassette was turning.

"Even before. Mine father, he shaved off his beard because the beard made you more noticeable. It wasn't a long beard, we weren't so religious, but a little short one." He gestured with his finger at his chin, outlining a goatee. "Because the Nazis in their brown shirts, the bastards, would rip the beards off Jewish men. Skin and all. It was like a sport. They did this on the first Rosh Hashanah of the war." He lapsed into silence.

Erica pictured blood seeping from the plucked, ruined faces, soaking into white shirts, dark jackets. On a day that you normally dipped apples and challah into honey, to ensure a sweet year ahead.

She took a deep breath to quell a rising tide of nausea.

"That must have been terrifying," she whispered.

"Everything was terrifying. It was one long terror for six years. And then some afterwards. When I find out that I have no one left."

A heavy silence fell over both of them.

"You were going to tell me about the forced labour," Erica finally said.

"It was I think almost right from the beginning. It was for all men, young and old. Before the ghetto, the thugs would hunt us down in the streets, and order us to scrub the sidewalks or pull their wagons, like animals. Mine parents kept me and mine little brother home, as much as possible. So mine father he took as much on himself as he could, to protect us. Mine sister, she had a job, so she also went out. I don't really remember where she was, or what she was doing."

"Do you think you were scared to know everything that was going on around you, and that you shut it out?"

"There are things you can never shut out, they are there all the time and for all time …. If you don't think about them or talk about them, you dream about them, which is worse. The day I saw mine parents and mine little brother Shmuel for the last time—this is what they call the liquidation—this is the worst day of mine life. One day I tell you about it, but not now. I have a meeting in a half hour, and if I start talking about this, I'm kaput for the rest of mine day. Can you maybe stay till one o'clock? I should be done by then and we could talk better."

Erica looked at her watch. It was twenty to ten. She shook her head.

"Our appointment was for nine. I'm sorry."

Melly furrowed his brow in displeasure.

"The first time we met, you said that something miraculous happened to you in the ghetto. Why don't you tell me about that?"

"Okay," he pouted, but stayed silent. Clearly put out at being thwarted, he began to chew on his lower lip. He rose abruptly and his chair thudded back into place. Running a hand through his coarse hair, he started to pace around the room, then threw himself back down in his chair.

"Mine first miracle was when I fell off a truck. And broke mine leg."

He placed his fingertips together, creating a small steeple on the desktop. Staring into the distance, he began talking in a softer voice. "What good are you with a broken leg in the ghetto? The pain first of all is terrible. And there's no one to help. I don't know how I get mineself to the ghetto hospital. You can imagine what sort of hospital. First of all, the first thing the Nazis did when they march into mine town is kill all the intelligent people. They arrest the doctors, they asked for them a ransom. After they get the money, then they take them away. So who do you think is left in the ghetto to look after us?" His voice trailed off and he stared off into the distance, lost in thought. "So there I am with mine broken leg in the hospital. And the doctor there is not from mine town, not from Radobice, he's a stranger. He looks at me, and he says to me in Polish, 'Where you're going from here, do you think it makes a difference if you go with a good leg or a bad one?'"

He trained his impatient brown gaze on Erica. "How about that? What do you think of that as a question for a seventeen-year-old boy? A seventeen-year-old in a lot of pain. They threw me out of there. Somewhere I got mineself a pair of crutches, don't ask me from where. And I'm thinking to mineself, how I'm going to go back to work in the quarry? Because if I don't show up for work, the police will come for me and arrest me. I was working then in a quarry, a terrible place where I wouldn't have lasted very long I'm sure, even with no broken leg. This is why it's a miracle what happened next.

"So I am lying in the road after they throw me out of the hospital. With mine crutches. Imagine, someone bends over me, crouches down. He is in the Wehrmacht uniform. A German officer. I figure this is the end. But no. No, he speaks to me so kindly, so gentle, in German, which I understand a few words at the time. He tells me I need to be in the hospital. I start to cry and say, 'That's where I've been!' He is with his private car and chauffeur. He writes a note for the hospital that I need a check-up. He says he wants a letter from them about what's wrong with me. Can you believe this?

"I don't exactly remember what the next thing was, but the upshot is that the hospital writes to him that I have a broken leg. I come back to him in the car with a chauffeur and the note from the hospital. He writes a new letter that he needs me to be fit for work. That they have to cure me."

Erica's eyes widened. Melly began to laugh. "Yes, you are right to look amazed! Back at the hospital, they were jumping around me like I was a big shot. For any money in the world you couldn't get such a service in that place at that time. The best is that the person who made my cast—he was a real shady character, though we didn't know it at the time—he was an informer to the Germans. A Jew. This man was a sort of half a doctor, he hadn't yet gotten his licence before the war, but still he was somewhat trained. And he hadn't wanted to help me before, but now he made a perfect cast for me, and I heal well. And also I don't work while it's healing. So I was saved from the quarry."

"And did you ever see the German officer again?" Erica asked.

"Never. He was like an angel that appeared when everything seemed to be lost. A plain miracle."

"And then?"

"And then? It didn't stay a miracle for long. One day I was told to report back to work. And then they threw me in a slave camp. Not that far from mine town."

"A slave camp? Which one?"

There was a discreet tap of the door, and Marie-Paule poked her head in. "Mr. Melly, the architect is here."

"Tell him I'm tied up. I'll be there in a minute."

He glanced at his watch, and stood up a little stiffly. "I gotta go. I'm running late."

"We should set up another appointment," Erica said.

"Book it with Marie-Paule." He was already almost

out of the room.

"The name of the concentration camp? Can you tell me?"

He mumbled something over his shoulder. It sounded vaguely like the word scar.

"Could you please spell that?"

Melly turned around to face her from the doorway. He stared at her as if he were coming out of a trance.

"Spell?"

"What you just said, Scar ..., I've never heard of it."

He furrowed his bushy eyebrows and glared. "G-e-h-e-n-n-a."

Erica looked at him blankly. "It was a terrible place?"

"Terrible beyond anything you can imagine. But I got lucky there. Which is probably why I'm here today."

He gave himself a little shake, as if consciously shedding the aura of the past. "Book another appointment with Marie-Paule," he repeated, suddenly brisk and businesslike. "I'll bet by then you'll know how to spell it." He grinned at her, now almost raffish. He did not need to say that he was paying her very well to find out.

5

Driving home along Lucerne, then Jean-Talon, Erica barely noticed that the skies had cleared or that traffic was light. Her knuckles were white on the steering wheel. Even if she'd been in the pink of health, this session with Melly would have unsettled her. A vision of beardless chins trickling blood from a thousand follicles kept flashing in front of her, as she gripped the wheel ever tighter. How could she have possibly undertaken this project, when it was a sure recipe for unleashing all the bogeymen of her childhood? How could she possibly fashion something true and authentic out of such episodic fragments as Melly was throwing at her? And why was he withholding information from her about the slave camp? Could he simply not spell? Or was he toying with her?

Yet, exasperating as he was, he had deeply moved her. The man had somehow survived, seemingly alone. He had lost everyone. She found that an ungraspable idea. *Everyone.* Mother father sister brother. And yet he still had it in him to build a completely new life, a life in which he showered such love on his family, a love that was patently reciprocated. For despite his arrogance and bombast, his children doted on him. She had only to remember that first meeting and how they had hovered around him.

Glen's motives she couldn't figure out at all. Last time, he had brought up the subject of his father's weak heart. Today he tried to deflect her from the Holocaust to Melly's career. But if you put aside his vulgarity and crude Darwinism, his ideas about the Holocaust were pretty much the same as those of her liberal and sophisticated older sister, Christine. When she heard that Erica was considering undertaking the Melly biography, Christine had pronounced, as she did on anything having to do with matters Jewish, "*Let it go, let that history go—what good has Jewishness ever been for us,* unter unser?" She pictured petite Christine with her neat features and tidy brunette bob, wearing a small, tight smile when pronouncing the German words from their childhood, a code for all their complicated, ambiguous family past. As always, in a voice that dropped to a whisper.

Between them, Melly and Glen had succeeded in catapulting her to a place of profound disquiet, a place that she had thought behind her.

Because stories about the war, the enormity of Jewishness, were matters freighted with significance, her family's great secret. But it was a secret she was privy to from the start of her life. Stretching back beyond the pale of actual memory, she was weaned on legends of survival. At the same time, a curtain of silence hid her origins from the world.

Without being aware of how she'd gotten there, she found herself at her driveway. Too exhausted to undertake parking the car in the garage, she needed the support of the handrail to get up the five stairs of the stoop. Inside, she kicked off her boots and collapsed in her reading armchair in the living room without bothering to take off her coat. Cinnamon Cat materialized out of nowhere and leapt into her lap. "There's a good animal," she murmured, and, lulled by his steady purring, fell into a deep sleep.

6

Marty Riess often thought his beloved Montreal, a multicultural metropolis of three million, was nothing more than a *shtetl*. If you were of that select club of English-speaking Jews of a certain age born and still managing to make a living there, you perpetually bumped up against the same people. Sometimes this gave you the warm glow of inhabiting a cozy, enveloping cocoon. At other times, it was like floundering in an algae-clouded gutter.

Perhaps if Marty hadn't been such a creature of habit or so resistant to change, it might have been different. If he hadn't, for instance, been going to the same barber for the past forty years. Marty knew Johnnie Miceli when Johnnie was still Giovanni and apprenticed in his father's hole-in-the-wall barbershop with the red and white spiral pole on the west side of the Main at Prince Arthur. This would have been in the sweltering summer of '59 when fourteen-year-old Marty was shoving cheap men's shirts into cardboard boxes in the stockroom of Riess Brothers, the *shmatte* factory owned by his dad and uncles next door to Miceli's. Johnnie learned to thin hair on Marty's then profuse black locks and practised his first clumsy brush-cuts on him.

When Leona and Marty were first married, and Marty (already thinning on top) was working days and going to Sir George Williams at night, Johnnie was also downtown, renting space on the ground floor of the Gordon Brown Building on Burnside. There were other barbers closer to the university, but Marty liked the way Johnnie cut hair. It did no harm either that Johnnie didn't charge an arm and a leg. And when the textile business moved north *en masse* in the early eighties to Chabanel, and Johnnie followed, Marty continued to give him his business. Even though he was in real estate by then, and had no real connections to the rag trade.

Johnnie's current salon—it was a salon, not a barber-shop—occupied a large, street-level storefront in a fif-teen-storey highrise of showrooms. Catering to designers and male models as well as the businessmen and factory workers who had been his original clients, he sold a dis-creet line of male cosmetics and employed five other styl-ists (four men and a woman), a female manicurist, and a girl trainee who washed hair, swept the floors, and served espresso. His rates were still competitive; he still gave an excellent cut.

Marty had been planning a trim for the Saturday af-ternoon before his date with Erica, but on Thursday af-ternoon he finished showing a lowrise on L'Acadie near Jarry earlier than he'd expected. There wasn't really time to go back to the office before his next client, and Johnnie was only minutes away.

"No problem," Johnnie said when Marty called. "I can do you now."

Yes, but how was Marty to know that Jerry Urbansky would also be getting sheared at the same time? Goddamn Jerry Urbansky, Marty's nemesis and all too real doppel-ganger in the alcove right next to Johnnie's. Mario, John-nie's partner, was solicitously snipping away at Jerry's leo-nine grey head.

Marty swore under his breath. In all these years, he'd never run into Jerry here before. His instinct was to turn on his heel and stalk out. Instead, he slid into the leather chair and forced his features into a rictus of a smile for Johnnie.

"The usual?" Johnnie asked.

"Just a trim," Marty said. A flicker of light swirled in front of his right eye. His right temple began to throb. Just what he needed. A migraine.

"So Marty," Jerry leered at him, their eyes meeting in the mirror. "How's tricks?"

"Things are fine."

"I didn't say how's things, Marty. I said, "How's tricks?" *Yuk, yuk, yuk.*

Funny how Jerry—eyes like black olives swimming in a plate of ruddy jelly—still had the same *punim* he'd had in kindergarten at Folkshule fifty years ago. He'd always been able to alter his features with the skill of a mime. The two of them had been the bane of every teacher's existence through their lacklustre careers at Northmount High.

O Montreal! *Shtetl* was too benign a moniker. Think mud puddle, think cesspool. And he and Jerry bottom feeders, preying on small female fishies.

Brushing Jerry's neck free of bristles, Mario removed the white smock enveloping his torso. Jerry retrieved his jacket from a nearby hook and ambled over to Marty. He slapped him on the shoulder.

"Why the long face, Marty? Can't you take a joke?"

Marty stared woodenly at his reflection in the mirror.

"Heard you and Leona were through. Too bad."

"Thanks."

"Then again, maybe congratulations are due. Nice seeing you, buddy."

"Want an espresso?" Johnnie asked as he cranked Marty's chair up a notch.

Normally he didn't drink coffee after three in the afternoon. But caffeine might just nip the migraine in the bud.

"Thanks, I will."

7

Plastered with sweat inside her down coat, and woozy from her unaccustomed nap, Erica woke with such a jolt that the cat jumped off her, yowling in protest. He stalked out to the kitchen, where she could hear him twirling his empty dish around and registering vociferous discontent.

She shrugged herself out of her coat, unable to account for the feeling of heavy foreboding that seemed to have settled on her chest like a brick. Then it came to her that she had been dreaming of her mother and her sister, though all she could remember of the dream was that they had been furious at her.

Not a very subtle dream, she thought wryly. Her mother would have hated the idea of her choosing to write another Jewish-themed book. Klara would have felt the threat of public exposure all over again, even if the subject this time were not as directly personal as *The Shadowed Generations* had been. And of course Christine, their parents' perfect and perfectly pragmatic daughter, had categorically declared herself against the Melly project. Not for Christine to root around in the family's Jewish past and then trumpet it far and wide in an autobiographical novel. Not for Christine to marry a Jew and then convert back to Judaism, as Erica herself had done. Dutiful, conventional Christine carried on the family business—medicine—and lived the ostensibly uncomplicated and unburdened existence that baptism and a carefully concocted pack of lies had been designed to assure.

Growing up in Budapest before the Revolution, the Molnár sisters had inhabited a no-man's-land of identity, clothed in protective camouflage woven by their parents. Dissembling was a fine art in which they were coached almost without being aware of it. It could be the way their mother rolled her dark-lashed eyes as she tied the sashes of their crimson aprons—symbols of the good Communists they were supposedly to become—and then placed a finger over her lips as she instructed them to say nothing in the school yard of what had been discussed at the dinner table the night before. Which could have been a reminiscence by her father of a daring escape from the clutches of an Arrow Cross goon in 1944, or of his being hidden for months in a hut under pain of silence, so that when he emerged, he was at first unable to utter a sound because of the long disuse of his vocal cords. But it could just as easily have been of the trashing of a Communist Party cadre or a scathing critique of one of General Secretary Rákosi's bombastic orations. Erica understood in her six-year-old bones that she could endanger her parents—no, not just her parents, *herself* and Christine, too—with one careless word.

This knowledge coexisted with the greatest trust in Klara and Tibor's ability to steer the course of their lives. Her parents had a clear knack for getting ahead. Virtually everyone in the family had managed to survive the war, an achievement due in equal parts to luck and cunning. Afterwards, the couple—both of them respected physicians—navigated the tricky shoals of life under Communism with sangfroid. The payoff was the four-storey villa that housed their offices and doubled as the family home on the appropriately named Áldás utca—Street of Blessings—in the Hill of Roses, one of Buda's choicest neighbourhoods. Trellised roses climbed its yellow stucco walls, gracefully trailing around the brown-shuttered windows. A tennis court took up a third of the back garden, the rest of it burgeoning in reckless abandon, the beds of iris, lilies, peonies, and jasmine planted in orderly rows before the war, now a jungle.

The prosperity they enjoyed—the Peugeot, the piano lessons, the opera, holidays on Lake Balaton—all this Erica understood to be the result of the wisdom of her parents. Their discernment manifested itself in her mother's daily warnings. As Klara embraced her daughters on the doorstep before hurrying back to the surgery, she whispered a final admonition. Some of their schoolmates were the children of prominent Party officials occupying even fancier homes perched yet higher in the Buda hills. Among them there might be child informers for the secret police. *You can never be too careful.*

Tibor had managed to avoid joining the Party, but Klara went along with it, though she was no ideologue. Hard-nosed and practical, she was a Communist in the same measure she was a Catholic. She kept her nose clean of politics; her Party job was to look after the Newspaper on the Wall, an innocuous bulletin board of clippings of professional interest at the faculty of medicine, where she taught pediatrics three mornings a week.

Just as, from an early age, Erica and Christine had figured out that there were shades of Bolshevik, so too they intuited that the world was divided into two classes of people: those who were Jews and those who weren't. Sometimes you could tell them apart by their looks, but mostly it was through intangibles. For one thing, all of Tibor and Klara's friends were exactly like them. Whether they had formally converted or not, they had all had their children baptized as a precaution against future potential Holocausts. But while donning Gentile masks, they remained really at home only among others like themselves. *Unter unser*. Among us. Erica always understood instinctively that this was the label signifying Jews who weren't Jews.

And yet they *were*. This was the truly curious thing. Though it was hush-hush, she knew it as a child, was perhaps even vaguely proud of it. What very clever survivors her parents had been for recognizing precisely when during the war to go underground, where to hide, when to trade in jewellery for false papers, false identities.

Somewhere along the way, the sense of not just living a lie, but of being one herself, began to gnaw at Erica.

8

In his bed at the Rockhill, wide awake at two a.m., Marty didn't know whether to blame the espresso, the fading but still persistent headache (he had taken the maximum dosage of Advil Migraine), his ancestors for bequeathing him a genetic predisposition for both sin and guilt, jitters about the upcoming date with Erica, or all of the above.

Every woman he'd ever slept with—Leona having been the first and Kim the hairdresser the most recent—was intent on making him a nocturnal visit. He, who was so accurate with the numbers, refused to tally the figures. A rough headcount would probably have yielded something in the ballpark of a hundred, but in his state of agitation he wasn't visualizing heads so much as bosoms and buttocks of all sizes and shapes, neat ankles and thick ones, smooth elbows and rough, curly triangles in shades of black, auburn, brunette, and sandy.

He groaned and counted the minutes until he'd see Dr. Winters at eight in the morning.

Encountering Jerry had made him realize there was no such thing as a fresh start or a second chance. He would always be dogged by the consequences of his actions. He was an impostor unworthy of the honours the shul had heaped on him by calling him to the executive, giving him a say in his community's future, allowing him to hold the precious Torah in its velvet dress on ceremonial occasions.

Tears pricked his eyes. He had so much been looking

forward to going out with Erica. Even though he knew he was investing way too much hope in her. She was totally out of his reach, a woman Dr. Winters described as having a rich inner life. (Dr. Winters followed her newspaper column closely and felt entitled to pronounce upon her psyche.) Until this afternoon Marty had merely been fretting about his own impoverished inner life, his shallow tastes, his years spent in front of the boob tube lapping up *Gunsmoke* and *The Simpsons*, his inadequacies as a reader. From now on he'd live in fear of running into Jerry Urbansky when he was out with Erica. It was unbearable to imagine Jerry looking her up and down, smirking at her knowingly, dropping hints to her about Marty. What if by some miracle Erica actually liked him—Marty, not Jerry—and then found out about his sordid adventures?

Marty reached for the alarm clock, pushed down the spring for light. The iridescent numbers winked back at him: 2:55. He groaned again, sat up, punched the pillow, then sank back down. In a gesture of defeat he slid his hand beneath the sheet and grabbed the one tried and true friend guaranteed to bring him mindless release.

9

Wonder of wonders, the next morning Dr. Winters didn't berate him. It turned into one of those rare, blissful sessions when the old man was actually compassionate. When, instead of tearing strips off Marty, he tendered balm.

"You can't undo the past," Dr. Winters offered, after Marty had ranted on about his sleepless night, his worthlessness, Jerry's sliminess, and Erica's ostensible purity. "You can only take charge of the present."

"But the past is all around me," Marty wailed. "Every corner of this city has some association with some squalid escapade or other."

"You exaggerate," said Dr. Winters. "Don't be so goddamn dramatic. When was the last time you went for a massage?"

Marty thought for a moment. "A week before I moved out."

"And was it a massage with extras or simply a massage?"

"Sometimes a massage is just a massage."

"So in other words, for more than six months you've done without them altogether."

"Well, yes," Marty said. "But we discussed it, you and I. The only way to stop was to stop altogether."

"There are many things that we've discussed, you and I," Dr. Winters said, "without you feeling compelled to follow through. That's what I mean about taking charge of the present. That's how we make ourselves over. Not in one fell swoop. We change incrementally. Small successes lead to new pathways."

"Yeah, but then I meet bloody Jerry Urbansky and I'm back on the same old pathway."

"Why's that? Because the guy went for a haircut and breathed the same air as you? And now you're going to go back to your old ways because he contaminated you while you were sitting in the barber chair?"

"N-o-o. But just seeing him brought everything flooding back. And it made me realize—one more time— what a minuscule world I live in. And how I'll always land in trouble when my old life catches up with me. I mean after I have a new life."

"What's this 'after-I-have-a-new-life'? A new life isn't like a new shirt or a new tie. Your new life isn't somewhere out there waiting for you. Your new life is right this minute. And Jerry Urbansky has only as much to do with it as you'll allow."

"But what if I meet him when I'm with Erica?"

"Really Marty, I'm beginning to lose patience with you. If you meet him when you're out with Erica, you'll nod pleasantly and move on. But I don't really think that's the issue, is it?"

"It's part of it."

"And what's the rest?"

The antique anniversary clock ticked audibly on the window sill. The mullioned panes rattled as a truck rumbled by outside.

"Erica thinks I'm one thing, a regular ordinary good guy. I'm not the man she thinks I am."

"Marty. Erica's going for coffee with you. I can almost guarantee she hasn't thought a great deal about you. She doesn't really know who you are."

"I have to tell her."

"*What!?* What do you have to tell her?"

"Everything. Everything. So she won't find out from someone else."

"That's a commendable impulse. Hrumph …. I hadn't thought of that. Yes, I think at some point, perhaps if your acquaintanceship progresses, if you continue to hold her in high regard and she isn't totally repelled by your lack of depth and intellectual rigour, you might indeed decide to take her into your confidence. I don't however suggest that you do it tomorrow night."

10

Rhoda called her Saturday afternoons with Faith adult playtime and, in pillow talk heart-to-hearts with Hershy, liked to muse about the relative merits of really good sex versus really good shopping. This particular expedition to Westmount was only moderately exciting: a pair of dangly peridot earrings at Folklore 1 for herself, some textured taupe tights for Faith at SoxBox, and a little preliminary research on behalf of Erica at La Cache. Erica had said she needed a white blouse and Erica hated shopping.

Adjournment over coffee was a mandatory requirement of Saturday afternoon outings.

"Second Cup or Nick's?"

"I have a yen for one of Nick's carrot muffins," Faith said. "The *kiddush* was disgusting."

They settled themselves into a booth at the back of the Greene Avenue diner.

"I really like your new haircut," Faith remarked after they'd ordered. "You haven't had bangs in ages."

"I asked Kim to try something a little different. Of course she made a pitch for doing away with the white. So I said she had carte blanche to do anything she wanted short of a dye job and this is what she came up with."

The cappuccinos arrived, along with a carrot muffin that Faith immediately offered to share. Rhoda waved it aside. She added sugar to her cup, scooped up a dab of foam with her spoon, and licked the spoon. "I think you're going to like this. Kim asked me to give her the lowdown on Marty."

Faith nearly choked. "*What!*"

"I said you'd like it."

"*Rhoda!* How could you wait this long to tell me?"

"I was only at the hairdresser at noon."

"Stop it! What did Kim say? How does she know him?"

"They're neighbours. He happened to have told her he goes to our shul. She put two and two together."

"Yes, well we can put two and two together too."

"We could make five."

"What exactly did she say about him?"

"Just that she has this new neighbour at the Rockhill called Marty Riess. Did I happen to know him? What was he like? He seemed very nice to her…. Not much to do arithmetic with."

"But he's taking Erica out!"

"Stop shrieking. That doesn't rule out dating all of

Montreal."

"But he's perfect for her!"

"Gimme a break, Faith. Why is he so perfect for her?"

"He seems the steady and devoted type. After Rick—"

"Don't even bring up that man! Marty might be okay, but what does he have to offer her? I mean really. She's an author—she's bound to have different interests than him. Even that Paul Ladouceur guy would be better. Just by way of a wild example."

"Her *editor*?" Faith pressed a hand to her generous bust, an expression of amazement on her round face.

"Yah? Why not him, for instance?" Rhoda gave a playful crooked smile.

"He's not Jewish."

"C'mon, Faith. That's *shtetl*-think. Do I need to remind you that Erica's not a stranger to non-Jews? Most of her *family* isn't even Jewish."

"They're not Jewish and they *are* Jewish …. Paul's so unfriendly and curt."

"So might you be in his circumstances. Erica thinks the world of him."

"His girlfriend killed herself. That's not a very good recommendation."

"Isn't that rather harsh? Erica says he was crazy about her. What was her name again?

"Maryse."

"Yeah, that's it. And he stuck by her through some really tough shit."

11

Saturday evening, Marty rang the doorbell of Erica's cottage on Connaught Avenue at the stroke of eight. She appeared immediately, not bothering to pretend she wasn't ready and waiting. As she bent over to pull on her boots, a faded orange beast with a tail like an exclamation point and whiskers flaring from his ears like wings began snaking around Marty's ankles.

"This old gentleman's Cinnamon," Erica said, "my comfort and joy."

"Hello, pussy," Marty said, edging away from the animal as he stifled a sneeze. He was violently allergic to cats.

"Do you have a cold?" Erica asked nervously. "I'm neurotic about catching anything right now."

"No, no," Marty said, stepping gingerly out of the cat's way as he helped her with her coat.

"Where would you like to go?" he asked in the car.

"Somewhere where I'm unlikely to meet Reconstructionists."

He looked at her sideways. Was she kidding?

"I was thinking maybe Brûlerie St-Denis," he said.

"On St-Denis? There mightn't be so many of them there."

"Actually I was thinking of the one on Côte-des-Neiges. It's become my neighbourhood café since I moved. But if you'd rather go to the one on St-Denis ..."

"No, no, that's fine."

"Do you have a problem with Reconstructionists?" he ventured after a few awkward seconds of silence.

"It's not that. I'm just leery of being the object of scuttlebutt."

Marty laughed. It came out too loud, like an explosion. "You have a very ... uh—poetic way of putting things. I would have just said, I'm worried about meeting a bunch of yentas."

She smiled. "Writers' style books would say your way is better because it's plain and simple."

By the time they arrived at the café, they were beginning to relax. Erica had been kicking herself all week for opting for coffee, instead of suggesting a movie. That at least would have given them a subject for conversation. But Marty surprised her by being easy to talk to. He even had a way with a story. Or at least of being a good reporter. In the car she asked him if he'd been to shul that morning.

"Yes, yes I was there. The d'var torah was quite instructive. Nate's clearly on a crusade. He's definitely harping on a certain theme."

"Are you talking about the new building?"

"Uh-huh. Today's parsha was Vayak'hel. He introduced it by saying that for several weeks in a row the Torah portions have been about these extremely detailed designs and decorations for the mishkan, the travelling Tabernacle. You know, for all the years in the wilderness after the Exodus. And he said how he's always found these descriptions terribly tedious and uninspiring, but now he realizes what they're about is a building project, so that's why every last little soffit becomes important and fascinating in the text."

"So that was his little joke?"

"Yeah, and it went over. He got a chuckle. And then he went on to kind of develop it. He spoke about the Reconstructionist notion of modesty and said something that I found interesting, that Judaism is about building cathedrals in time, not cathedrals in space."

"Meaning?"

"Meaning observing Shabbat and the holidays is where we place the emphasis, as opposed to actual edifices."

"Oh yeah? So then why can't we make do with the edifice we've got?"

"Wait, there's more. He said despite this modesty, when you read the specifications for the mishkan, they're very fancy, silver and gold, and onyx and brilliants. And now here's the clincher, the part that we read today was actually about how there was this great outpouring from the people. They brought all their valuables in great droves to Moses because they cared so much about the beauty of the sanctuary. In fact there were so many gifts that Moses finally had to say, 'No more. It's too much. Take it back.'"

"Well, that is a bit rich. And how was this homily received by the faithful?"

Marty, who had been driving rather fast, braked as they turned onto Côte-des-Neiges. A car pulled out from a spot directly in front of the Brûlerie, and he chortled.

"Our faithful," he echoed Erica's words as they made their way indoors, a little awkward side by side, both of them careful not to touch, "were, I would say, more than a little sceptical. There was some kvetching during kiddush."

A hostess showed them to a little round granite-topped table past the glass pastry display. A pleasant buzz of conversation filled the long and narrow room. The place smelled tantalizingly of coffee beans.

"They didn't like the hard sell?"

"Well, we don't yet have a formal endorsement of the project from the congregation. I'd say no, they didn't like it."

"But you think it's going to go ahead?"

"I do, yes."

"And you're in favour?"

"Yes, yes, I am. Aren't you?"

"I've resigned myself to it. Nate wants it so badly, he'll get it by hook or crook."

"It's not only up to Nate."

There was a lull between them. A waitress with very short, very yellow hair, a gold stud in her nostril, and staples in her ear brought a menu which they perused with more attention than it warranted. Marty asked whether she'd like a bite or dessert. She shook her head. She still had no appetite after the treatment; she'd try a décaf allongé and a biscotti. Marty would have loved a double espresso, but decided on discretion. He ordered a chocolate mousse cake and a tisane.

They eyed each other warily. A middle-aged woman and man may indulge in small talk and gossip for a while, but if they're at all interested in each other, they'll inevitably pick up the trail of the past.

At the next table, a young couple burst into laughter. Beyond them, behind the counter, an espresso machine hissed loudly. Marty cleared his throat, then gave Erica a particularly intense and searching look. She returned it measure for measure, her pale eyes narrowing slightly before she withdrew her gaze.

—*Are they green or grey, her eyes?*

—*He isn't handsome. Not like Ricky. But he has a kind face. And I like the way he carries himself, with his shoulders pulled back. It gives him an air of confidence that's kind of attractive.*

The waitress brought their order. The dishes clattered against the granite of the tabletop. Marty emptied a sachet of sweetener into his tea. "I reread *The Shadowed Generations* this week," he said. "It's a very revealing book. I feel as though I know you well."

"Everybody always says that," Erica said, skittish. "But they should realize that a writer only reveals as much of herself as she wants. You only know what I'm willing to tell. And anyway, it's fiction."

"Any resemblance to actual persons living or dead is purely a coincidence?"

"Yes." They both laughed.

"In that case," Marty said, "let me tell you a little bit about me. This isn't fiction. I'm fifty-three, going on

169

fifty-four. I've lived my entire life in Montreal, which is partly why I'm fascinated by your family's history. So much dislocation, adversity, so much *insecurity*. I've had such a humdrum life by comparison. I didn't do well in school and was always getting into trouble. I eventually wised up and put myself through university, with the help of my wife. My ex-wife, I should say. I tried this, I tried that before I sort of fell into real estate. It's volatile and demanding, but I've done okay at it."

"I understand you've done more than okay."

"Who told you that?"

Erica blushed. "Oh, Faith, probably." She looked away. She had very fair skin that began turning pink in stages, the flush showing first at the neckline of her white, round-collared top, then rising towards her chin and high cheekbones, and upwards to her hairline, like an elevator going up. She was wearing her hair pulled back with a couple of tortoiseshell combs at the side, from which her mane tumbled to her shoulders. She seemed so vulnerable in her embarrassment, Marty wanted to put his arms around her. He refrained.

"I work hard," he said, "and I've been lucky once or twice. Faith's parents' bakery was located in a building I later came to own. She probably assumes I'm a wealthy man."

"I'm sorry," Erica stammered. "I just meant that you have the reputation for being successful in your field."

"You didn't say anything wrong. I just don't want you to get an overinflated sense of my worth. And if we're on the subject of worth, or I guess I should say worthiness, I'd like you to know that I've made mistakes, all kinds of mistakes. The biggest one is the failure of my marriage, for which I take a large measure of responsibility." He picked up his teacup, took a sip, then played around with the remaining dollop of whipped cream on his plate. He laid his fork down and pushed the plate away, without finishing.

"I've made a mess of things, Erica. But I'm trying to make important changes in my life. I've been seeing a therapist and he's impressed upon me how I've wasted so much time, that I no longer have any left to waste. I don't want to badmouth Leona, but we weren't happy together, and I really don't know what it's like to be in a serious and meaningful relationship. And that's what I'm looking for now."

"How long were you married?"

"A very long time. Thirty-two years."

"And you have children?"

"Two sons. And I have a little granddaughter in Boston. My older son and his wife are there. Ian, my younger boy, lives in Vancouver."

"I find it very hard to believe that you were married that long to someone and never experienced any fulfilment. You must be angry and bitter, so you've forgotten the happy times."

"I *am* angry and I *am* bitter. But Leona and I really weren't good together. That's not only her fault, of course. Look, the reason I'm bringing this up is not to wash my dirty linen for your benefit but to lay my cards on the table. I'm glad I finally got out of my marriage. But I'm lonely. I'm looking for a partner in life."

"I'm sure you'll make some woman very happy with that kind of declaration, Marty."

"I'm not interested in some woman. I'm interested in you."

"I'm flattered. But I'm not ready for anything along the lines of—what did you say?— 'meaningful' and 'serious.' Not right now anyway. I'd like to go to the movies maybe, or out to dinner. Just like that. Company. But I'm not ready for anything more."

"What went wrong in your marriage?"

Again that disconcerting flush.

"I wish I knew. I've tried to figure it out and of course my friends are armchair psychiatrists. Especially Faith, who has some claim to the chair. We were also married way too young. I wasn't twenty-one yet. And we were from very different backgrounds, but that was something we enjoyed, our different backgrounds. We were crazy about each other—"

To her horror, her eyes welled up and spilled over. "Oh, please excuse me." She began rummaging for a tissue in her purse.

"I'm sorry. I shouldn't have asked."

"No, it's okay. I cry like Niagara, it's one of the things Ricky can't stand about me. A long list."

"I find that hard to believe!"

"Oh, believe it," she said, as she blew her nose emphatically. "Hindsight tells me that we had problems from the beginning. I'm no angel but I put up with a great deal over the years that I now wish I hadn't. But at the time I didn't know it was going to end this way. And at the time it didn't seem like other people were so much better off."

"Well, I can certainly relate to that," Marty smiled. "I tried and tried. We did couple therapy, we did marriage encounter groups, we tried every last gimmick in the relationships business. How did you meet your husband?"

"Promise you won't laugh?"

"Scout's honour."

"Were you ever a boy scout?"

"Never."

"We met at Hillel House, at McGill."

"But I thought, reading between the lines of your book, that you weren't brought up Jewish?"

"I wasn't. This was the first step of my great rebellion. Checking out Hillel. To find some Jews who were Jews. If my parents had known, they would have locked me up. Imagine, they'd moved heaven and earth to make themselves over, they'd had me and Christine, my sister, educated at Sacré Coeur, Jewishness was supposed to have been laundered right out of us, and what do I do at the first available opportunity? I go on an anthropological expedition in search of Jews who aren't Christians. But I didn't have to do too much exploring because I ran into Ricky there and I was the answer to his prayers. If he'd been into praying at the time, which he wasn't."

"Why?"

"Because he was into his very own adolescent revolt. Which meshed perfectly with mine, as it were. Ricky ran away from home. He came from a very religious family in Mile End. He was the oldest of seven kids. He was brilliant, I don't know how old he was when he was reading Spinoza, nor how he got a hold of Spinoza. None of the religious practices of his household made any sense to him. And he hated his father, who, among other things, beat his mother. One fine day he ran away. And the only place he could think of to run was Hillel. There was a wonderful chaplain there at the time, Rabbi Schreiber. Who actually took him in for a time and who facilitated bursaries, because he'd already won a university scholarship to McGill.... He was quite brilliant."

"So you've already said," Marty said, his face clouding over.

"Yeah, well, this is more information than you need."

"No, no, I want to know everything about you."

She began to laugh. "I assure you, there's not much to know. Really. We married. We had a civil ceremony. My parents were beside themselves, because here I was marrying someone who for all intents and purposes was a *Yiddishe bocher*, the kind of Jew there hadn't been in our family for at least a hundred years. But they needn't have worried. Rick was totally irreligious. This became a great bone of contention between us over time. He thought he'd married a *shiksa* and got all agitated because I was keen on rooting around in the Jewish past. I went to see his parents—against his will—to try to patch things up between him and them. I began to study Judaism. Eventually I converted. I had to, if I wanted to be Jewish, because I'd been baptized as a baby. Weird stuff, eh?"

"It's fascinating."

Erica shrugged. "Not really. Everybody has a story. You probably do too."

Marty was silent. He was biting his tongue. Then he nodded. "Of course. Perhaps one day I'll tell it to you."

Erica felt a great wave of fatigue washing over her. The idea of listening to his story was totally overwhelming. She glanced down at her watch. Marty immediately noted the gesture.

"You're tired, aren't you?"

"It's only ten, but I'm bushed."

"Let me just pay up and I'll take you home."

"You don't have to pay for me."

"But of course I do."

Once again, he insisted on holding her coat for her. She wanted to be irritated by his dogged chivalry, but there was something touching about it. They were just about to leave the restaurant when the door swung open from the outside to admit Reisa and Rabbi Nate. In the flurry of cheek kisses and handshakes, Erica noted Nate's dancing eyes and Reisa's smothered smile.

"We've just come from the movies," Reisa said.

"We haven't seen you in shul for a while, Erica," Nate said reproachfully.

"Yes, but I'm kept *au courant*. I understand you're taking inspiration from the story of the *mishkan*. Onyx and brilliants, silver and gold."

It was Nate's turn to blush, and he did a spectacularly good job of it.

12

Dear Erica,

When you started to cry tonight over your oaf of a husband—who didn't deserve you, how could he if he had a long list of things he disliked about you —I vowed you'd never cry over me, if, that's to say, things progress between us in the direction that I'd like. In the direction you're not interested in—the serious and meaningful direction—because, if I get your drift, you're still seriously and meaningfully stuck on that putz.

This letter I'm writing tonight I can't send you because if you were to read it now, that would be the end of our relationship before it's even started. I'm writing it a) because I can't sleep; b) because as a result of my work with Dr. Winters, I've got in the habit of writing out what's bothering me; and c) because one day I will *give it to you. That's to say, if we have a second date and a third and a fourth. I think by the fifth, I would have to put this letter into your hands.*

Earlier this evening, I told you I wanted to know everything about you. I really do. And even if you don't want to know any-thing *about me, I need you to know me in full. I'm a decent guy, Erica, at bottom. Which is already to start with the excuses. A woman like you, a fine, sensitive, genuine person, should only enter into a relationship with a lowlife like me with her eyes wide open. I feel obliged to tell you the worst things about me, right now, because I can't take a chance that someone else, someone like Jerry Urbansky, would do it down the road.*

Marty stopped writing and flexed his wrist, staring at his fingers. Then he resumed again, in a burst.

Forget I just wrote that bit about Jerry. I'll get around to him and Hank Srulowitz and Barry King in due course.

And I'll qualify that bit about the lowlife. In many ways I'm exactly the kind of man I appear to be on the surface: polite, hardworking, helpful, with an almost pathological desire to please. That's the real me: an ordinary, middle-aged Jewish guy with receding hair, a humpy nose (broken in a boxing match years ago when I was in better shape), and pot belly. A better than average father, devoted grandfather, hardworking realtor. I think I have a pretty good sense of humour, and I'm interested in all sorts of things—art, opera, drama. Shakespeare's become my passion; McGillicuddy, my English teacher, whose side I was a thorn in for my five years at Northmount—I flunked grade 10—would drop dead if he knew. He probably already is dead, but if he isn't, he would.

So, yes, an okay guy—a card-carrying blood donor, a member of B'nai B'rith and of the Liberal Party of Canada. But— here's the rub—with this really huge blot in my scribbler.

I could start with the family stories, my parents' histories in Ukraine, my birth, what have you, but you'd know I was stalling. I can tell you about all that on dates two, three, and four. But I'd better at least level with you a little about my marriage to Leona, which will give some context to these sordid disclosures.

Marty put his pen down again. "I can't go through with this!" he muttered.

He buried his head in his hands, then jumped up so abruptly he upended his chair. His desk in the den had a small built-in wall unit over it. Inside one of the lacquered cabinets, next to a neat stack of writing paper, note cards, envelopes, and a stamp box, were secreted a couple of shot glasses and a bottle of Johnny Walker Blue Label. He reached in, poured himself a finger of the scotch, and took a gulp. Warmth bloomed at the back of his throat, then down his esophagus. Nirvana.

He glanced at his watch. It blinked 2:20 at him. He couldn't write the whole sorry tale out now. No. He'd make an outline. What was the rush? Date number five was at least a month off. Assuming he hadn't already blown it tonight, seriously and meaningfully.

Married, June 1966.

Jason born January 1967, weighing 8½ pounds. (Shotgun cliché, see movie <u>The Graduate</u>, same year.)

Leona, a looker (in those days).

Never crazy about her the way you say you were about the schmuck. Something lacking in me then. <u>BUT NOT NOW.</u>

TIME TO BITE BULLET HERE ALREADY, RIESS! Introduce those 3 pillars of community who mentored your career as seriously flawed husband.

Exhibit A, Hank S.

1. Hank's the easiest to describe, since he's no threat (poor guy).

2. Keeled over his computer a couple of years ago

during tax season.

3. Terrible shock, a year younger than me.

4. A mensch and a fine accountant, not easy to replace at short notice.

5. Used to see him regularly at the Snowdon Y. Type A, always out of breath, rushing, pushing hard.

Exhibit B, Barry K.

1. Moved to Toronto in '77, making dark predictions about those of us who stayed on here. (Wasn't altogether wrong, since my kids and almost everyone else's that I know haven't been able to find jobs in Montreal, just like he said. BUT Quebec still part of Canada, I'm still making a living, and the PQ hasn't put the Jews in concentration camps, nor nationalized the banks.)

2. Done OK in TO. Got into video franchising on the ground floor and built himself quite the palace overlooking a ravine in Richmond Hill.

3. Not such a bad guy—especially since I'm unlikely to bump into him any time soon.

OK, back to Jerry. Exhibit C (but really he's THE ONE).

1. Ran into Jerry at the barber last week—but could run into him anytime, anywhere, even when I'm out with you.

2. Jerry and I the downfall of every teacher at Northmount High. Pair of smart alecks and practical jokers—maybe one day I'll tell you about our stunts. (Better not.)

3. Lost sight of Jerry after I finally graduated. He went to McGill right out of high school, and I, after a detour, ended up at Sir George.

4. Meeting up again as young family men in Chomedey. Same shul. Renée, Jerry's wife, a good egg—willing to put up with Leona.

5. Double dates with Renée and Jerry. One awful night at their place for dinner, just like *Who's Afraid of Virginia Woolf.* Leona really giving me the gears. I remember 3 things:

    a. I worked too many hours for not enough dough,

    b. I was developing a bald spot and running to fat, *and*

    c. *—get this!—I couldn't peel a pineapple without leaving in the bracts.*

6. We're getting to the bad stuff now:

    ·   A week after this dinner party, meeting of the shul's Brotherhood.

    ·   Afterwards Jerry suggests we go for a coffee. We stop in at Chenoy's.

    ·   It's late on a weekday night, dead quiet. We sit in a booth near the back. I order a smoked meat sandwich and a cherry Coke.

Jerry sips his coffee, and gives me this long, shrewd look. *"Leona's a bitch,"* he says, *like he's stating a self-evident fact rather than insulting my wife. "You ever want a woman to make you feel good all over—*

Suddenly the pen in Marty's hand assumed a heaviness it didn't have before. It fell from his fingers onto the parquet floor.

Marty laid his head down on the desk and groaned. He was horribly tired. His right hand ached, and he clenched and unclenched his fingers to try to get rid of the cramp. His watch said it was four in the morning.

"I really can't go through with this," he said out loud again. He shoved aside the two sheets of foolscap he'd covered with his crabbed backhand. He stretched, rubbed his eyes with his fists, then once more pulled open the cabinet that held his liquor and stationery supplies. From a box of note cards, he selected one of a pre-Raphaelite woman with a mass of auburn curls sitting in a field of flowers, a book in her lap.

"Dear Erica," he wrote, *"I so enjoyed our evening together and apologize if I was too forward in playing the commitment card. I'd like to see you again soon, and promise to not be too serious about the subject of relationships until after we've exhausted a lot of good restaurants and movies. I'll call you later in the week. Sincerely, Marty."*

The synagogue membership list lay on his desktop. He riffled through the pages looking for Erica's address.

13

Monday evening Erica was whisking eggs for an omelette while tuned to Katie Malloch's *Jazz Beat*. The kitchen smelled pleasantly of sautéed onions, mushrooms, and thyme, and she was considering pouring herself a glass of wine from the remnants of a bottle Tamara and Bob had left in the fridge on the weekend. The immortal Ella was crooning about a wrong song and a wrong smile, and Erica hummed along, congratulating herself all the while on feeling not the slightest nostalgia or melancholy. "It's All Right with Me" elicited thoughts of neither Rick nor Marty. The only man in her life at the moment, she told herself, was Melly. But when she thought of him, she stopped humming and nixed the glass of wine.

Spread out on the desk in her small office off the kitchen was a jumble of books, papers, and maps in the happy disarray that testified to work well in hand. There was the trilingual (Hebrew, Yiddish, English) *Black Book of the Martyred Jews of Radobice*, opened at a page depicting a fuzzy snapshot of men and women in overcoats, caps, and flowing head scarves, carrying suitcases. It bore the caption "A group of Jews at the ghetto of Radobice on their way to forced labour." There was *My Life under the Nazi Occupation,* a self-published memoir by a landsman of Melly's in Toronto. There was Martin Gilbert's paperback tome *The Holocaust*, its bulk pinned open by a ceramic coaster on one side and an agate paperweight on the other, to a page on slave factories. And most importantly there was a sheaf of photocopied pages from a history of Nazi forced labour camps that had arrived that afternoon by courier from Paul. With no fanfare save a yellow post-it beneath the heading "Skarzysko-Kamienna". In gangly script, it said, "Might this help?"

Last week, after she interviewed Melly, she had complained to Paul that she really didn't think she had the skills to piece the story together. She was a lowly English major out of her depth with all the convoluted history and the source materials in Yiddish and Polish, German and Hebrew. She couldn't even figure out the place names anchoring Melly's dreadful wartime odyssey. The more she talked to him, the more at sea she felt.

Paul sounded neither impressed nor sympathetic.

But today he had sent her a map and a description of the camp that indeed began with the sound *Skar*. Only the fact that she now had some hard information on which to pin Melly's story could give her cheer at knowing about it. And, of course, the fact that he had said that he'd been lucky there. Luck being a relative concept.

Melly had been right. It wasn't that far from Radobice and it was indeed a hell-hole. The place was a huge armaments factory. Originally, Jewish slave labourers were employed there only for building roads and barracks and for clearing forests. But as the war wore on, Jewish manpower began to be used in the ammunition factories themselves. And womanpower, too, for men and women had slaved together in conditions so appalling that, in some sectors of the camp, life expectancy was a mere three months. The toxic nature of the product poisoned those handling it. Which appeared to be part of the plan: destruction by work. Paul's source calculated that over a span of two years, between 18,000 and 23,000 prisoners perished at this one site. The mind reeled at the figures. But stupefying numbers blunted your feelings. Her job was to make readers ponder one life, bring that life into relief, and then extrapolate imaginatively to what that might mean. But could she do it? Could she fashion something worthwhile out of the raw data of her interviews and the context of her research?

Erica wandered away from her prospective supper back into the office. She began flicking through the archaeological dig of papers piled up on her desk, hunting for the notes from her latest interview.

EM: Tell me what happened next, when you say that they threw you into this slave camp. Tell me.

MD: They took us by trucks over there.

EM: It was at night, it was in the daytime?

MD: They take me out, it's two o'clock in the morning. It's dawn when we get there, that I remember, and the terrible heavy smell of the acid. Picric acid, it's called. I read about this once in a book after the war. I never saw the workers with mine eyes, but they were slaves for sure, these unfortunates. They turned yellow all over from the gases that the acid made. I read that no one would go near them, the other prisoners in explosives wouldn't let them get near. Because anything they come into contact with turns yellow. And even the food—what they called the food—goes bitter in the mouth.

EM: But you never saw this yourself?

MD: Never, I just read, and maybe I heard rumours while I was there.

EM: And so what happened to you?

MD: A miracle, a plain miracle. I was given a trade. Don't get me wrong. This place was a hell. But about five of us from Radobice, we were picked to repair trucks and machinery. We weren't actually in the ammunition place. We were nearby. And so I had better conditions. First of all, instead of twelve hours a day, I worked eight, that was a big thing. And they ordered for me double soup.

EM: But why?

MD: I was good with mine hands, and I caught on good what they want from me.

EM: But why were you so privileged?

MD: The trucks and the cars of the Nazis were coming back from the Russian front in bad shape. And we fixed them up. This was important. But you know, something that is lucky for you doesn't mean you're not suffering. First of all this is after the liquidation, and I have nobody left in the world. And even if I'm somehow surviving here, it is a terrible place. There was sabotage from the Jews. They were unbelievable brave some of those people. In front of the eyes of the guards, they smuggled stuff out to the Polish. The Resistance. And so then there were executions. With mine own eyes I have to watch mine own people hang. And from one day to the next, you don't know what's coming.

Returning to the kitchen, Erica realized she had left the element on, and chided herself for thoughtlessness. Distractedly, her mind still on Melly, she poured the eggs into the omelette pan, tilting it to and fro. A wave of heat and a tantalizing smell of butter and eggs wafted back in her face. The phone rang. She considered not answering, but then pulled the frying pan off the hot element. She picked up on the fourth ring.

"Erica, it's Marty."

"Oh—hi. Could I maybe call you back in half an hour?"

"Erica, I need to talk to you right away, if you wouldn't mind. About something ... something very difficult for me."

"Okay. Just hold on a minute."

Erica turned back to the stove and switched off the element, glancing with chagrin at the arrested omelette. She wiped her hands on a dish towel and returned to her office. She sat down at her desk and picked up the receiver there.

"I'm sorry, Erica. I'm probably interrupting your supper."

"It's okay. What's this about?"

"Look. It's hard to explain, but I have this insane cleaning lady...."

"Yes?"

"Mila. I've inherited her from Leona. She's a very good cleaning lady. Excellent. Portuguese. They're the best."

"Marty?"

"I'm going to have to fire her. She's always tidying, reorganizing me. She has this unfortunate habit of knowing better than me what I want and need ... Look, it's like this. I wrote you a note on Saturday night and addressed it. But I didn't seal it or put a stamp on it or send it. There were some other papers on my desk. Mila decided they were for you, put them in the envelope, and mailed the whole shebang to you this afternoon."

"But why would she do that if the other stuff wasn't for me?"

"Well—it was actually addressed to you. Not *addressed* like with a mailing address, but the salutation, well that had your name in it…. Erica, I'd like to ask you to please not open the letter when it comes."

"Of course not, if you don't want me to."

"I don't want you to."

14

As she washed the supper dishes, Erica's thoughts roamed away from Marty's odd request. Still under the spell of Melly's account of Skarzysko, she found herself wondering how she had allowed herself to be persuaded— by whom? Paul? her agent? the Graces?—to undertake *another* Holocaust-themed title. In an earlier day, Rick would have kicked up a terrible fuss over it, and, in fact, she hadn't breathed a word to him about *The Shadowed Generations* until she was too far advanced in the project to be derailed. As for her parents and Christine, she had kept them in the dark altogether, until almost the date of publication. If you were reared in secrecy, you knew how to keep a secret.

But why hadn't she thought more deeply about the potential of Melly's story to shake her up? She would certainly not work on it any more tonight; that would be a certain recipe for insomnia, or nightmares.

Suddenly, in her mind's eye, she saw not her neighbour's lights glowing across the span of two suburban snow-covered backyards, but a scene straight out of her childhood: the Buda Jewish cemetery in high summer.

One of the great paradoxes of her upbringing had been the Sunday pilgrimages on which her father had led her and Christine. Despite Tibor's paranoia about Jewishness, a visit to the graves of their ancestors was an unfailing weekly ritual: the first stop on what was usually a day of outings—either a hike to the higher reaches of Buda, or a dip at the mineral baths on Margit Island, or a trip to the zoo. If anyone were spying on them—if the affairs of the Molnár family intrigued any Nazis waiting to make a stealthy comeback or any Party functionary nursing a grudge—the Molnárs weren't making it hard for them. It was as if the family's past were an open book for anyone who cared to read it.

Tibor and the girls set out early in the bottle-green Peugeot, Christine and Erica in their Sunday best sailor outfits taking turns in the front seat with their father. (Klara never came along, never let down her guard.) In the early 1950s, this part of Buda past Széna tér—Haymarket Square—past the southern railway station, still had the character of a placid village. A smattering of modest single family homes dotted the landscape. Chestnut and fruit trees blossomed in spring, and an abundance of poppies, daisies, hollyhocks, and sunflowers bloomed over the course of the summer.

About halfway up the steep incline, the hill plateaued into what once must have been a meadow where now two cemeteries, one Christian and the other Jewish, were planted side by side. Tibor parked the car by the stone wall, and he and the girls strolled past flower stalls, where peasant women in layered skirts and bright kerchiefs offered up violets, carnations, or gladioli, according to the season. Visitors heading for the Christian cemetery paused to purchase posies, but the Molnárs always did the Jewish thing. Before setting out from home, they had filled their pockets with pebbles, one or two for each of the graves at which they paid their respects.

The cemetery was neat, well-maintained, leafy, and the weekly visits matter of fact, with few displays of emotion. They spent a half hour wandering from one monument to the next along the narrow pathways, placing a stone here and there. Tibor held forth a little at each stop. Here was his grandfather Fülöp, that gentle, kindly man. Look at this, Fülöp's was the only family marker with square Hebrew lettering on the veined marble. And note too that their great-grandfather's gravestone was one of the few etched with the historic family name, Müeller. Beginning with Tibor's father, Ignác, their name changed to Molnár and the Hebrew content ceased.

Ignác's monument was the only one at which Tibor grew silent. Erica could just dimly remember her grandfather, who died when she was four, "of a broken heart," Tibor said. Ignác had never recovered from the loss of Tibor's older brother, the only member of the family to perish in Auschwitz. Albert's name, dates (1905-1944), and the words, "beloved son and brother, martyr, and hero" were inscribed on Ignác's sandstone monument. Here Tibor would stand longer than at any other place, his arms loosely resting on the shoulders of his daughters. His lips moved soundlessly. Years later Erica persuaded herself that, despite his growing devotion to Catholicism, he had been mouthing the Kaddish.

They pressed on to other graves, to sorrows blunted by time and circumstance. A cousin of Tibor's who had died as a young woman, leaving a tiny baby. A favourite aunt and uncle, their children also victims of death camps. Everywhere Tibor murmured a few words, characterizing the departed, bringing them briefly to life.

These childhood memories had left an indelible mark on Erica. In hindsight, she attributed the seeds of her inspiration for *The Shadowed Generations* to these graveside visits. As a child, though she didn't have the words to formulate it, she had chafed at having to bear the burden of a secret past without the compensating joy of belonging to an old and rich tradition. Perhaps it also had to do with having children of her own and wanting to raise them free of the lies that had shackled her, made her at times hate herself for being a fraud. Perhaps it had to do with striking out on her own, in her bid for independence from Rick, who frowned so determinedly on religion and who had found her perplexing background so appealing.

For her novel, she had spun whimsical daydreams about unknown graves stretching back in time over centuries before the great rupture that tore her family from its roots. She did not dwell on that rupture in the story, leaving it largely to the reader's imagination. But Melly Darwin was dragging her into the thick of it now. Piecing his history together, anecdote by anecdote, detail by factual detail, was forcing her to grapple with a new disloyal thought: no matter what her parents had endured in forced labour and hiding, in harrowing escapes and privation—Christine was born in 1944, and Klara had given her over to Christian friends for safekeeping—no matter how shattering their war had been, it was tame compared to Melly's.

15

Rhoda let herself into her mother's house and called out loudly—Leah Gutner refused to wear a hearing aid— "I'm here, Ma."

"Did you bring the nuts?" Leah stood at the top of the curving staircase, fiddling with the clasp of a thick gold chain from which hung a medallion in the shape of a stylized gourd, its lower half round as a pregnant belly. Once statuesque like Rhoda, she was now bent under a prominent dowager's hump. But her hair, almost as thick and long as Rhoda's, was still dyed her old ash blond, and she was still immaculately groomed.

"I did. *And* baked brownies. And if you come down here, I'll even help you with that clasp."

"I *told* you only nuts. You hate baking!"

"That's not true. Are you coming or not?"

Leah gripped the banister tightly as she began her progress down its broad sweep toward the square landing midway. She had once been a sultry heartthrob with a flair for making a grand entrance. She still had the knack, but part of this particular moment's drama was unintentional. Rhoda held her breath as she watched her mother teetering on the steep, carpeted risers in high patent-leather pumps. Useless to point out that a three-storey heritage property was not the best domicile for an arthritic octogenarian. Leah wouldn't hear of moving.

At the foot of the stairs, she tried to straighten her shoulders. She accepted a perfunctory peck on the cheek, then sighed as she bent forward again, allowing Rhoda to fasten the necklace.

"Every day there's something else I can't do."

Rhoda sniffed dismissively and gestured toward the dining room. The table was covered in white linen and laid with Leah's best bone china.

"Seems like there's still plenty you can do."

"I didn't get round to setting up the card table."

"That's what I'm here for. Certainly not for my bridge game."

"I don't have time for your nonsense, Rhoda. They're going to be here any minute!"

"Ma. 'They' are Auntie Ellie and Joan."

Ever since Rhoda could remember, bridge had been a fixture in her parents' lives.

Tuesday nights were dedicated to deadly duplicate

games at the club. Sunday afternoons were more laidback but still competitive affairs played either *en famille* with Josh's sister Ellie and her husband Harvey, or with a few other congenial couples from the club. These gatherings were held in the library of the Gutners' home on Belmont Avenue. Snuggling in her father's arms and helping sort his cards first into colours and then into suits, Rhoda had learned to recognize a good spread of hearts before she could read. By the time she was eight, she could take over her mother's hand when Leah left the room to put on the kettle.

Even seven years after her father's death, Rhoda found it hard to speak of him without (as she put it) blubbering, and each year the anticipation of his *yahrzeit* and the inevitable visit to the cemetery still oppressed her. He had been her sun and her moon during her childhood, a tall, pleasantly ugly man who had spoiled her to bits. She surely didn't need to play bridge to keep his memory alive, but it was a good way to spend friction-free time with her mother. She and her cousin Joan—Ellie and Harvey's daughter—had devised the occasional foursome to bring the widowed sisters-in-law together. The two old women loved the game, though by no means each other. There had once been an extended period of bad blood between them that Josh had eventually managed to paper over. But the nature of memorable feuds, even when they are papered over, is that they bubble up like groundwater in an earthquake.

Ellie was dealing the hand, her blood-red fingertips

sliding rapidly over the new cards. The evening was no longer young. Her prominent jaw was clenched tight.

"It's only a game, Mom." Joan, as gentle as her mother was ornery, said soothingly.

"But down *three*, Joanie!"

"Vulnerable and doubled," Rhoda goaded, her eyes glinting.

"Behave yourself, Rhoda," Leah said. She turned towards Joan, "It's not *only* a game, Joan. I heard an *authority* on the *CBC* say the other day that bridge is even more challenging than chess."

"But, Ma, there's luck involved in bridge," Rhoda said, "not just skill."

"Not in duplicate."

"Who dealt this?" Ellie sounded outraged.

"You did, Mom."

"That's it—this is definitely the last hand."

Over brownies and Leah's famous lemon squares, Joan heroically tried to deflect the conversation from the fact that Leah had come in first and Ellie last in the final score. "How are the plans going for your new synagogue, Rhoda?"

"Are you finally going to get some proper pews in that place?"

"Well, some of us like our camp-like arrangements as they are, Aunt Ellie."

"Camp! That's exactly what it was like the time I was there. Folding chairs! My tush went numb."

"Being a bit uncomfortable keeps you awake."

"You probably need all the help you can get doing that. Your rabbi certainly isn't an orator. At least when Moish Stipelman was in the pulpit, you could hear the man."

16

Hershy was watching the hockey game in the living room and eating a bowl of Shreddies when Rhoda got home.

"For God's sake turn the volume down!"

"What?"

"Turn it down, or I'll do it for you."

"Bridge game go badly?"

"No."

"Better call Erica."

"She called?"

"Sounding more than usually weird."

"How do you expect me to hear her with the god-damn TV blaring like that?" Rhoda threw the comment over her shoulder, with no particular animus but just for form's sake, as she mounted the stairs. She pushed speed dial to 3. 1 was Faith. 2 was her mother.

Erica answered right away. "Thank God."

"Whoa! What's Rick done now?"

"It's not Rick. It's Marty."

"Oh, goodie. Something new."

"Rhoda! This is serious."

"Well?"

"Look, I'm not proud of myself. Some information

has come into my hands that I'm not really supposed to have."

"Whew! What sort of information?"

"Well, I can't exactly make out, but Marty has some kind of tawdry secret life."

"I don't believe it. Who's been snitching on him?"

"No one. He's written a kind of outline for a confession."

"Go on! How d'you get a hold of it?"

"It's complicated! It's a very crazy story. He wrote it for me, but then he asked me not to read it— "

"Wait a minute. If you weren't supposed to read it—"

"I was ... overcome by curiosity. I steamed open the envelope."

"I do not believe what I'm hearing. Like some third-rate detective story? You steamed an envelope open. With what?"

"With a kettle. What else?"

"E-R-I-C-A!"

"Don't you want to know what it said?"

"*No!* ... Well, yes."

17

Email from erica.molnar@script.net to rhoda.kaplansky@lbpsb.ca

March 18, 1999, 9:45 a.m.

He called, like you predicted he would. He

asked to come by to pick up the letter. I followed your orders and told him that I had opened it. There was an appallingly long silence. I then departed from your script. (I shouldn't have.) I grilled him in my strictest journalistic style. He was FURIOUS with me but came clean. It's bad. I never want to see him again. Ever.

Email from rhoda.kaplansky@lbpsb.ca to erica.molnar@script.net

March 18, 1999, 12:20 p.m.
    Don't be such a drama queen.
    What did he say?

Email from erica.molnar@script.net to rhoda.kaplansky@lbpsb.ca

March 18, 1999, 12:22 p.m.
    What he said isn't for email consumption at the school board! Can you drop by on your way home from school? If not, are you free for tea tonight?

Email from rhoda.kaplansky@lbpsb.ca to erica.molnar@script.net

March 18, 1999, 12:59 p.m.
    I was planning to pick up steaks from Noam

on my way home, but I could skip it. Hershy will have to make do with veggie spaghetti. Could be at your place by 5 p.m.

Email from erica.molnar@script.net to rhoda.kaplan-sky@lbpsb.ca

March 18, 1999, 1:00 p.m.
    Kettle will be on.

18

Erica poured tea into Rhoda's mug, then into her own. Marty's card with the pre-Raphaelite maiden on the cover and his foolscap notes lay spread out on the knotty pine table. Rhoda bent over one of the blue-lined yellow sheets.

"So who are these guys Hank S and—what's his name?—Barry K? Marty's right about one thing. It's a small world. Renée Urbansky used to be Hershy's hygienist. Nice woman."

"Well this nice woman's husband is a pimp. And these other guys, Hank and Barry, are also pimps. Or were. One of them's dead. Even if they weren't actually making money off the proceeds, they were directing their buddies to girls whose services they'd bought and liked. Marty went to someone called—let me check …."

Erica stood up and dived into her cubby office off the

kitchen. A minute later she emerged with a small spiral-bound notebook.

"You took *notes*?"

"I sure did. After he left, so I could tell you. The first one was Micheline. Urbansky told Marty to say to her that Hank S had sent him. Even though it was actually Jerry. And later it was Barry K he was to refer to, although it was always Jerry. He said that knowing that these so-called 'young pillars-of-the-community-in-training' were doing it sort of emboldened him."

"He gave you all these details?"

"He clammed up after a while. He got mad."

"Why did you go after him like that, for God's sake? I didn't tell you to do that."

"I told you already, I departed from the script. I said to him that on our date he'd led me to believe his marriage was kind of dead in the water, not that he'd been cheating on Leona. He actually tried to defend himself and say that because he 'paid for it,' it wasn't like a girlfriend with whom he had an emotional bond. I kid you not."

"Whew, that's some fancy footwork.... So what about Micheline?"

"Let's see: executive secretary at Steinberg's head office—there was still Steinberg's in those days. Lived in the east end. Turned tricks on the side to save up for a trip around the world! He liked her and would have liked to get to know her, but that wasn't part of the deal."

"Erica, I realize this is a shock for you, but where d'you get this tone of high moral outrage? You promised him you wouldn't open the letter. You have a lot of nerve throwing the book at him. Was there more?"

"Quite a bit. An older woman, a masseuse in Ahuntsic. But he was starting to get testy and didn't say much about her. And oh yes, later he no longer took referrals from the boys because—let me quote him—'*massage parlours and escort services began advertising openly. All I had to do was consult the classified section of the paper you write for.*'"

Rhoda picked up the notecard and laid it next to the first page of Marty's confession. She took another sip of tea and then fixed Erica with a long, blue-eyed stare. "You know something? This guy's got a massive crush on you. He says here that he's working on his issues. He wants to make a clean break with his past and live a different kind of life. You weren't supposed to get this confession of his until sometime down the road. It's not a pretty picture. But he's honest. Very honest."

"Oh, yeah, right. And now I know what I was supposed to learn later. There won't be later."

"Well, I can see you might feel that way about it." Rhoda cupped her fingers around the earthenware mug and looked off into the mid-distance. "But I actually think it makes him interesting."

"You *do*?"

"Absolutely. Way more interesting than his butter-wouldn't-melt-in-his-mouth public image. A man with a secret, a man trying to redeem himself. Besides, Leona Riess is such a nasty piece of work."

"That doesn't entitle him to cheat on her."

"You're right. But you know what? I think human beings are hardwired for infidelity."

Erica's eyebrows shot up. "You do? Since when?"

"Have you *never* been tempted?"

"No! Attracted, maybe. But actually tempted? Uh-uh. Rick's entire professional life was one long testimonial to the fall-out from affairs."

"But what if you fell for somebody else?"

"Well, it's academic now, but I don't think I'd have been able to live a double life. I grew up with lies—not about love, but about something maybe even more important."

"You mean about Jewishness?"

Erica nodded. "Who we were to the outside world was one big fat lie." She began doodling in her spiral notebook. Without seeming to realize what she was doing, she drew two small interlocking hearts. "You know something, Rhoda?"

"What?"

"I think I'm hardwired for fidelity."

"To *Rick*?!"

"Not to Rick exactly. But I have this stupid ideal of true love. Like my parents. They were childhood sweethearts. Whatever mistakes they made, they were always faithful to each other. It wasn't a perfect marriage. My mother dominated the show, but my father adored her. And she him, really. I always had that model of harmony before me. Even in the worst times with Rick, I believed it would work out between us. In my bones I felt it was possible."

"But people sometimes have a fling—and it can actually strengthen a marriage."

"Are you telling me something?"

"No. I'm just being contrary. Listen, I gotta go. This has been quite the conversation. By the way, when are you going to tell Faith?"

"I'm not telling her."

"You're not telling her?"

"*And neither are you.*"

"Since when do the two of us have secrets from Faith?"

"Rhoda, you know Faith. She can't zip up her mouth the way he can't zip up his pants. I'm done with him, but I'm not vengeful."

"You have *nothing* to be vengeful about!"

19

Outside in the crystalline cold, the snow crunched beneath Rhoda's boots. The last vestiges of pink and purple from the setting sun feathered the sky. *I almost told her*, she thought as she walked slowly toward her car. *It's the nearest I've ever come to telling anyone, even Faith.*

She got into the car, switched on the ignition and began scratching off the frozen condensation on the inside of the windshield with her scraper. Little flecks of ice, like dandruff or dead skin, cascaded onto the dashboard where they melted as the engine began to thrum.

For a moment she sat motionless, overcome by lassitude, her mind blank.

Does every family have to have a secret?

With an angry flick of her fingers she cut the engine, and stared, unseeing, at Erica's white garage door. She suddenly didn't want to go home, skirmish with Hershy, cook spaghetti. She didn't want to think about the turning point of her life, or about how infidelity could actually strengthen a marriage. How did that *chanson* go? She began softly humming to herself. *Plaisir d'amour ne dure qu'un moment. Chagrin d'amour dure toute la vie.*

Part Three

I sang "Come, O Sabbath bride" on Friday nights with a bridegroom's fervour.

—Yehuda Amichai

1

According to the gospel of Mordecai Kaplan, modern Jews live in two civilizations. On the one hand, they swim in the swirling waters of mainstream society. On the other, they cling with varying degrees of tenacity to the shores of their idiosyncratic particularity. Overall, Rabbi Nate enjoyed this tension. However, as his eyes skimmed over the gathering in his dining room from his spot at the head of the table, he reflected that it was a little trying when New Year's Eve happened to fall on a Friday night and January 1st on a Saturday. Tomorrow morning he would have to preach a sermon about the millennium—as fundamentally un-Jewish a concept as could be invented. Tonight, arrayed around his lace-covered table, bathed in soft incandescence, were eight guests assembled—as it were—by the dybbuk of Y2K. Although, of course the invitations had been issued by no other gremlins than himself and Reisa.

How was he to have known that she was asking Abigail Rosen at the very moment he was on the phone with Moish Stipelman? Reisa should have touched base with him before placing that call! He distinctly remembered having a discussion with her about the invitations. They agreed two weeks ago that it would be a mitzvah to have a set of old-timers for Friday night/New Year's Eve: the Stipelmans *or* Abigail. Naturally they were motivated by a spirit of *chesed*—loving kindness—though, to be honest, neither he nor Reisa would have been broken-hearted if turned down.

Both Moish and Abigail had accepted with alacrity, Abigail requesting to bring along her daughter visiting from Victoria. Moish was of course accompanied by the stern and censorious Sylvia, now glaring at Abigail across the table.

If Reisa's head weren't perpetually in the clouds of Jewish mysticism—she taught a course on Kabbalah at McGill—she would have recalled that in the interlude between Moish's first marriage and his second, well before Nate's connection to the shul and her own, Moish and Abigail had had a torrid affair, the steamy details of which were to be found in "Song of Delight," a sonnet interred in Part One of Abigail's *Collected Works*.

Grinning unnervingly at some private joke of their own (or perhaps merely relishing the image of Moish's and Abigail's intertwined limbs and hearts with which the sonnet had ended), Helen and Jeff Stern sat together, on Nate's left. Helen was wearing a most peculiar outfit, black elephant pants crowned by a strapless spangled top demonstrably contrasting her white chins with her bronze head. Wiping the smirk off his face with difficulty, Jeff began interviewing Abigail's daughter Cynthia about her job in market research. A heavy-set woman with big hair and dark bulging eyes, Cynthia responded in monosyllables while turning her fork over and over with one hand.

Thank God for Susan and Aaron Leibovitch, without whom this evening would be nothing but a penance. The original idea—and it had been a good one—had been to invite a few young (okay, youngish) congenial couples like the Leibovitches and Faith and Al Rabinovitch. In their midst, Moish or Abigail would have been quite neutralized. But then Faith begged off, citing family obligations. (A likely story.) As for the Sterns, they were a political afterthought. Since they'd thrown their collective weight behind the building project as few others had, it was wise to cultivate them. Reisa hadn't thought they'd accept, but clearly they didn't have more exciting plans.

"Nate, darling," Reisa said gently, "don't you think we should start?"

Nate started from his reverie and gave a nervous tug to his beard.

"Yes, yes, please join in everyone," he said and began singing, "*Shalom aleichem.*" He beamed at Reisa, as if seeing her for the first time that day. She looked more than usually pretty, her face serene and her eyes bright. She smiled back at him and joined her voice to his, and the others around the table took up the melody.

The repetition of the timeless words about the angels of peace conveying the blessings of the Majesty of Majesties was balm for Nate's spirit, the tune like a soft breeze wafting in from some preternatural source of comfort. Ah, Shabbat, Shabbat the queen. You kept this, the most beloved of days, because you were so enjoined; it was a central commandment. But more importantly you kept it because it kept you. The millennium celebration would be over in the small hours of the morning, but Shabbat would return to restore your parched soul until the end of days.

At the conclusion of the last *ha-kaddosh baruch hu*, Moish, his voice full of emotion, asked if he could say a *shehecheianu*.

"Of course, of course," Nate waved expansively. "I should have suggested it myself."

Pushing his chair back, the old man creaked slowly to his feet. Sylvia clucked and fussed until Nate got up from the table to fetch Moish's cane from the hall. Since his accident a year ago, Sylvia seemed bent on turning her husband into an invalid. Nate thought the stick was more for her than for him, but Moish obligingly leaned on it when it was handed to him.

"My dear friends," Moish began, his voice still thick with passion or phlegm, "I'm an old, old man of waning powers, so bear with me if I ramble. At this stage of my life, every day is a bonus. It's an extraordinary thing for someone born in the horse and buggy age to reach the end of the century and the millennium and be obliged to worry whether his computer's going to crash at midnight." A delighted ripple of laughter rewarded this preamble and Moish, encouraged, cleared his throat.

—*He's off and running now,* thought Reisa. *There goes my roast.*

"It is, as I say, an extraordinary gift to reach this marker and to do it with my dear wife by my side—"

At this, Abigail, as if on cue, began coughing and spluttering. Sylvia fixed her with a scornful look, but it remained unacknowledged. Abigail's explosion was nearly drowning out Moish, who—either oblivious or deliberately offensive—was insistently carrying on with his peroration.

"—and here with my surrogate son, Nate, and dear Reisa, and other dear friends—"

On either side of Abigail, Cynthia and Nate were offering her glasses of water. Abigail, her rouged and weathered face turning purple, grabbed Nate's drink from him, splashing some in his lap. She took a theatrical sip and, with dramatic heaves of her bony shoulders, gradually recovered.

"I was thinking, as we were singing *Shalom aleichem*," Moish continued, unperturbed, "that I must not only thank God for allowing me to reach this historic turning point, but I must express my gratitude that we've arrived at a juncture when we may indeed dare hope that God's angels of peace have alighted upon the face of the Earth, since peace seems to be breaking out all over it. Most especially and importantly in that little corner of the universe that is so close to all our hearts. I'm thinking of the resumption of talks between Israel and Syria after a hiatus of many years, so that at long last there are some real hopes for peace in the Middle East. Let's also pray that with the gradual subsiding of the crisis in the Balkans, we may look to—as our Christian brethren like to say—peace on earth and goodwill to all men. And there are more grounds for cautious celebration, here too in Quebec, since the tide of separatism seems checked, and so the prospects look encouraging for more of our young people choosing to stay and make their futures here.

"Not of course that there aren't huge challenges ahead for the world, but the lull in hostilities will allow leaders and statesmen an opportunity to concentrate on creating conditions for social peace, and attempts to assuage environmental distempers and fight the scourges of poverty and dislocation and intractable diseases.

"And so I thank you for your indulgence and ask you to join me in a *shehecheianu*, as once again my heart overflows with thankfulness that the Eternal has brought me to this day. *Baruch ata Adonai, Eloheinu melech ha-olam shehecheianu v'kiemanu v'higgianu lazman hazeh*."

2

"I'm not sure how I got here," Rhoda said. Sporting a striped Paris-Bistro apron over her jeans, hair pulled back into a neat ponytail, she was rolling out filo pastry on the kitchen counter.

"As in what's the meaning of life?" Hershy rinsed one of the champagne flutes he'd bought that afternoon at IKEA. It hadn't been as insane a project as Rhoda had predicted. The expected monster crowd hadn't materialized; the store, in fact, had been like a ghost town. On the afternoon of New Year's Eve, consumers had finally stopped shopping and were hell-bent on preparing for the blowout of a thousand years.

"No, idiot," Rhoda grinned sidelong, exposing her crooked uppers. She stuck her pinky in a bowl of spinach filling and licked it before waving the pepper mill over the bowl. "I just meant, how did we come to be hosting this party when I hate New Year's? I've never been able to understand why people go into an orgy of celebration over turning a page on the calendar. Everybody's got this idea we're on the verge of something wonderful. When the reality will probably be something quite nasty."

"Oh, lighten up, Rhode! This doesn't even qualify as a party. Just Erica and this editor of hers and Faith and Al. And you and me. And the only reason we got to be hosting it is because you and Faith have taken it into your heads to be matchmakers. And also because Al's too cheap to treat Faith to a big night on the town."

Rhoda burst out laughing. "With the teensiest encouragement she'd be seeing in the new year on a volcano in Guatemala, like she says *The New York Times* recommended. Or at the very least an evening at the Ritz."

"That'd be the day. Al, the great ex-hippie, forks out a couple thousand bucks for Dom Perignon and truffles and the big band sound of an orchestra you've never heard of? I don't think so."

3

Erica squinted at her image in the mirror as she carefully applied mascara to her (ever thinning) lashes. The trouble with having once been beautiful was the dimming of your allure. Age was a great leveller. Take Rhoda, who had been so skinny and gangling when they first met, but who, over the years, had grown into such a handsome woman. Her hawk-like features had softened, and her silver hair set off her unusual combination of blue eyes and olive skin far better than her original dark locks had ever done.

Erica ran a comb through her curls which, unlike her lashes, were luckily still abundant. She was deliberately going easy on the makeup—a bit of foundation, a touch of blush, some copper eye shadow. And she was dressing simply: velour pants and a turtleneck. The idea was to be warm—it was going to be freezing on the mountain later.

And anyway, why dress up for a house party with your buddies?

Even two years after the fact, the memory of her fiftieth birthday party still stung like a slap in the face. That particular occasion had cured her of getting excited over extravagant festivities. Now, in front of the mirror, she bit her lip in an effort to hold back the stupid tears that would ruin her mascara-thickened lashes. What an idiot she had been, missing all the clues—Ricky's crazy hours and his sudden zeal for showering in the middle of the night when he came home, supposedly from the office. And yet he'd gone to such great lengths to organize a beautiful event for her, inviting everybody they knew to Chez Lévêque for the evening. There was sensational food, flowing booze, impeccable service. He had planned all the details, down to the party favours of gilt quills and miniature dictionaries.

She had had no idea that her birthday party was in fact a swansong for the marriage. Two days later, she intercepted an email between him and the used-car heiress, a client whom he'd helped part from her ex.

"But why, why did you make this party for me?" She couldn't take it in. Stingy Ricky, spending a fortune on her while *shtupping* Sandra.

"Because you deserved it," he shrugged, a breathtakingly double-edged answer.

"But why did I deserve it, if you want to leave me?"

"You weren't supposed to find out, and I don't want to leave you. You're throwing me out."

It was like a bad play, a soap opera.

"So go already. Go."

But he wasn't in a hurry to go. He moved into Raichie's old bedroom—a feminine bower, all pink frills and ribbons—and then, when Erica objected to sharing the upstairs bathroom with him, down to the basement. Every nerve in her body jangled when she heard the front door click open in the middle of the night, as he nonchalantly returned after tomcatting with the Queen of Refurbished Jaguars.

She sought legal advice, and the breezy female attorney told her there was no way to make him leave and that fighting the nastiest family lawyer in the city was going to be uphill work. That little jab got under Erica's skin. No one except her was allowed to say bad things about him.

The day she came home to find his side of the bedroom closet entirely empty, she stared at the hole he'd left behind—the bare scuffed wall at the back of the cupboard, the narrow strip of hardwood where his shoes had sat—and howled. Not since giving birth to Tamara had she made a noise like the one that emerged from the back of her throat. She frightened herself with it; if she wasn't careful, she'd disintegrate altogether.

She tried to work, but the columns she churned out were insipid. Was it any wonder, considering she was staring at the page of a book or at the computer screen without noticing that a couple of hours had elapsed? To her amazement, Paul didn't complain about her copy.

And yet there were good things in her life as well. Her friends, her father, her sister, the kids, all treated her with the tender solicitude reserved for a sick child. Somehow she managed to get through the days, even if by evening her vocal cords were strained from too much talk, her eyes red from too much crying. But at night she lay rigid and wide-awake, primly keeping to her side of the bed. She refused to admit to herself how much she yearned for the animal comfort of Rick's body next to her, spoon style. The only person who could really have comforted her was the one who had shoved her into this hackneyed, preposterous, totally unacceptable predicament.

Then her cancer diagnosis completely eclipsed the divorce. At first she couldn't believe that life could outdo art so extravagantly. What self-respecting novelist would have stooped to such a cheap trick, piggybacking malignancy onto heartbreak? The day her endocrinologist called saying the biopsy showed suspicious cells vaulted to the top of her short list of worst days of her life.

And so, for a while at least, cancer cured her of Rick. It put his betrayal in perspective. So he preferred a wealthy woman for whom he'd arranged a handsome out-of-court settlement to herself? *Let him.* Consumed by blood tests, ultrasounds, and visits to the surgeon, she had no time for his tawdry tricks. After the surgery there were post-op appointments and scans by large-eyed machines scrutinizing her body for more rogue cells. When none was found, she was pathetically grateful to the technicians, the doctors, *God.*

Whenever and wherever she thought of it, she prayed. Out on a walk, she'd furtively check that there was no one nearby, then approach a solid looking tree and touch the veined bark for luck. *Dear God, give me back my old life, it's not as bad as I thought it was.*

"*Let me live that I may praise You.*"

I'll deal with the shambles of my marriage, just don't abandon me.

"*Do not hide Your face from me, or I shall become like those who descend into the Pit.*"

From being a desultory worshipper, she became a regular at shul. She joked that synagogue attendance was the high point of her week. At the very least, it anchored her weekends. The structure and predictability of the service, the rabbi's attempts to decode the rich and problematic text, the kindness of strangers—were these prosaic but actual experiences of the divine?

Well, *hardly*. And now there was the Marty factor to contend with as well. Far from divine Marty. She avoided him; not that he was seeking her out. She wouldn't stop going to shul because of him; how would she explain it to Faith? And she'd miss it too much. Just her luck. The one guy who'd asked her out since Ricky was as kinky as a skein of unravelled wool. Maybe that's all there was out there, seriously flawed people. Like Rick, once a runaway *yeshiva* boy in search of a mixed-up Jewish *shiksa*. And now a warped real estate agent who settled scores with his wife by trying to get laid in massage parlours.

Getting laid was becoming an issue for her too. Since Ricky's departure, she had more or less convinced herself that she'd be unable to function with anyone else. But two weeks ago she had a disconcerting experience at the annual Quebec English-language literary gala. Covering the event for *The Gazette,* she ran into Gilles Lemay, the literary columnist of *La Presse*. Literally. Dashing towards the phone to call in her quotes to the night desk, she collided with Lemay in the narrow indoor corridor linking the nightclub in which the award ceremony was held and the adjoining bistro. "*Pardon!*" they both exclaimed and laughed, embarrassed. With an innate courtesy Lemay grabbed her lightly by the shoulders to keep her from falling. The embrace lasted perhaps ten seconds before he'd righted her and they each hurried off in opposite directions.

Phoning in her story, Erica felt the imprint of Lemay's fingers on her arms as if he'd handled her with hot tongs. "I was practically swooning," she later told Faith (who naturally reported it to Rhoda). "It suddenly came to me. I haven't been touched by a man in nearly *two years*."

The dream she had the night following this collision she disclosed to neither Faith nor Rhoda. (There were limits.) She was in shul, the Torah reading had just ended, and Marty was called up for the honour of *hugbah*, to hold aloft and exhibit the sacred scroll to the congregation. Only men with broad shoulders and strong arms were equal to this task, the scroll not only being heavy, but at certain times of the year, dangerously lopsided. Marty, outfitted in a beautifully cut chalk-stripe suit, braced himself on the *bimah*, bending from the knee slightly to lever his load. Hoisting the twin spools high in the air, he turned to face the Ark, flinging his arms apart as wide as they would go so as to show off the text. As he did so, there was the sound of fabric ripping, and his jacket disintegrated into jagged strips to reveal a back ropy with muscle. The congregation was singing lustily. *La mazikim bah, v'tomcheah m'ushar.* "A tree of life to those who grasp it; those who uphold it are made happy." Everyone except Erica appeared oblivious to Marty's straining, sinewy bare torso.

At this point Marty's trousers slipped down to his ankles. He was wearing paisley print boxers and black knee socks. What was visible in the expanse between briefs and socks was quite promising—sturdy looking legs dappled with dark curly hair that wasn't even slightly repulsive.

In the morning Erica lay in bed replaying this scene. It wasn't erotic, she told herself, not at all. It was a dream in which she exposed Marty for all the world to see. But the world, or at least the part of it represented by Congregation Emunath, remained unruffled. They were paying attention to the word of God on display, no one but herself distracted by Marty's nice broad shoulders and paisley shorts.

4

Marty—in serviceable white cotton briefs and undershirt beneath jogging suit and warmest parka—was dousing four Hygrade frankfurters with mustard and relish. Inside the oversized van parked at the corner of Ste. Catherine and University, it reeked of hot dogs, cigarettes, and b.o.

Actions speak louder than words, his mother used to say. Apparently this had been a cornerstone of the thinking of Poppa Joe Teoli's mama too. That coincidence had been a little surprising the first time he'd spoken to Poppa Joe. Of course it was nothing compared to the amazement he felt at conversing at all with a bona fide Catholic priest. And at being face to face with the founder of the Alley Mission.

Marty harboured a deep distrust of the Catholic Church, if not actually of Catholics. He knew better than to say that some of his best friends were Catholic, especially since none were. Over the years, however, there had been colleagues and acquaintances (his trusted dentist Denis Vaillancourt, his barber Johnnie Miceli) who adhered at least nominally to the Church of Rome. But the *idea* of Catholicism and the reality of occasional attendance at Catholic weddings and funerals conjured up in Marty a race memory of auto-da-fés, the smell of burning flesh, and the tainted odour of the crypt.

He had been drifting more or less since the disaster with Erica. During the course of innumerable sessions with Dr. Winters, he beat his breast over his sullied past. He raged at Erica for opening his letter. He vowed never to go near her again. (Winters was in wholehearted agreement.) And then he beat his breast some more.

One day, Dr. Winters said to him, "Enough of this self-flagellation! *Do* something." Then he'd added, "Atonement isn't just for the Day of Atonement."

In somewhat different terms of course this was always the gist of Nate's High Holiday sermons. And though March wasn't the season of Jewish repentance, it became the time of Marty's resolve. Erica had blown up in his face like a giant firecracker because of his own fixation on confession and absolution. (And of course because of stupid Mila. Whom, in the event, he didn't fire.) Maybe Winters was right. Doing something might help—not with Erica, but with the sickness inside him.

But when the idea of taking action occurred to him, he didn't think of Emunath's Social Action Committee, or Hanukkah Food Basket Drive. He thought of Poppa Joe's *Mission dans la ruelle*, the Alley Mission.

He'd heard an interview with Poppa Joe on the radio. How, ten years earlier, at a time when the priest was considering retirement from active work, he had bought an old Winnebago with a personal loan and with it began ministering to Montreal's street kids and runaways. How great the need was and continued to be and how, along with filling kids' bellies, he gave them nurturing and respect. He talked to them, listened to them, "As if they were guests in our home. We give them a little hospitality. Something to eat and drink. As if the van were a family kitchen. And in this modest way, we hope to offer them solace, a sense of acceptance ... even love."

The priest's words struck a chord with Marty, and before he could change his mind he called *Ruelle* about the possibility of volunteering. He was amazed when he was vetted by Poppa Joe himself. The priest looked a few years older than in his publicity photos, an aging paesano with more salt than pepper in his handlebar moustache. The brown eyes he trained on Marty were both kindly and sharp.

"Why have you come to us?"

"I want to be useful," Marty said, keeping to the narrow truth and delighted to find himself free of any desire to bare his soul.

"Tell me a bit about yourself," Poppa Joe prompted.

Marty sketched a short bio of himself, beginning with his uninspired career as a student. It was a sore point with him, but a sort of point of pride as well. The unspoken subtext—*I wasn't supposed to amount to anything, but I've worked to make something of myself*—hung in the air, a silent offering to the priest.

"Ah yes," Poppa Joe said, "I know something of this kind of failure myself. D'you know, I was thrown out of not one, but two seminaries in my time? It's a dubious distinction in my line of work."

And so Marty found himself accepted not only as a volunteer but as a real person in the eyes of this down-to-earth, good man. There weren't many conditions or much formal orientation. You learned on the job, committing to one night a week for twelve months. He'd been doing it ever since, with a double shift the previous week at Christmas, when a Jewish *bénévole* was a particular asset. Though he wasn't obliged to cover New Year's Eve, he was relieved to have a place to go.

"*Hey Marty, dépêche-toé! Où sont mes quatre steamés avec relish et ketchup? Il m'en faut trois encore avec mayo et moutar'.*"

"*J'arrive*," Marty said, stifling a smile. Claudine, who took the orders at the front of the van, was an excitable twenty-year-old student at UQAM. She had a nice touch with clients, but gave short shrift to older volunteers. He slipped the hot dogs into wax paper envelopes and hustled to the front of the bus.

The smell of stale sweat became more powerful as he neared a couple of scrawny boys seated side by side on a bench in the middle of the bus. Marty tried not to breathe too deeply as he passed them, telling himself that if the stink became unbearable, he'd step out of the trailer and let the wind give him an airing.

He handed the hot dogs to Claudine, a strapping young woman as tall as himself. Behind her he caught sight of a girl perched on the stairs of the bus. She seemed like a bird arrested in flight—apparently unwilling to enter all the way in and ready to bolt back out into the cold any second. Her narrow face and slight build made him think of a sparrow.

Girls seldom came to the van. Poppa Joe had told him they were more likely to seek help at *Ruelle*'s day centre. The fragility of this waif in her black pea jacket open at the neck sent a pang through Marty's jaded heart. He couldn't tell how old she was, fifteen or twenty-five. Though he had never picked up anyone underage, a wave of guilt engulfed him, and he was overcome with shame. With all his might and against all reason, he hoped she didn't work these streets.

Claudine nudged him with her elbow. "Marty, what's with you tonight? *As-tu oublié?* Three more with mayo and mustard!"

"Right away. What about … her?" he added, shrugging his shoulder in the direction of the girl.

"*Calvaire*, Marty! Who do you think they're for?"

5

"My New Year's resolution should be about Bridget Callaghan. But I don't know what to resolve. Actually, I wish I could just start off all over again with her," Faith sighed, dipping a zucchini stick into the guacamole on the coffee table. There was a holiday sheen about her, from her dangly earrings, to her form-fitting black jumpsuit and pointy-toed stilletos. She had shed twenty-five pounds in the past six months and was looking svelte, seated on the pouffy couch in Rhoda's living room. Al lolled beside her, one arm draped casually over her shoulder, a tumbler of scotch in his other hand.

"Well, maybe that would be just the ticket," Hershy suggested. "Share that wish with her, and try to win her over."

"You don't have a clue what you're talking about," Rhoda said. "As usual."

"Stop it, you two," Al said. "Faithie, this is no time to be talking shop.

"And it's not very interesting anyway," Hershy looked daggers at Rhoda.

"Are we revisiting Bridget Callaghan yet again?" Erica breezed in from the kitchen, bearing a platter of cheese straws. She offered one to Paul. "May I tempt you?"

"Thanks," Paul said, taking one and giving her a searching look from beneath bushy black brows. "Who's Bridget Callaghan?"

"Oh God," Al groaned. "Don't encourage them! She's one of their mutual thorny cases that they insist on chewing over ad nauseam. I've had her coming out of my ears for the past year. Her and her son Sean and his hair fetishes, and his delays. Why don't we just change the subject? Erica, how goes it with Melly Darwin?"

"Do you really want to know?"

"I said I did, didn't I?"

"I'm still trying to prise the story from him. For a smart man, he has an awful lot of trouble being coherent."

"Isn't it taking awfully long?"

"Not really!" Erica sounded defensive. "I have to somehow fit my research in with my *Gazettte* work. And there's so much checking and double-checking of the war background. It's a real pain."

"But don't you find it interesting?" Paul asked.

"Yes. But it's also ghastly. It seems like every time I talk to him, there's some new horror."

"Like?"

"Like, after managing to scrape by in a horrendous work camp for nearly a year and a half, he's shipped back to his home town, only to be shipped from there to Auschwitz. And on the cattle car, the poor guy develops an abscessed tooth that drives him insane with pain. And guess what? He's lucky, he says. Because there's a vet in the car, and another guy who happens to have a pair of pliers. And so they extract his tooth with the pliers, while everybody holds him down. And he says to me, 'Such a thing would maybe kill somebody from infection today with all our conveniences. But I survive there, in those conditions, whether I want to or not.'" Erica trailed off, as if she'd forgotten where she was. She gave herself a little shake. "Sorry."

"I'm the one that's sorry," Al said. "As a topic of conversation for New Year's, even Bridget Callaghan was an improvement." He looked at his watch. "It's after ten, you guys.

225

If we're going to do fireworks, we'd better get a move on."

"It's too early," Rhoda said. "We'll just stand around, freezing."

Everybody started to talk at the same time.

"It's not like you're going to get a better seat, if you go early. You're going to be looking up at the sky."

"There's bound to be piles of traffic. They've closed off the mountain."

"And you have to find parking."

"Have we decided on the reservoir, or should we try Fletcher's Field?"

"Nah, too many trees on Fletcher's Field. They'll obstruct the view."

"And there'll be scads more people there."

"Okay, okay. So how're we getting there?"

"We could all fit in my van."

"That'll be too tight. Why doesn't Erica come with me?"

6

"I didn't know you even had a car, Paul. You always take the Métro."

"I do, usually. Or my bike. The car's a total indulgence."

"It's nice. What is it?"

"A Mazda Miata. I got a deal on it. One of the copy editors had a baby. She figured her sports car days were over."

Light snow was splattering on the windshield. Paul turned on the wipers. "I have a good mind to break away from the others and opt for Fletcher's Field instead of the reservoir. How about it?"

"I couldn't leave my friends!" Erica exclaimed. "Don't you like them?"

"They're okay. I just thought I'd like to have you to myself a bit."

Erica stared at the rubberized wipers, hypnotized. They were sweeping the snow off to the sides of the windshield, drawing neat half-moons in the middle of the window. In the sudden conversational lull, they thudded like a noisy heart. She held in her breath, then sneaked a quick sidelong glance at Paul. His eyes were fixed on the road, and his gloved fingers clenched the steering wheel as if his life depended on it.

"Do you always do everything by the book?" he burst out finally, sounding bitter. "No, forget I said that. I *like* that you're such a straight shooter. It's a reassuring thing, predictability in a woman."

He frowned in concentration. The road was slick and slippery, and he skidded turning onto Westmount Avenue.

"How're you doing these days?"

"Ask me again next week," Paul said, his square jaw grimly set.

"It must be just about a year now."

"Yep. A few days ago.... And you, how're you doing? Have you spoken to Ricky at all?"

"A couple of weeks ago. He wanted some stuff from the house, paintings and CDs, stuff like that. But my lawyer told me not to make little side deals. She said we have to come to a settlement."

"You know, I still find it hard to wrap my mind around it. You and Rick were together all those years. We had such great times together. When Maryse heard you were splitting up, she said it was like someone had torn a strip off her heart."

"She was a really fine sensitive person, Paul."

"Too sensitive.... How's this project of yours really going?"

"I wish I knew. Sometimes I think he's toying with me. I've asked him about other people to interview. And he says that's a good idea, and then he just smiles. Sort of blandly. I don't know whether he's got something to hide, or whether he's testing me, to see if I know what I'm doing."

"And have you found other sources?"

"I'm in the process. There's someone in Toronto who's written a self-published memoir of his war experiences that's actually quite good. I've spoken to him. His name is Stein, Peter Stein. And he says he doesn't know Melly—he insists on calling him Meyer—but he says the person I should be speaking to is a guy called Gershon Lieberman. Someone right here. And I suppose I *could* speak to Faith's parents as well. To her father, anyway. Apparently they didn't know him, but in a roundabout way everybody in Radobice must have known everybody else, even if there were nearly twenty-thousand Jews in the town. I mean, here in the Montreal community we keep on bumping into each other every time we turn around, and we're five times bigger."

Paul drove in silence for a minute or two, his jaw even more grimly squared. "I'm not sure why this guy should be testing you and not cooperating. As I recall, he was very eager to engage your services. Has he paid up the advance?"

"Oh, I don't get it all at once! It's all in increments for different stages. On signing, on completion of interviews, and so on."

"And is he paying up on sked?"

"Well, so far, there's only been one instalment, because I'm still interviewing. And then there will be a separate schedule when I start writing. He was a bit slow coughing up the initial payment, but yeah, he paid."

On Cedar Avenue, icicles hung from the eaves of limestone mansions, catching the dancing lights from the coloured bulbs framing windows. The evergreens in front of the gracious old homes wore mantles of thick ermine. Clumps of snow lined the crooks and wide branches of the mature maples and stuck in patches to mottled trunks.

"What were Al and Faith carrying on about traffic?" Paul asked. "There's no one on the road."

"Not no one," Erica pointed and laughed. "Look at that couple!" A man and a woman bundled up in parkas and tuques were clambering along on the snow-clad sidewalk in snowshoes. Each had a small child strapped on in a backpack. Erica waved at them and they gave a thumbs-up sign in return. "I wonder if they're heading our way."

"We're going to be way early," Paul said on Docteur-Penfield. "You're sure you don't want to try Fletcher's Field in the meantime?" He was teasing her now.

"Quite sure," Erica said firmly.

They found a parking spot easily on McTavish, in front of Thomson House. She waited on the sidewalk for Paul to lock up. He ambled towards her, a portly figure in tan sheepskin, and before she knew it he had clinched her in a bear hug. He kissed her hard, then stepped back. His visored cap was askew, and his dark eyes bore into hers with longing and trepidation.

"You taste like cigarettes, not as if you've been drinking," Erica said, breathless. "But you're acting like you've lost your mind." Her heart was pounding madly.

"I don't think I've lost it. I think I've just found it."

She stared up at him, flabbergasted.

An errant snowflake lit on her eyelash and she dashed it away, feeling a glow radiate through her body even as her cheeks and fingers registered the brisk cold. *Is this how your life changes from one moment to the next?*

"Come on, let's look for the others," she said, taking his arm.

7

By a quarter to midnight, a camaraderie had sprung up among the revelers gathered in Rutherford Park on the reservoir. Al was bantering with a clutch of students swigging beer and tossing snowballs. Faith, wrapped in faux ocelot, was offering candy from her purse to the cherubic twins of the couple on snowshoes Erica and Paul had passed in the car. Erica and Paul were stamping their feet to ward off the cold and studiously ignoring each other.

"Look!" Rhoda exclaimed. The students had begun to set off firecrackers, little trailing silver rockets pop-pop-popping like an opening act for the main event. A cocker spaniel belonging to a woman in a long black mink whimpered at the noise until she bent down and scooped him in her arms.

"C'est minuit!" someone exclaimed.

The sky above the mountain exploded in a blitz of colour.

"This really was the right place to come," Erica breathed.

"You can't see the cross from here," Paul grumbled. "We'd have been able to from Fletcher's Field."

"You and your Fletcher's Field!"

"Look at that!"

Whorls of purple and green chased each other above. Hoisted onto their parents' shoulders, the twins clapped their hands. The students hollered enthusiastically and guzzled their St. Ambroises.

I'm always going to remember us like this, thought Rhoda. Maybe I'll tell my grandchildren some day how we were all here together, at this epochal moment—yes, it's epochal. I'd never say it out loud, I'd sound like Erica, and Hershy would never let me hear the end of it. But here we all are tucked arm in arm, at the instant one century meets the next, at the moment one millennium greets another.

A hush descended on the hillside as an eerie glow lit up the entire sky. On the hump of the mountain the silhouette of each rockface and tree smouldered like embers left in the wake of a great firestorm. There was something awesome, even frightening, in this post-nuclear radiance that lingered for a few moments and then gradually subsided to darkness.

"Wasn't that something!" Faith said. "I wasn't sure till this minute that I was really having fun. In case anyone's interested, I am really having fun."

"I've got some champagne back home," Hershy said. "I want to see you dance on my coffee table."

8

In Paul's bedroom across town in Mile End, Erica kept her eyes squeezed tightly shut against the soft light. *I will not think of Rick. He has no place here. This is about me. And Paul. Period.* She opened one eye cautiously. Paul was kissing her with an expression of such concentrated absorption that she wanted to laugh. Half naked, she was wedged against his buttoned pillow shams (one of the buttons was digging into her left buttock), while he, propped on one elbow, was stroking her breast through the thin fabric of her bra.

Really, it was quite startling how similar the mechanics of the act were, even when you changed partners. Not that the two men looked the same. She supposed Paul was handsome if you could appreciate a furry, bulging chest and legs like a prizefighter's, but she felt a wave of homesickness for Ricky's lean, athletic form. The small imperfections that the years had appended to it—the love handles, the slight stoop—had just made him more lovable, more hers.

By the light diffused through the crimped folds of the lampshade on the bedside table, she saw herself going through familiar motions. It was almost like watching a movie, the delicate strokings, the parting of lips and thighs. It was very odd to be doing this with Paul, whom she cherished in a fond, comradely way. Her anxiety about being able to function with someone new was dissipating as the anticipation of release mounted from the tips of her toes to her taut nipples. She tingled all over. But as she eased off Paul's briefs, the sight of a foreskin on the emerging and erect penis was a shock. When she reached for it tentatively, he groaned, climbed on top of her, and entered her with a shuddering sigh. Afterwards he was tenderly apologetic.

"It will be better next time," he said, caressing her cheek.

"Uhm," she murmured.

He sat back to survey her from the foot of the bed.

"Let me look at you properly at least. You're gorgeous."

"There must be a condition called post-coital dim-ness. Like temporary insanity."

"What are you talking about? You've got a great body. And absolutely amazing red hair."

"Corinne will be so pleased to hear that."

"Corinne?"

"My excellent and very expensive hairdresser."

"What, you have yourself styled and coloured down here?"

She slapped his hand away and yanked the sheet up to her chin.

"I'm a little fresh?"

"Yes!"

He crawled back into bed beside her and took her in his arms. The sheet dropped away as he nuzzled her neck.

"Can you see my scar?"

He propped himself on one elbow, and with his other hand adjusted the lamp to give better light. "Is this it? Or is it a tiny wrinkle? I can't tell."

"I had a great surgeon."

He gave her a worried glance. "But you're okay, aren't you?"

"I sure hope so."

8

"So the man clearly has a weakness for cheese straws," Hershy said, scooping leftovers into a plastic container.

"You noticed that too!" Al, bloodshot and rumpled, sprawled back in his armchair.

"Yeah," Rhoda said, "he looked like he was having some kind of revelation. Like he was seeing her for the first time."

"I think she must have been sending subtle signals his way," Faith said. "Is there more of this champagne left? I love it."

"What subtle signals?" asked Hershy, rolling his eyes and swivelling his hips in a grotesque stab at a belly dance.

"I read about it in *The New York Times*," Faith said, holding out her champagne flute to Rhoda, who emptied the dregs of the bottle into it. "Women send out these understated scents I guess they must be. Sex hormones. Pheromones, they're called. We give them off without knowing it, when we're in a receptive state. If you know what I mean. And men kind of get ideas only after they pick up the message."

"Woof, woof," Hershy barked. "Fee fi fo fum, I detect the odour of pheromones."

"Get up off the floor, you idiot," Rhoda said, doubled over with laughter.

I won't admit it to Hershy or anyone else, but this party was okay. Even if it was New Year's.

Part Four

After Auschwitz, no theology:
the numbers on the forearms
of the inmates of extermination
are the telephone numbers of God,
numbers that do not answer....

—Yehuda Amichai

1

The evening of the general meeting to approve the design for the new building was fiercely hot. Nate had debated wearing a tie, but in the end opted for an open-neck sports shirt, despite the magnitude of the occasion. He couldn't recall an event of greater consequence for the future of the congregation. As he waited impatiently for Faith to call the meeting to order, it occurred to him that the heat could only advance his cause. The muggy sanctuary begged for air conditioning.

Finally, finally Faith was getting to her feet and heading for the mic. She looked very trim in a loose skirt and clingy tank top, over which she wore some kind of bolero thing. There are faces that shrivel and crinkle after a diet. But Faith's recent weight loss became her in every way. Her skin was smooth and tan, her eyes sparkled with anticipation.

Below the *bimah*, the members of the building committee were arranged behind a long table. Faith introduced them in turn: Helen Stern, the chair. Melly Darwin and his son, Glen, experts in the management of properties, old and new. Sally Lightstone, representing donors. Stan Shifrin, the architect. Elliott Namer, the capital campaign co-ordinator. And "last but not least," Rabbi Nate.

Faith was supposed to hand the meeting over to Helen at this point: there was a long agenda to get through. Instead, to Nate's surprise, she cleared her throat and began to speak.

"We have so much to discuss tonight, but if you'll humour me I'd like to share a small parable with you. The Talmud tells the story of a sage called Honi, who lived at the time of the second Temple. One day, this sage saw an old man planting a carob tree.

"'Why are you planting a tree whose fruit you'll surely never see?' Honi asked the old man, knowing full well that it takes a lifetime for such a tree to mature.

"'I was born into a world full of carob trees,' the old man answered. 'I enjoy the fruit of trees that have been planted by others. The time for me to plant for the generations yet to come is right now.'

Faith flashed a big smile at the audience. "I see in this little fable a paradigm for our situation tonight. *A sapling is a commitment to the future, and so is building a shul that will outlast us.*"

A flutter of applause greeted her words. Nate was thrilled but amazed. What had persuaded her to give this little homily? Had she really put her reservations aside? As she returned to her seat on his right, he gave her a spontaneous hug.

Helen Stern was already launched on a history of the process that had brought them here: the purchase of vacant land on either side of the existing lot, the needs' assessment questionnaire members had filled out, the canvassing of major donors, the hiring of an architect and development of a design.

Next it was Glen Darwin's turn. A strong and silent type, Nate guessed, since he hadn't heard him utter more than a few token grunts on the occasions they had exchanged so-called pleasantries. It was surprising that he took the floor, rather than his father, but he acquitted himself honourably enough. Scowling at his notes, he spoke in a husky baritone about the questionnaire that had gone out in the fall. The wish-list compiled out of the returns included air conditioning (here a ripple of laughter ran through the stifling sanctuary), a social hall, function rooms, and better kitchen facilities. The membership would soon hear from the architect how the present design concept fulfilled those specifications. Glen concluded with some motherhood statements about how Les Entreprises Régales, his family's company, would lend its expertise in a hands-off supervisory mode if the project went ahead. When he sat down beside his father, Melly slapped him on his broad back. Glen flushed with evident pleasure.

Short and slight, with a little mousy goatee, Stan Shifrin was up next to make the major presentation of the evening. At the time of Stan's hiring, there had been controversy over his selection. Marty Riess (*such a detail-oriented fusspot!, thought Nate*) had argued that the job shouldn't go to an architect merely because he was a shul member. Especially in light of the fact that Stan had never designed a synagogue in his life and had worked exclusively on restoring heritage buildings. Marty had recommended striking a search committee for an architect and issuing a call for submissions for a design competition. This would have taken way too long, Nate countered. Besides, Stan was an excellent candidate, an up-and-coming talented partner in a vigorous young firm, who just happened to belong to Congregation Emunath.

As it turned out, Stan had been a fount of creative ideas. Easy to work with, too; he was exceptionally accommodating about scaling back the design when all that to-do was made about its purported extravagance last year.

Now Stan wore tailored jeans, an expensive looking cotton shirt, and a small suede kipah over his fair hair. In order to explain his visuals, he faced the large screen at the front of the room and thus had his back to the audience. Soft-spoken and ill at ease, he quickly roused the ire of the older members.

"Speak up, man, speak up," Simon Herscovitch growled, punctuating his demand with emphatic bangs of his cane.

Once he got going, Stan warmed to his subject. He used words like palette, envelope, and footprint in ways that required you to listen carefully. The palette for sanctuary décor would be neutral beige to warm blonde, the envelope bone-coloured brick, and the footprint one and a half times that of the current building. His most persuasive point was to explain how his firm's expertise in restoration architecture would benefit the current project. Because a historical perspective governed his approach,

Stan said he looked to the past to inform the present. As he projected the images of ancient synagogues on the screen, he identified three traditional design features of synagogue architecture: a courtyard, two columns at the entrance, and something left unfinished to remind the faithful of the destruction of the Temple.

There were murmurs of approval as he illustrated his points with sketches and perspectives of the new building. It would have a minuscule courtyard in the rear, two minimalist columns at the entrance, and one interior wall that would be left unplastered. Without labouring the details, he cleverly mentioned that this was a second-stage design that had been pared back without compromising either aesthetics or the needs of the community. He sat down to measured and respectful applause.

Helen took the floor again. "What an act to follow," she twittered. Since her job was to talk money, Nate tuned out a bit. All that business about soft and hard costs, long-term maintenance, contingencies, the endowment fund, mortgages, loans—so many hundreds of thousands and millions of dollars, he'd been hearing variations on these figures for years. It was very important, yes, yes, but it was so tiresome. Everybody talking of bottom lines, Marty and Helen and Elliott and even Faith.

Nate's private bottom line was that the money would be found. *Somehow.* In his mind, the project had reached the point of no return. By the time you convened a meeting like this, brought the community together, showered them with 3D images of a building that was so superior to the one they were obliged to inhabit, the momentum was too powerful to be checked.

He came out of his reverie as Helen, her copper face shining with sweat and the wings of her lacquered coiffure at half-mast, was going on about the cup being half full or half empty. At the entrance to the sanctuary, a large drawing of an orange-coloured pitcher with black graduated markings showed the figure of three million dollars at the midway mark. "Do the arithmetic yourselves," Helen coaxed. "We are three hundred family units, with an outstanding balance of two and a half million dollars.

"Elliott and our canvassers will be calling all of you shortly. Think about what you planned to give. Double it. Then double it again."

Restive murmurings suddenly rose in the hall, more or less drowning out the half-hearted applause.

The Rabbi was the last speaker. Nate stood up, smiled down at Helen and Faith on either side of him. Opening his arms, he gestured to the congregation to rise. People shuffled to their feet, looking puzzled, peeling away damp skirts and slacks from their legs. Many of the women fanned their faces with their agendas.

"I'd like it very much," Nate said, "if you would all say *Aleinu*."

"*Aleinu*."

"Please be seated again."

Amid much scraping of chairs, two hundred people sat back down.

"As you know, *Aleinu* has been the closing prayer at

every Jewish service since the middle ages. It is a beautiful prayer that affirms God's sovereignty over us and looks to the day when the Eternal will reign in harmony over all the peoples of the earth. The word *Aleinu* with which it begins means *it is up to us*.

"It is up to us," Nate repeated. "It's up to us to rise to the challenge. Forty years ago, some dozen forward-thinking Montreal Jews answered an ad our beloved rabbi emeritus, Moish Stipelman, placed in the paper, calling for the formation of a Reconstructionist *chavurah*. The group that came together was composed of bright, curious, energetic community-minded men and women who had little notion that they were trailblazers or pioneers. At the time they were simply trying to meet their own needs for an egalitarian shul where they could worship as modern Jews. A few months after that first meeting, they and some of their like-minded friends held High Holiday services in the basement of Mountainview High. Within five years they had reached a vital critical mass with the resources and vigour to erect and support our current beloved building. By then, I believe they were able to foresee that they were building not just for themselves but also for us, the next generation.

"So now it's up to us to take the next step. It's not just a matter of having outgrown this physical plant. We need to be able to keep on growing in every sense of the word. We need to develop into a beacon of light—certainly for our local community here in Montreal. But we must do more than that. You may not realize that the legacy of our founders has reached well beyond the boundaries of Montreal. In a few weeks, Reisa and I shall be travelling to Eretz Israel. We are to be guests of Kibbutz Darchei Noam which, through serendipity and word of mouth, has heard of our congregation and has chosen us as spiritual inspiration for how to be Jews in the modern age."

At this moment of full rhetorical flight, Nate happened to glance down at Faith. She was looking up at him, elbow bent and chin resting on her thumb. From the vantage of the audience she must have been a model of rapt attention. Only he, intercepting her gaze, could see the merriment in it, and note the derisive flaring of her nostrils. As soon as his eyes locked on hers, she glanced away, but it was too late. Or perhaps not. Stung by her scorn, he brought himself back to earth. No, this wasn't the Gettysburg address. This was a meeting to endorse a design. Had he scuppered it by getting carried away?

Apparently not, because his sudden silence elicited a wave of applause. He smiled uncertainly, tugged at his beard, and sank into his seat.

Faith chaired the question period, a mostly tame affair. There were some mealy-mouthed inquiries—nothing dangerous—about why the anticipated costs were so high. Stan handled them deftly, at one point even suggesting that, being only at the concept stage, when working drawings and schedules were refined, the project could conceivably cost less than expected.

One of the stickier questions came, naturally, from Abigail Rosen. She declared herself in favour of the project before launching her zinger.

"I happen to be a pensioner on a fixed income, but I'm not asking on my own behalf. I can only congratulate Stan. This design is quite lovely and so resonant in its historicity. But I'm speaking on behalf of several of my friends who are too embarrassed to own up publicly to being unable to give anything at all."

Helen stood and said, "Tell your friends that no one will be pressured to contribute if they can't afford it."

Cheering and resounding clapping followed this promise.

At this point, Faith recognized a question from Rozalee Zelniger in the front row. *Sans* walker tonight, Rozalee squinted in the direction of the chair. "I've heard repeated references this evening to needs assessment, to questionnaires," she said. "But no one's bothered to ask the Social Action Committee, of which I am the chair, for our input."

Faith turned towards Helen.

"An oversight," Helen said.

"We're very anxious to give you our suggestions," Rozalee brayed. "We have a strong ecological mindset. We want to see as much recycling of existing materials as possible."

Faith said, "You've heard how Stan plans to make use of our existing stained glass windows."

"We've also heard how he plans to put in air conditioning. Air conditioning is highly pernicious to the environment. We want something that will enhance the health of future generations."

A buzz of rising impatience rippled through the hall.

Faith held up a hand. "We hope to have the full input of your committee, Rozalee. It's a very important committee, and surely must have many valuable ideas to offer. May I suggest we break for refreshments at this time, and continue the discussion over coffee? And you'll all want to take a look at the sketches of the design that Stan has mounted on the back wall."

2

The Graces were grouped around Rhoda's kitchen table. The Tiffany lamp bathed the room in soft light. Rhoda was cutting a thick slice of carrot cake with cream cheese icing in two. On the plate in front of Faith lay a shaving of mandelbroit.

"Faith, you're responsible for my increasing girth," Erica complained. "We used to share a piece of cake like this three ways."

"A balanced diet should include some sugar and fat. Also additives," Rhoda said. "Just tell me you're not going to stay off cake forever."

"Yes, forever," Faith said, "except for the most special occasions. And even then, just a tiny piece."

"Well I think this is a special occasion," Erica said. "You did great yesterday."

"Don't get me started on yesterday," Rhoda snorted. "A beacon of light! Yup, that's our little collectivity for sure."

"'We've been chosen by Kibbutz Darchei Noam as a spiritual inspiration for how to be Jews in the modern age,'" Faith tugged at an imaginary beard on her chin.

Erica choked back a laugh, looking guilty. "Stop it, you two. Cut the poor man a little slack."

"Please," Rhoda said. "We're cutting him a building that's a shrine to his inflated ego. And what the hell does Darchei Noam mean anyway?"

"Ways of pleasantness," Faith said. "It refers to the Torah …. Speaking of pleasant ways, how's Melly Darwin these days, Erica?"

Erica started. "Melly," she said and then trailed off, looking ill at ease. "Melly is … Melly. You know. Cock of the walk, tough, and full of himself. I had another interview with that guy your father knows."

"The policeman?" Faith asked, immediately curious.

"Yes, and this time his wife was also there."

"And what's she like? Another lovely Bubbles?" Rhoda said sarcastically.

"Not at all. A nice lady. Grandmotherly, friendly. She served cookies and homemade bubke and very good coffee. There were doilies under everything."

"Did she add anything new to the picture?"

"N-not really." Erica began fiddling with an amber ring on her right hand. "Nothing useful about Melly."

3

In the car on the way home, Erica was conscious of how evasive she had just been. She had always found it best to hold things in, not to talk them out, when getting close to the core of her subject. And so the more her thoughts circled around Melly, the less she wanted to discuss him. But there was something else she needed to keep back. At least until she'd talked about it with Paul or perhaps with Rhoda. Something Gershon Lieberman's wife had intimated.

She had located Lieberman's address and phone number quite easily. He was listed in the phone book on Shalom Street in Côte St. Luc. But before placing a cold call to him, she decided to broach the matter with Melly. Without his blessing, she could hardly approach other sources.

At the tail end of a dryly factual session about his arrival at Auschwitz—"we had heard of the place and would rather have been anywhere else"—she hesitantly dropped Gershon Lieberman's name. She was sitting across from Melly in his office, her equipment spread out on his huge untidy desk.

"Would it be all right," she asked, "for me to speak with Lieberman regarding the book?"

Melly cast her one of his mercurial glances.

"Some time I've been waiting for this question. It's taken you long enough."

Erica felt herself flush. "What do you mean? If you

wanted me to speak with someone, why not say so?"

"People who work for me, I like to make sure they know their business."

Stung, Erica stood up and began packing away her gear with indignant emphasis. She pulled the mic out of its stand and wrapped it with exaggerated care inside its small, soft-cloth pouch. She stowed the recorder in her briefcase.

Squaring her shoulders, she looked him in the eye. "I work for myself, Mr. Darwin."

"Sit down and don't be so huffy. I'm pulling your leg. Good for you for finding him. What have you turned up?"

"I've learned that he's quite a bit older than you, well into his eighties. So I should speak to him as soon as possible. If he's willing to speak to me, that is. And also, that he was a Jewish policeman in the ghetto."

Melly picked up a pen on his desk and began tapping rhythmically against the dark wood. "You've done quite well. There's something else important about him, but perhaps he'll tell you that himself."

"How do you know he'll even see me?" Erica was still rattled.

"I don't *know*. But I will call him to let him know who you are. And I'll tell him you're a smart lady. That should get you through the door."

Though it was late April when she looked up Lieberman, Erica still needed her winter coat. Shalom was a residential street lined with large, newish brown-brick duplexes. A Filipina housekeeper opened the door and escorted her to a spacious ground floor den. Erica had not been sure what to expect, but it was certainly not a floor-to-ceiling book-lined study furnished in leather. A cozy fire roared in the electric fireplace, and the man she had come to see rose to greet her from behind a solid looking desk piled with a stack of Yiddish newspapers. He was tall and still well built, and his handshake was firm. Soft, silver, tufts of hair stuck out from the sides of his nearly perfectly bald pate, over which he wore a small black kipah.

He asked where she wanted to sit, and she gestured toward the armchair for herself and the sofa for him, so she could place her apparatus on the coffee table between them.

As she set up the tape recorder, she felt herself being appraised by keen, pale blue eyes. She tried to square her imaginings about the former ghetto policeman with this well dressed, dignified old man in his tailored white shirt and neatly pressed slacks, his hearing aid, and liver spots.

It was Faith's father Ziggie who had relayed to Erica through Faith that Lieberman had been a member of the Jewish police force in the ghetto. The Internet helped to enlighten her about what that meant. With typical cunning and efficiency, the Nazis had ordered the various Jewish Councils under their control to organize a special constabulary to keep order in the ghettos. At first it appeared that the recruits might be of actual service to their community, but step by step they became cogs in the machinery of terror, executing for the Germans the daily tasks of control and destruction. Senior members of the Radobice force were imports—German or Austrian Jews—with no ties to local people and a rabid enthusiasm for ingratiating themselves with their masters. Sadism and corruption were rife. But according to Ziggie, Lieberman had been a local boy who kept a low profile. Ziggie thought he had likely joined up in order to secure a preferred situation that might provide him with freedom of movement, immunity from forced labour, and opportunities to lay his hands on food and money. "Lieberman was relatively benign," Ziggie had said.

"So Melly has sent you to see me," Lieberman said with a wintry smile. "How black a picture did he paint?"

"I'm writing a book about him," Erica said, "but I'm not at all sure why I'm here. He said he'd provide me with an introduction to you, but it was Peter Stein in Toronto who originally told me to see you. In what way are you part of Melly's story?"

Lieberman studied her with unhurried interest. "Do you maybe have two or three days to spend here?"

There was a silky, almost sinister undercurrent to his voice. Erica was nonplussed. He did not appear to be joking.

"Perhaps you can tell me a little bit about yourself first?"

"My life, like that of every other Jew in Radobice, was broken in two. The part before the war, and afterwards. And what came afterwards is so complicated, you would need many different kinds of experts to make sense

252

of it. So perhaps I should stick to where my story connects to the Wiener family. You do realize that used to be Melly's name: Meyer Wiener?"

Erica nodded.

"I was maybe five years old when I was first in their house. It was after the birth of Melly's older sister, Sarah. Mrs. Wiener, as I later learned, had had a series of miscarriages, and this was her first live birth. And, as I later also learned, it had been very difficult, Sarah's birth. Melly has had a lot of luck in his life, and perhaps this was his first piece of luck, that he even ever came into the world, because his mother had so many problems in the female department."

"How did you come to be in their house at such a time?"

"I was getting to that. It was the custom among the Jewish people there that when a baby was born, some *cheder* boys were picked to visit the home and to say a prayer. And me, being from a middle-class family, I was one of the ones picked. Now, you might ask, what is middle class in Radobice at that time? You have a roof over your head and food to put on the table, that was middle class. Us little boys stood around the bed where Monia Wiener lay with the baby beside, and the custom was the lady passed out candy, red and white striped candy. So everybody got one. And I was the smallest child there. She called me back, as we were trailing out. 'What's your name, little boy?' I said my name is Gershon. 'Whose boy are you?' I said, 'I am Leibish Lieberman's.' 'Oh,' she said, and she smiled. She was a very pretty lady. And she gave me another candy. Because my father and her husband *davened* at the same *shtiebel*. We lived not far from them. And so this was my first time there, and being a little boy I didn't pay much attention to the baby. But Sarah grew up and she became my wife."

Startled, Erica sat bolt upright in the leather arm chair and stared at him. She was too surprised to say anything.

"I see Melly has left it up to me to fill you in. Typical." He made a large circular gesture with his hand. "Sarah was a beautiful girl, but not just beautiful. She was a great reader and a dreamer and an idealist. Hashomer Hatzair. Socialist, Zionist, she would have made a great pioneer in Palestine. We were sweethearts in the ghetto. She was not in favour of my volunteering for the Jewish police force. But I saw the way things were headed, and I knew that that family needed a protector. By then, I was on my own. My own mother died when I was ten; my father remarried and had not much use for me. And Sarah's family, well let's just say that her father—Melly's father—with his big-shot store on the main street, Mademoiselle de Paris—well, Bronek Wiener was a strong man in good times. But in the time of the struggle, he was good only for catching typhus. He was not just sick in his body, but all the spirit went out of him. Monia, now she was a force! Fierce and beautiful. But in the end, she couldn't do anything for Melly or for the little boy."

"Little boy?" Erica whispered.

"Melly didn't tell you he had a little brother?"

"Yes, yes, of course he did. Seven years younger than him. I just didn't connect."

"They needed somebody to look after them. And don't you believe Melly's story about miracles. There were no miracles in German-occupied Poland. I was the one looking out for them. Me—the Jewish police man—and the Germans. Who do you think sent that German officer to save him with his broken leg? And how do you think he landed in an auto repair shop in Skarzysko? But of course all he can do is blame me for when things went wrong."

He made another large gesture with his hands. "It was all luck. One misstep, and we were finished."

The fire had died out, and the room had become gloomy and cold. Lieberman suddenly looked shrunken into himself on the couch. "I told you, you need two, three days for my story."

Erica began to gather up her things. "I've tired you out. I'm sorry. But may I ask you just one more question?"

Again, a frosty smile. "I have reached the point in my life where attention, even if it's disturbing, is welcome."

"If you and Melly are on bad terms, why are you talking to me—and why did he send me to you?"

"Melly and I don't see our past in the same way. But I owe it to Sarah's memory to speak to you. To tell you about her. And to tell you things Melly doesn't know. The Baal Shem Tov said, 'Forgetfulness leads to exile, but remembrance is the secret of salvation.' Remembrance, Ms. Molnar, is a sacred obligation."

Erica forgot her resolve to ask no more questions. "Are you a believer, then?"

He gave a short, dry laugh that sounded like a bark. "Why? Because I can quote the Baal Shem Tov?" He raised a bony finger to his bald head. "Because I wear a kipah? After all I saw and experienced, what to believe in? Goodness? Let's just say I believe in remembering."

Paul kept Erica busy with a string of spring books and their authors, so she had almost no time to work on the Melly project. But she often found herself wondering about Gershon Lieberman. She'd been hired to tell Melly's story, not that of his former brother-in-law. She felt almost guilty at finding him more interesting than her actual subject. The idea that he had been a collaborator repelled her, yet she had found herself unaccountably liking the man. Or perhaps it wasn't unaccountable. She appreciated his honesty with her. Over and over, she dwelt on the fact that he had used his position of power in order to help those close to him. What might she have done in like circumstances?

Melly saw it differently. After she had been to see Lieberman, she asked Melly about his sister. Though she intuited that the story must be painful, she did not anticipate Melly's response.

Sitting behind his desk, he buried his head between his hands.

"What happened to her?" Erica whispered, unnerved by this departure from his normal brash persona.

He raised his head and looked at her, his eyes swollen. Reddish splotches were breaking out on his forehead against the bristling silver hairline.

"She was executed."

"*Executed!*"

"Yes. Because of him. Because he tried to play a double game, and he got caught. He hooked up with the Polish Resistance. I think probably to please mine sister. She never wanted him to be working with the Germans, carrying out their orders.

"Mine sister, mine beautiful sister. Whatever she wants, she was the top. Mine father sent her to private school, because she was exceptional, very intelligent. She was always reading books. That's how I see her in mine memory. The early morning sun was coming into the room, and her bed was by the window, and she would get up at dawn, and read books. As soon as she'd wake up, she had a book. She wants to know everything what's going on."

"How? How was she executed?" Erica could barely get out the words.

"It was public. I only heard afterwards, because I was still in Skarzysko. It was a public hanging. Him, Gershon, they didn't kill. At gunpoint they made *him* prepare the scaffold. And afterwards, right after, they shipped him to Auschwitz, as a political prisoner. This was before the liquidation. He was there in Auschwitz longer than anybody else from Radobice. I don't know what he did to survive all that, but the idea was not to kill him, but to let him live because that was worse."

He turned a piercing gaze at Erica. "*Why are you crying?!* Mine sister died because of him. She might have had a chance, if he hadn't tried to be too smart. And now he goes around full of religion, how you say, holier than thou?"

Shortly before the annual general meeting, Erica returned to the duplex on Shalom. This time, the windows of the den were flung wide open, and the sounds of bird song and the scent of orange blossoms heralded the finest time of year. She found him waiting for her, already seated on the couch. When he rose, his movements were stiffer than she remembered, and he seemed more fragile.

"So you've come back. I did not expect to see you again."

"I had to tell you that I never heard of anything so cruel."

"Never say that. When you try to wipe out a whole people, there are uncountable ways of being cruel.... I will tell you something that nobody else knows except for my wife, Chavaleh. Sarah was pregnant. Very early. She didn't show yet. I don't want that you should write this in your book, if you write about this at all. Because it would seem to lift the burden of guilt from my shoulders, a little bit. And I don't want it to appear in any way lighter. But because she was pregnant, by the time of the liquidation she would not have been chosen to go to the right, with the living. She would have gone straight into the gas."

Erica sat as if turned to stone. Was there no end to this chain of horror? She felt chilled to the bone, despite the balmy June air wafting in from outside.

There was a tap at the door. A plump, pleasant looking elderly woman smiled at the threshold. "Gershon, remember what the doctor said."

"This is my wife, Chavaleh. She worries too much about the doctors."

But, as if in accordance with doctors' orders, he stood up, wincing a little.

Chavaleh entered the room, bearing a tray of refreshments. Lieberman shook his head when she asked if he wanted a snack. For a moment he held Erica's gaze with his pale blue eyes. He said he looked forward to reading her book, and left the room.

Chavaleh was generously proportioned, her white hair drawn back in a tight bun that pulled at her half-moon pencilled eyebrows. Her broad lips were painted plum, and they smiled readily, though there was a hint of guardedness in her brown eyes. She said she was not from Radobice, but that she had met her husband in a DP camp after the war.

"We all had stories, and most of us were left all alone. He was always a quiet man, mine husband. It took a long time for me to learn what happened to him. I can only tell you that he has been a very good husband and you couldn't find a kinder or more generous father."

She poured coffee into a rose-sprigged china cup and changed the subject.

"Your friend Faith, I knew her mother in one of the camps. Did she tell you that?"

"Faith doesn't talk very much about her mother, Mrs. Lieberman."

"Call me Chavaleh. Everybody does. Yes, that's too bad what's happened to Freda Guttman. She was such a smart woman. And strong for someone so tiny! When I first saw her I never could have thought she'd recover from what happened to her."

"What happened to her?"

"Oy, if you don't know it's not my place to say."

Erica also thought it wasn't her place to gossip about Faith's mother with a near perfect stranger. But it had been this cryptic allusion that prompted her to speak so cagily about Chavaleh Lieberman with the Graces on the night after the annual general meeting.

4

After Erica had left, Rhoda and Faith adjourned to the living room. Faith curled up on the couch, tucking her small feet beneath her. Rhoda sat opposite her in her favourite comfy wing chair with its fat plaid cushions.

"I don't know how she can stand doing this," Faith muttered. "I know I egged her on in the first place, but I still don't know how she can go through with it. I know I wouldn't be able to. You know it was the Jewish police who carried out quite a bit of the Germans' dirty work. Horrible stuff like burying people in mass graves and rounding up people for transports. He couldn't have had a choice, but I wonder if any good can be served by bringing this stuff to light."

"You mean," Rhoda said, "that it's better to sweep it under the rug and not talk about it in front of the *goyim*?"

"Oy Rhoda! Who said anything about *goyim*? I don't know what I mean. It's just that Melly's such an *operator*. And she's going to have to dress him up and make him look good 'cause that's what he's paying her to do."

"Don't worry about Erica. She may not know where she's going with all this, but she's starting to sink her teeth into it."

"I'm not worrying. I just wonder how it'll all turn out. And if you want to know the truth, the whole subject of the war fills me with fury! If I really let myself think about it hard—and I don't usually, because what's the point? Why think about it when you can't change what happened and it's over? Even if it's not done with, it's over.

"But if I think about my parents, and what they went through. It's true that if it wasn't for the war they'd never have got married, and I'd have never been born. Or not as me.... And it's not like they'd have had such fantastic lives, either. My mother would have had a dozen children and lived under a wig and waited on her husband hand and foot. And my father—well, actually I can't imagine him without my mother. I can't imagine what he'd have been like if they never met."

"How did they meet?"

261

"Back in Radobice, right after the war. But that's not the first time they saw each other. They passed each other on the street many times before the war. They caught each other's eye, they liked the look of each other. But they never spoke to each other 'cause my mother was *Hasidisheh* and my father was a Zionist—and that would never do!

"But of course none of that mattered anymore when they met afterwards. And they did fall in love and somehow found their way to Sweden. That's where they were married. She was pregnant with me by the time they arrived here. And she said that I was her reward for having gone through the war."

Faith took a deep breath and rubbed her eyes with her knuckles. Rhoda felt her own eyes prickle. The chair creaked as she stood up and moved over to the couch next to Faith and took her hand.

"I'm sorry," Faith said, her lower lip quivering. "It's just so hard with her now. And I know there were things she wanted to tell me and I didn't let her. I think she never spoke of them to my father because it would have hurt him too much. Female things."

"What are you saying, Faithie? That she was raped?"

Faith shrugged.

"Something happened. She tried telling me, she dropped hints. All I needed to do was ask the right question and she would have said. You know what great friends we were before she became someone I don't even know anymore. But I didn't want to hear. I didn't want to know. I actually still don't want to know, except that I wish I hadn't let her down by not listening."

There was the sound of a key turning in the lock. Rhoda let go of Faith's hand.

"Here comes the conquering hero from his squash game."

Hershy stood in the doorway, surveying the room.

"What are you two doing sitting in the dark? Where's the third Grace?"

He flicked on the overhead light.

"What's wrong, Faith?"

"Nothing," Faith said, bending over to search for her sandals on the floor and hiding her wet face.

"Erica went home early," Rhoda said. "We were just sitting here reminiscing."

"*Reminiscing?* Are you coming down with something? No wonder Erica left! Are you sure she went home? Maybe she made an early getaway so she could have a little roll in the editorial hay in Mile End."

"Hershy, really! That's all over, as you well know."

"Don't *Hershy really* me! Maybe that's what you need too!"

"I'm leaving," Faith said. "Have a good time, you two."

5

Hershy was sprinting around the bedroom in his shorts, his chest bare, lobbing imaginary balls at the full-length mirror. He could see Rhoda's reflection in front of him. She was sitting up in bed, three fat rollers on the crown of her silver head, applying cold cream to her neck in deliberate upward strokes. He turned a pirouette, then feinted once more with his racquet towards the mirror.

Rhoda rolled her eyes and tried to suppress her urge to grin. This was an ancient routine of Hershy's, and she knew what was coming next. The fact that she knew didn't negate how hilarious she still found it.

"I played with my gynecologist tonight and I destroyed him."

Hershy's gynecologist was Murray Goldfarb, a retired obstetrician he had met at the Hampstead Squash and Racquetball Club. In his time, Murray had delivered thousands of babies. He had no idea that half of Jewish Montreal called him Hershy Kaplansky's gynecologist.

"Cut it out," Rhoda said. "It's late and I've got to be at a school in Beaconsfield for eight tomorrow."

She switched off the light as Hershy grumbled his way to the bathroom. "Don't lose your sense of fun, Rhode. If you stop laughing at me, we'll have nothing left."

She rolled onto her stomach, her favourite position for sleep, but she knew it wasn't going to come easily tonight. She was much more upset over what Faith had told her about Freda than she had allowed herself to show.

Did every family have these pockets of vital information kept hidden even from each other?

She had known Faith's parents longer than she knew Faith. Their bakery on Monkland and Grand was a favou-

264

rite destination for her father on Sunday mornings. Josh Gutner used to say it was the only place for a decent loaf of kimmel west of St. Lawrence Main. He used to drive over from Westmount with her to pick up a few loaves for the freezer, along with Guttman's prize party sandwiches and chocolate rugelachs. Her Dad liked to chat with the owners. Tiny Mrs. Guttman always had her blonde hair tucked under a hair net. Her spare, dark-haired husband was always smiling, always cheerful.

Rhoda met Faith in first year McGill in Moyse Hall. A cross between lecture hall and theatre, it was the setting for English 100 and the histrionics of Professor Walker, an actor manqué who swooped about the stage in his black academic robes like a great bat, declaiming Shakespeare. A corps of bloodless teaching assistants took attendance, which was mandatory. To make their task easier, seating was by alphabetical order. Rhoda Gutner sat beside Faith Guttman.

Faith was the first member of her family to go to university, and she took to heart the dire warning at freshman orientation that one-third of first-year students flunked out. She was an assiduous note-taker, while Rhoda sat back, closed her eyes, and relied on her memory. Faith privately thought Rhoda was riding for a fall. Rhoda smiled her crooked smile and assumed Faith was a drone. At the end of term, when the marks were posted, they were tied for third place. By the end of the school year they were fast friends.

Rhoda never connected Faith to the bakery until she

was invited to Friday night dinner at Faith's house. Faith had been reluctant to issue the invitation. Though Rhoda wore torn jeans and work boots to school, she sported chunky gold pieces around her neck and her curly head was shaped and straightened at Charles of Westmount, her mother's hairdresser. Everybody knew Bijoux Gutner on Greene Avenue. But still Freda and Ziggie urged Faith to bring her friend home, and she finally gave in.

Rhoda loved Faith's parents, their demonstrativeness, their sweet and funny accents, their absence of affectation. She had never witnessed a blessing of children and watched, her mouth slightly agape, as Ziggie placed his hands first over Faith's diminutive head and muttered a benediction, then reached up to bless Daniel who, though younger than Faith, was a head taller than his dad. Rhoda's Bubbie had used to light *Shabbos* candles, but after her death the custom fell by the wayside at home. Now Freda, echoing the gesture Rhoda could just recall, swooped her arms over the lit candles, then covered her eyes with her fingers and sang the blessing under her breath.

Rhoda enthused so much about the Guttmans at home that her parents, who were always a soft touch where she was concerned, reciprocated the invitation. If Leah looked down her elegant nose at Freda and Ziggie, she never said so. A back and forth began to take place between the family on the hill and the one in Snowdon. Each attended the simchas of the other: the girls' weddings, the *brises* and bar mitzvahs of the grandsons, and Andrea's bat mitzvah.

Rhoda started awake, one arm bent awkwardly underneath her trunk, her face hot. Hershy was snoring on a stentorian scale next to her. She poked him but he continued to wheeze and gasp, so she jabbed him, less gently this time. He rolled onto his side, taking the bedclothes with him.

Her mind was processing the cacophony she had just woken from, its jarring notes still reverberating in her head. There she was, pacing up and down on a stage, garbed in graduation gown and mortar board. The stage was actually a classroom with a blackboard behind her. Children sat in a row on the floor, but all sorts of adults crowded around them. Faith and Erica were there. So were Rhoda's parents, a youthful Leah in a white sundress with a scooped neck, her blonde silky hair tumbling to her waist. Curiously, Josh—jeweller's loupe in his eye— looked grey-haired and old.

Rhoda jumped off the stage and, arms flailing, began haranguing Erica. "But don't you see, fidelity isn't natural at all!" she was yelling. "It's infidelity that's our default setting. And that goes as much for women, too—otherwise who would the assholes be doing it with?"

Part Five

Try to remember some details. Remember the clothing
of the one you love
so that on the day of loss you'll be able to say: last seen
wearing such-and-such, brown jacket, white hat.

—Yehuda Amichai

1

Al brushed Faith's lips with his as he headed for the door.

"So shall we have a bite out tonight, like we said?" Faith asked.

"Sure. When the kids are away, we can play even in the middle of the week! Bye, Seymour," Al patted the dog, whose black tail was wagging enthusiastically. "Bye, Faithie."

Faith was almost out the back way through the garage, when she turned around to switch the radio off in the kitchen. It was tuned to 88.5. Dave Bronstetter was interviewing a pundit about the possibility of a fall election.

The phone rang.

She picked up on the third ring. Her heart jolted when she realized it was Bridget Callaghan. Bridget had a kind of throaty hiss that, even if she hadn't come to dread it, Faith would have easily recognized.

"Why are you calling me at home?" she asked.

"I tried you at the hospital but you wasn't there."

"I wasn't there," Faith said, "because it's not even eight o'clock."

"I need to talk to you."

"This is ridiculous," Faith said. "This is harassment."

"It's not harassing. I need to get through to somebody. None of youse pay attention. No one wants to help." She was weeping.

"Has something happened to Sean?"

"Has something happened to Sean?" Bridget stopped mid-sob and did a perfect imitation of Faith's soothing professional voice, down to its slight Jewish singsong. "Something is *always* happening to Sean."

Faith felt her face reddening. Waves of heat began rolling over her. She broke into a sweat.

"I'll call you from the office."

"Look," Bridget said, "I'm trying to tell you something. All youse at the hospital just don't wanna get it. He isn't getting better. Not with Ritalin, not with Prozac. He's started collecting hair from my hairbrush and from Maureen's hairbrush. He sleeps with it under his pillow. Last week he cut her hair off in her sleep."

"He cut his sister's hair off?"

"Yup. Her long beautiful pigtail. He cut a huge chunk off."

In spite of herself, Faith felt herself being pulled into the story. "Did he say why?"

"Just that he likes it because it's soft. That's what he always says."

"Bridget—I'm going to give Sean's case some further thought and also brainstorm with my team. I promise to call you from the hospital. But now I've got to go."

"You better come up with something good. I'm at the end of my rope—"

"Yes, I recognize that," Faith said and replaced the phone in its cradle on the freckled kitchen counter. She turned her back on her beloved kitchen: the hanging spider plants in the bow window overlooking the deck, the light oak cabinets, the island sink. Al had finally capitulated last spring about having it renovated, and it was giving her so much pleasure. She turned swiftly on her heel in her new three-inch sandals. Her pedicured toenails were the exact same shade as its thin mauve straps.

She took the back stairs more quickly than usual. This part of the house was cramped and dark, the risers on the staircase steep and curved. But Faith knew every one of these steps intimately—in the past twenty years she must have negotiated them ten thousand times. The third rung down had been rickety for two years. For some reason— haste? agitation?—her right ankle buckled when she put her weight on it, and she gave a little scream as she pitched forward. Her arm ought to have broken the fall, but it didn't.

2

Faith lay crumpled on the yellow painted planks of the landing that led to the garage. Seymour licked her face and whinged uneasily. In the meantime Al hummed cheerily to himself in briskly flowing traffic on the Ville Marie Expressway, mapping out in his mind the article he was preparing for next spring's issue of the *Canadian Journal of Political Science* about the fallout of Mike Harris's Common Sense Revolution in Ontario. Rhoda snored gently into her pillow, luxuriating in summer vacation's relaxed schedule. Erica at her computer pored over notes about the roots of Radobice's Jewish community, in preparation for writing her introduction.

Only Faith's father, Ziggie Guttman, experienced a frisson of foreboding. On his knees, gently pushing Freda's left foot into her beige walking shoe, he tenderly caressed the stockinged instep—still high, still after all this time, desirable—and was suddenly assailed by a wave of nausea. Was there an odour escaping from her toes, or shoe, or pantyhose this hot and sticky morning to account for his queasiness? No, no, Ziggie staggered to the living room couch and collapsed on it at the exact moment that Faith—her neck neatly broken—stopped breathing. Later, after the police had come and gone, Ziggie remembered that sixty years ago, as a boy of fifteen in the early days of the ghetto of Radobice, he had felt the selfsame upsurge of malaise, followed by the same exhaustion, at the instant that, unknown to him, his father was felled by a heart attack across town.

How could Ziggie sense death, without knowledge of it? How is it even possible to be alive one moment and be gone the next, without warning, without preparation, without a struggle?

3

When Faith didn't show up at clinic, it caused a flurry of annoyance. After all, an important element of her many-faceted job was running an efficient clinic. At 9:30, a harried Charles Levitan asked Yvette, the secretary, to call her at home. When there was no answer, he shrugged and looked angry. Appointments were backed up; it was hard to know exactly what to do without Faith directing the flow of patients.

Charles wasn't a worrier, but at 11 a.m. he told Yvette to find Al's number for him. It took a while to trace Al, a new phone system having been recently installed at the university. The voicemail bypassed the poli-sci receptionist, who, in any case, was on vacation.

Al picked up the phone reluctantly when it rang. He had just given birth to an excellent sentence excoriating Harris's cuts to social assistance and predicting the creation of a marginalized and radicalized underclass that would rock Toronto's public weal down the road.

It was hard to grasp what Levitan was carrying on about. Faith not at work? Not possible. She had to be at work. There was nowhere else for her to be.

4

Nadine Benloulou lived across the street from the Rabinovitches in a split level the mirror image of theirs. She was watering her wax begonias when Al drove up, burning rubber. Shirttail bunching over the belt of his jeans, he tore out of the car, leaving both its door and that of the house flung open.

Nadine took an ardent interest in the doings of her neighbours. She and her husband Jacques were on excellent social terms with Faith and Al. Jacques, a kosher restaurateur, had catered the Rabinovitch children's bar and bat mitvahs and Faith and Al's twenty-fifth anniversary party.

When she heard an agonized cry emanate from inside Al's house, Nadine hesitated the merest interval before crossing the street and letting herself in. The cool, air-conditioned interior was refreshing after the heat of outdoors. The piercing keening grew louder as she mounted the front staircase that led to the living area and kitchen. She followed the sound to the stairwell winding down to the basement. When she saw Al doubled over a mound on the landing and Seymour whimpering next to him, she backtracked to the kitchen and dialled 911.

Word of an accident spread at the speed of tongues clacking. By the time the ambulance arrived, Nadine was in her own home, galvanizing the community. She called Congregation Emunath, where she spoke with Rabbi Kaufman. Then she called *The Gazette*. She and Jacques were friends with Vikram Mukherjee, the assistant managing editor who also wrote a dining column in which he had lauded their restaurant. Vikram immediately advised Paul, who'd just returned from lunch, and who, moments later, was on the phone with Erica.

Erica was caught off guard. For months now, her interactions with Paul had been strictly professional. Their breakup, ostensibly over the awkwardness of carrying on a love affair in the workplace, had been polite and civilized. Which was not to say that she didn't draw her breath in sharply when she heard his voice on the line.

"An accident?" she repeated stupidly, staring at her screen where a chapter about Melly's postwar black-market exploits had begun to float and whirl. "What accident?"

"Something to do with Faith and Al. There's no details yet. Vikram's calling the hospitals. I'll get back to you as soon as I know what's happening. I'm sorry, but I have the impression it may be bad."

Erica's hands shook as she dialled Rhoda. Voicemail kicked in after the first ring: Rhoda must be on the phone. Erica rocked from side to side in her swivel chair, hugging herself in front of the computer. *Don't let it be Faith, please don't let it be Faith.*

A moment later the phone rang. She jumped, then reached for it.

Rhoda's voice was barely intelligible. "Have you heard?"

5

Erica's new shortlist of the worst days of her life: today.

This was worse than the day her mother died. Way worse, though she would never say that to her father. Klara had been ill for a long time. They had said their goodbyes. If death wasn't a blessed relief, it was the full stop to a complete life. This was a tear in the fabric of the world.

Rick's betrayal compared to this, something mendable. Perhaps.

Cancer? Terrifying, a reminder to get on with things.

This, now, this aching void, this is an assault on the natural order.

I shall never see you again, never take another walk with you, never pick you up for shul. You'll never again tell me what to do, what to wear, whom to trust.

I can't take this in. It's unacceptable. Impossible.

6

In the house on Rosedale, Rhoda dragged a lazy boy armchair from Max's room into Andrea's. She knew she would be unable to sleep; let her at least sit vigil over Faith's daughter. Earlier in the day, she and Hershy had driven to Huberdeau in the Laurentians to break the news to her at the Y Country Camp, where Andrea was head counsellor. Max, farther afield at a photography workshop in Banff, had to be briefed by phone. That task had fallen to Ziggie, because Al was prostrate with grief and quite unhinged by guilt. The rookie police officers who turned up at the house at first considered booking him for murder, until they grasped that he was babbling about a wobbly stair.

They had had to trace Andrea to a club in St. Jovite. It was her night off, and they found her on the dance floor, gyrating under the strobe lights to a mechanical techno beat. When she became aware of them, her face—so much like Faith's at the same age—lit up for an instant, before she turned white and became motionless with dread.

Now she lay breathing deeply and evenly in her narrow bed, the streetlight outside illuminating features smudged with tears and the party makeup she hadn't bothered to remove. Al's sister, Debbie, had sedated both her and Al. She would no doubt drug Max too when he arrived home in the morning. Frozen with misery, Rhoda felt this was all wrong. When the worst thing in the world happened, shouldn't you feel it in every pore of your body? Shouldn't the pain sear and scald? Wasn't it your *job* to suffer unanaesthetized?

She thought back to a night last week. She and Faith and Erica were having coffee together.

For the last time. (How could that have been the last meeting of the Three Graces? And how many Last Times have to be endured in a lifetime?)

They'd been discussing holiday plans. Faith and Al were planning a trip to Banff to visit Max and do a spot of hiking and white water rafting. Rhoda suggested they might want to hook up with her and Hershy in Stratford on their way home. Why didn't Erica do the same?

Faith began to quiz Erica about the progress of the Melly manuscript. All the while, she was—typically— scoping the room for items of interest. They were at a new place, the Java U café on Sherbrooke West. Everything in Faith's body language spoke of approbation: the ear to ear smile baring strong white teeth, the sparkle in her brown eyes, the energetic bobbing of her close-cropped head. Recently she had started to wear her hair very short, playing up her finely sculpted Nefertiti profile. She was looking around the cave-like room with its molded stainless steel tables and elegant clientele. To their right, a party of three older women raised martini glasses in a toast.

"I've been watching them for some time," Faith had said in a hushed voice.

"Naturally. We expect nothing less of you," Rhoda said.

"Aren't they wonderful?" Erica said. "Every hair in place."

"I want to be like them when I'm seventy-five," Faith said. "They've got class. They're here to celebrate the life of a friend who died recently. She loved martinis."

"How do you know this?" Erica looked disbelieving.

"I've been following their conversation. I think it's really a beautiful thing to just kind of sit around and share memories and raise a glass."

"I don't. Assuming you're right and can read lips that effectively," Erica said. "I think it would be much better if their friend were still alive and enjoying her martini with them."

"In our case, we'd have to do it with a *shtickel* cake," Rhoda said, pointing to the crumbs of chocolate cake on their plates. She had divvied the one piece into three slices. Faith had actually accepted the sliver without protest about her diet.

Rhoda felt tears burning behind her eyelids, though they refused to shed. *She should have had a whole piece of cake. She shouldn't have deprived herself of anything.* She bent over Andrea and was suddenly engulfed by a wave of despair about the profound injustice of everything. A vision of

Sean Callaghan, that adorable and exasperating child, floated before her eyes. Why had the universe singled him and his family out for suffering?

Rhoda bit down into the back of her hand, hard. Until the skin broke. *I'm crazy.* She began sucking at the fang marks she'd etched, then adjusted the light duvet covering Andrea with her other hand. Andrea stirred, snuffled, and turned her face away, leaving a streak of mascara on the pillow.

7

As he turned off the Décarie service road and headed east along Jean-Talon towards Paperman's, Rabbi Nate felt glad of just one thing. At least he wasn't in the air on his way to Eretz Israel as he was supposed to be. If this tragedy had occurred even one day later, his vacation would have already begun and he'd have to have come back from Jerusalem to bury Faith. Because there was no way at all that he could have abandoned his community in this demoralizing hour.

In his twenty-odd years with the shul, Nate had witnessed plenty of wrenching life passages. Sheba and Steve Shizgal's stillborn child. Charlotte Tobin's stroke at age thirty-seven. The suicide of poor Bernie Kahane last year. He had officiated at umpteen funerals, but never one like this. He would do his utmost to console the bereaved, but he was one of their number as well. As a doctrinaire Reconstructionist, he didn't actually believe in a supernatural deity, but he felt an irrational urge to shake his fist at the sky.

Driving along in the early afternoon haze, he barely registered the car dealerships, muffler shops, service stations, and wholesale outlets lining this ugly stretch of Jean-Talon. He was still marshalling his thoughts for the eulogy. Perhaps the Book of Lamentations, customarily read at the approaching fast of *Tisha b'Av*, would make the best introduction. In Hebrew, Lamentations is called *Eikhah*, from the first word of the book which is "How."

How?, he shouted to himself in the empty car, gripping the steering wheel with unnecessary force. How could this happen to *Faith*? She is—*was*—the epitome of vitality, a woman just bursting with life.

Impossible to begin his eulogy with the accustomed teaching of Rabbi Tarfon from the Ethics of the Fathers, the one about the shortness of the day and the reward of the righteous being a fruit of the world to come. He would instead cry out *Eikhah!* and quote some of the tragic verses of Lamentations, using his own free translation. The words, attributed by tradition to Jeremiah, mourn the destruction of Jerusalem and the devastation of the Temple, but they would, he thought, also resonate with a terrible aptness today.

Nate scoured his memory for his early impressions of Faith. She and Al were among the first couples to join Congregation Emunath after he took over from Moish. He had attracted a lot of young people back then, being himself so young and energetic. Al had thick sideburns and beetle eyebrows and was skinny as a rake at the time. Nate remembered Faith's huge smile and her salt and pepper hair. Plump and buxom, she might still have been breastfeeding Andrea. Andrea, in fact, was one of the first baby girls he'd named, a little bundle he'd held aloft on the bimah and rocked back and forth to everyone's delight.

Faith began showing interest in synagogue life when Max started preparing for his bar mitzvah ten years ago. He'd been an engaging child, bright and inquisitive but also volatile, given to pranks and outbursts. Nate liked to think that Faith was impressed by his handling of Max in the pre-*B'nei Mitzvah* workshops. At the same time, she got her feet wet in the shul's Social Action Committee, organizing the sponsorship of a Nicaraguan family immigrating to Montreal. She quickly moved up to the programming committee. (What had she said about her rapid rise in the shul hierarchy? *If you get full marks for attendance, they'll make you chair as your prize.*)

God, how he was going to miss her. They had had their differences, but in the end he'd won her over about the new building. He slammed his hand down on the steering wheel in a burst of frustrated rage and accidentally touched off the horn. The guy in the car next to him rolled down his window, waved his arms threateningly, and unleashed a string of invective in French. Nate squirmed and stared ahead, avoiding eye contact. (*Anti-Semite? No, no, calm yourself. The idiot's taken the honking personally.*)

Traffic was really heavy east of Lucerne. Maybe he ought to have come by way of Côte-des-Neiges? He glanced at his watch. No need to worry. He'd left himself plenty of time.

He reached into his pocket for a tissue and mopped his forehead. It was a similarly oppressive day last month when Faith chaired the special meeting to approve the revised design. What a trooper she had been as m.c.! Even if she did end up deflating him, she proved herself a staunch ally. In his mind's eye, he pictured her beaming, and then conjured up her impromptu homily about the sage Honi who planted the carob tree he'd never see bear fruit. *A sapling is a commitment to the future, and so is building a shul that will outlast us.*

What had possessed her to say this? How thrilled he had been by her words then. But now that cryptic comment made him shiver despite the heat.

Yet no one had even given it a second thought at the time.

The last block on Jean-Talon between the Thrifty car rental and the turnoff for Paperman's was backed up bumper to bumper. It was dawning on Nate that the reason for the congestion was Faith. Again he checked the time: only ten minutes to spare. Again his stomach clenched. He would have to use the washroom before the service.

Nate knew it was going to take every ounce of his training and self-control to not break down while conducting this ceremony. He and Faith were colleagues rather than friends; he wasn't even sure she liked him. He smarted at the notion that she scorned him for his ambition, maybe despised his desire to make his shul the biggest and the best. Perhaps he had asked too much of her, taken her for granted? Fuming as the light turned red once more, he was all too aware that he could no longer make it up to her. His eyes stung and the pit of his stomach released a sour tang of guilt.

8

Paperman's main chapel was packed to capacity, the back and side walls of the hall lined with standing latecomers. Erica's daughter, Tamara, her eyes bloodshot, jabbed her mother with her elbow. "There's Dad," she whispered. Erica snapped her head around. She saw a sea of faces, men's heads covered by black kipahs, women's with black lace doilies. Old Moish Stipelman, Noam, the butcher (barely recognizable in a black fedora and without his apron), Marty Riess (in sunglasses), Abigail Rosen, Melly and Bubbles Darwin floated into view, all as unreal as a desert mirage. Ricky was slouching at the very back, the tiniest of skullcaps adorning his silver head. He gave her a limp wave of his hand. Erica nodded and turned away quickly, but not before catching the eye of Helen Stern in the row behind her. Wearing a complacent smile, The Lovely was also surveying the scene.

"Isn't this something?" Helen said. "Well, of course, we did call everybody."

Erica gave her a withering look and The Lovely instantly erased the smirk from her face. "If it were up to me," she added quickly, "I'd be sitting in the last row, but Jeff—" she indicated her husband, seated on the aisle— "is a pallbearer."

Good God, Erica thought, *this can only be happening over Faith's dead body.* What could Al be thinking? Faith had had no use for Jeff Stern.

She turned away wordlessly from Helen, towards her father on her left. It had cost Dr. Tibor Molnar considerable physical and psychic effort to drag himself on his two canes to Paperman's today. For a man of ninety-one, funeral services were chill reminders. As a good Catholic, he seldom frequented Paperman's. Like other identifiably Jewish institutions, the place pierced his conscience, stirred up associations that would likely haunt his sleep tonight. Painfully he screwed his great bald head, curved low by osteoporosis, towards Erica. His dark, mournful, intelligent eyes tried to convey encouragement. He reached out one bony hand, pressed hers, then extended his palm beyond Erica, searching for Tamara's fingers, squeezing them tight with his.

For all his reluctance to be here, Tibor had insisted on coming. Over the years, he had met Faith and her parents many times. The code he lived by dictated the need to pay his respects, as it did to stand by his daughter, who had no man to lean on.

Tibor counted the failure of Erica's marriage as a misfortune of his old age second only to the death of his beloved Klara, whom he grieved as much today as he did on the day she left him five years ago. That he should have so misjudged his son-in-law of whom he was fond despite his undesirable background was living proof of the necessity for humility that Christian faith prescribed.

Tibor shook his head sadly. Why must passion die? His ardour for Klara had never wavered from the time of their innocent courtship, playing pitch and catch on the Hill of Roses, until he closed her eyes on her deathbed. When Erica first brought Ricky to meet him and Klara, he didn't disparage the romance as puppy love to be outgrown. "First love, true love," he said to Klara, patting her cheek. She brushed his hand away. "Is this why we had her baptized? So she could go to Hillel House and bring a *bocher* home?"

He didn't put up a fight. Klara never gave up a point easily, least of all about the bane of Jewishness, which, after the war, she had come to equate with the mark of Cain. As for Tibor, in his most private of selves, he had felt a soupçon of satisfaction over Erica's choice of mate and her eventual conversion to Judaism. It was as if, by reverting to her roots, she righted an imbalance in the universe, repairing a breach that he and Klara had created.

Tibor's musings were disrupted by a sudden silence amidst the flurry of whispers.

A man in a black suit was entering by the side door.

"Please rise."

At the sight of the gleaming oak casket rolling into the room, a collective gasp swept the hall. Despite the evidence, the idea that the polished box housed Faith's compact form seemed entirely ungraspable.

"You may be seated."

Rabbi Kaufman, accompanied by a cantor, took the podium.

"At last," Erica muttered. "What's taken him so long?"

The cantor chanted the Twenty-third Psalm, holding the notes mournfully. Next to him, Nate looked down at the crowd, feeling emptied out, as if it were all over instead of just beginning. When the cantor stopped, Nate began, not as he had planned with an agonized cry, but very softly.

"'*My eyes flow copiously,*
My heart is confounded with grief,
My whole being laid waste
Over the ruin of the daughter of my people.'

"This verse from the Book of Lamentations is an outpouring of grief bemoaning the horror that marked the destruction of Jerusalem. In Hebrew the Book of Lamentations is called *Eikhah*.

"*Eikhah* means *how*? Surpassing even the agony of loss we are experiencing, we are overwhelmed by our shock, horror, and disbelief. *Eikhah*—how could it be that we are here to cry out at the tragic passing of such a keenly alive, such a *spirited* woman as Faith Guttman Rabinovitch? *Eikhah*: how could this outstanding leader, this fine and upstanding human being, this beautiful person have left us so abruptly and so meaninglessly in her prime, when she had yet so much to contribute to and draw from life?"

Off to the left of the podium, the bereaved family was seated in an alcove with an excellent view of the rabbi but shielded from the eyes of the public by a screen panelled in dark brown. In the front row Al had his arms around Andrea and Max. All three of them heaved with suppressed sobs. Behind them were Freda and Ziggie, with Faith's brother and sister-in-law. In the next aisle, Al's parents, and his sister Debbie huddled with her husband and three children. At the very back of the bay, Rhoda and Hershy were holding hands. Andrea had specifically asked them to sit with the family.

For two nights and three days, from the time she heard the news until the funeral, Rhoda had been unable to sleep or touch food or shed a tear. But once Nate kept on repeating the word *Eikhah*, Rhoda began to shiver. Her teeth chattered as if she had fever. Hershy wrapped both his arms around her but she kept on shaking. When Nate pronounced Faith's full name, Faith Guttman Rabinovitch, Rhoda dissolved. Faith never used the two surnames together; she'd always said it was too much of a mouthful. But for Rhoda the name Faith Guttman brought it all back, all the long years of friendship from Moyse Hall on, all the expectations—unspoken, unthought—that friendship is forever, world without end.

Rhoda wept great gulping sobs. It was all, all true. *Eikhah*—how would she go on without her?

At the cemetery it was only worse. Much worse. Rhoda knew she'd blank on the details afterwards—in fact, even as it was happening, she wanted to shut out the sounds and images. Maxie—in the past couple of days, she had reverted to calling him by the childhood pet name—was shrieking at the grave into which the coffin had just been lowered. "No.... No, no, no, no. No." Ziggie, his face stamped with sadness beneath an impeccable black fedora, stepped forward, abandoning Freda for a moment. Despite the heat of the sun beating down, he was garbed in heavy dark formal clothes, as if death had to be confronted in full regalia. A picture of stoic dignity, he took his grandson in his arms, rocking him back and forth like a baby. "It's all right, Maxie," he crooned. "It's all right. You will get used to it."

Nate, more sombre than Rhoda had ever seen him, called on all who wished to participate in the mitzvah of burial to come forward. Al, Max, and Andrea all stepped up in turn and pitched token shovelfuls of earth into the pit. Ziggie followed half-heartedly. Nate again urged the others on. "It's a way to say your last goodbye." She thought Nate was crying too, but wasn't sure. She caught Erica's eye. They nodded at each other. *Yes.* They would do it.

Before they had a chance to approach the grave, Daniel, Faith's brother, strode up to the open trench. A tall, strikingly good-looking man, Daniel Guttman had so far barely said a word to anyone. Now he grabbed the shovel from the pile of earth where Ziggie had stuck it. Like someone possessed, he began hurling spade after spade of dirt on top of the coffin. His eyes gleamed bright with rage, and he seemed determined to finish the task single-handed. Nate watched him warily for a while, then observed diffidently that Rhoda wanted to partake of the ritual. Without a word Daniel planted the spade into the soil and stalked away, a spot of red burning on each high cheekbone.

A stray breeze lifted the black lace doily off Rhoda's

head as the first heapful of earth she mustered landed in the grave. Erica stepped up to her and, hip to hip, they clutched on to each other.

And then comic relief—*how could there be comedy at a time like this?* Queenie Maislin, dressed as for a garden party in a broad brimmed straw hat and espadrilles, swept up to her at the graveside. Rhoda had never spoken more than two words to Queenie. Queenie landed a brisk kiss on each of her cheeks.

"If there's anything I can do to help—with meditation and healing—please don't hesitate to call." She whipped out a business card. Rhoda stared at it in disbelief.

Queenie Maislin, Family Therapist
Holistic therapy.
Bereavement counselling.
Reflexology.
By appointment only.

In the meantime, Abigail Rosen, crone-like over her cane, accosted Erica. Erica was standing forlorn and aimless, her arm linked through Tamara's, wondering if it were time to go yet. Face seamed with wrinkles, flaccid caves beneath her deep-set liquid brown eyes, Abigail fixed Erica with a searching glare and pronounced in her deep, almost masculine voice, "I have never been able to understand why you've always rebuffed me, when I've only wanted to be your friend."

Erica gaped at her, mouth open.

"I just want to assure you that I hold no grudges."

Having imparted this piece of good news with regal serenity, Abigail continued without skipping a beat, "Do you see Marty Riess in this crowd? He's promised to drive me home."

9

At 7:25 on the morning after Faith's funeral, Marty hesitantly let himself in through the unlocked front door of Al's house. A white sheet hung over the mirror in the hallway and muted female voices and the clatter of crockery came from the nearby kitchen. The air was fragrant with the aroma of coffee.

The first to arrive, he entered the living room, a place he'd frequented a handful of times to attend the odd meeting or drop off documents. He had the eerie expectation that any minute Faith would poke her bobbed head around the corner. Yes, any minute she'd call the meeting to order at the long dining room table in the far end of the room.

Marty unzipped his navy *tallis* bag, donned his kipah, draped his prayer shawl over his shoulders, and started pulling the phylacteries from his bag. It was years since he'd attended a morning *minyan*—ten years, to be exact, when his dad died—and whatever knack he ever had for laying *tefillin* was mostly lost. At least he remembered enough to stand while strapping them on.

The front door creaked open, announcing new arrivals: Daniel Guttman, bringing Freda and Ziggie. Soon Nate, too, appeared, and the room began filling up. Hershy Kaplansky came over to shake Marty's hand. When he saw Marty entangled in the leather straps, he couldn't resist a token jab.

"You're a pro, Marty. I can tell."

"It's like this," said Jeff Stern, already wearing both hand and head pieces, and making the rounds of the room, his chest puffed out. "Once you've knotted it around the bicep, like so, and it faces your heart, you say the *bracha*—"

"I know," Marty said.

"—and then there's one twist above the elbow and seven twists between the elbow and your wrist...."

Who today loved God with all his heart and all his soul and with all his might, thought Marty, the words of the *Shema* whispering through his being. All around the room his co-religionists—the men anyway—were arraying themselves in tribal gear. Not all adhered strictly to the injunction to bind the *tefillin* as a sign upon the hand and as frontlets between the eyes. Melly Darwin wore only the head *bayit*, dispensing with the arm straps. (*Quite a surprise to see Melly here.* He seemed frailer than Marty remembered him, the collar enclosing the bull neck hanging loose. Had he lost weight, was he ill?)

Daniel Guttman put on a *tallis*, but shook his head when Ziggie, in a broken whisper, asked him if he'd brought phylacteries with him. Marty wondered if, after all that life had dealt him, Ziggie still loved God with all his might? Last night, at the evening service here at the house, Marty overheard Ziggie questioning Nate. In a bewildered voice, his brow furrowed, he asked while he stroked Freda's hand absentmindedly (she was latched onto his arm, both of them looking spent), "But Rabbi, why do we do all this? Why do we hide the mirrors? Why must *shiva* be seven days? Tell me how this is all supposed to help?"

And then, after prayers were over, after the rabbi had taken his leave, Marty happened to glance in the direction of Erica, as he too was about to depart. The old man was sitting beside her, sunk into a corner of the sectional couch. Speaking to no one in particular, he observed, "You know, for me, this is like a second Holocaust."

Now Ziggie's *shel yad* and *shel rosh* were in place just so, the requisite loops and knots on arm and hand, the black box pointing upward from his forehead, the ends of the head straps lying on his chest against his crisp white shirt. Facing east, with his hollowed eyes, stubbled cheeks, and outlandish get up, he was an alarming sight. *But then, we all are,* thought Marty. What could be weirder than a bunch of unicorned men with zebra-striped arms?

Nate, jumpy with nervous energy this morning, was glancing surreptitiously at his watch. He couldn't very well start without the immediate family, who were nowhere to be seen. On the other hand, it being a Monday, everybody else was on a tight schedule. Timidly, he edged towards the swing door to the kitchen. Inside, Rhoda and Erica were busy preparing the post-service breakfast. Coffee in a large urn was perking on a side counter. Erica was arranging lox on a platter, Rhoda scooping seeds out of a cantaloupe. When the rabbi explained his predicament, Rhoda laid the spoon aside and said she'd venture upstairs.

A couple of minutes later, Al, Max, and Andrea trooped down. By now, the living room and hallway were crammed. Alienated by the bizarre appearance of their menfolk, the women had exiled themselves to the hall.

Andrea marched past them, dashing tears from her eyes. She had on a *tallis*, richly embroidered in shades of blue and purple. She and Faith had purchased it in New York eight years ago, for her bat mitzvah.

"You don't have to stand off to the side, you know," Andrea said to the women through clenched teeth. "My mother would have hated that."

Spunky kid, Marty thought.

He tried to avert his eyes from the sight of Al. His shoulders bowed, Al looked a mess, like an old man. Unshaven, as required by the rules of mourning, unkempt, grey, and crumpled, he appeared to have slept in his clothes, the same shirt and black pants as last night. His only concessions to Jewish practice were his black kipah, and the riven black tie, loose at the neck and askew, so that the place where it was slit by the beadle at Paperman's lay just over his heart.

The service was austere. The dawn blessings, thanking God for our bodies and our souls, enjoining ethical living, praising the Eternal for creating us in His image, for creating us as Jews, for creating us free, for giving us courage. Then came the *Shema*, the keystone of faith. And so on, and so on, until the *Kaddish*.

You shouldn't gape at the face of a mourner, Marty remembered his father telling him. This teaching was stamped into Marty's skull, so that even now, fifty years later, he could feel the heavy imprint of his father's hand compelling him to shift his gaze. The first time Simon Reiss took him to shul for a *yahrzeit*, that of Marty's Bubbie Rivkah, he couldn't have been more than six. How was he supposed to know where not to look? His father's great paw—Marty had those hands now, broad, long-fingered, each nail etched with a neat half-moon at the base—clamped down on his head, forcing his eyes to his shiny penny loafers twitching on the dull wood flooring of Beth David.

Beth David on St. Joseph Boulevard was a dim and shadowy place, a dour place. Scion of a long line of strict and critical patriarchs, his father was a dour, closed man. Marty was never to discover why he and not his two older brothers was chosen for these occasions; Simon Reiss wasn't much of a shul-goer otherwise. Maybe it was to impress dutiful behaviour. His father's stern features had never softened in grief. His disapproving pale eyes never filmed over as he raced through the *Kaddish* at the frenetic orthodox rate.

Heeding the old injunction, Marty now studied the bold square Hebrew lettering of his *siddur* intently, although of course he knew the words of the *Kaddish* by rote. (His left arm was going painfully numb, he must have cut off his circulation by winding the straps of the *tefillin* too tight.) His heart twisted to hear the voices of Max and Andrea. The murmurings of Ziggie, Al, and Daniel were barely audible, but the two young people were barking out the prayer like a harsh manifesto. *Oseh shalom bimromav, hu ya'aseh shalom aleinu ve'al kol yisrael....* There was such a disturbing dissonance between the consoling language—"May the One who creates heavenly peace create peace for us and for all Israel"—and the stark reality.

Marty didn't linger after the service. He unwound the *tefillin*, massaged the welts on his arm, slipped his *tallis* and kipah into his *tallis* bag. It was tempting to stay for breakfast, but he didn't want to see Erica. And Rhoda gave him the heebie jeebies. He'd caught her observing him from beneath hooded eyes and wondered what she knew about him.

10

Marty had first heard the news about Faith from Helen Stern, who had stepped up to assume the presidency. After the initial heart-stopping shock, his mind leaped to Erica. He saw her and Faith together after the service last Shabbat, doubled over with laughter by the *kiddush* table. He had no idea what was so funny. At first, when he used to see them laughing like that, he imagined he was the butt of their humour. But as time went by and Faith treated him the same as ever, he calmed down. Perhaps Erica had said nothing to her.

It was three in the afternoon when Helen called. He had a house to show in Hampstead in half an hour. He dialled Erica's number. He hadn't spoken to her since the fiasco of his confession, had avoided her as much as possible. But this was different. She couldn't construe this call as anything but what it was meant to be, an acknowledgement of shared tragedy, an expression of genuine concern.

There was no answer. He thought of leaving a message on her voice mail, but decided against it. He didn't have any claim on her, and he wasn't trying to push his way in. It was too late to cancel the appointment in Hampstead. Besides he didn't know what else to do with himself. The smoked meat sandwich from lunch burned in his chest. He needed to belch but couldn't.

The house, a five-minute drive from his office on Queen Mary, was on Cressy Road, in the heart of old Hampstead. It was a limestone beauty, with lozenge-shaped leaded windows and gorgeous woodwork. Though it hadn't been updated in twenty years, it was well kept and fairly priced. His client, for whom he had to wait a few minutes after he let himself into the house, was a vapid woman, a *tsatske*. She had a helmet of big hair and a big capped smile. She was coming out of a divorce and moving down from Devon Avenue in upper Westmount. So far she hadn't liked anything he'd showed in her price range.

This house was no exception. It was too small, too

dowdy, requiring too much work for her budget. (He assumed she was down to her last couple of million.) By the time he'd finished showing the property, his jaw ached from a surfeit of politeness. She asked him to take another look at his listings. He suggested she think about the possibility of the Circle Road area. Or even—he took a deep breath at his own audacity—Montreal West.

From his car, he tried Erica again, and still only got the recorded message.

At six, the daughter picked up.

"This is Marty Riess. I know your mother from synagogue."

"Yes?"

"May I speak with her?"

"She's not here. Something's happened."

"I know," he said. "That's why I'm calling. I'm terribly sorry."

There was silence on the other end.

"I just wanted to tell your mother—Do you know when she'll be home?"

"She's at the Guttmans'. Faith's parents. She said she'd be home around eight."

Trying not to think of Faith, he worked an hour on a closing for the next day. He felt the beginnings of a migraine, closed his eyes, and saw bright flashes. He laid his head on the desk and to his shock was overcome by tears.

At a quarter to eight, he parked in front of Erica's house. It was a beautiful summer evening, the heat of the day fading, the light still golden. A gentle breeze rustled the pink lilies that encircled the base of a young magnolia tree on the front lawn. A pair of cardinals trilled their four-note song at each other. When he'd been here last winter, he was left with an impression of neatness and order. Now, as he waited—he must be crazy to be coming here; she'd think he was stalking her—he noted that despite the obvious care lavished on the garden, the cream paint of the shutters was peeling and the red bricks needed repointing.

Erica turned into her driveway at a couple of minutes before eight. She got out of her car slowly. When she saw Marty approaching from the street, she dropped her keys.

By the time she straightened up, he had joined her on the lawn. She did not look happy to see him. There was a cross-hatching of little lines beneath her eyes, which looked like oddly matched slits.

"I tried calling you, Erica, to say—to say, I have some small sense of what this loss must mean to you. I don't have really close friends like you and Faith are. I've always admired your friendship, the three of you. I am so very very sorry."

Erica blinked.

"I won't keep you. Please don't think badly of me for coming. If there's the smallest practical thing I can do—give lifts or do errands. Or anything at all that might be helpful." His voice trailed away when she made no answer.

He placed a business card in her hand and for an instant closed his big paw around it. Then he turned on his heels.

11

Other than his decision about volunteer work, Dr. Winters disapproved of most of Marty's recent initiatives. He was icily contemptuous when Marty decided to reciprocate his neighbour Kim's earlier invitation to dinner. The morning after, he described his labours in the kitchen to Winters. He drew out the details of tossing the mesclun in lime juice and coating the inch-thick rib steaks in Montreal Steak Spice. This way he was left with less time to report on the ignominious bedroom callisthenics that had followed the steaks. Dr. Winters got predictably agitated and, his face purple, gave his patient a brutal tongue-lashing.

Trying to heed the advice he was spending lavishly to acquire, Marty lined up two women whom Winters deemed more appropriate. (It was curious how adamantly he was bent on seeing him fixed up with Jewish women. Marty was tempted to ask him if he thought his urges too gross to visit upon Gentile females. Then he thought better of it.)

So he dutifully squired Millie Brody, a washed out, rather pretty platinum blonde widow a year or two his senior, to the symphony. He wasn't particularly optimistic about Millie but Stephen Kovacevich was performing Mozart on a rare North American tour, so the evening would at the very least be redeemed by the music. In fact, all the way home Millie was one long gush about the two concertos and invited him in for the inevitable nightcap.

She lived in a small townhouse on Rembrandt Avenue

in Côte St. Luc, across from a condo building where he had sold a unit a week earlier. Her place was chock-full of bric-a-brac, antiques, and overstuffed needlepoint cushions she'd been unable to part with when she liquidated her large home a year ago. Now she donned a frilly pink apron and fussed around him with jiggers, ice bucket, and a silver kidney bowl of pistachios. She had clearly refreshed her perfume and smelled like an orchard when she finally alighted beside him on the floral loveseat and tucked her stockinged feet beneath her. Marty sneezed three times.

"Is that strawberries you're wearing?"

"No," she smiled. "Coconut."

She fixed the glass of white wine in her hand with an expression of studied candour. "I like you a lot, Marty," she said, "but it's still awfully soon for me after Bernie. But if you'd like to you know, have sex, I think I could cope with that. I mean, while you're looking around for someone in a serious way. Because I can't be serious yet. But I actually believe it would be helpful for me. Sex, I mean. You know, healing the body as a first step to healing the heart."

Marty gave his gin and tonic a long stir with a swizzle stick shaped like a rapier. "That's really good of you, Millie, to offer. I'll beg off tonight, if you don't mind. But I'd like to take a rain check on that."

If she was disappointed, she hid it. He broke the awkward silence by inquiring about the photo of a baby with gargantuan cheeks in a studio portrait on the Louis XV coffee table. While he downed his drink as quickly as decently possible, they compared stilted notes about grandchildren.

The following Saturday, he asked Myra Schachter to *Waiting for Godot* at the Centaur. He had known Myra forever. She was a few years behind him at Folkshule, and they overlapped by a year at Northmount High. He remembered Myra as a brain; she placed first in the PSBGM's high-school-leaving examinations in, it must have been '63, no '64, the year the Beatles turned up on the Ed Sullivan Show. His mother had passed him her picture in the *Star* when he got home from work one afternoon. Northmount Girl Leads City, the headline read and there was dumpy little Myra in cap and gown, peering out owlishly from behind a pair of sequined butterfly-shaped glasses.

Now decades later, Myra was still short and stout, though she'd rid herself of glasses. Her eyes were a fine deep blue, and she still had thick sandy lashes. She gazed at him quizzically through them after they adjourned to the Second Cup on Greene Avenue, a stone's throw from her cottage.

Myra taught cross-cultural studies at McGill and had been married to a colleague of Dr. Winters at the Institute. Marty wasn't sure what cross-cultural studies were and didn't think this was the time to ask.

"So Marty, what did you make of the play?" Her tone was playful but her expression stern; he was clearly on trial. She had thin lips. He associated narrow lips with lack of libido. Perhaps even with meanness of spirit, though that was belied by the soulful eyes.

"It was pretty bleak, wasn't it? I mean the acting was good and the set was well done. Arty, with all that faux exposed brick. But if you really want to know, I prefer Shakespeare to Beckett."

"But you can't live on a steady diet of the bard!"

"Well, maybe not a *steady* diet, but you can go a long way. What I particularly like about Shakespeare is all the activity on stage, the buffoonery, the swordplay, all that stuff. And the huge casts. This modern pared-down business, I can't make head or tail of it. What was it Estragon said somewhere in the middle tonight? 'Nothing happens, nobody comes, nobody goes, it's awful.'"

"That was irony. When something does happen, it's worse than when nothing happens. Beckett was exploring the aesthetics of meaninglessness."

"I guess I get more out of Viktor Frankl's search for meaning."

"You've read Frankl? I wouldn't have thought it was the kind of thing you'd be interested in."

"I have a psychoanalyst who sets great store by Frankl and meaning and purpose in life."

"So your interest in Frankl is more utilitarian than pure?"

"Is there something wrong with trying to find—I don't know—guideposts for living?"

"It's a bit simplistic to think such guideposts exist. I perceive Victor Frankl as being a kind of highbrow Mitch Albom. You've heard of *Tuesdays with Morrie?*"

"Isn't that a best-seller? No, I can't say I've read it. Would you like to tell me what I've been missing?"

Myra coloured and looked away. She narrowed her fine blue eyes. There were deep circles beneath them, the skin dry and puckered. "In my line of study, I have to keep my finger on the pulse of popular culture, you know."

Driving home alone, he felt unutterably tired. Rain was pelting down in sheets as he drove uphill on Atwater. This wasn't what he'd expected of the single life, this feinting and sparring. What *had* he expected? He didn't know anymore. It was Winters's fault for encouraging him to leave Leona. Leading him on to believe he would find a woman of substance to share life with, someone kind and compatible he could hold on to and cherish for whatever time was left.

Someone like Erica. On that date they'd talked about real things, themselves, their failures, their expectations, not about Beckett and Shakespeare. But he'd shot himself in the foot with Erica. Or in the head.

He couldn't blame that on Winters.

The streetlights on Côte-des-Neiges cast shadows onto the slick road. A fork of lightning zigzagged on the horizon to his right, above the cemetery, and thunder rumbled in great drum rolls. As he turned into the parking lot of the Rockhill, the sky opened up with a vengeance. He ducked out of the car and was instantly drenched. Acknowledging the doorman with a curt nod, he stood waiting for the elevator, dreading the moment he'd step into his apartment. It would echo with emptiness and smell stale. There would be nothing in the fridge but half a loaf of week-old gefilte fish and the dregs of a bottle of Coke. The solitary bed almost made him long for Leona.

No, it didn't. Her lawyer, that *bulvan* Rick Aronovitch, had had him served with divorce papers at the office the previous week. He couldn't believe that she didn't have the courtesy to warn him that the bailiff was coming. As if he were some deadbeat who'd been shirking his responsibilities, instead of depositing a sizable cheque in her account on the first of every month.

No, he didn't miss wretched Leona. And he didn't hanker after Millie or Myra or Kim. Maybe a serious meaningful relationship just wasn't on the cards. At this particular moment, turning the key in his lock, he didn't give a fuck any more. What he craved at this particular moment was businesslike and anonymous. He wanted expert professional hands—the hands of a Micheline or a Céleste—to iron the kinks out of his back and neck, to touch him ever so lightly in a few strategic places, and make him come like a geyser.

12

"She needn't have worried so much about getting Alzheimer's," Al said. He and Rhoda were sitting in his dining room on a warm, late summer night. Beyond the open window, the crickets sawed a soothing melody.

"I've thought of that, too." Rhoda laid down five

tiles. They clicked gently against each other as they met the T on the board.

R-E-G-R-E-T.

"I hope you realize I'm not making any points off this move at all," Rhoda said. "I'm selflessly developing the board for you."

For the month that Andrea and Max were at home, Al bestirred himself to buy groceries and walk Seymour, but once they returned to school and work a couple of weeks ago, he let the dog out the back and cleaned up his mess or not. He didn't leave the house at all, said he'd get his groove back by the time term began. That was still three weeks away.

Rhoda and Erica took turns dropping by with casseroles and treats, otherwise he forgot to eat. On her watch, Erica washed the day's accumulation of coffee cups and plates strewn about the living room, and wiped the jam and honey off the kitchen counters. Rhoda didn't bother with the dishes—*a little activity would do him no harm!*—but she often stayed on into the evening. Occasionally, she suggested a game of Scrabble.

"You're a saint," Erica said to Rhoda when they talked on the phone late every night. Erica was in the throes of the final push of the Melly second draft. Apparently determined to restore their old platonic friendship, Paul still read every word she wrote. He said she was doing a great job. It was going to be a real book, not a puff piece. She hoped he was right.

"I can't be around Al." Erica said to Rhoda. "I just

can't bear all his mea culpas. *Yes, yes, yes!* I agree with him. He should have fixed the stair. Oh how I wish he had! But he did *not* kill her. It was an accident. It was random. It was senseless. Very true, she managed not to fall all the other times. My heart bleeds for him. *For him, for the kids, for you, for me. For her parents!* But most of all for her. For Faith. She fell right out of her own life. How many times are we to go around this particular circle?"

"He's like a wounded animal," Rhoda said on the phone. "He's nursing his wounds."

The wounded animal brushed the tiles off the dining table with a violent swing of his arm. They skittered in every direction on the floor. Seymour yelped from the corner. He trotted over, leaped to Al's knees, and began licking his hand.

"I can't *do* this," Al said. "How insensitive can you be? Bugger this *Regret*."

"Al, I'm sorry," Rhoda said. "We can't bring her back."

"Stop patronizing me."

"I didn't mean to patronize you.... I'm not patronizing you."

"Tell me, are you happy with Hershy?"

"Where does Hershy come into this?"

"You're not, are you? *Well, are you?* Faith was my heart, she was my everything. If we hadn't been so good together, if we hadn't been so perfect for each other, if we'd been like other couples, it wouldn't hurt so much. I could manage somehow."

"You're managing. You can't expect—"

"Stop preaching at me! You think you know everything. You know nothing. Not one damn thing!"

13

Melly Darwin hunched over the rosewood table in his home conference room and pulled a pencil from behind his ear. He circled a word, then underlined it, then scowled, then crumpled up the sheet of paper and lobbed it in the corner where it joined at least a dozen similar creased balls.

"Bubbles," Melly yelled, "Come here. Right now! Please."

Bubbles appeared with uncharacteristic speed. "What now?"

"I'm not a big reader, Bubbles."

"You called me here to tell me that?"

"Bubbles, in the very first chapter, she hasn't said a word about me."

"I know. I told you before. She's setting the scene. She's writing about Radobice, she's creating a background. Atmosphere. Mood."

"Yeah, well, she's describing Sarah's birth, and some business about Gershon and candies."

"'Cos Gershon said to her your mother almost died giving birth to her. It's a miracle you were born at all."

"I don't see nothing here about a miracle. *You* were the one who found her, you and your fancy book club!"

"This is just the first couple of chapters. It's still rough."

"Why's it rough? She's had all this time. And not a word about me being a war hero! Not a word about mine career in business."

"She'll lead up to it. That's the way books work. You lead up to things."

"I'm not paying her to lead. I'm paying her to write. About me. Not about Gershon."

14

Though it was past 11 p.m., Erica was at her computer.

Since Faith's death, she stayed by her desk longer and longer, putting off going to bed where she knew she would lie with her eyes wide open, her mind like a revved motor, her limbs tensed. In the office it was easier to push away the vision of Faith toppling downstairs, stifle her cry, delete the broken body at the foot of the stairs. For some reason the image of Faith's dainty mauve toenails—that cute last pedicure—particularly tormented her. To think Faith had gone to her maker wearing that very pretty shade of light purple. But of course she hadn't. Someone at Paperman's would have rubbed away the polish with cotton balls and remover.

Erica shuddered and forced herself to focus on the screen.

Melly was breathing down her neck. According to the terms of her contract, she had submitted the first two chapters, for which she was now due payment. He had said that he wanted to see the whole manuscript, but she was unwilling to show it in draft form, particularly since she was still working on the parts that were most problematic for her. The atrocity sections.

And anyway, according to the contract, she only had to submit the rest once he approved the sample material.

Ever since she found out what had happened to Sarah and Gershon, she had become invested in the project in a way she had never been with anything before. She felt a great urgency to craft something really good, at the same time as she was overcome by a choking despair that her words were entirely inadequate, that in fact, all words were inadequate in the face of the enormity of suffering she was called on to write about.

Yet words were all she had. She had spent the whole day combing through her files in search of information on the liquidation, but now late at night the books and notes were stacked in piles on the floor and her desk. She willed the stored information to float from her memory to her fingertips, and began typing with her eyes closed.

Late August 1942.

At the edge of town, near the railway tracks, fields of wheat were fattening for harvest. Out of the blue, a division of German soldiers scythed the crop to the ground. And then the empty freight cars began arriving, manned by unknown guards with unknown insignias.

For weeks, there had only been one topic of conversation in the ghetto: would its inhabitants be sent away, and if so when? "Away" didn't signify Auschwitz or Treblinka, it was held to be relocation to the east, possibly to Ukraine, where there would be much hardship, but still a chance to survive. Only the odd cynic muttered from time to time, "You fools, you daydreamers, you're wilfully blind. They're going to find a way to do away with us. We're all going to die."

On Shabbat, the Chief Rabbi preached an exceptional d'var Torah. He was an old man, much venerated, a gentle soul who rarely raised his voice, yet on this day he preached with a feverish intensity. "I see before my eyes a great fire, a conflagration out of all control. I see the bright flames engulfing the gates of the ghetto. Soon, soon, our ghetto will burn, and if we don't look out for ourselves, we too shall be consumed. In times of the gravest trouble, all rules are suspended. It's now every man for himself. Save yourselves! You must do whatever it takes to live." The force of his words was such that it was on the lips of everyone in synagogue that morning and spread throughout the entire population. And then to the consternation of every Jew in Radobice came the news that the Rabbi had been felled by a stroke. He was dead before the following morning.

The years of war had hardened Melly. Living by wits as much as by brawn, he developed a sixth sense for survival, especially since Gershon had been shipped away, God only knew where. If there was a God.

At the age of nineteen, Melly realized that he was to be the head of his family. His father had sunk into apathy long ago, and the fate of his sister had completely demoralized his mother. It was up to him to protect them, and his little brother, Gedalia, but when the Aktion came, he failed them. He would never forget, no matter how hard he drove himself to create an empire, to measure his success by making more and more money. That day would haunt him forever.

They woke to the howling of hounds and the cracking of whips. Hoarse voices barked the order Raus! over and over.

Grabbing whatever came to hand—a crust of bread, a bag of potatoes, an heirloom necklace—the Jews of Radobice streamed out of their homes. His mother took her one remaining piece of jewellery, a gold chain, and kissed it before giving it to him. "This is the only thing I have from my mother. Sell it for food for you and Gedalia."

Outside, women were rushing with infants in their arms, their older children hanging on to their skirts. The streets thronged with people of every size and shape, herded pell-mell in the direction of the field by the railway tracks. Gedalia trembled from head to toe. Melly grabbed his quivering hand, and Gedalia clung to him, frozen. Their parents, oblivious to everything except the need to follow orders, hurtled ahead, dragging between them an ancient carpet bag of raggedy clothing.

"Raus! Raus!" The staccato commands were reinforced by shots. Melly picked up the terrified child, and began running. The pavement was slippery. It suddenly came to him that he was sliding in blood. He faltered for a moment, stumbling over a head to which a long white beard was attached. "Close your eyes," he whispered into Gedalia's ear. "Don't look." He scoured the multitude with his eyes, but he could no longer see his parents. They had merged with the formless crowd, which was being driven to the outskirts of town.

By the field of dry stubble where the tall grass had swayed in the wind last week, SS officers wearing skull and crossbones badges on their caps brandished guns and clubs, and stalked amid the cowering crowd. He could see that the majority were being pushed toward the tracks.

An officer strode amid the crowd, snarling. "Hand over the jewels! Hand over the money!" A woman holding a baby protested the loss of her wedding ring.

One efficient bullet dispatched both mother and child.

The lesson took instantly. Trembling fingers ripped watches off wrists. A young woman nearby reached into her pocket and surrendered an amber necklace.

At the same moment, a German poked Melly on the shoulder with the butt of his gun.

"Papieren!"

Melly's heart sank. He had a pink worker's ID, but Gedalia, small for his age at twelve, didn't. The officer had already yanked the child away. Melly took one step towards his brother and the butt of the gun caught him in the face. He—

Erica came out of her trance to the sound of mad rattling at the front door. There was a murmur of voices, then Tamara, in polka-dot boxers and matching T-shirt, poked her head sleepily into the office.

"Do you realize the doorbell's been ringing for five minutes?"

"No.... Who's at the door at midnight?"

"Daddy."

"*Daddy*? Here? Now? Why?"

"I don't know. I wish you'd settle your affairs at a decent hour. Or that you'd answer the door when it's for you. In case you've forgotten, I've got to be at camp for eight tomorrow."

When did your kids start to sound like your parents? Also why does your heart start racing in overdrive because your estranged husband has turned up on your doorstep in the middle of the night? You shouldn't care that you probably look wasted after your recent time travel to Radobice, that you're not wearing makeup and that the polish on your bare toenails is chipped. After all, it's only two-timing, smooth-talking Ricky.

15

Rick slouched in the hallway, surveying the living room.

"You've rearranged the furniture."

Erica shrugged.

"That's a new picture. Aren't you at least going to ask me in?"

She gestured towards the living room, where he settled into the couch, crossing his legs. She perched gingerly on the arm of the easy chair on the other side of the coffee table. He leaned over it to hand her an envelope.

"Here's the support cheque for Tammy."

"It's an odd time to bring it."

"I'm a couple of days late. I thought you'd appreciate it if I dropped it by."

"You could have pushed it through the mail slot."

"I could have. But then I wouldn't have seen you. Actually, I've been meaning to call ever since I found out about Faith. It's just a terrible thing."

Erica nodded.

"Look, this isn't easy for me. The reason I've come so late—I've been driving around for hours tonight. I was working late, and then I wasn't up to going home. So I started driving around, and thinking…. I drove past our first apartment downtown. Don't you remember being so happy there? And then I went up Côte-des-Neiges to Ridgewood—you remember that's where we were when I was called to the bar. When Raichie was born. I thought about her birth and how worried I was, and how magnificent you were, and how I loved you more than I could have thought possible for pushing that little person out into the world. And then I drove up the mountain and parked at the lookout, and thought of all the times we went there the two of us, and then with the children. And I thought of seeing you at Paperman's with your father and Tammy last month…. I miss you, Erica. You're my family. You've been my family for more than half my life. And the situation I'm currently in, it's not a family situation. And it won't ever be one."

"What's wrong, your heiress isn't sharing the goodies with you?"

"That comment is beneath you, Erica, and I'll ignore it. I came to ask if it's possible to rethink our positions? I know you've had a little fling with Paul. So that kind of evens things out between us."

"I beg your pardon?"

"I mean, you've made your point. What's sauce for the goose is sauce for the gander. Or however that expression goes."

"I hardly think that my relationship with Paul—*whatever it is*—can be mentioned in the same breath as yours with the used-car queen. I wasn't cheating on anyone, when Paul and I…. It's none of your business what Paul and I…. I totally resent you mentioning him in the same breath as that woman."

"I stand corrected." In a small voice he added, "But it doesn't change the matter at hand. I'd like to come home, Erica. Let me come home."

"Just like that? You leave, and when your hormones have settled, you decide you're coming home?"

"Do you want me to crawl on my belly? Even if I did, it wouldn't undo what's happened. Doesn't it make more sense to come home and make it up to you? This awful thing that's happened to Faith, it's like a sign. A warning about what counts. Who counts. I know who counts now…. Say it isn't too late."

Ah, that honeyed tongue of his! He was always so good at pleading, so persuasive, a paragon litigator. And it was so enticing to believe him, to turn back the clock. Forgive, if not forget.

He'd always been adept at cajoling her. And this theatrical emergence from the wings—he'd always had a flair for drama. Right from the beginning, running away from home, jettisoning his past. At a social at Hillel House, he'd latched onto her like a limpet. (Okay, okay, so she'd latched right back.) And just as it said in Genesis, he left his father and his mother and cleaved to her and her family. Yes, Klara had been slow to warm to him, repelled by the stereotypic swarthy complexion, hook nose, and curly hair. But her father had embraced him like a son, perhaps because he'd always yearned for a son, perhaps because his Jewish air was something Tibor actually valued.

To Erica he had had all the exotic grace of a prince of the Orient then. But now the yellow glow cast by the lamp on the coffee table revealed grey stubble on seamed cheeks.

When did he acquire those jowls? He's definitely beginning to show his age.

But silver curls go really well with dark skin. And he's still trim around the middle.

So what? It has nothing to do with me!

"You can't just arrive on my doorstep in the middle of the night and ask to come home."

He got to his feet. "Can I at least kiss you?"

"No!" she exclaimed. But when he reached out for her she didn't pull away until an involuntary wave of lust coursed up her belly. Flushing, she pushed him towards the front door.

Why did she have to feel this instant chemical response? Why hadn't this adrenalin rush and buzz struck with Paul, ever?

"How about dinner tomorrow night at Milos? You always love their snapper." He was trying to suppress a triumphant little smile by biting his lip.

"No. Good night."

"I'll call you tomorrow."

She pushed the door shut behind him and turned off the light in the vestibule so he wouldn't see her peering after him as he strode away with his characteristic loose-jointed gait.

Once he turned the corner, she opened the door and stepped out on the stoop. The August night already hinted at fall, and the cool air on her arms made the small hairs rise. She took a deep breath and sat down on the top step, hugging her knees and tucking her bare feet under her.

She used to wave him off to work from this spot every morning for years. When had she stopped doing that? Probably after his affair with the tennis-playing architect, after the success of *The Shadowed Generations*. She remembered the scenes between them at the time—yes, she also had a flair for drama—"You think I'll always be your good little wifey, no matter what you do? You think I'll forgive you no matter what you dish out? Who do you think you married, the bloody forgiving Virgin Mary?"

But she had. She forgave him then, or thought she did. Was that the residue of her Catholic upbringing? But maybe it wasn't forgiveness at all, just a question of being pragmatic, of allowing herself to be wooed back. Not with the yellow roses that he bombarded her with—she was offended he'd even assume unfaithfulness could be papered over with flowers. He won her back with the gift of aptness. The card with the roses read, "And ruin'd love, when it is built anew, Grows fairer than at first, more strong, far greater."

He swore up and down that his misguided adventure had taught him her true value, had in fact deepened and strengthened his feelings for her. The tennis-playing architect meant nothing to him, she wasn't about anything real or profound or true.

He also won her back in bed. They had the most electric sex of their marriage in the months after that affair ended. The clinging vestiges of his religious upbringing suddenly dissolved. And she couldn't get enough of him, turned on—by what? The whiff of another woman on him? His expanded repertoire?

Edgy with arousal now, she asked herself if she was programmed to mate for life with this one particular man, even if she held him in contempt. Was her body teamed with his? How could physical love flourish without trust? How could bodies still meld and mesh and find release, when good sense shouted caution, danger? *Maybe quite easily.*

A flash of fur brushed her ankle as it streaked by her from behind.

"Cinnamon," she shrieked. "Bad cat!"

The cat nipped down the stairs and began grazing on the grass beneath the magnolia tree that she and Ricky planted together, after he broke off with the architect. When she tiptoed downstairs towards him, he took off into the neighbouring yard. "Ridiculous animal," she muttered under her breath, her toes splayed in the cold grass. "Stay out all night then. See if I care."

But she knew she would care. She'd go in, turn off the computer, brush her teeth, and then come back down again with cold cream on her face. She'd doubtless find him by the rear door by then, meowing balefully at her for the delay. Within minutes he'd barf up mucousy grass onto the kitchen floor. She'd clean up the mess and scold him, then carry him down to his chequered basket in the laundry room.

The anticipation of this banal conclusion to the day steadied her. It was true she didn't trust herself with Ricky, but she wasn't obliged to do anything about him either. Tomorrow she might ask Rhoda for advice. Or not. (She had a pretty good idea what Rhoda would say.) Maybe she'd talk to her father instead.

It came to her with a sudden jolt that what she really wanted was to hear Faith's take on Rick. Right now. Because she couldn't guess what Faith would say—her opinions were less predictable than Rhoda's. A sharp longing for Faith seized her, a kind of soul hunger. She was still fixed to her spot in the grass and she shivered as she looked around her and whispered, feeling foolish, "Where are you now?"

A breeze rustled the leaves of the magnolia and, uncannily, the cardinal whom she hadn't heard for weeks—and never at night—answered in a sweet, clear tremolo.

Just once.

Part Six

The heavens are the Lord's heavens
And the earth He gave to man. But
Whose are the gold and marble houses of prayer?

—Yehuda Amichai

1

Rabbi Nate stood by the picture window of his office on the second floor of the synagogue, lips drawn into a thin line, eardrums vibrating. The window was the one feature of the building that he was still fond of. Its height and width made the room bright and airy, and its size gave a great vantage point on the street below, should he need inspiration for an upcoming sermon. At the moment, however, the view from his window was anything but inspiring.

He desperately wished he were still on vacation. He wished he were at the meditation retreat in Jerusalem. Or admiring the bougainvilleas and pomegranate shrubs at the Baha'i Temple grounds in Haifa. Or watching the dolphins cavort in the pristine waters of the Red Sea.

The nightmare scenario unfolding across the street had been inconceivable a few months earlier, and even at the time of his departure for Israel he had somehow remained in the dark. Yes, he had known that Rabbi Alter's Centre for Jewish Spirituality had bought the empty lot opposite Congregation Emunath a year ago. But then the Town of Hampstead had successfully blocked Rabbi Alter's band of Hasidim from beginning construction. Not that Hampstead was anti-Semitic. Hampstead was overwhelmingly Jewish, but also overwhelmingly disdainful of the ultra-Orthodox. Balking at the idea of bearded men in furry *shtreimls* and snooded women encumbered by broods of children establishing a toehold in their midst, the sleek and buffed members of the town's council had successfully mired the Centre for Jewish Spirituality in a thicket of feasibility studies.

But then the tide turned. An anonymous benefactor sought legal advice on behalf of Rabbi Alter's congregation. The Charter of Rights and Freedoms was invoked. Despite opposition at Town Hall, a defunct study which earlier ruled in favour of a new building was revived.

Perhaps if he'd stayed at home he might have done something to avert the catastrophe across the street. But it had all transpired through stealth and subterfuge, double-dealing, *sneakiness*.

Nate sank his front teeth into his lower lip and tugged at his beard. He was a liberal man. He had nothing against Hasidim. The Baal Shem Tov and Nathan of Bratslav were personal heroes of his. Rabbi Alter was a decent man (he supposed), albeit very hirsute and mystical. Nate hoped that this supposed paragon of piety had converted Margo Darwin and her infant son because she had evinced a sincere desire to join the Jewish people, not because Kabbalah and woven red bracelets were the latest rage in Hollywood.

The lot across the street was crawling with men in yellow hard hats. He could count twelve of them. His head clanged from the noise produced by the derrick pointed in his direction. That's to say, it wasn't a derrick, it just looked like one. Actually it was a pile driver. Stan Shifrin had been by to commiserate and had clued Nate in about the correct terminology. All day long, it boomed, it jounced, it reverberated, over and over. The operator in the cage teetering on high must surely be deaf by now. And bored out of his skull. Imagine spending your life suspended in the air, negotiating an enormous steel cylinder battering that row of piles. Knocking them in like nails, an inch at a time until they hit bedrock. Bang, bounce, echo. *Bang, bounce, echo.*

Nate felt as if he'd hit bedrock himself. He was jangling all over. Stan said the new shul didn't mean Congregation Emunath's expansion was doomed. Imagine, the architect was reassuring him, the rabbi!

"He's given them five million dollars," Nate whispered. "And he's *loaned* us three hundred thousand."

A vision of the hoarding at the side of the site flashed before his eyes. Mounted on top of a giant easel, a colourized perspective depicted an edifice built of exquisite, golden Jerusalem stone (no question of penny-pinching, no niggling economizing). It had a jutting upstairs balcony that resembled the one the Queen liked to wave from at Buckingham Palace. Two mighty pillars supported it and were flanked by a couple of massive arched colonnades. What an eyesore the whole thing would be when finished. How ostentatious, how tasteless. Were they trying to emulate the Taj Mahal? "No," Nate groaned, "Not the Taj Mahal. Solomon's Temple itself."

Bold black lettering at the bottom of the drawing proclaimed to the world:

The Melly and Bubbles Darwin
Centre for Jewish Spirituality

In smaller, lighter type, there was a quote from the Psalms:

Sing unto the Lord with thanksgiving,
Sing praises upon the harp unto our God.

2

Reisa entered the den and turned on the light.

"I can't bear to see you eating yourself up like this," she said. "It's just a setback, not the end of the world."

Nate was hunched in fetal position on the couch. He raised himself on one elbow, covering his face with his other hand, surreptitiously wiping away tears.

"Nate, darling," Reisa said, stricken. "It's just a building."

"I know. *I know.* I keep telling myself, no one's died. But we seemed so close.... And how can I face the congregation at Rosh Hashanah? What will I say in my sermons?

"But nothing's changed! The capital campaign is still on."

"Everything's changed! Faith is dead. She finally got behind the idea—and now she's gone. And Helen's a total dud. And we'll never be able to get the go-ahead from the town with that monstrosity going up on the other side of the street. They won't allow two public buildings in such close proximity to each other in a residential area."

"You're not thinking straight. They've already allowed it, implicitly. By giving the go-ahead to Rabbi Alter. Everybody knows we aren't going anywhere. Everybody knows we're planning an expansion."

She sat down beside him on the couch and began caressing his arm and talking coaxingly, as to a sick child. "It's so unlike you to give up…. Come, let's go out on the deck. It's such a beautiful evening. I've brewed some fresh mint from the garden for tea. And we've got to discuss who we're having for Friday night dinner."

3

Rhoda said to Erica on the phone, "I wish Hershy and I could wiggle out of this invitation."

"You can't," Erica said.

"If at least Al would come."

"I know. But he won't. He keeps pushing everybody away. The Kaufmans are only trying to be kind."

"But what are we going to talk about for three hours with them?"

"That's easy. Melly Darwin and Rabbi Alter."

4

"Nate, I hope you don't mind. I've invited Marty Riess as well for Friday night."

"Whatever for?"

"I was short a man. Al Rabinovitch said no."

"You know you always strike out when you try to be a *schadchan*."

"I'm not being a *schadchan*. I just happen to be short a man."

5

Marty had never before been a guest at the Kaufmans' and wondered, as he pulled up and parked, if there were some deep political reason for the invitation. He couldn't think of one. His stint as treasurer was up. No one had asked him to stay on for another term, which piqued his vanity, though it actually suited him. Working alongside pushy Helen Stern had echoes of being married to Leona, and he was glad to be out of it.

One of Marty's last acts as treasurer had been to approve a generous salary hike for the rabbi, which Nate had negotiated with hard-nosed confidence in his professional worth. You could see that he knew how to put a dollar to good use. The Kaufmans owned a lovely home in Hampstead, adjacent Snowdon, a half-hour's walk from the shul, so they could get there without driving on the Sabbath. Originally a detached duplex, it had been remodelled as a spacious single family house in the French-Canadian style with a mansard roof and a wraparound veranda. Two spectacular rows of floppy-headed yellow dahlias lined the front walk. The white elyssum border beneath them perfumed the dusk air with a subtle fragrance.

Nate accepted the bottle of kosher wine that Marty handed him with a wider smile than usual, and patted him on the back. He ushered him in the direction of a den towards the end of a long corridor, from which came the murmur of voices. Rhoda and Hershy Kaplansky and Erica were grouped together on a comfy couch. Reisa, wearing a frilly apron over a long black skirt, introduced him to a couple he didn't know, who turned out to be Reisa's brother and sister-in-law.

Benjy Cohen, the brother, was tall and broad-backed, a handsome, vigorous looking man in his late fifties, who taught engineering at McGill. Essie, his wife, was tiny and fragile, glinting with diamonds in her ears and on her fingers. She had thick, glossy dark hair and was wearing a well-cut pantsuit and spike heels.

"Shall we begin?" Reisa prompted, "Now that we're all here."

They trailed after her into the dining room, where she lit the candles on the sideboard. In Reconstructionist style, everyone—men and women alike—sang the blessing with her and then joined in chanting the *kiddush* with Nate. Moments later, Marty found himself seated between Rhoda and Essie and, beyond a centrepiece of pink and yellow tea roses, directly opposite Erica.

Erica didn't look well. Though he still thought her an uncommonly pretty woman, he noted lines of strain around those light green eyes with their flecks of grey. In repose, her skin, usually so delicate and creamy, puckered into pleats on either side of her mouth.

She and Benjy Cohen, on her left, were deeply involved in a conversation that had begun before Marty's arrival, about a vacation that Benjy and Essie had just returned from.

"Maybe it's my age or something in the water that suddenly made me all gloomy," Benjy was saying. "Essie and I've never been to Eastern Europe. Our parents—Reisa's and mine—came to Montreal a long time ago, in the Twenties."

"Where were they from?" Erica asked.

"From some little town in Ukraine."

"Their parents were Bundists. They hated religion," Essie said *sotto voce* to Marty. "You should get Benjy to tell you about how they used to celebrate Yom Kippur. Their father sent them out to buy bread on *Kol Nidre* night and made them ham and cheese sandwiches for supper."

"Essie," Reisa warned. "It's *Shabbos*."

"This apartment in Budapest we were staying in," Benjy went on, ignoring Essie, "we figured out used to be in the heart of the Budapest ghetto. It was a fantastic flat, by the way—tons of atmosphere and every convenience. But after we toured the Great Synagogue and the Jewish Museum, I put two and two together. This building must have been what they called a 'Jewish house' in the war.

Maybe someone from this very apartment that I was trying to sleep in had begged Wallenberg for false papers, or been shot into the Danube."

Marty cast a surreptitious glance at Erica. She was staring at Benjy motionless and had gone pale.

"The next day I went around gawking at people on the street, calculating how old they were. I gave dirty looks to anyone older than me. What had they been up to in the war?"

Benjy gave his handsome head a little rueful shake. "Sorry, everybody. Seeing Erica made me think of it."

At the head of the table, Nate gestured toward Erica. "What's it like for you when you visit Budapest?"

Her face flamed. "I—I've actually never been back since we left in 1956 …. When I was seven."

"*Never?* But it's your hometown! And it's such a gorgeous city …. And your novel—"

"That was all just research. And imagination. I boned up on as much as I needed to. I can read Hungarian, you know. I went to school for two years in Budapest. But," Erica appeared more and more flustered with each word, "I don't actually consider Budapest my hometown anymore. It has too much of the wrong kind of history."

"Is it *true*," Rhoda broke the strained silence that had fallen over the room, "that Rabbi Alter has converted Margo Darwin?"

"Not just Margo," Essie said with evident relish, "her baby, too."

Reisa pushed her chair back forcefully and began

gathering up the salad plates. "Nate, would you help me bring in the soup?" She cast an exasperated glance over her shoulder at her sister-in-law as she left the room.

"What exactly happened with Margo Darwin?" Rhoda mouthed.

"Exactly we don't know," Benjy said. "But it appears that Glen Darwin enrolled in one of Rabbi Alter's classes on Kabbalah, and Alter hooked him but good."

"Glen?" Erica said, astonished. "Have any of you ever met Glen Darwin? He's a loudmouth. He's a racist. Faith would have called him a *pig*! Are you *sure*? He once made a big point of telling me that he had no use for Judaism."

"Well, he must've seen some kind of light," Essie said lightly, "or perhaps he was inspired by Madonna. She's really into that stuff. All the glossies are full of it."

"Maybe I shouldn't pry, but what did your Bundist parents think of Reisa marrying a rabbi and teaching Jewish mysticism," Hershy was asking Benjy in a low voice, while their hosts were out of the room.

"Danken Gott, Nate was a Reconstructionist," Benjy responded in a stage whisper, making a comic face. "They were good people and tried not to hold it against him."

"So what did they have to say about Reisa specializing in Jewish studies?" Rhoda asked.

"That wasn't a problem. They loved Jewish culture. It was, in a manner of speaking, an article of faith with them. The Yiddish language especially. And Reisa only began teaching Jewish mysticism after they were gone."

"But does she believe in it?" Erica asked.

"You'd have to ask her that yourself. I think she's found it possible to reconcile the conflict between our upbringing and her intellectual interests through a scholarly pursuit of mysticism. A real mystic would search for the so-called realms beyond through the emotions."

"It's strange, isn't it," Erica said, "how we try to reinvent ourselves as the antithesis of our parents, and we end up like our ancestors. Or some modern version."

"Speak for yourself," Hershy said. "I personally come from a long line of Romanian idiots, and Rhoda will be the first to tell you that I conform to type perfectly."

"Hershy," Rhoda warned, her eyes gleeful. "Don't start."

Marty coughed. "How's Al doing?" He was looking at Erica, while fiddling with his napkin. *What nice hands he has,* she thought, startling herself. They were large, well-shaped, and long fingered. Her father's hands had looked like that before arthritis disfigured them.

The rabbi returned carrying a tray with soup bowls.

"Yes, how *is* he? We wanted him here tonight, but he said he wasn't up to it."

"He's very low," Rhoda said. "I'm just hoping that going back to work will help. He needs some kind of structure. He's completely lost."

"In a way we all are," Nate said. "I still expect Faith to walk through the door at board meetings."

"What's in this soup, Reisa? It's delicious, *so* refreshing," Essie trilled after a pained silence.

"Cucumber."

"How's your Melly Darwin project going?" Marty asked, trying to restore the flow of conversation.

"My Melly Darwin project is dead in the water." Erica tried to smile, but couldn't pull it off.

"What!" Nate's soup spoon clattered against his plate. "What happened?"

"He hates it. It wasn't what he was expecting at all. And he's reneged on a good chunk of money he owes me. My agent wants me to sue, but I can't afford a lawsuit. Nor do I have the stomach for one."

"But why does he hate it?" Reisa asked.

"I think he must have expected something grander, more heroic. I've tried to tell it very simply. That's where its power lies."

Erica became aware that Nate had become very still. His eyes were suddenly swimming behind the tortoise-shell frames of his glasses. Marty, across the table, appeared to be holding his breath.

"These poor people went through so much just to get from one day to the next," she added in a rush. "And then most of them died anyway. People think this story's about numbers, mass graves, victims with empty eyes staring from photographs I wanted to tell one person's story. And that ends up being about…." She trailed off, looking into the middle distance.

Marty said softly, as if thinking out loud, "being left all alone, with nothing to live for but the next unbearable moment."

Erica nodded, her eyes opening wide with recognition.

"Can't you make changes to the manuscript?" Reisa asked.

"He's flatly rejected it."

"I'm really sorry," Nate said. "I got you into this."

"It's my own doing. I had misgivings from the start. I shouldn't have entered into it. But it's a big financial loss, because it's not only the money he owes me. It's also what I stood to make if I'd completed it." She sighed. "This is turning out to be the summer from hell. Faith dead. And now this stupid thing."

6

The evening at the Kaufmans' wound down with a subdued *Birkat ha mazon* and a half-hearted round of Shabbat songs. As the final notes of *Yom Zeh le' Yisrael* were plaintively drawn out, Rhoda's cell phone rang. She ducked out into the hallway, then returned to beckon Erica out of the room. "Simeon's sick. I'm going over to his place. We won't be able to take you home."

"Not to worry. I'll call a cab."

Marty, on his way to the washroom, overheard her and offered to give her a lift. She protested that he'd be going out of his way, but he insisted it would be no trouble. She regretted it almost immediately, when she caught a smirk on Reisa's face as she and Marty said their good-byes to the group.

In the car, Erica racked her brains for what to say. Suddenly beset by images of Marty on a massage table, she was about to blurt out that she was planning to put her house on the market, when he said, "I'm really disturbed by what you told us about Darwin. I always thought he was basically honest. Stiffing you is disgraceful."

She was surprised by the vehemence of his tone.

"He shouldn't be allowed to get away with it. If you need a lawyer, I have a couple of good people to suggest."

Erica flushed. "Actually, Ricky has sent a letter."

Marty's jaw tightened. He kept his eyes on the road. "Your ex-husband?"

"Actually, we're only separated, not divorced."

"Right. Of course."

Marty didn't say another word until they arrived at the house. She thanked him for the ride. He nodded and wished her goodnight, reversed back to the road, and then idled while she rummaged in her bag for her keys.

At the same moment, a car door slammed on the other side of the street, and a tall figure emerged from a parked vehicle. As the man crossed the road, the streetlight caught the shine on a head of abundant silver curls and for an instant illuminated the morose features of Rick Aronovitch.

Erica and Rick exchanged a few words that Marty couldn't catch, even though he'd opened the window of his car. Then Rick followed her into the house.

Marty pulled away, his tires screeching.

7

"I've had one hell of a day," Rhoda said to Hershy in the car. "I really hope there's nothing wrong with Sim."

"You've had a hell of a day, and Erica's having a hell of a summer. That's quite a lot of hell floating around."

"Her hell is part of my day."

"Is that some kind of riddle?"

"Hershy, listen for heaven's sake! Erica got the results of a routine blood test this morning. A count that shouldn't be up is way elevated."

"What does that mean?"

"It could mean some kind of serious problem. But it's also possible the test was inaccurate. Apparently that sometimes happens. So they'll repeat it in a couple of weeks. And then she'll have to wait another couple of weeks for results."

"She didn't look so hot tonight."

"Neither would you if you thought you had metastatic cancer."

"It's too bad.... What else about your day?"

"I was reviewing my files this morning, refreshing my memory and in general tidying up. A bunch of reports always comes in over the holidays. So I open one up and it's from Faith."

"From *Faith*!"

"Exactly. She'd written it the day before she died, and it didn't get processed until now. I nearly passed out when I saw her handwriting, all loopy and curved. You know she had such a unique—"

"Rhode, I'm sorry. I can't stop the car here."

But then he did brake and pull over. The car behind swerved wildly, and its driver fired a long and loud honk. Hershy hesitated, trying to decide whether to respond with a blare of his own or to attend to Rhoda. She was folded over, hugging herself into a ball, choking back great gulping sobs. Hershy began to pat her head tentatively. Rhoda shook him off.

"It's just so unbearable, it gets worse instead of better," she said, her voice muffled from beneath her arms.

"What was the report about? That kid Sean Callaghan?"

Rhoda sat up, dashing the tears from her face.

"No. It was about a kid called Mikey Delaney she and I don't see eye to eye about." Rhoda reached into her bag for a tissue, and blew her nose noisily. "*Didn't* see eye to eye about. He's going into grade four. Nice, nice kid. Not a behaviour problem at all, but he's got huge learning gaps. Lots of difficulty reading and writing. I've always believed he's attention deficit. Faith and her people at the clinic say no, it's visual and perceptual impairment. Towards the end of last year, I begged her to come and see him in the classroom. I was convinced if she saw him wiggling around and falling off his chair, she'd change her mind. And so she finally came, and this was her report about it."

"Did she agree in the end?"

"Are you kidding?" Rhoda smiled a sad, sidelong smile. "No, she stuck to her guns. She says that because of his perceptual difficulties he can't look at a blackboard and sustain attention and copy from it to a paper. And the reason he falls off chairs and crawls under desks is because he is frustrated. Maybe she's right. But it's not what's in the report that surprises me—it's the shock of getting it. It was just like she's still here."

8

"I'm scared," Erica said to Rick. They were sitting across from each other at the knotty pine table in the breakfast nook, blue earthenware mugs of steaming chamomile tea in front of them. The mugs had been a gift for their twenty-fifth wedding anniversary from Raichie and Tamara.

We're having tea in the kitchen together.

Ever since Dr. de Costa called midmorning, Erica had been in turmoil. At the sound of his soft, Spanish-accented voice, her heart had stopped and then begun lurching violently. "I don't want to alarm you," he said, but to her ears he sounded alarmed. She knew him to be cautious and meticulous to the point of obsession. Two years ago, in the era of her diagnosis, he wore his anxiety like a badge, never once offering reassurance through a diagnostic process that was drawn out over months. Only after the removal of her thyroid gland did he relax. When, after her surgery, he dropped by her bedside in the recovery room, he was wreathed in smiles. He touched her swathed neck delicately and said, "You'll see, you're going to be an old lady one day."

All day today she had recited his words like a mantra. She was murmuring "old lady one day" when she went through two red lights. The second time it happened, an angry pedestrian gave her the finger. She stopped the car. Closing her eyes, she pulled her shoulders away from her ears and breathed deeply. It would hardly do to maim somebody or kill herself while agonizing about the length of her lifespan. Remember how Faith had worried about Alzheimer's?

Faith had been just amazing in Erica's crisis. She took the day off work to accompany her for her first visit with the surgeon. She ran interference for her with the clerk who scheduled the operation. She beamed hope and encouragement. It wasn't until after the surgery that Rhoda told Erica what a wreck Faith had been that day at the hospital, all strung out with fear for her.

Ricky had, of course, been nowhere. He and she were busy unmaking their marriage, taking it apart brick by brick. And now? Now he was having tea with her in the kitchen, looking preoccupied and husbandly.

"Have you spoken to your father about this?" he was asking.

"No. He'll push the panic button. It's the last thing I need."

"Why do you baby him so much? He's a doctor. He could give you advice, provide perspective."

"For God's sake, he's ninety-one. His perspective is he doesn't want to bury a daughter."

Ricky took a gulp of tea, tapped his fingers on the

table. "You'll be all right, Erica. Not just all right. Look how well you've done since your first bout. It's probably just a blip anyway, some incompetent technician who can't interpret a printout."

Since your first bout. Erica's eyes filled with tears and she pushed herself away from the table and turned her back, so he shouldn't see. It served her right for telling him. He was the last person she should have told.

He'd been calling her every day since their dinner at Milos. When he phoned that afternoon, in a weak moment she let it out of the bag. He immediately insisted on seeing her at night, not to be put off by talk of her evening at the Kaufmans. No problem. He'd stay late at the office and drop by around ten.

Blotting her eyes in the powder room, Erica was seized by another fit of sobs. *Since your first bout.* How many bouts would she have to face before the final bout? Couldn't he think before spouting stupidities? But what had she expected from him? There never was anyone to beat him for tactlessness.

She went back to the kitchen, her shoulders drooping. Cinnamon Cat was ensconced in Ricky's lap, purring like a little engine as he stroked the top of his head.

Ricky sent her a long searching look. "You've been crying."

Erica shook her head.

"Look, it's not the end of the world. So they'll treat you again. One way or another, you're going to be okay. You've got to be, for me and the kids."

9

Though it was the tail end of summer, the cardinals were still calling insistently to each other at dawn. Drugged from a sleeping pill she'd taken at three, Erica rolled onto her side, but kept on dreaming.

A curious kind of bird has flown in through the bedroom window. It has a long jagged red scar running down its swan-like, iridescent blue and yellow striped neck. It flaps around the room, causing a great rumpus. Erica manages to shoo it out and it lands on the lawn below. Drawing itself upright with great dignity under the magnolia tree, it fans out its resplendent tail, revealing itself to be not a swan but a peacock. Its scar magically healed, the bird stretches its graceful neck this way and that before carefully picking its way down the street.

As the bird retreats, Ricky enters the picture. She tries to tell him about the magnificent apparition, but he won't listen. "I just want you to know," he says harshly, "that I never intended to stay with you forever. It was never my intention."

"Of course not," she answers, equally nasty, "you were going to keep me around to raise the girls and then get rid of me after I'd outlived my usefulness."

The phone rang again and again at nine o'clock. She groaned and picked it up in a daze. Raichie in Toronto, all apologies.

"I thought you'd be up by now, Mom. Don't you always go to shul on Shabbat?"

"I've had a horrible night. I couldn't sleep. I turned the alarm off after three. I figured I'd skip shul."

"Is there something wrong you couldn't sleep?"

"It may be nothing, but my TSH was elevated on the last blood test."

Raichie was quiet for a minute.

"I was talking to Tammie last night. She didn't say anything about this."

"I haven't told her yet."

"Mom, the thing Tammie and I were talking about last night—maybe I shouldn't tell you. Especially if you're already worried about your bloods."

"Is there something the matter with you or with Tammie?"

"No, Mom! We're *fine.* It's just that Tammie and I don't see eye to eye about this. Tammie says you've been seeing Dad."

"Just a little. Yes."

Again Raichie was silent.

"What's going on, Rache?"

"It's just that…. If you and Dad are planning to get back together again," Raichie gulped and then continued in a rush, "there's something you need to know."

"We're not planning anything, but he's certainly been very attentive lately. It's rather refreshing."

"Did he tell you that Sandra's thrown him out of the house?"

"What?"

"I figured you didn't know. And Mom, you *should* know."

"Damn right."

"Tammie said it wasn't our business. She says I have no boundaries."

"Fuck boundaries."

"Mom!"

"When did this happen?"

"Two, three weeks ago. He's been living at the office."

"The bloody cheapskate."

"Mom, don't swear. It's not becoming."

"Why?"

"Why's it not becoming?"

"Why'd she throw him out?"

"Promise not to swear."

"Raichie!"

"He's been, uh … he's been 'dating' on the Internet…. Mom, are you still there?"

"Raichie, it's not nice of you to pull my leg at a time like this."

"I'm *not* pulling your leg! Sandra caught him on some escort site on the Internet. Or she intercepted some emails between him and some … some girls."

"How do you know?" Erica didn't know whether to laugh or cry.

"What's really bizarre is Sandra calling me and Tammie to tell us that our father's a total shit. It's totally inappropriate."

"She should have called *me*."

Rhoda held the phone away from her ear. Her mother had no idea she was shouting.

"*Not* chicken soup! What can you be thinking?"

"I thought it was supposed to cure everything."

"*Not* stomach flu! Poor Simmie. I'll make him some applesauce, and you can take it over for me."

Rhoda rolled her eyes, and put the package of raw chicken pieces back in the fridge. "Don't bother, Ma. I can buy some."

"Not like mine, you can't! I know exactly how Simmie likes it: not too much cinnamon, lots of nutmeg. And lemon zest. Don't deprive me of the pleasure."

When Rhoda arrived at the house on Belmont, Leah, her hair in curlers beneath a little lace cap, was mopping her forehead. There were two mason jars of applesauce cooling on the kitchen counter, plus a fruit nappy filled to the brim. The house smelled of apples and spices.

Leah pointed at the little bowl. "That's for you. Eat."

"You're acting like some parody of the Jewish mother," Rhoda said. Smiling her sideways smile, she opened the cutlery drawer, took out a spoon, and plunked herself down opposite Leah.

"Uh-m, I like the nutmeg. I keep meaning to tell you, Joan wants to know when we can play bridge again."

Leah's chin began to wobble with indignation.

"I'm done playing with Ellie. Such a hypocrite! She does me a favour by eating my food, but I can tell she despises me. She looks down her nose at me like I'm a fallen woman."

Rhoda dropped her spoon. It clattered against the bowl.

It had been years since her mother had gone to this place. Years.

She stared into Leah's grooved face. The faded blue eyes met hers for an instant before skimming away, but the jaw remained set at its most infuriatingly uncompromising. Rows of neatly aligned curlers left naked ridges of pink skull under her lace cap. Suzy Homemaker transformed into a witch.

Rhoda bit back the words that threatened to burst from her lips. *Playing drama queen in rollers and a daisy-patterned duster doesn't work.*

She stood up. "I've got to go."

For form's sake, she brushed her lips against Leah's sunken cheek before picking up one of the Mason jars. At the front door, she shot a backward glance over her shoulder. The staircase curved away from the foyer in a lavish sweep, halting at a square landing. A banquette covered in blue velvet was tucked into the alcove under the leaded window. As a child, she had often crept there after she'd been put to bed. Burrowing into the fat needlepoint cushions, she'd curl up and listen to the ebb and flow of her parents' conversation. Even when she couldn't make out a word, she derived comfort from it. Later, they'd find her there asleep, and her father would carry her back up to bed.

A wave of memories washed over her and she was back again, sixteen years old on a summer night in 1967, the night she tumbled out of her childhood Eden.

For much of that year, Expo 67 made an international tourist destination of the city. The house on Belmont was a hub of visiting friends and relatives. One of the guests was a cousin of her father's from Boston. Sid was funny and debonair, a urologist who specialized in male infertility and taught at Harvard Medical School. *Recently divorced*, the grown-ups whispered, shaking their heads. Divorce was rare in their circle.

He stayed at the Queen Elizabeth but came to dinner a couple of times on Belmont. In turn, he took the family out to a restaurant in Old Montreal. He teased Rhoda, a picky eater, into trying the *escargots*, paid homage to Rhoda's Bubbie, and drew out Josh—always modest to a fault—about the success of his business.

Leah volunteered to escort him about the exhibition site when the weekend wound down and Josh went back to work. That evening she phoned home at six and told Rhoda she'd be a little late. Rhoda should order a pizza from Pendeli's for her and Daddy.

When Leah tiptoed into the house at a quarter to midnight, Josh and Rhoda were sitting in the darkened living room. Rhoda jumped to her feet, shaking.

"*How could you?* I wanted Daddy to call the police."

"I called."

Rhoda stared at her mother. Leah's lips were swollen, her cheeks streaked pink. She plopped into an armchair

346

and crossed her legs, releasing a cloud of lily of the valley fragrance.

"Six *hours* ago you called. You said you'd be a little late. *A little late!* What happened to 'Always phone if you're delayed'?"

"Rhoda, that's enough," Josh said. "Mummy's home. Go to bed, sweetheart."

"*How could you?*" Rhoda flung over her shoulder again, as she stomped out of the room and took the stairs three at a time.

She halted at the window seat, the refuge of her childhood. Caught between fury, curiosity, and a sense of impending doom, she collapsed on the banquette and curled into a ball. Her parents, who never fought, kept their voices low, so she only heard little bursts and snatches of words.

I've never lied to you, Burble burble burble.

It's not him, it's us. Burble blah burble.

I don't know if I love you anymore. Pause. *I don't know if I ever loved you.*

All this from her mother. Rhoda had squinched her eyes together against the prickling of tears: she had not imagined this. This was like the time she'd been thrown off her bike into traffic. You ached all over, and still there was the premonition of worse to come.

Her father's bass was too low to distinguish. And then she heard him raise his voice and the tone pierced her heart as much as the anguished words.

Don't leave me, Leah. Whatever you do, don't do that to me.

347

And then a noise she couldn't decode. She'd never heard a grown up cry before. That her father was responsible for these strangled yips of pain was unbearable. Rhoda covered her ears and ran to her room. Flinging herself on the bed, she didn't bother to undress. It must have been hours before the door handle turned, and her mother sat down on the bed.

"Are you going to leave us?" Rhoda wept.

"I would never leave you," Leah said.

11

Though Erica had told Raichie she wasn't going to shul, she thought better of it when confronted with the prospect of a morning spent trying to concentrate on the Saturday papers while her mind buzzed around Rick's betrayals and those of her own body. In the shower, she held her breath as she soaped and palpated her neck. It seemed smooth and free of lumps, but what did she know? She'd never felt anything when she'd had her *first bout*. Besides it might not be localized in her neck. By now it could be everywhere.

She ought to go to shul and *daven*. Never mind her health and her fury at being taken in by Ricky (again), wasn't a Jew's place in synagogue on Saturday morning?

All the way there, she held an internal discussion with Faith.

— *Why'd you have to die? Who can I talk to about this? I didn't tell Rhoda in the first place, because I knew what she'd say. ("How many more times are you going to get burned by that putz?") But, Faithie, he truly seemed to have repented. He was so broken up by your death. I know he wasn't pretending about that. I do know him that much!*

— I'm not impressed. So he was shaken up! You know what my mother always used to say: "The self does not change." What he once did to you, he's now doing to Sandra. Serves her right.

— I'm such a chump.

— How does it help to call yourself names? You just don't want to get it that the two of you are well and truly through. As in forever. You're not going to live happily ever after with him. It's not in the cards. It hasn't been since he started cheating on you. Whenever that was.

The Torah service was in full swing by the time Erica arrived. Faith would have thought it inappropriate to turn up this late: yentas would say she was more interested in the *kiddush* than in the worship.

I'd have been more punctual if you were still here.

On the *bimah* at the front of the room, Jonathan Vineberg, the *Baal Korei*, a stocky man with a head of close-cropped grizzled hair, was chanting from the Torah. The rabbi and the Lovely Helen stood on either side of him. Marty, probably the recipient of the last *aliyah*, was up there as well. All of them were following the Hebrew text closely, ready to pounce and correct the least error.

Erica hesitated at the back of the dim, near-empty room. It was evident that few members of Congregation Emunath shared her opinion that shul was the place to be this morning. It was a bright day, one of the last golden flashes of summer. The large square windows of the sanctuary were open to admit a mild breeze, and dust motes danced in the streaks of light. In precisely two weeks there would be an overflow crowd in this room for Rosh Hashanah, but today it held only a few elderly congregants.

Erica tiptoed to the spot on the aisle beneath one of the open windows where she and Faith always sat. She craned her neck around to get the page number from Maureen Segal in the row behind her, leafed through the *Chumash* to the right place, and began to read.

It wasn't long before it crossed her mind that she should have stayed home. In a low, hurried voice, quite dissimilar from his usual booming delivery, Jonathan was intoning the harshest, most awful verses of the Torah, a litany of what would befall the Israelites if they didn't follow God's commandments to the letter.

"The Lord will make pestilence cling to you, until He has put an end to you ... and you shall become a horror to all the kingdoms of the earth."

Erica flipped back and forth a few pages, trying to find the context for the passage. She gathered it was part of Moses's peroration immediately before the entry of the Children of Israel into Canaan. The *parsha* began pleasantly enough, with a description of a ritual of thanksgiving to the Creator, offering God the first fruits of wheat, barley, figs, pomegranates, and olives upon the arrival of the Hebrews to the land of milk and honey. There followed feel-good sections promising that, upon faithful observance of and conformity to all decrees, a heap of blessings would rain down on them—in the city and in the country, in the womb and the kneading bowl, etc. "The Lord will make you the head, not the tail; you will always be at the top and never at the bottom—if only you obey and faithfully observe the commandments ... and do not deviate to the right or to the left ... and turn to the worship of other gods."

If only, Erica thought: but there are hundreds of commandments!

And hundreds of curses—scores anyway—for non-compliance. What a fevered imagination the Great Redactor of Deuteronomy had possessed. Or perhaps he intuited a preview of the cataclysmic future of the Jewish people?

"The Lord will let loose against you calamity, panic, and frustration in all the enterprises you undertake, so that you shall soon be utterly wiped out because of your evil-doing in forsaking Me. ... The Lord will bring a nation against you from afar, from the end of the earth, which will swoop down like the eagle—a ruthless nation, that will show the old no regard and the young no mercy...."

Erica slammed her *Chumash* shut with a bang. If she'd been in a different frame of mind, she might have pored over the glosses, seeking enlightenment from learned commentators. It occurred to her that she must surely have been in shul on other occasions when *Ki Tavo* was read, but she had no recollection of it or of any great sense of previous outrage. Today, however, she felt personally rebuffed. In lieu of uplift and consolation, the tradition had delivered a frontal whack.

It made her think of Melly. He had lived through ghettos and crematoria and work camps and death marches that somehow echoed and were evoked by the painfully detailed curses. Was witnessing and enduring suffering on an epic scale in some way extenuating? If you had survived by hanging on with your fingernails, by theft, subterfuge, cunning, and sheer luck, were you to be henceforth exempt from the normal niceties of good behaviour?

And then, unbidden, she had a flash to her mother, not as she tended to think of her now, a wasted wraith racked by terrible pain, but vibrant and beautiful, sending her and Christine off to school, tying up their red sashes, and then placing a warning finger first on her lips, then theirs: *Thou shalt not speak of who you are, or of what we say here in our home. On pain of death.*

Klara and Tibor too had endured the times when the Lord brought to their door a nation from afar, a nation that swooped down like an eagle, and showed no mercy. For the first time in years, perhaps for the first time ever, Erica understood, understood *in her bones* the terror that would make you leave the faith of the ancestors, leave the legacy that brought upon your head the hatred of the nations. And blend into blessed innocuousness and anonymity.

She stayed for *kiddush*, though she wasn't sure why. *Kiddush* had only been fun with Faith. Faith knew everybody and liked to schmooze at length after services, with Erica tagging along, a bemused sidekick. There was no pleasure in hanging around today, feeling marginal, but she couldn't face going home either. And if she stayed she could thank Nate for last night's hospitality in person, instead of by phone.

As usual there was a clump around the Rabbi. Jeff Stern had buttonholed him first and was making emphatic gestures with his hands and leaning in so close that his moustache almost grazed Nate's cheek. (*Space invader*, Faith used to say.) Marty stood on the periphery, waiting his turn, and, it seemed to Erica, avoiding her. She went over to say hello, racking her brains for something to say.

"It was very kind of you to drive me home last night. I'm not sure I said thank you."

"You did."

"I ... I think you may be angry at me."

"I have no reason or right to be angry with you, Erica."

"It was a nice evening last night at the Kaufmans."

"Yes. I was just about to say thank you to Nate. But if you'll excuse me, I'll come back a little later."

Whew, he's really pissed off. Well, he's right. He's got no right to be mad at me. Even if I were getting back together with Rick. I owe him zip.

She caught Nate's eye and moved in a little closer. Jeff was still expostulating.

"I don't want to intrude," Erica said.

"No, no, you're not intruding. Jeff and I are—"

"Just about finished," Jeff said and strode off abruptly, chest thrust out combatively.

"What's his problem?" Erica said.

Nate smiled and diplomatically held his counsel.

"It was lovely last night, Nate. Thank you for asking me."

"It was our pleasure to have you. You must come again."

"Did we exhaust Reisa? She isn't here."

"She had a headache this morning. She's prone to headaches, I'm afraid."

"Nate, I want to ask you about the Torah portion. I had a lot of trouble with it."

"So did I," Nate smiled wryly. "I do, every year."

"I found it really upsetting today."

"Isn't it awful?" Nate said disarmingly. "I'm afraid I copped out a bit by focusing my *d'var Torah* on the beginning sections—the first fruits—"

"And the tithe. The importance of shouldering our commitments and responsibilities to the community."

"Did you have a problem with that?" Nate spoke a trifle too quickly.

"Not exactly. Only that I was preoccupied with the idea of belonging to an accursed people."

"I see. Well. Yes. Is everything all right with you, Erica? I mean aside from this nasty business with Melly? Reisa and I thought you didn't seem quite yourself last night."

It was Erica's turn to be taken aback.

"Actually, things aren't completely all right."

"Would you like to talk to me about it?"

"I, I might, actually," Erica stammered. "Should I call your office for an appointment?"

"You could do that," Nate said. "But you could also—" He looked down at Erica's feet and then shook his head, disappointed. "I had a thought—but you can't in shoes like that. I was going to suggest you walk me home. It's a beautiful day. But you're wearing those heels."

Erica dimpled and for an instant the lines of strain lifted from her features. "I always keep a pair of running shoes in the trunk of my car for exercise class."

"Well, then," the Rabbi said. "Shall I meet you out front in about fifteen minutes?"

12

Normally Erica wouldn't have dreamed of discussing her private life with Nate. But this wasn't normal. Not that he wasn't already thoroughly in the know about her family.

As she bent down to tie her shoelaces by the curb, her dying mother's face—the sallow, translucent skin, the emaciated cheeks—swam before her eyes. She saw Klara swaddled mummy-like in a pink striped flannel blanket and could almost smell the reek of putrefaction that no amount of airing could dispel. In the final stages of her illness, Tibor had rented a hospital bed for her and moved out of their room into the den. Once he could no longer cope with caring for her on his own, a private nurse attended her round the clock,

Drifting in and out of consciousness, Klara still man-

aged to stay mostly lucid. The disease had ravaged her vocal chords and by the end she could only produce a thin
squeal. In this mouse's squeak she ordered Tibor to call up
Dr. Winters. She had something urgent to discuss with
the analyst who had reassembled her after Erica's book
unmasked her before the world.

Crusty old Dr. Winters actually took it upon himself
to pay a house call and, once he was gone, Klara stunned
her family by asking to see a rabbi. It fell to Erica to find
one. It was before she and Ricky had joined the shul.
Faith put forward Nate Kaufman's name.

A cloud of secrecy shrouded that meeting. Only after Klara's funeral—at the Loyola Chapel—was the veil
slightly lifted. Back home after the burial on the mountain, Tibor sank into his favourite armchair in the den
and in broken, halting phrases took Erica and Christine
into his confidence. Klara had suffered from terrible
nightmares—morphine induced hallucinations he called
them—in which she was haunted by those shadowed generations Erica had dreamed up in her novel. And so Dr.
Winters suggested that she unburden herself to a rabbi.
What she and Nate said to each other remained between
them, but it appeared that it had given her a measure of
comfort and peace.

Nate's delicacy and understanding on that occasion
were reason enough to trust him now, Erica thought, as
she paced in front of the shul waiting for him. She kept
her gaze firmly averted from the offending building site
emblazoned with Melly's name across the street. Nate was

the last person to emerge from inside, and he blinked several times in the sudden sunlight.

His automatic smile for Erica didn't reach his eyes, which remained sad and distant behind the tortoiseshell frames. He must have regretted having asked her to accompany him, Erica thought. She felt a jolt of irritation with herself for having placed them both in this embarrassing predicament.

They both started to speak at once.

Erica said, "I don't want to bother——"

Nate began," What's troubling——?"

They both laughed. "Which route are we taking?" Erica asked.

"Let's get off of Hillpark right away. I can't wait to turn my back on that monstrosity across the street. We'll take Finchley as far up as you like, it's a pretty route.... Now don't beat around the bush, just tell me what's wrong."

She told him about the blood test. He listened gravely, bending his head forward in concentration, occasionally tweaking at his beard. "It will be tough waiting out the results," he said, and then peppered her with questions. "Do you have confidence in your doctor? Will you have chemo? Will you have to lose your wonderful hair?"

Erica recoiled. "It depends what the results are. I don't want to go there unless I have to."

They walked in silence for a few moments. Across the street a *frum* couple were shepherding a family of tots along. A baby and a toddler shared a double stroller pushed by the wife, a nicely dressed woman wearing a dramatic hat. The father was a bear of a man with a curly beard. Two little girls in frilly dresses hung on to his hands. A boy of about six brought up the rear, dawdling.

"That's Rabbi Alter," Nate observed quietly. He nodded curtly in the vague direction of his nemesis.

"*Gut Shabbos, gut Shabbos,*" the bear shouted back amiably.

"This thing with Rabbi Alter and Melly, is it really getting to you?" Erica asked.

"Yes, I can't pretend it isn't. But I really do want to talk about you right now. It was insensitive of me to talk of chemo. Cancer preys on all our insecurities."

"Thank you for saying that! It's like I tucked away all this information about cancer, or associations with it—I've been collecting them all my life, way before my mother's illness or anything to do with me. And now all these bits and pieces are coming out to ambush me."

"Like what?"

"Well, for instance, there was this novel I read years ago. It was kind of light and fluffy, maybe a mystery. But there was something in it of substance. The best friend of the main character has had a mastectomy, but she's fine. She's a regular character with a life. And then in the middle of the novel she has a recurrence. The book isn't really about her, it's about her friend, this is just a sub-plot. And so the main character is very upset and goes to see her family doctor and tells the doctor what's happening and asks about her friend's prospects. And so the doctor says,

'Prepare to say goodbye.'"

"But it isn't like that today!" Nate said, too quickly. "There've been all these advances."

"Yeah, I know. But I've figured out that no matter what statistics they throw at me—eighty per cent survival rate, or ten per cent, it doesn't really matter. Either I've got what they're looking for this time, or I don't. You don't have cancer eighty percent or ten percent. It's a fifty-fifty chance you've got it one hundred per cent."

They walked on in silence for a few minutes. Then Erica spoke up again, "There's something else. You asked me if anything was wrong. Well, you know that saying about sorrows coming not in single spies but in battalions. The thing is, Ricky and I've been kind of working on a reconciliation. At his initiative, not mine. And—I don't want to get too specific—I've realized that I've been a great fool. Again."

Nate stopped in his tracks and looked at her searchingly.

"This might sound strange coming from a rabbi, but haven't you drunk enough from that particular well?"

Erica gaped at him. A rabbi, her rabbi, advising against salvaging her marriage? She couldn't believe her ears.

And then to her immense surprise, she burst into rollicking laughter. She felt out of control. Maybe she'd never be able to dam this crazy wave of hysteria. It reminded her of that moment when Hershy had pronounced the words "Ricky Who?"

After a while, Nate, too, began to chuckle. It was

some time before they resumed walking.

Nate said, "It's none of my business of course, but why would you want to go there, Erica, when someone else is so clearly interested in you?"

"You mean ... *Marty*?"

"Uh-huh. I'm just an observer on the sidelines, but I do notice things, you know, and he's a fine guy. Dependable as a rock and, I would guess—though I'm hardly an expert—that women would find him attractive."

"Is the fact that someone admires you a reason for you to give that person encouragement?"

"*Yes!* Why not? Unless for some reason you've absolutely and categorically ruled against that person."

"But shouldn't you feel a strong attraction?"

"Sometimes you can feel a strong attraction, and it can even lead you astray. No, not astray—that's the wrong connotation. I don't know how best to put it. I guess what I'm trying to say is that making rational choices in relationships is easier to do when the hormonal impulses remain in the wings for a while. You'd be surprised how they emerge when the drama's allowed to play itself out. Anyway that's what I've noticed in many mature romances."

"But what if someone's done something ... shameful?"

"*Shameful*?" Nate raised his eyebrow and stopped in the middle of the road again. "Whatever has Marty done to make you say that?"

Then he held up his hand like a policeman stopping traffic. "No, no, don't tell me. I don't want to know."

They walked on some more. By now they had reached Ellerdale, and begun heading east.

"You know, Erica, the longer we live, the more opportunities we have to make mistakes. By the time we reach our age, pretty well everyone's done something questionable."

"Even you?" Erica teased.

"Even me, the rabbi. But it's easier to accept another person's failures and flaws if we weren't the party they stuck it to. Don't get me wrong. I believe in working hard at marriage. The Talmud says, 'When a man divorces the wife of his youth, even the altar sheds tears.' As a Reconstructionist, I'm happy to paraphrase that to 'when a woman divorces the father of her cherished children.' Still, as an observer, I'd say that sometimes you simply have to wipe the slate clean and start all over."

13

Dressed in an ancient pair of jeans, a white cotton hat with a visor shielding his eyes from spattering paint, Paul Ladouceur was perched on a stepladder in his spare bedroom, humming gently to Tom Waits on the radio. He arced the roller on the diagonal, filling in a broad stripe of yellow next to a matching band of green, and grinned. The rainbow mural was taking shape nicely.

Sun come up it was blue and gold. Tom not growling. Tom's voice rich and mellow. Tom suddenly a balladeer. How perfect was that? And how perfect this song. Paul wanted to shout his happiness from a rooftop, or at the very least his balcony, but even more he wanted to hug it to himself, keep it secret. Let him not tempt fate this time, or invite ridicule, or have someone puncture his hopes.

He wiped his forehead on his sleeve, laid the roller back in the pan, and went in search of a Griffon in the kitchen. And there she was, her picture not in a frame like in the song, but stuck to the fridge by a strawberry shaped magnet. His miracle woman, the embodiment of the Polish saying his mother so often quoted, the gist of which was that there's no event too awful for something good not to come of it.

Her name was Norma. He liked to tease her that she was just like her name, an exceedingly *normal* girl. To which she'd respond, "Not girl, Paul, *woman*." He didn't know whether she was sticking up for feminist language, or simply stating that she wasn't that young. Nearly forty. To her, that was ancient. To him, a girl.

He wandered back into the spare room and picked up the roller again.

Breathtaking that, if not for Faith dying, he'd never have met her.

It was the last evening of the *shiva*. When he'd come the first night, the place was still too jammed to do more than shake hands with Al and the children and give Erica a big bear hug. He intended another one for Rhoda, but she darted him such a poisonous glance when he approached that he ended up merely stammering stock condolences.

Mess with my friend, you mess with me, the steely eyes said.

Erica made her peace with you, but not with my blessing.

He could only assume that she had taken his breakup with Erica in a distinctly vengeful spirit, quite unlike Erica herself.

This second time he had a chance to press the hands of Faith's parents and brother as well, but after a few stilted sentences—he could tell they had no idea who he was, or how he was connected to Faith—he retreated to a corner couch occupied by a solitary woman.

She wasn't drop-dead gorgeous like poor Maryse, nor did she have the exotic appeal of one striking feature, like Erica's curls.

He hadn't yet told Erica about her, but he would soon. It gave him a pang each time he thought of Erica. He wasn't the praying sort, but the other day at lunchtime, he'd actually stepped into Notre-Dame de Bon Secours Chapel to light a candle for her. The idea of her undergoing treatments, losing her hair.... The thought of losing her altogether hovered on the edge of his new happiness. He had a lot of trouble keeping it at bay. He knew now that he would always cherish Erica as a dear friend. And he blamed himself for his impulsiveness in stepping over the professional divide that normally guided his relations with female colleagues.

It had taken a great effort by both of them to step away from the brief affair that carried them from New Year's Eve to Valentine's Day. Over a steak dinner at his place, she let him off the hook by saying it was a misguided idea, work and romance didn't mix. But she had clearly intuited his change of heart, though he hoped she'd never know the real reason. Her scar, always camouflaged by a thin gold chain, was the culprit—that tidy little seam at the base of her throat. It symbolized mortality for him almost as much as a tub full of poor Maryse's blood had. He couldn't risk becoming hostage to that scar more than he already was by token of being Erica's friend.

And then a few months later, there was Norma, sitting on a couch in Faith and Al's living room. (Beneath Rhoda's loyal, glaring radar. He suspected that she understood his craven heart, even if Erica didn't. She was a witch, that Rhoda.) He asked how she was connected to Faith and Al. She explained she was a multimedia artist who paid the bills as an art therapist. She consulted at various facilities, one of them the Children's. That's how she knew Faith.

She was pretty in a natural, wholesome way, with regular features and nut-brown eyes. They were probably the only two Gentiles in the room, which made for a bond of sorts. She seemed impressed by his journalism background. "I love editors," she said, and then laughed shame-faced, catching herself lest she was being too forward. She seemed to think that being an editor at *The Gazette* was important and glamorous.

He tried, but not too hard, to disabuse her. The paper had recently been bought by a Western media mogul who was slashing and burning and gutting the product, hellbent on turning it into homogenized corporate pap. Erica as columnist was viewed as too elitist, too intellectual.

Paul's budget had been cut; he was resorting to more wire copy than he was comfortable with. Forget glamorous; his job had never been less fun.

All the more reason that it was flattering to be admired.

She seemed direct, easygoing. An outdoorsy woman without a complicated past, who liked to kayak and hike. Yet she read his section, and had some lively opinions about Erica's last column. Apparently she didn't just love editors, she loved books.

"What's your schedule?" he asked.

She looked back at him blankly.

"I mean, when can I call you?… Can I call you?"

He called the next day, which was a Friday. They went for dinner. And despite his best resolution for no more impromptu beddings, they made love on her lumpy living room sofa.

They didn't take precautions.

Which is why he was now giddy with joy, painting his spare room in nursery colours, and crooning softly.

I love you baby and I always will
Ever since I put your picture
In a frame.

14

Business was brisk at the butcher shop the Sunday before Rosh Hashanah, but Noam had two extra men flying about the store, so he had a moment with Erica. It was the first time they were seeing each other since the funeral, and he beckoned her to a corner by the square cabinet freezer.

"I'm really sorry about Faith." His face twitched, as he hoisted a bag out of the cooler.

"Oh, Noam, thank you. I can't think of the holidays without her. I keep on going over what happened, over and over. How *could* she fall? Why did this happen?"

"There is a plan. That was the plan."

"Noam, *no*! What an awful idea. There was no *plan*. It was an accident. God is sad over this."

Noam smiled pityingly at her. He hoisted another bag of meat from the cooler, preparing to help her to her car.

"Don't get me wrong, Erica. You and I, we don't agree too much about God. You Reconstructionists, what do you mean by God, anyway? I've heard people say you *daven* to To Whom It May Concern. Oh, you like that! You haven't heard that one?

"The Lubavitcher rebbe taught that we're here on earth for one purpose," Noam continued earnestly. "To reproduce. To have children. So after that it makes no difference, really. Now the rebbe, he was married for years and years. But he had no children. But all the things that he did good in the world, all over the world, they're his children. Faith did on earth what she was supposed to do."

"You mean, just because she had children? She didn't even see them grow up properly! She didn't see them get married. She didn't have grandchildren. *Among other things,* that was also what she was supposed to do."

"That's very sad. But look at it my way. She has a son to say *kaddish* for her. In her life she was involved with many good things. She did a lot for your synagogue. Okay, it's not my synagogue—but still. And she helped a lot of kids with problems at the hospital. She made a difference. That's her legacy."

"But—"

"Erica! Hello. I was just thinking about you."

Erica looked up, startled by the voice behind her. Marty had walked into the butcher shop and was staring at her with open concern.

"I didn't know you bought meat from Noam," Erica said, casting about for a straw.

"I don't usually," Marty said *sotto voce*, looking awkward as he tried to ignore the butcher in his apron. "My son and daughter-in-law and little granddaughter are coming in from Boston for the holiday. They'll be at my place for the second night. I'm not much of a cook, but I got a recipe for chicken soup off the Internet and I thought it would be nice to go kosher for *yontiff*."

"Say no more, mister," Noam stopped pontificating in a flash and became the soul of professional concern. "Do you mind if I get one of the boys to help you to your car, Erica?"

"Why don't I do that?" Marty picked up the two bags, "and maybe you can start by cutting me up a chicken?"

"Mister, you're gonna need at least two for a proper soup."

"Okay, so two."

The sun was beating down with pleasant warmth as they headed towards the parking lot.

"Like I said, you've been on my mind a lot, Erica. I'm terribly sorry to hear that you may be having a recurrence."

"Whoever told you that!?"

"Nate. He's worried about you. So am I, it goes without saying."

"What a yenta!"

"I've been called many things in my time—"

"Not *you! Nate!* If a woman can't talk in confidence to her rabbi—"

"Erica, please. Could you tell me what your Hebrew name is?"

"Whatever for?"

"I'd like to make a *mishebayrach* for you. A blessing for your good health."

Erica gazed at him dumbstruck. It was as if she were seeing him for the first time. The long rays of the sun were blinding and she shielded her eyes with one hand. Had she ever taken stock of him properly, this large, middle-aged man with a receding hairline, beaked nose, and pouches like bruises beneath his eyes? Worry was written all over his face and furrowed his high forehead, but what held her in this intent exchange was the simple compassion radiating from those almond-shaped eyes.

After all the snubs she had subjected him to, he had still found it in him to make this crazy, corny, amazing request.

She bit her lip, hard. If she started crying now, she might never stop. Faith dead. Cancer a second time. *Prepare to say goodbye.*

"I'm touched, Marty."

"I don't want to overstep, but as much as I've tried, I haven't been able to stop thinking about you."

"Even now? I'm a pretty poor risk."

"Yeah, well," he said drily. "In a different way, so am I.... So what's your Hebrew name then?"

"Ruth. Ruth bat Avraham ve Sarah."

15

Marty's cellphone rang just as he arrived at the office. He answered while letting himself in.

"Melly Darwin, here. Is that you, Riess?"

"It is."

"You're the agent for that lowrise on l'Acadie and Jarry."

"I am."

"We have a project in mind. We'd make an interesting offer for the owner."

Marty didn't say a word.

"Are you still there?"

"Yup," Marty said, thinking hard.

"*Nu?*"

"There are ... conditions to that property."

"What's this *conditions*?"

"I own it."

"So—and I want to buy! At a decent return to the seller, already I told you."

"Well, that's very good. But the thing is, I have a condition for selling it. Or rather for selling it to you. I understand that you owe Erica Molnar some money."

"What the hell does that have to do with what we're talking about?"

"Pay up. It's a condition of the sale."

This time it was Melly who remained silent.

"I'll … think … about it," he said. Then, just before the phone cut out, in a low voice he added, "*Shmuck*."

16

Rhoda having decided that Erica needed a new outfit for the High Holidays, on Sunday they went shopping. Erica hated everything she tried on at Boutique Arnelle and declared she was a hag in the chartreuse silk dress that Rhoda said fit her perfectly. At Papaver bleu there was a Chanel-style suit that Erica thought might do, but Rhoda said it looked like a flight attendant's uniform. Erica then announced that that was all the shopping she could handle—she had a wardrobe full of clothes to make do with. Rhoda insisted that they should try Quelles Sensations on the off chance. There she kept up a steady patter with the owner, while studying the racks with narrowed eyes. She pulled a mid-calf brown skirt, a form fitting leopard print top, and a long tawny cardigan off three different racks and thrust them into Erica's arms.

"This top is more Faith than me."

"Humour me. Try them on."

Erica did so and had to admit that Rhoda was right.

Re-energized by this success, Erica agreed that the afternoon was still young. They headed for Greene Avenue to look at shoes. Rhoda was at the cash at Tony's, paying for a lovely pair of button-up ankle boots, when the manager touched her elbow from behind.

"What's happened to your friend—what's her name?—I haven't seen her in ages."

Erica stepped up and put her arm around Rhoda's waist. For a moment Rhoda, taller, more sturdily built than Erica, buckled against her.

"Faith," Rhoda whispered. "My friend's name is Faith Rabinovitch."

Erica spoke into the silence. "Our friend Faith—died ... very suddenly ... in July."

"I just couldn't say she'd died," Rhoda said, looking pale on a couch at the back of the Second Cup. "The words just wouldn't come out."

"That woman wanted to fall through the floor when I did tell her," Erica said.

"I had a feeling something like this might happen one day," Rhoda whispered, "I just didn't expect it now.... Yesterday my mother, and today this. And tomorrow just happens to be my father's *yahrzeit*."

"What's wrong with your mother?"

"Nothing's wrong with her, she just said something

really outrageous." Rhoda took a gulp of coffee, stared at Erica without appearing to see her, and then tried to straighten her spine against the soft cushions. "Listen, I'm going to tell you something I've never told anyone. And I don't want you to comment on it. I don't need you to be philosophical, or deliver an opinion. I just need you to listen."

Erica placed her mug on the coffee table.

"Okay?"

"Okay."

"My father adored my mother. You know that."

Erica nodded, completely baffled.

"He had this massive crush on her in high school. He could have had any girl he wanted—this was the way I heard it from my aunt Ellie, not from him, he'd never make that kind of a claim. He was the nicest person alive, and he was an all-round athlete and he was bright. He might have gone to university if my grandfather hadn't died when my dad was in his last year of high school. Ellie was still in elementary school. There were three other kids.

"My grandfather had been a watchmaker and owned a hole-in-the-wall jewellery shop on Ste. Catherine East. My dad learned the basics of dismantling and cleaning watches from him. And so when my grandfather died and my Bubbie took over the shop, my dad had the *chutzpah* to present himself at Birks. He got a job at their repair bench, but every spare minute he was watching and learning from the goldsmiths working with their gems. He wanted to be a master jeweller. There was a guy called

Serafino there who'd apprenticed at Cartier in Paris, who took him under his wing. My Dad was ambitious—but I have a hunch that really he was just dying to create beautiful baubles for my mother.

"He was obsessed with her. And I think she liked him, too, but she wasn't having any of him. Her passion was for climbing out of poverty. She'd had a bad childhood. My other grandfather had done time, and my Nana was simply a beaten-down woman."

"Beaten?" Erica ventured.

"Beaten down, not beaten up. He was a petty thief and a gambler and a drinker. There was never any money. And my mother was this beautiful girl. I think her great allure for men, Jewish men anyway, was that though she was Jewish, she didn't look it at all. Blonde hair, blue eyes, upturned nose. And she must have been a bit of an ice maiden. She dated older guys with better prospects than my dad. She liked him, but she didn't want to go steady with him.

"He wouldn't give it up. My Bubbie scolded him up and down about her. Bubbie'd say that Leah Spanier, the daughter of a *goniff* who'd served time at Bordeaux, had a lot of nerve turning up her *shiksa* nose at him."

Here Rhoda gave the weakest of chuckles and drained the last drops of her latte. "But he tuned her out and asked my mother out again. And I guess in a weak moment, she said yes. By this time, under Serafino's eye, Daddy was crafting the odd ring and brooch of his own. And one found its way into Birks' side window, in a famous Birks blue box.

"After the movie let out at Loew's, for once he didn't hide his light under a bushel, and he steered her by the shop window and pointed out the ring. It was a pretty flashy number, a star sapphire I think, between two diamonds in a wide platinum band.

"And my mother was astute enough to recognize talent. I think she figured that, with a push in the right direction, he just might make it. And she was going to give him that push.

"She was working as a bookkeeper in a large financial-collection company. Mr. Black, the owner, probably had a crush on her. A lot of men did. In any case she told him that her boyfriend worked with a master jeweller who'd trained at Cartier in Paris. Between them, the Cartier guy and her boyfriend could produce one-of-a-kind jewellery at a fraction of the price that it cost at Birks.

"And so one thing led to another. In the romance between them—and in my father's career. He never did become a master jeweller. At first he peddled Serafino's creations to the Blacks and to their friends. Literally. He'd call on couples in the evening, showing off his wares in a customized attaché case. It turned out he had a real flair for sales. And like I said, one thing led to another. They got married. Daddy took over his father's old store, and then he rented space on Bernard, and then eventually he became Gutner's on Greene. And later, Bijoux Gutner.

"We had a nice life. I had a great childhood. Not just because I had nice things and we lived well, but because I understood how loved and cherished I was. By my father especially, but my Mom, too. Before I was born she'd done my father's books and he always discussed every step he took with her, but she stopped working when I was born. Which—" Rhoda stopped and looked pensive for a moment, "may have been a mistake."

She took a deep breath.

"D'you want another coffee?" Erica asked.

"No. Do you?"

"No."

"You're probably wondering where this is all heading."

"A little."

"Where this is going is she got herself royally laid by my father's cousin Sid over the course of a day and a night during Expo. And she made sure that my father and I would know it. She rubbed our faces in her crotch."

"Rhoda!"

"*Not* a word, remember?"

"Sorry."

Rhoda's eyes filled with tears. "I'm sorry, Erica. I shouldn't have said that." She bent down to rummage in her purse, found a tissue, and rubbed her eyes.

"How's my mascara?"

"Smudged."

Rhoda made a valiant attempt at a lopsided grin, but with her blackened eyes and ravaged features she ended up looking grotesque.

"You don't have to tell me more," Erica said.

"Nah, you're not off the hook. Besides, there isn't that

much more.

"My father was shattered. He aged ten years that summer. His hair began falling out. He lost so much weight, his clothes hung on him like on a scarecrow. When people asked if he was sick, he couldn't be bothered making up stories. He told my Bubbie that her charming nephew had seduced my mother."

"'What can you expect of the daughter of a jailbird?' my Bubbie said. 'The little slut.'"

"She said that? How d'you know?"

"Ellie. Ellie was the fly on the wall, the whole time.

"My father stood by my mother through it all. He told my grandmother to cut it out. He said, 'She made a mistake. Have you never made a mistake?'"

"'There are mistakes and there are mistakes,' my Bubbie said. 'Mistakes like this I haven't made.'

"That has stayed with me," Rhoda said. "'Mistakes like this I haven't made.'"

"You never told anybody about this?" Erica said, after it appeared that Rhoda was done.

"No."

"Not even *Hershy*?"

Rhoda shook her head.

"Why not?"

"Why should I?"

"But what kind of a marriage is that—when you carry around this big secret—?"

"It's not a secret! All kinds of people know—"

"This big story, the biggest story in your life. And

you don't tell your husband? Don't you trust him?"

Rhoda shrugged. "I trust him, but I don't want him to know how much something like that can hurt. Can hurt me. Did hurt me."

"But don't you want to share everything with him?"

"There's way too much emphasis on sharing in marriage. Marriage should just be a pact. Like, I want to have children, I want to have a certain standard of living, I want someone who can make me laugh, and I want someone who'll stick to his side of the bed."

"And what about romance? Passion?"

"*That* is precisely what I distrust. My father loved my mother too much. Right from the get go. It's a stifling thing to be loved like that. A risky thing. Loving and being loved like that, you could get burned, you could get burned up...."

17

Rhoda bent down to place a couple of pebbles at her father's cool, marble headstone. It read:

JOSHUA GUTNER,
Yehoshuah ben Yekutiel,
1920-1992

Beloved Husband,
Incomparable Father,
Devoted Grandfather.

Each year on his yahrzeit, she was in the habit of having a little monologue at this spot, catching him up on the family news. Breaking down.

"Hi, Daddy," she said now. But instead of launching into her bulletin to the hereafter, instead of pouring her heart out to him about poor Faith as she had planned, she was tongue-tied with shame.

She had not called her mother for two days. She had not picked Leah up and brought her along to the cemetery as she always did. In the hereafter—about the existence of which Rhoda was highly dubious—her father would be sorrowful.

Head bowed, Rhoda stood, her fingers still lightly touching the monument, remembering the night of her father's death. A massive coronary, completely out of the blue. She and her mother were back at the house on Belmont, back from Emergency at the Jewish General. Both of them stunned by the suddenness of the attack, and by the futility of the measures taken to save him. She helped her mother ease out of her clothes, as she might have done a small child, then slipped the cotton nightgown over her head. From the bathroom she brought her a glass of water and a sleeping pill. Leah grabbed hold of her hand.

"Don't leave me just yet."

"I'm not going anywhere, Ma. I'll be next door."

"Not yet. Stay with me for a while."

Rhoda sat down at the edge of the bed.

"Every night—from my wedding night, until last night, your father and I were together. Every night.

D'you know what I'm saying, Rhoda?"

"I think so," Rhoda said. What was that expression kids had these days? *Too much information. Please don't say another word.*

"But he never, you know, satisfied me until after Sid. I didn't even know what it was."

"So now," Rhoda said through clenched teeth, "Now will you get together with Sid? There's nothing to stop you now."

"You don't understand the first thing, Rhoda. Not the first thing about me. I didn't love Sid."

"You didn't love Daddy, either. I heard you say it with my own ears that night. You know which night. 'Maybe I never loved you.' That's what you said to Daddy.'"

"I never said that. You're mistaken. I never said that. I always loved your Daddy. I just loved him a whole lot more after Sid. After Sid, I didn't just love him for what he could do for me as a provider. I loved him for the way he stood up for me. And for the way he gave me pleasure."

In the cemetery, Rhoda dashed tears from her eyes. She would call her mother. She would go fetch her. They would return together to pay their respects, as they did every year.

Part Seven

I believe with perfect faith that at this very moment
millions of human beings are standing at crossroads
and intersections, in jungles and deserts,
showing each other where to turn, what the right way is,
which direction.

—Yehuda Amichai

1

Rabbi Nate stood on the *bimah* Rosh Hashanah morning waiting for his flock to come to order for his *d'var torah*. A sea of faces swam before him. Some gazed back at him with expectation, some with disparagement, others with boredom. In the front row to his right sat Reisa with their son and daughter and with Nate's parents. In the central bank of seats, in the middle of the front row, old Moish Stipelman's bald pate caught a ray of sunshine. Behind Moish and Sylvia and Frances and Mark Tannenbaum, Melly Darwin and Bubbles wore an air of complacent self-righteousness—

What was Melly doing here?

The younger generation of Darwins must be cozying up to Rabbi Alter at his headquarters in Snowdon (Solomon's Temple would take some months to complete), and Nate had assumed that Melly and Bubbles would defect as well. What did their presence signify?

Abigail Rosen, a garish turban wound about her head and her eyes burning with a feverish light, sat in her customary place a few aisles back, and Marty was seated behind her, a doting smile on his face, as he dandled a tot on his knee. Nate reflexively scanned the room for Erica and found her in one of the back rows of the section to the left, sitting between Raichie and Tamara, near the Kaplanskys and their sons. He searched in vain for Al Rabinovitch. No trace of him, not even in the rafters.

Nate had struggled hard with his sermon this year. He was in the habit of bouncing his ideas for this most supercharged address of the year off Reisa and any half-way intelligent soul he could corner for a few minutes of agonized discussion. Faith had always been a great sounding board and had helped him fine-tune many a half-baked notion into insight.

Faith was constantly on his mind. He didn't want to base his most important sermon of the year exclusively on her, yet her tragedy underlined the need for *heshbon ha-nefesh*, taking stock of the soul, the core theme of these Days of Awe. And so of late the ghostly melody and dread litany of the *Unetaneh Tokef* prayer had become the default setting for his mind, as he found himself waking to its haunting strains from troubled sleep and humming it under his breath as his thoughts strayed this way and that, but never far away from what he would be saying today.

Finally he had decided to give in and allow himself to say what was really on his mind. "*Hayom harat olam*, our prayers tell us, 'Today the world was born.' Rosh Hashanah, our New Year, celebrates the birth of the world and the birth of humanity. However, our celebration is accompanied not by the partying fanfare of the secular New Year but by solemn soul searching. It is a holy day. Later we will chant the *Unetaneh Tokef* prayer which begins with the words "Let us recount how utterly holy this day is."

"*Unetaneh Tokef* has a tragic origin. It's attributed to Rabbi Amnon of Mainz, a great scholar who lived in the eleventh century and who was martyred for his faith.

"The metaphor of a Book in which God judges us and records our deeds and seals our fates comes to us from the remembered words of Rabbi Amnon. In this, one of our most solemn prayers, we are reminded of the fragility of our lives as we are assessed and brought to account.

"On Rosh Hashanah humanity's destiny is inscribed, and on Yom Kippur it is sealed: how many shall pass away and how many shall be brought into existence; who shall live and who shall die; who shall come to a timely end, and who not; who shall perish by fire and who by water; who shall be at peace and who tormented.

"Against this grim pronouncement, *Unetaneh Tokef* also speaks of God's throne being founded on loving kindness and truth. In the face of uncertainty, the prayer offers a ray of hope. Its refrain teaches that repentance, reflection, and good deeds can mitigate a dire judgment.

"We don't need *Unetaneh Tokef* to tell us we are going to die: we know it in the marrow of our bones. But we don't know how and when. This prayer with its litany of possible deaths brings us face to face with our mortality, and confronts us with a challenge. Since we will not live forever, we must try to turn towards the kind of life we want to lead. *Unetaneh Tokef* prods us in the direction of making the best of our lives.

"But how are we to do this? There are so many claims

on us, so many ways for our good intentions to be dissipated. In a poem called "A Man in His Life," the great Israeli poet Yehuda Amichai, who died just a few days ago leaving a gorgeous body of work, framed this dilemma in a litany of arresting paradoxes:

> *A man doesn't have time*
> *to have time for everything....*
> *A man needs to love and to hate at the same moment,*
> *to laugh and cry with the same eyes,*
> *to make love in war and war in love....*

"Somehow we must find a way to live in fullness, nourishing our inner lives by committing ourselves anew to our faith, our families, our community. We must create! Those of us with books or symphonies inside us must get them onto the page. And we must build. As a congregation, we have dreamt of building a new home. We need but take it one step further now to make this communal aspiration a reality. Working individually and together, we must bring all our worthy strivings to fruition. And if we live intensely and fully, to paraphrase the poet, we will

> *...die as figs die in autumn,*
> *Shriveled and full of ourselves and sweet,*
> *the leaves growing dry on the ground,*
> *the bare branches pointing to the place*
> *where there's time for everything.*

2

It was a couple of weeks later, a Monday morning. Erica was pulling on her sneakers, just about to leave the house for a yoga class, when the phone rang.

"Ms. Molnar, Dr. de Costa is on the line."

Erica's heart stopped. This was the call she had been dreading and anticipating for a month. Her legs began to shake. Her throat tightened.

"Erica, are you there?"

"Yes," Erica whispered.

"You're okay! These new readings are completely normal!" She had never heard him so jubilant.

"The TSH? The Thyroglobulin?"

"Perfectly normal. Everything. Relax. Get on with your life. Don't give it another thought."

Don't give it another thought.

She replaced the phone in its cradle and leaned for a moment against the wall in the hallway, as tears trickled out the corners of her eyes. Then she kicked off her sneakers. There was a yoga class at seven in the evening that she could take instead.

There were people who would be thrilled with this piece of news. First she called Raichie's school in Toronto and left a message with the secretary that Raichie should be told, in these words, "Mom is fine. Yes, that's right, 'Mom's fine.'" Then she dialled Christine's pager and got her sister on surgical rounds at St. Joseph's.

"Fabulous! Excellent! I'll call you back in an hour."

Erica hung up. She was dying to talk to somebody, but the rest of the world was gainfully employed.

She went into her office and shot off a rapid-fire emails to Tammie at school, and Rhoda at work.

And then, she took a big gulp of air and decided to tackle a task that was the equivalent of a dive from a high cliff. She pulled open her desk drawer and began to rummage in the cubby where she kept an assortment of business cards in disarray.

The one she was searching for was near the top of the pile. Martin Riess Realties. There was a plethora of numbers on it—office, home, cell. She opted for the cell.

He answered on the first ring.

"It's Erica."

There was a brief silence.

"Yes, Erica…. How are you?"

"I—I'm fine…. Is this a terrible time for you? I mean, are you in the middle of something?"

"I'm in the office. It's not a terrible time."

"I wanted to tell you—my doctor just called. I'm okay."

"*Baruch hashem!* That's wonderful. I really appreciate hearing it from you like this."

Erica was quiet and then spoke in a rush.

"Do you have another minute? Are you sure I'm not disturbing you?"

"I have another minute."

"This isn't the easiest thing to say to you. I've been thinking a great deal over the course of the past few weeks. I simply can't put out of my mind that letter of yours …. You know, the information that came to me inadvertently? You know what I'm talking about?"

There was an exceedingly long silence. Then Marty spoke in a strangled voice.

"Yes," he said.

"But really, I realize now that I wasn't supposed to get that letter until after the fifth date. Do you remember that?"

"Yes," Marty whispered.

"I wondered," Erica continued haltingly, "I wondered—that is if you're still keeping an open mind about me—I wondered if perhaps you'd like to consider date number two?"

There was a sound like a pent up sigh being released. She wasn't sure if it was coming from him or from her.

"Did you have something in mind, Erica?"

She allowed herself a tiny giggle. "Perhaps coffee at the Brûlerie St-Denis?"

"Should we try the one on St-Denis this time?" he asked. "If I recall, you thought it less likely that we'd meet Reconstructionists there. Not, of course, that you dislike Reconstructionists. Just that you prefer to avoid—what was that word again?"

"Scuttlebutt."

Epilogue

And now they come together – what might have been
and whatever was – and the two become one....

– Yehuda Amichai

A tall woman bundled into a fur-trimmed coat braced herself against the wind that was sweeping through Rutherford Park.

"I'm not crazy," she said out loud. "Please don't call me crazy, Faith. Hershy's already read me the riot act about this. And no, I wouldn't let him come with me. This is just between you and me. I had to come back here tonight. For you. There's no way I could go to a party. Even if it's at Erica's. Even if she means well.

"Just look at those stars, they're bright and hard like diamonds. On account of it's so cold and clear. Like last year, but even colder. And no fireworks this time.

"You know how I've always been fascinated by stars. They represent all that's out there, all that's unattainable, all the vast reaches of what I'll never know. All those things I'd like to understand, like Nietzsche's theories and the big bang.

"Where are you Faith? Where are you *really*? I mean I know you're in Beaconsfield, in the ground, under the snow. And I think I'm over, or mostly over, thinking about your crumpled little body down there.

"Maybe you're aware of the recent activity around you. Moish was buried near you a couple of weeks ago. The old guy apparently collapsed in shul on a Saturday morning and died of a cerebral haemorrhage the next day. As the new cemetery committee chair, Marty thought you were lonely in that corner by yourself. The logic escapes me, since you and Moish didn't have much to do with each other, but now you have him for company.

"I went to Moish's funeral, mostly to see you. I need to repeatedly drive it home to myself that it's really really true. But actually the hardest place to believe you are dead is right there. There's no stone yet, just a little marker with some dried-up flowers from the summer. (Al says placing pebbles on your grave is barbaric. For your birthday, he took you roses, and some of those magenta geraniums you were so excited about last spring.) But it still seems as impossible, as unbearable as on the day it happened. That you're down there. In the frozen ground....

"But maybe you're up there with the stars, in the ether?

"Or maybe you're somewhere near me right now, in which case I needn't be talking quite this loud.

"That's why I came tonight, or one of the reasons. My New Year's resolution is to stop talking to you. You'd be the first to say it's sick. You're dead five months and five days, and there's been not one day out of the 158 (I counted them up today) that I haven't talked to you. Usually in the car, when I'm alone, but sometimes at home, when Hershy's in the basement watching TV. (I think he's overheard me a couple of times. I've caught him staring at me sideways when he thinks I don't notice. For all I know he's preparing to put me away.)

"You're pretty much up to speed from my reports about what's been going on—." Here Rhoda paused in momentary confusion, appalled at her own turn of phrase. She could no more tell a lie to Faith on the other side of life, than she could have done if she were there in the flesh. She'd just pointed out two minutes earlier that it wasn't normal to talk to a person who had died five months and five days ago. But that wasn't the only reason she had to stop talking to her.

She had been censoring herself with Faith ever since a Saturday in early November, but she didn't think she could keep it up much longer.

What had happened was this. After checking out a great Lancôme promotion at Holt Renfrew, she popped into the Première Moisson on Sherbrooke for a takeout of their fabulous tomato flan for supper, and to her consternation—

Don't go there now! She'll read your mind in a sec.... But maybe where she is, it doesn't matter anymore? Maybe she doesn't even care a bit.

She began talking extra fast, gulping down the frigid air in great slugs.

"Have I said how much I miss you? The whole world misses you. A witless cowboy is about to take office in the White House and a second intifada is raging in Israel. Erica is carrying on and on about how we need your leadership now, more than ever. She's like a broken record about how you kept the spirit in her when the Scuds burst into flames in Tel Aviv during the Gulf War. She says she was watching it live on TV and was on the phone with you at the same time and she was completely hysterical and you talked her down. She says you were true to your name, you had faith that we would all come through it. One way or other, the Jewish people would survive.

"Faithie, there's a great hole in the world without you, but it still keeps on going on and on and round and round. No one seems to care *enough* that you're gone. Maybe I'm as bad as everyone else with my new coat and these nice new boots I got on Boxing Day—do you like them? But at least I'm not at a party! Erica said we had to come together, raise a toast to better times ahead, life is for the living—that's what her mother always said. Etc. Well *sure*. Klara Molnar was quite the philosopher of survival! A Communist when it suited her one day, and a Catholic the next. Life at all costs and nothing but life!

"You know what? I don't think life's just for the living. The dead add heft to our lives. My father's still a big part of me. He's in my thoughts and heart every single day. I would maybe even say that I continue to have a relationship with him. The living have a responsibility to all of you. *That's* what I think!

"The rabbi's running around like a regular Energizer Bunny now that he's managed to breathe life back into the building project. Guess what? Melly coughed up the dough for us after all! Rumour has it that he was inspired by the Rabbi's Rosh Hashanah sermon. Apparently he's hedging his bets about which way salvation lies. And, wonder of wonder, he's paid Erica the money he owes her. Even though she's walked away from the project. No-body can figure that one out.

"One theory is that those paradoxical, contradictory concepts Nate preached about from the Amichai poem—love and hate and laugh and cry and forgive and forget and remember—people are saying that Melly took them as a sign that he should give to us as well as to the Kabbalists. Frankly, I don't think Melly Darwin has a gift for poetry. I doubt very much that it was Amichai or the rabbi who inspired him. I think it's more likely his accountant or lawyer.

"The shul's going to be demolished next month. Everything is being scrapped except the stained glass. The rabbi's got his way after all, and his head will swell to three times its size—well, maybe only twice. Having the Kabbalists across the street will keep him in line.

"As for Erica, the scare over the recurrence seems to have focused her. That life of hers that's been reprieved: she wants to put it to use. She's writing in a white heat, finally, *finally* working on a new novel. She's very coy about it, but when I really press her, she says it's about the many faces of love. Could she actually mean to write about Marty? Or, here's an original thought! Maybe it's about you?

"I wish you could see her and Marty together. You'd get such a kick out of them. Saturday mornings they sit primly on opposite sides of the sanctuary, making googly eyes across the room at each other. After services they exchange restrained cheek kisses at the buffet table, for the diversion of all who care to follow the unfolding of this little romance. The clincher comes on Saturday night when, I have it on good authority, they fall upon each other at Marty's love nest at the Rockhill.

"When I remind her that Marty isn't her physical type at all, she smiles a demure smile and says a woman's tastes can evolve. And then she dimples up and adds that such developments are just part of life's rich pageant."

Rhoda clamped her lips shut. If her heart ached because Faith wasn't able to see how good Erica and Marty were together, she could take a measure of comfort from some events that were also most likely veiled in the hereafter. Presumably Faith hadn't seen Al that particular afternoon at the back table in Première Moisson with his arm flung over the shoulders of a very cute girl. The girl he was bringing to Erica's party tonight.

It's not because of Al and his little grad student that I'm not going to that party. I'm not going because I've never had any use for New Year's and I made one exception—and that night, that millennial night will always be summed up by my memory of Faith, her eyes sparkling, her cheeks pink, welcoming the year which is now coming to an end and in which she came to an end.

"Faith, I can't stay any longer, my toes are falling off. I just have to tell you one more thing. Erica's editor, Paul, the one who had the chutzpah to jilt her, is—I have to admit—redeeming himself. He's gone and hooked up with a very likable woman and apparently managed to knock her up on the first try. They act like they've invented pregnancy. Apparently, anyone who comes within walking distance is subjected to ultrasound images of the baby.

"If it's a girl, they're going to call her Faith."

Acknowledgements

I gratefully acknowledge a generous grant from the Conseil des arts et des lettres du Québec that facilitated the writing of *The Book of Faith*.

For kindly sharing parts of their life stories with me, I thank Mary Rona, the late Dr. Stephen Rona, Henry Schaffer, and Linda Schwartz. I am also indebted to Bryan Demchinsky, Jane Lewis, and Monique Polak for reading early versions of the book and for their valuable comments and sustained encouragement. As always, my agent Daphne Hart has been a fount of excellent advice, for which, as always, I am grateful.

A special thank you to Linda Leith for giving *Faith* a happy home, and for her editorial vision and wisdom.

I am grateful to Rabbi Ron Aigen for all that I have learned from him about the ways of the Jewish heart, and wish to acknowledge that he inspired the best of Nate Kaufman's *divrei Torah*.

For helping me keep faith in general, I thank Philip Beck.

For his unwavering belief and trust in me, I am humbled and forever beholden to Archie Fineberg.

Elaine Kalman Naves
Montreal

RECYCLED
Paper made from
recycled material
FSC® C100212

Printed in May 2015
by Gauvin Press,
Gatineau, Québec